A ki... ...ing
A ste... ...re
advanc... ...ongoing fight.
She stra... ...again to force her stubborn limbs into
motion. Right as her would-be-killer stepped in for
the strike, an object slammed into the top of its head,
crushing half its face and driving it to the ground.

Akina's maulaxe clanged down beside her. A clatter
of armor pieces fell after it, with her ram's helm as the
last to land.

Izthuri's call rang out. "Found it."

Akina grabbed the maulaxe handle and pulled herself up. "Lady, whatever you are, I like your timing."

Ignoring the rest of the armor for the moment, she
slapped the helm over her head and hefted the maulaxe in trembling arms. Screaming wordless defiance,
she ran for the nearest of Nullick's warriors. One flung
crystal wedges at her as it backed away. Two wedges
shattered as she ran past, spraying her with slivers. The
third clipped her arm and spun away. She threw her
maulaxe ahead, and it struck one of the little monsters
aside. As the crystal-flinger drew another shard, she
drove it to the floor and clamped a hand on its wrist.
It struggled with wiry strength, but she flexed its arm
until it gasped and dropped the crystal. She grabbed
the wedge and crunched it through the waiting neck.

Nullick laughed. "Such a good game. But you've only
found one set of gear and I've summoned more to play
on my side. Shall we try for a second round?"

The Pathfinder Tales Library

Forge of Ashes

Josh Vogt

To Cait —

Stone Endures!

paizo

Cover art by Eric Belisle.
Cover design by Emily Crowell.
Map by Robert Lazzaretti.

Paizo Inc.
7120 185th Ave NE, Ste 120
Redmond, WA 98052
paizo.com

ISBN 978-1-60125-743-7 (mass market paperback)
ISBN 978-1-60125-744-4 (ebook)

Publisher's Cataloging-In-Publication Data
(Prepared by The Donohue Group, Inc.)

Vogt, Josh.
  Forge of ashes / Josh Vogt.

   pages : map ; cm. -- (Pathfinder tales)

  Set in the world of the role-playing game, Pathfinder and Pathfinder Online.
  Issued also as an ebook.
  ISBN: 978-1-60125-743-7 (mass market paperback)

  1. Dwarfs--Fiction. 2. Kidnapping--Fiction. 3. Brothers and sisters--Fiction. 4. Underground areas--Fiction. 5. Battles--Fiction. 6. Pathfinder (Game)--Fiction. 7. Fantasy fiction. 8. Adventure stories. I. Title. II. Series: Pathfinder tales library.

PS3622.O48 F67 2015
813/.6

First printing April 2015.

Printed in the United States of America.

To Robert and Beth Vogt, who gave me a lifelong love of stories, and who have never stopped believing that my own tales are worth telling.

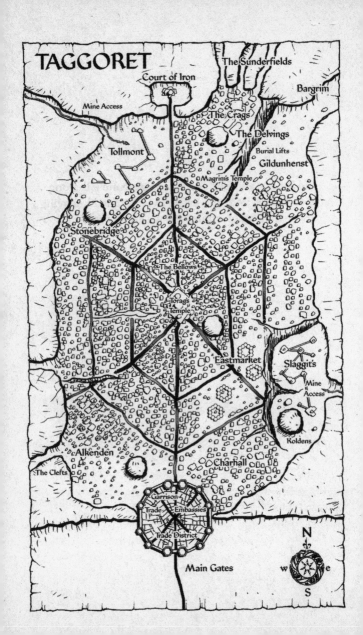

Chapter One
Homecoming

Akina hefted her maulaxe and pointed to the iron gates visible just down the mountain road. "I swear, if you don't say something by the time we get there, I'm pounding you into the ground—head-first—and leaving you to rot."

Ondorum's soft smile, barely visible in the shadow of his hood, tightened her irritation into a prickling knot of anger. He looked down at her and then over at the dwarven city of Taggoret—at least, its surface level. He spread his hands and shrugged. She'd put up with his ridiculous vow of silence long enough to understand that this gesture simply meant, *Really?*

Huffing, Akina strapped the maulaxe to her back and plodded onward, iron-and-leather armor creaking. "Stop calling my bluffs. And next time you want to sell our horses and toss all the coin to a few beggars, you damned well ask me first. Think I wanted to walk all this way? And stop dragging me into your penance. Not your fault they died. How many times do I have to tell you?"

Ondorum kept his gaze forward, but his gait grew heavier. Akina sighed. Fool of a monk. His ridiculous commitment to "attaining perfection" had manifested in stubbornness before, but this took it to unbelievable heights.

He strode beside her, his hood and voluminous sleeves hiding most of his features, but dusky gray skin peeked out from time to time, streaked with emerald-hued veins. His deep brown robe, stained by weeks of travel, added to the illusion of his having been dug up from the earth. With his stocky frame, he had the size and sculpt of a man chiseled from stone—fitting for an oread, she figured, with an earth elemental for an ancestor. However, he moved more like a mountain river than a boulder.

Compared to him, Akina clomped along like a miniature avalanche, kicking up enough dust to blind an eagle. As Taggoret's gates neared, she straightened her helm. Shaped in the likeness of a ram's head, complete with horns curling back around the sides, it was one of the few mementos she'd kept from their years with Durgan's band, exchanging blood for gold.

Realizing she was fiddling with the strap, she dropped her hands and made fists. Since when did she let nerves get to her? Why should returning home make her feel more on edge than facing down a pack of rabid wargs?

Ahead, several caravans and a stream of lone travelers worked their way in and out of the main gates. The towering iron and stone had been worked by hammer and hand, filling the mountain pass from wall to wall with images of dwarves bent over the anvil or over fallen foes. Faces of the city's leaders stared out with graven eyes, features embellished with precious metals. All around them rose the peaks of the Five Kings Mountains, a mix of harsh scree- and scrag-spotted wilderness along the upper slopes, with verdant fields and forests in the valleys below. The peak of Mount Langley reared above Taggoret itself, one enormous bluff carved so the likeness of King Taggrick watched over Kingtower Pass.

Akina sucked in a deep breath, savoring an earthy scent she'd thought she'd forgotten these past ten years. Snatches of dwarven language filled the air as they neared the gates. With brisk efficiency, the guards inspected everyone, hammers and shields readied. Their helms and breastplates bore the symbol of the Five Kings Mountains, a noble peak adorned with a five-tined crown. Two guards blocked their path.

"Name and business?"

Akina stepped forward, chin lifted. "Akina Fairingot. Business is personal. Taggoret's my home."

The other dwarf tilted his head. "Fairingot? The one who went off to the Goblinblood Wars?"

Surprise jolted through her at being recognized after so many years, especially since there'd been at least a hundred volunteers from Taggoret in her cohort alone. She studied the guard's features, but didn't think they'd ever met. "So?"

"Huh. Many thought you dead. Some will be glad to hear it isn't so."

She furrowed her brow. Many? Some? Before she could ask, the guard waved for the next group of travelers to come up.

"Pass on and welcome home."

The other guard thumbed at Ondorum. "What about him?"

When Ondorum just bowed, Akina sighed. "His name's Ondorum. He's"—*a crack-brained fool!*—"taken a vow of silence."

The dwarf peered up at the oread. "What for?"

Akina leaned in and spoke in a stage whisper. "He was cursed by a mad wizard. Now his voice makes warriors weep and children hide and dogs howl. So we figured it'd be best if he just kept his trap shut."

Ondorum drew his hood back, revealing a sweep of gray hair a shade darker than his skin, and ridges of alexandrite crystal shards instead of eyebrows. Malachite-green eyes gazed out beneath these, thoroughly unamused.

Akina contained her chuckle. She'd been working on rounding out his sense of humor ever since they met. Whatever monastery he'd been raised in, the monks there had certainly striven to grind any mirth into dust, replacing it with the nobler pillar of grave contemplation. Not that they'd needed to do much. With earth magic fused to their bloodline, oreads not only resembled stone, but also often shared its sense of humor. Hard to make a mountain laugh, after all. Ondorum readily admitted to his failings there, though he'd become more nomadic than most of his kind, partly due to Akina's influence—as well as the events that spurred him to leave the monastery in the first place.

The guards shook their heads in sorrow.

"Pity to hear," said one. "Might be the temple could help."

As they passed through the gates, Ondorum pointed back, frowning.

She smirked. "If you don't want me to lie, tell the truth yourself, hm?"

She ignored him and took in the sights of home. Taggoret's surface had been built on a gentle slope until it butted up against a cliff. The central road ended in another set of gates that led to the main subsurface dwellings. Little of this topside portion held her interest, except for faint nostalgia. Most of the buildings and shops were part of the trade district, shipping out the city's famous iron.

Dwarves bustled about, carting crates and wagonloads of armor, mining gear, or refined ore. Guards patrolled the thoroughfares, keen eyes scanning the visitors to the many inns and taverns. A handful of humans and gnomes mingled, and even one elf glided through the crowds, several bodyguards keeping in step. The stone buildings blended into the mountain while engravings and murals adorned almost every wall and rocky surface—results of the dwarven drive to transform the raw hills into eternal works of art.

Akina glanced at Ondorum, wishing he'd tell her what he thought of the place. Pure delight shone in his eyes, and his broad smile elicited one of her own, easing some of the tension simmering in her bones.

As they passed one frieze, his smile slipped and he pointed. There stood a carving of a female dwarf clad in golden armor, poised before a fleeing army.

Akina's marrow chilled. The image looked like her. It didn't just depict her build or broad features, but also the streak of platinum that shot through her otherwise dirty blonde hair. An inlaid strip of white marble created the effect.

She edged over to study the piece. Ondorum joined her, brow raised in question.

"Must be my mother's work." She brushed gloved fingertips over the smooth stone. "Looks like she's doing good business; it's an honor to mark the city itself." Was this a way for Jannasten to remember a daughter gone off to war? Akina tamped down a swell of guilt.

Ondorum stroked the image of her face, then turned and did the same to her cheek.

Flushing, Akina jerked her head away. "Come on."

They passed through the inner gates, exchanging sun and sky for cool tunnels blazing with torchlight. The passages had been decorated with reliefs, so walking down them felt like crossing through dwarven history. One detailed their emergence on the surface millennia before. Another showed the founding of the Sky Citadels.

Yet after they left the main tunnel, Ondorum pointed out several more carvings that looked eerily similar to Akina. The art often placed her in scenes of battle, fending off everything from orcs to hill giants. They passed a row of wall niches, and a small statue of Akina stood in one like a city guardian. Her appearance accompanied many other works, but care had been taken to subtly set her apart, especially with her distinctive hair.

With each image of herself she saw, Akina's unease grew. Why had her mother toiled to add her to the bedrock of their people? She didn't deserve any such honor. She didn't deserve to be treated like a revered ancestor, especially not after she'd surrendered that heritage to seek a violent fortune in the world beyond.

Her pace quickened. She locked her eyes forward, refusing to give the art any further regard until she burst out of the tunnel's end. She paused to slow her breath as Ondorum caught up. The tunnel exited onto a ledge with switchback stairs leading down several flights to the main level. Their perch provided a perfect vantage to see across the cavern. Stone columns jutted up to the rocky ceiling far above, and the non-load-bearing pillars had been carved out to provide dwellings for thousands of dwarves. Everburning lamps and torches cast most areas in a golden glow, blazing from doors and windows as well as from posts set at intervals along the roads. Worked every hour of the day, hundreds of forges lit swaths of the cavern.

Several deep rifts cut through the cavern floor, with massive bridges set across them allowing for steady streams of foot traffic. Further dwellings and workshops had been dug directly into the sides of the cavern, connected by stone ramps and stairs. More tunnels bored deeper within the mountain, connecting to other city districts. The smell of hot iron filled the air, underlain by the nose-crinkling stink of scorched beards. Bellows and laughter echoed through the cavern, punctuated by the metallic music of hammer on anvil.

Akina pondered her next move as she soaked in the familiar sensations. Find her mother and get it over with? No. She wanted a clearer head first. Wouldn't do to make her first homecoming act a demand for explanations—especially since she owed the bigger one for her extended absence.

She fixed on the central temple to Torag, where the smithing fires forever roared in honor of the dwarven god. Her brother, Brakisten, had just begun serving there as a cleric when she'd left. Akina assumed his position had since changed, but they'd no doubt have his name and current station noted in a duty roster.

She led Ondorum down into the city proper and had to reorient herself only twice before they reached the front court of the smithing temple. Here, dwarves worshiped the Father of Creation by fashioning magnificent works of art, powerful tools, and equipment for war. Unlike many clerics Akina had encountered during her travels, ones who kept their robes clean and hands unsullied by labor, Torag's faithful milled through the temple in dirty aprons, faces stained with soot. Their roaring chants rang out as loud as the clang of their tongs and pounding of their hammers on the consecrated anvils. The whole temple thudded with a fiery heartbeat.

Akina paused within the main chamber to let the sense of the place engulf her, memories sparking in her mind, stories and legends and history she'd given little thought to ever since leaving home. All dwarves of the Five Kings Mountains grew up with abundant reminders of their heritage. Even outside the temples, countless statues, murals, and anvil-shaped altars celebrated their maker and god, Torag, whose forge hammer had birthed their race within the Darklands and who'd given them a simple prophecy:

When the ground shakes beneath your feet, you must leave the caverns of the world behind and journey upward at all costs.

For even though dwarves still toiled beneath the earth, in ages past they'd existed far deeper, and knew nothing of the surface. When earthquakes wracked the world, her people had embarked on the grand Quest for Sky, traveling for three centuries and braving monstrous dangers to finally answer Torag's call.

Though not all of them had done so. Akina frowned, but her reverie was interrupted by a sweat-stained cleric who escorted them to a side room where they could hold a conversation. A grin split his black beard as he focused on Ondorum, giving an excited bob of his head.

"A son of the earth! We're blessed to have you with us. Have you come to ply your strength in Torag's honor?"

Ondorum bowed with a rueful smile. At the dwarf's quizzical look, Akina explained the monk's vow of silence and then presented her own inquiry.

"I'm looking for my brother, Brakisten Fairingot. He served here awhile back."

The cleric's beard sagged.

Akina removed her helm and clutched it against her side. "What's wrong?"

"You must be Akina." The cleric drummed fingers on the hammer strapped to his belt. "We're blessed to have you back with us, but your brother has fallen out of favor." At her scowl, he raised calloused palms. "It isn't my place to speak his deeds, but I can direct you to him. Please, tell him he's not beyond redemption. But he must be willing to go through the fire of renewal if he wishes to work beside us once more."

Akina stepped closer. The cleric gripped his hammer but didn't draw it.

"Where is he?" she growled.

Chapter Two
Brother's Keeper

Akina rammed a shoulder against the tavern's front door and tromped inside. A single lamp flicked shadows across the simple bar and the tender who gawked at her from behind it. Rough-carved tables and chairs littered the area, and it took her a second to scan the assembled riffraff. Her brother wasn't present.

Ondorum waited by the doorway as she marched over to the barkeep.

"Brakisten Fairingot," she said. "He here?"

The dwarf scowled through a bristly beard. "If you're looking to collect, you'll have to wait a few. Snuffstone's boys already have him out back, and I doubt he'll have much left to pay with by the time they're through with him."

Akina chucked her chin at the back door set off to one side. "That way?"

"You want to poke around in Snuffstone business, go out the front and 'round the side. But they don't like being interrupted."

"Right. They'll have to get used to disappointment."
Ignoring the bartender's bark of warning, she clambered over the counter and strode through the back storeroom. Another door deposited her into the broad alley behind the tavern, filled with rubble and scrap.

Three dwarves already occupied the space, and Akina barely recognized Brakisten as one of them. He stood with an arm locked behind his back, held by one of what she assumed to be the Snuffstone brothers.

Brakisten wore a tattered robe stained yellow and green down the front. His black beard and hair had grown wild, hiding most of his eyes and cheeks. He breathed heavily, and his eyelids drooped.

A Snuffstone brother tangled a fist in Brakisten's beard and growled threats until the other nodded Akina's way. He spun, scowling.

"Off with you," he said. "This don't concern you."

She reached back and gripped her maulaxe. "That's my brother you're working over. You've business with him, you've got it with me."

"This lout's your kin?" His grin exposed a silver tooth. "Never figured anyone would admit to being related to this soppy soul. Don't you know what he's done?"

"Let me guess: he owes you money, hm?" Akina hid her dismay behind the nonchalance, pained to see Brakisten in drunken disarray. How had he fallen in with these ruffians?

The Snuffstone brothers shared a look. The one holding Brakisten let go and whacked him across the back of the head as he dropped. Brakisten curled up on the ground, shivering and whimpering.

Akina bared her teeth. "I might expect surface folk treat him this way. But not his own kind in his own home."

The first Snuffstone prodded Brakisten with a boot. "You wouldn't claim him as kin if you knew. He got kicked out of the temple years back for stealing from the coffers. Then he started raving about Droskar and how we're all doomed to burn in the Ashen Forge. He's nothing but a mad traitor."

At her snarl, they put hands to the blades at their belts.

"Don't you dare accuse him—"

"It's true," Brakisten whispered. "I've stolen from Torag himself. Droskar will take our souls. I've seen it . . ."

She stared in horror. Mentioning the Dark Smith, much less proclaiming doom in his name, equated to blasphemy for some dwarves. And her devout brother admitting to thievery? It had to be the ale addling his senses.

When the other Snuffstone reared for another kick, she stepped closer. "Touch him again and I'll break your knees and knuckles."

"Oh, the little lambie thinks she's a wolf." The lead dwarf blocked her path while his companion laid a blade across Brakisten's throat. "We're the ones with fangs, see?"

Akina trembled in rage. It'd be so simple to let it wash over her and leave these two as quivering piles of pulp. If the fury claimed her, though, she might hurt Brakisten before she regained her wits.

The dagger-wielding dwarf nicked Brakisten's neck. "Brak. Brak! Lookie here. This little lambie claims she's your sister."

Brakisten dribbled drool over his beard. "Sh-shut it, you lying bastard. Just leave me alone. Lemme sleep."

The dwarf chuckled. "That's rich, it is. Calling *me* a liar."

One of Brakisten's eyelids peeled upward, revealing a bloodshot eye. He stared at Akina, then closed his eye again.

"Go away. You're a ghost. Everyone's a ghost now. All darkness and ghosts."

Grinning, the lead Snuffstone crossed his arms. "Seeing as you're so protective of this poor soul, how's about we strike a bargain?"

She curled fingers into fists. "How much does he owe?"

He scratched the tip of his nose. "With interest and whatnot, I'd wager right around a hundred gold."

Akina sputtered. "What kind of crook are you?"

"Aw, c'mon, little lambie." He rapped knuckles on her ram-shaped helm. "Can't you see he's had a hard time? Why not make it easier for all of us? Do your sisterly duty, pay his debts, and we won't have to chisel it out of his hide."

She hauled her maulaxe free. The Snuffstones drew their blades, but she just held out her weapon.

"This is worth at least a few hundred. Here. Take a look."

One stepped in, eyes narrowed but head cocked in curiosity.

She dropped the maulaxe headfirst onto his foot with a thud. Even as his howl rose, she dove at the second dwarf. A wild dagger slash clanked off her breastplate. She grabbed his beard and yanked his forehead down against the curve of the ram's horns. Eyes rolling, he staggered and crashed to the ground.

The first dwarf roared as he turned and charged—straight into her cheek-cracking punch. He dropped alongside his brother. Akina heaved breaths as she stood over them, wanting to pummel them into scrap. Her vision fuzzed around the edges, and her nostrils flared, scenting sweat and blood and smoke.

Then Ondorum shifted into view at the alley's end, worry etching his features. While Akina's fury didn't vanish, it ebbed at the thought of him watching her beat the two dwarves senseless. So she tended to her brother and let the violent cravings become a background buzz.

She grabbed Brakisten's stained robe. He grunted and tried to bat her away, but she gripped his chin and forced him to look at her.

"Brakisten. Stand up. We're going."

Groaning, he slumped. Then he clawed upright, using her armor as handholds until he stared blearily at her face. She chuffed at his rank breath and tried to ignore the embers that simmered in her gut. At last, the disorientation cleared from his eyes and he took her into a hug.

"Akina! My big sister. You're alive! Let's go inside and buy a round to celebrate."

She grabbed an arm to guide him out of the alley. "Let's get you home. Where's mother?"

Brakisten choked a laugh. "Mother's dead, Kina. Been dead years now."

Akina froze. "You're drunk. She can't be dead; I've seen her work across the city. Some of it's recent."

He staggered free and leaned against a wall. "That's not her work. It's Gromir's."

Her fingers twitched. "Whose?"

He dropped to his knees, buried his face in his hands, and wept. Aghast, she stared at this wreck of a dwarf while a mocking voice whispered in the back of her mind.

Welcome home, Akina.

Chapter Three
Graven Images

As Akina hauled Brakisten back up, Ondorum came over and took his other arm. She nodded in silent thanks, not trusting herself to speak.

They maneuvered him out into the street. It saddened her to discover that almost everyone they passed recognized Brakisten in this state; a few even knew her, though they treated her with an odd reticence, as if unsure whether to congratulate her homecoming or not. Perhaps her return reminded them of the many warriors Taggoret lost during the Goblinblood Wars.

Muttered requests got her directions to where he lived. When they arrived, her face flaming with shame, she kicked the door wide and they stumbled into a stone hovel. Two rough-hewn rooms contained little more than a rickety bed in the back, with a dry wash-basin and small dresser in the front. Ratty clothes and boots lay piled in one corner. Not so much as the tiniest anvil altar to be seen.

She dropped Brakisten onto the bed. He snored, and she resisted the temptation to shake him awake. He'd be useless like this. However, she knew where to get more answers.

Grimacing, she turned to Ondorum. "Not how I expected things to go."

He frowned in sympathy and tapped his temple.

She shook her head. "No. It didn't take me that time. That was necessary."

His expression remained dubious.

"I could've done worse and you know it. I'm fighting the rage better now. It doesn't control me as much."

He tilted his head.

"At least, I think so." She stared at her hands. "Hope so. Sometimes it seems life is nothing but fighting. Fighting the rage. Fighting myself. Fighting idiots who can't see how badly outmatched they are. I thought coming home would give me a rest." She puffed her cheeks. "Apparently not. At least those fools will think twice before threatening Brakisten again."

At his deeper frown, she pounded a fist against the nearest wall. "Don't tell me I can't be angry for my brother! Nobody died. Besides, if you'd really been worried, you would've stepped in. I know you were just around the corner." She headed for the door. "Right. My mother's old workshop shouldn't be far. I need to go figure a few things out. Make sure Brakisten doesn't wander off to get cockeyed again, hm?"

Ondorum looked over at her brother and mimed lifting a bowl to his lips.

"I'll find a meal, sure. Lucky I saved a few coins before you gave the rest away."

He reached out, offering a parting embrace, but she pretended not to see as she strode out. Once the door latched behind her, she squared her shoulders, swallowed hard, and set off to discover her family's fate.

As she dredged up old memories, remembering which roads connected where, she fought against the sense of being a ghost, as Brakisten had accused. While the city remained similar in many ways, most of the faces had changed. She avoided those she recognized, though plenty of people pointed her way, even with her helm in place. A handful of other architectural pieces featured her, from archways to cornices to door knockers. With each one spotted, the urge rose to smash the ornamentations to shards. She'd never earned that honor. Maybe she never should've returned.

She rounded a corner onto the street that ended at her mother's workshop. Her heart bumped up at the sign hanging over the door. *Janna's Handworks*. Light burned in the front windows and from the workshop in back. She fought to keep her pace steady. Her mother lived. Brakisten had been rambling nonsense after all.

She entered, and a greeting died on her lips. An unknown dwarf stood at the counter, dressed in a simple violet robe, her reddish hair pulled back into a ponytail. She smiled at Akina and spoke in a husky voice.

"Can I help you?"

Akina locked eyes with her. "Who're you?"

The other dwarf frowned. "I'm Selvia, the shop assistant. You've business with the master?" She waved at the curtained entrance to the back rooms.

"Master? This is my mother's shop. Jannasten Fairingot. Where is she?"

Selvia's eyes widened. "You're . . . oh my, you're her. I should've realized." She bowed her head. "I'm . . . I'm so sorry for your loss."

Akina came up to the counter. "What're you talking about? Where's my mother?"

"Selvia? We have a customer?"

The curtain parted. For a long moment, the newcomer joined in a three-way stare-down. Wiry for a dwarf, and with a sparse, golden beard, he wore trim work leathers over which he'd donned a cerulean robe. A bandolier peeked out from under his robe, strapping throwing axes across his chest. A tuft of darker yellow hair peeked out from beneath his tunic at the base of his neck.

A memory flashed by of Akina's fingers tangled in that particular patch. She shoved the image away, not needing the distraction. Ancient history.

He twitched a hand. "Selvia, please see to the latest invoices on your desk."

Selvia curtsied and slipped past him. He rounded the counter, hands raised as if framing her in his mind.

"It's you. It's really you." He clapped once in delight. "You've returned!"

Akina pressed fingertips to her forehead. "Gromir. Dust and drudgery, what're you doing in my mother's shop?"

"Well, I—that is, I run it now, in the wake of . . ." His face fell. "No word ever reached you, did it? I sent letters all around, but we had no idea where you might be. Or if you were even still alive to receive them."

"What word?"

"Your mother. Her . . . her death."

Akina's shoulders slumped.

Gromir wavered, looking torn between wanting to embrace her and respecting the years between them now. She remembered how he'd held her once before at a time like this, after she'd learned of her father's frozen body being pulled from the avalanche debris. How she'd used him to wear her out until she was too exhausted to feel grief anymore.

She firmed up, refusing to show weakness this time. "Brakisten told the truth, then."

"You've seen him? I wish you'd have come here first; I could've prepared you."

"Prepared me? For finding my brother's been kicked out of his temple for theft and is now a blithering drunk?"

Gromir cleared his throat. "That, unfortunately, summarizes it rather well." He raised arms and stepped forward. "I'm sorry, Akina."

She backed up, and her maulaxe bumped against the door. "What're you doing?"

He hesitated. "Welcoming a dearly missed and beloved friend home?" When she continued staring, he lowered his arms. "My apologies. I thought . . ."

She adjusted her maulaxe straps. He'd always been a bit clingy during their time together. Apparently that hadn't changed.

"I'd welcome some straight answers," she said. "What happened to my mother? What happened to Brakisten? Why are you running her business and sticking my likeness all over the city?"

He perked up. "You've seen them, then? Do you like what I've done?"

"Like it? Gromir, what in Hell were you thinking? What's going on?"

He clasped hands behind himself. "You've been gone a long time, Akina."

"Right. Tell me the one thing I do know."

"Hear me out, please." He bowed his head. "After you left for war, once my guard post expired, I returned here to continue my studies. I never had your prowess in battle, and hoped I might find success in the magical arts. However, it proved an expensive effort. Jannasten supported my studies by hiring me, and we kept the business quite profitable. I eventually became her apprentice on top of my other pursuits." He moved back behind the counter and gazed up at various stone and metal panels decorated with icons and runes.

"When most of the surviving volunteers returned after the war—minus yourself—we feared the worst. No one had any idea what had happened to you."

"I joined up with a few mercenaries. Seems I'm pretty good at that sort of work."

Gromir twitched. "Ah. That's quite . . . enterprising of you." He coughed. "But after five years passed, we were certain you were a battlefield casualty. I convinced your mother to let me honor your sacrifice in our work—a way to also uphold your ancestors' dignity as Brakisten's crimes became known."

"So he really stole from Torag's temple? And started prophesying about Droskar?"

"I wouldn't call it prophesying. More like disjointed rants."

"My brother never had visions before."

Gromir splayed his hands. "Your brother is sick in mind and soul. Drink dragged him down, but he hid it well until they caught him pilfering straight from the temple coffers to pay his debts. That in itself might not have been enough, but then he turned violent against anyone who wouldn't listen to his ravings. It almost broke your mother, but she threw herself into the work even more fervently. I joined her, but when she disappeared—"

"Disappeared?" Akina stepped closer. "You said she was dead before. Is she dead or just missing?"

Gromir sighed. "Will you please just let me tell you? Here's the full of it: You know your mother loved this shop and her craft, but she loved seeking out new materials just as much—better-quality stone and ore to work with. Whenever she wasn't plying her trade here, she was out on some excursion or another. The last time, she told me she'd found a particularly valuable vein, but needed more proof to claim the strike. She swore me to silence, fearing competition. She knew the area well, so she said, and could navigate alone. Once she had the claim protected against jumpers, she'd take a proper team down. Despite my own worries, I'd seen her succeed numerous times. So she went. And never came back."

"Nobody went after her?" Akina's voice came out hoarse.

"Many people hunt down strikes and never return," he said. "Janna's bold—almost reckless—reputation was well known. Like mother, like daughter." He gave her a meaningful look. "People warned that she was risking the inevitable. That she should rely on survey

31

teams; she never listened, of course. She always wanted to be the one out there, making the discoveries, seeing what lay beyond Taggoret, whether out across the peaks or in the depths."

Akina bowed her head. That certainly sounded like her mother. Forever caught between her craft and a restless urge. When Akina had signed up for battle training, Jannasten had celebrated, as it'd provide the perfect way for her daughter to see the world as well— so long as she came home. That'd been the unspoken stipulation. But things changed. Akina was her own dwarf. She'd made her own choices.

So why did she feel like she'd failed her mother's legacy?

"Once we realized she'd been away too long," Gromir said, "a few cries went up for search parties and the like, but most accepted it as a logical consequence. The world's a dangerous place. People die. We try to live on as best we can."

"How long ago?" Akina asked.

"Just over three years now. Time enough. I held out hope for awhile, but I knew she'd never abandon her work and home for so long."

Akina narrowed her eyes. Was that an accusation?

"Since then, I continued to do what I could to bolster your family's name. I kept the business open, even though it meant diverting focus from my studies. I've also kept an eye on Brakisten, providing meals and a small abode he can rest in when he's sober enough to take advantage of it." He coughed. "Don't worry. The property's under my name, so he can't sell it for more drinking coin."

"Why, Gromir? Why go to all this effort?"

He spread his arms again, though this time as if displaying himself. "Isn't it obvious?"

"You're kidding. After all this time?"

"We loved each other once. Might we not do so again?"

Akina couldn't contain her snort. "We were infatuated over a decade ago. Big difference."

Gromir's face tightened. He exhaled through his nostrils. "Can I show you something? It'll only take a moment."

Scowling, she followed him into the back. Selvia glanced up from where she bent over a desk, ticking off figures with an inked quill. Gromir nodded for her to continue as he led Akina past the workshop filled with marble blocks and iron slabs. He showed her into a darkened side room. Lifting a hand, he whispered a command, and a sphere of pale blue light flickered into being above their heads.

Statues, medallions, masks, and more crammed the shelves, all positioned to face the middle of the room. Akina spun a slow circle, gaping.

"What's this?"

Gromir kept his gaze down. "I suppose you could call it my private collection. Pieces I've crafted but can't bring myself to sell."

Akina picked up the nearest statue, feeling the polished stone. "They're all . . . me."

"They're a gift. A way to honor your memory and what I felt for you. Still feel."

She stared into the false eyes of her miniature and imagined Gromir at work, night after night, forming

33

idols he then stashed. Convincing her mother to plant Akina's image around the city so he could see her wherever he walked. Practically building an altar in her image. This went far beyond his clingy nature. In fact, when she'd left for war, it had been something of a relief to learn he planned to stay behind—a fresh start for them both. But apparently he'd never truly let go of their past. And what had she become in his mind since?

She swallowed her rising gorge and set the statue back down with a click. "This is a little . . . obsessive."

His expression blanked for a moment before his eyes flared. "Not obsession. Devotion! Something you obviously have no comprehension of." He froze for a moment, gaze darting all over. Then he sagged. "I shouldn't have said that. It's just been difficult, and this kept me focused on what really mattered."

"You should've moved on a long time ago. You should have a family by now. Younglings."

"I do have a family." He sniffed a laugh. "Not the traditional sort, no, but it's the one I've chosen."

So she'd left and, instead of shaping his own life, he'd supplanted hers. Who did he think he was? What gave him the right to claim her family as his own? What gave him the right to turn her into some sort of icon?

She hefted her maulaxe and pointed at the collection. "You chose to be stuck in the past."

"Akina . . ." He closed in, but she thrust a hand into his chest. He stumbled out the door and caught himself on the threshold. When he tried to reenter, she blocked his way with the maulaxe head. His eyes widened. "What're you doing?"

She pondered the wisdom of her actions for half a heartbeat. After all, they had been friends and lovers once. Did he deserve to be punished for dreaming of an impossible future with her? She cast the misgivings aside. Wisdom had nothing to do with it. She needed this. If she'd killed those dwarves in the alley, the consequences could've been costly. Here, though, she at least had a safe target, an outlet to keep the fury from consuming her for a little longer.

"I'm freeing you from me." She spun and slammed the maulaxe down on a mask of her likeness, turning it to powder. She swept a shelf to the floor and proceeded to pound and crush it all into shards.

"Please, don't! No!"

He cried for her to stop with every smash of her maulaxe, wailing as if she struck him instead. Yet Akina didn't cease until the last piece of the twisted hoard lay broken, her features obliterated. Fragments crackled under her boots as she lurched out of the room.

Moaning, Gromir slid to his knees, hands shaking as he stared at the ruined art. Selvia peeked down the hall, but ducked back out of sight at Akina's glare.

As she moved by, Gromir snagged the edge of her sleeve. "Wait. Where are you going?"

Akina pulled away and didn't look back. "To pray for my mother's soul."

Chapter Four
Contemplation of Stone

Ondorum watched the snoring dwarf for a little while after Akina left. He looked for any sign that Brakisten might wake, or even be sensible enough to work the door latch if he did. He studied Brakisten's twitches and briefly wondered what he might've been like before drink, deception, and grief took such a harsh toll. Little use, however, in questioning what might have been. Better to focus on what could be.

Ondorum searched the rooms for stashed alcohol, but the den lacked any hiding places he could discern. He guessed it'd be a while yet before Brakisten woke. Perhaps he could use the time to explore a bit on his own.

While he'd encountered other dwarves besides Akina, he'd never visited one of their kingdoms before. What glimpses he had so far proved fascinating. He'd been looking forward to meeting Akina's family—at least, the brother and mother. She'd told him how her father had died while she'd been in battle training, buried in an avalanche during a Kingtower Pass patrol. In the years they'd traveled and fought together with the swords-for-hire, she'd occasionally spoken of her home and remaining kin. Her tone had initially been dismissive, but had grown increasingly wistful until her return had been inevitable. Her asking him to come along had been one of the great joys of his existence, but he possessed no certainty of how long it'd last.

Best to make the most of it, then.

Believing it safe to stroll for a bit, he bowed to Brakisten and prayed to Irori that the dwarf might have a soothed mind and soul when he woke. Then he stepped outside and took a moment to orient himself. Fortunately, he had an excellent sense of direction, a talent the mercenaries had often put to use when navigating unknown territory.

As he wound through the district, he admired the roads and bridges. The dwarves had fashioned well-situated thoroughfares, yet their constructions retained the sense of having sprung whole from the earth. Studying the dwarves themselves, he almost believed the legends that their earliest ancestors had been formed of living stone with fire baked into their hearts. He sensed their joy and peace in knowing who they were and where they belonged—a peace he knew Akina no longer held. Even though she'd never said it outright, he reckoned she'd hoped to regain that centering of herself by coming home. Could she still, he wondered, despite the unfortunate beginnings?

An inconsistency nagged him as he wandered. Something about the city itself . . .

Ah! Of course. The light. He should've realized. Akina said her people worked all hours, taking shifts to ensure the forge fires never dimmed, the mining carts never rolled in empty, and the tunnels and buildings never stopped being strengthened or lengthened. While Ondorum knew dwarves could see in the dark just as well as he could, the artificial light displayed their handiwork in far greater glory.

He paused on the corner of a four-way intersection atop a rise. From here, he could see down one of the massive rifts dividing the city. Structures appeared to be built into the depths of the rift itself, with chain-and-pulley lifts providing transportation up and down. Mining entrances? Homes?

He gazed upward and let himself feel the weight of the cavern. Not a claustrophobic press like many humans or elves complained of after spending time underground. To him, it offered a soothing weight, like a warm blanket beneath a frigid sky.

It seemed a city an oread might be right at home in. Oread culture was a loose thing, in itself. They had no central government. No real inclination to congregate with others of their kind. Most, like him, chose their own paths. He'd heard of other oreads finding homes among dwarven settlements, their inclinations toward stone helping them blend in well enough. He'd even heard of oreads and dwarves who'd married and had children, though he and Akina had never discussed such. Not that they'd been talking much lately.

Guilt cracked his concentration at that thought. He knew Akina detested his self-imposed vow, sometimes opining that he must've taken it just to provoke her. But did she realize how much it tormented him as well? Ever since they'd first begun traveling together, he'd enjoyed the steady way they'd drawn ever closer. Now he'd distanced them in a way neither of them could bridge. In the pursuit of perfecting himself, did he now fail her?

Trying to restore a more contemplative focus, he shut his eyes and visualized his ki as a golden ball at the core of his being. Palms opened to the ground, he imagined lines of ki stretching out into the stone, connecting him with the essence of the city. A futile effort to gain a sense of the place, perhaps, since he'd only seen a fraction of Taggoret, but all lessons began somewhere.

As he attempted to meditate, a memory of screams teased his thoughts. Past mistakes and failures rose to taunt him, as they so often did. The golden ball of ki turned to granite. He fought to corral the riot of sudden emotion and steady his breathing, but everywhere he turned, regret threatened to overwhelm him. Akina. The monastery. The village. All of them hurt or lost despite his best efforts. The wrong words. The wrong actions. Yet he still struggled to know what he could've done or said differently in the circumstances.

Irori, please. I'm trying. Truly. I've ever believed yours is the hand that should guide my path, but it can be so difficult to know which way you're pointing. Is Akina's solace more important than my silence? Is my vow meant to be broken? Or is this a test to refine both of us?

He waited, listening for an answer, memories still haunted by screams. Then he opened his eyes, realizing some screams weren't in his mind. A faint roar sounded nearby, followed by a cry and crash. Someone in trouble?

He reached into his robe and drew out an iron rod no bigger than his thumb. He carried a small collection of

such metal rods and chips to be employed when circumstances required. While he could fight decently
enough with empty hands, he knew better than to
overlook the advantage of an extended reach.

Calling on his elemental heritage, he let earthen
power flow through him and infuse the metal, giving
it the potential to be so much more than it appeared.
The rod lengthened into a full quarterstaff. While it was
a temporary transformation, and one he could only
repeat after a lengthy delay, it could help if he needed
to intervene in a scene of violence.

So armed, Ondorum stepped out into the middle of
the street, looking for the source of the disturbance. A
dwarf walking by jumped aside, fists cocked. Then he
gave a grating laugh.

"Flaming beards, boy. Thought you were a statue."

Ondorum pointed down the road and cupped a hand
to his ear. The dwarf frowned, but then brightened. "Oh,
that's the Scarred Knuckles. Best fighting hole in all
the mountains. There's a tournament tonight. Was on
my way, myself." He sidled up and nudged Ondorum.
"My bet's on the Silver Skewer, but it'll be a good fight
either way. For some of us, blood gleams brighter than
gold, eh?"

Quarterstaff tapping along, Ondorum fell in step
with the dwarf, who talked as they went. The dwarf
didn't seem to notice the oread's failure to reply as
he guided Ondorum to one building and ushered him
inside. The noise quadrupled in force, and Ondorum
tried to let the cacophony flow over and past him. At
least two hundred dwarves crammed into multi-tiered
seats surrounding four sunken arenas. Each ring held

a pair of fighters. The crowd loosed another roar as one combatant hit the ground and didn't move.

His dwarven escort cackled. "Remember! All bets on the Silver Skewer."

Others called out names such as The Haunch and One-Nostril. Ondorum shifted through the crowd as the audience slapped and pounded one another in revelry, celebrating with what would've been bruising—or bone-breaking—force for many other races.

Ondorum's attention fixed on a cage set off in a corner. At first, it appeared to contain nothing but darkness; then the slightest movement suggested a figure huddled within. Ondorum got closer until he discerned the captive.

Clad in filthy rags, the person looked dwarven in shape and size. However, his skin was a dull gray, and what hair remained in his beard hung in white patches. He lay curled up beside a chamber pot, withered arms and legs weighed down by chains bolted to the stone wall. The wrinkles and heavy folds of his forehead and cheeks made him seem practically ancient.

Duergar. Ondorum had heard of the dwarves' fallen cousins but never seen one before. By the look of him, this one had been kept there as a spectacle for many years. The duergar stared out past the cage bars, dark eyes unblinking, face slack.

Ondorum frowned, uncomfortable with seeing any creature imprisoned. Akina had once entertained the mercenary band with tales of the outcast race. Once dwarves themselves, they'd rejected the call of Torag to seek the surface millennia ago. They'd remained below and, to survive in the treacherous Darklands, sworn themselves to Droskar, the Master of the Dark Furnace. Now the duergar continued to toil down in the Darklands, ruling their fell kingdom in cruelty and malice.

After a few minutes, he moved on, realizing he wasn't about to solve the ancient enmity between the two races with a little sympathy for a prisoner. He approached one of the nearer rings and looked easily over the heads of those crowding around it. The two fighters exchanged a barrage of hits and kicks before stumbling back from each other. The brief pause gave him a clear view of one bare-knuckled combatant and her platinum-streaked hair.

Akina.

The crowd might as well have vanished as he focused on her in dismay. Her half-crazed eyes, the flex of her jaw, and the hunch of her shoulders told him she rode the edge of fury. Ondorum gripped his staff, uncertain. Even if he broke his vow to shout her name, his voice would be lost in the riot. She always thought she could control her rage, and so often proved herself wrong as she rode the swell up and over into temporary madness. The others here didn't know the danger, and would find out too late.

Akina howled in glee as her fist cracked across her opponent's cheek, sending him somersaulting. Every landed blow meant more coin added to the wagers on the bout. She didn't know her enemy's name. Didn't care. She bounded after and forced him up against a wall to pummel his belly while he beat at her skull. Might as well have been knocking stones against stones.

Here. She belonged here, dealing pain to any and all.

The longer her blood boiled, the more the world altered around her. Her nostrils flared as she picked out others by their sweat, by the auras of smoke clinging to them, by their reeking fear. The air itself felt like a rich current of magma through which she flowed as easily as thought, while those around her slogged and stumbled and burned.

With an incoherent battle cry, her opponent sprinted in. She took the hit and tangled fingers in his thick hair. Turning with his momentum, she drove him face-first into the wall. He rebounded, and she threw her weight into another slam. Then another. He went limp after the fourth, but she held him upright and cracked bone to stone, wanting to smash his skull through and beyond. Blood spattered her and the wall. He gargled in her grip as she reared back for a final thrust.

A hand grabbed her shoulder. She dropped her victim and spun, aiming a blow, but something slapped her fists aside and threw her off-balance. As she recovered, the newcomer scooped up the fallen dwarf and threw him out of the ring.

Akina shook bloodstained fists. "No! I was winning!"

Cheated on the brink of victory. For a moment she thought she recognized the new enemy, but then it didn't matter. Yet as she charged, he stood solid and took her strikes as they came. Open palms intercepted her fists; his arms didn't even as tremble at the hits. When she tried to grapple him to the floor, he stepped aside and let her sweep past.

"Stand still!"

Each missed attempt stoked the fires higher.

"Stand—" One moment to the next, the flames in her belly turned to a block of ice. The cold weight of it dragged her to her knees. She shook her head, hands planted, trying to rise. "No, I was winning . . ." Quivering limbs refused to support her.

As she collapsed, a pair of hands caught her. She blinked away the gray haze long enough to focus on Ondorum before a curtain of ashes enveloped her.

"Sorry," she said. "It's the only way I know how to pray."

Chapter Five
Harsh Words

Akina groaned as she tried to open her eyes. Someone must've switched her head for a war drum while she slept. The incessant pounding vibrated through her whole body. Even her teeth and toenails thrummed in exhausted agony. Who? Where? These were important questions to answer, but simply lying there felt like the less-painful option. Which meant she should kick herself out of such a weak-willed state and get back on her feet.

She sat up, hoping her surroundings might clue her in, and then hoping her surroundings would stop spinning and let her actually get a good look at them. When the world realigned its orbit, she recognized Brakisten's hovel of a home. She lay on the overturned dresser in the front room, with a bundled robe stuffed beneath her for cushioning.

A glance aside showed Ondorum seated in a meditative position, taking up most of one wall. Eyes closed, he wore a simple loincloth.

She recalled the first time she and her hunting party had encountered him, similarly poised outside the gates of a hillside temple. Until he'd moved to greet them, she'd thought him an actual statue carved in breathtaking detail.

His lack of clothing exposed alexandrite crystal ridges across his ribs, down his sternum, along his shins, collarbone, shoulders, and forearms. His granite-colored body appeared carved from stone and, when clenched, his fists looked like boulders. When open, as they were in meditation, she could barely cover his palm with her whole hand. It was a beautiful sight—to her at least.

Ondorum opened his eyes, looking straight into hers. Akina dropped her gaze.

"Didn't mean to let it get that far. Hit harder than I thought." Seeing his questioning look, she sighed. "It was . . . I was just . . ."

He leaned forward, hands on knees. She swallowed the rest of the words, realizing she'd be making excuses where none were needed.

"Nobody died in the ring. Right?"

He shook his head and gestured to her gear and maulaxe stacked in a corner. Akina eyed the jumbled heap of leather and iron pieces, topped with the breastplate and ram's helm. The shells she wore to keep the world at bay.

So strange how the overwhelming rage frightened and disgusted her outside of a fight. Not the fighting itself—a dwarven warrior could find great glory and honor through battle. It was the way she abandoned all sense of self and principle. She hadn't been reared that way. She'd been taught to fight for a purpose. For her people. For those she cared about.

Her chest tightened to think of what her mother would've thought, seeing her like this. Jannasten had the occasional temper too, but even when her mother got angry, she'd kept it contained. She'd funneled it into her art, into constructive pursuits. Akina had once imagined herself capable of that sort of control. Yet now, when a fight began, she craved letting the fury consume her. It burned away everything else. She didn't have to think. Didn't have to deal with any complicated emotions beyond the rage itself. Life got easier. Kill or be killed. Simple.

But then it always deserted her, forcing her to deal with the consequences. She'd hoped her destruction of Gromir's idol collection would provide temporary relief, but it had just cracked her shell enough to let the rage seep in and sweep her away.

She retrieved her equipment. Whatever her struggles, it didn't feel right to go without wearing her gear for long. As she strapped everything on, she explained what she'd learned at her mother's old shop and her encounter with the still-smitten and more-than-a-little-obsessed Gromir. Ondorum's expression dipped into sorrow on hearing of Jannasten's supposed death. Akina left out details about Gromir's shrine, but stated she'd made it clear she wanted no more pieces resembling her placed around the city. She also reassured Ondorum she wouldn't deface the already-existing work.

As she finished dressing, her brother groaned on his cot in the other room. He jolted upright, sticking a hand against the wall to steady himself.

"Who? Where . . ." He fixed on her. "So. It wasn't a dream. Just a nightmare."

"Good to see you too." She crossed her arms. "So. What do I say when I find my brother has disgraced the Fairingots?"

He slumped. "I dunno. What am I supposed to say when my sister vanishes for ten years?"

"I didn't vanish, Brakisten. I went to war."

"Sure, but then you never came back." He looked aside. "And when you do, it's too late to matter."

She bit the inside of her cheeks, tasting blood. She hadn't saved her brother's life to threaten it herself for a few snide comments.

"You knew about Mother and Gromir?"

"Of course." He shrugged. "I'd probably have jumped down a ravine years ago without his help. But I didn't pay much attention to him until she died."

"She disappeared. That's not the same as dying."

"Doesn't matter."

"Doesn't matter," she echoed. "What matters to you anymore, hm?"

Glaring, he staggered to his feet. "I'll admit, it's a bit disappointing waking up day after day and finding I still haven't managed to drink myself down into the Abyss. If you want to see the death certificate, I signed off on it a year ago. The debate's closed unless she turns up in another decade or two." He scrunched one eye. "Why is a naked oread listening to us?"

"Oh for . . ." Akina snatched up the robe and tossed it to Ondorum. He slipped it on and secured the belt. "He's with me."

Brakisten cocked a bushy eyebrow. "*With* you? In what way?"

"That's not your business."

"And that says everything."

"I said it's not your business. He's a companion. My friend. My . . ." She struggled for the right word. ". . . balance."

"Balancing? Is that what they call it these days?"

"Shut it."

"You haven't introduced him to Gromir yet, have you?"

She frowned. "No, why?"

"I just know Gromir doesn't take well to your friend's kind. Oreads, that is."

"What?"

"Way he tells it, during his studies, he came to feel that oreads were . . . well . . . cheap imitations of dwarves. The subpar result of humans trying to mimic Torag's creations." Brakisten grimaced. "Don't know that many agree with him, but figured I'd warn you. Especially seeing as you're letting a mountain man under your armor and that clod is still pining over you."

Akina cleared her throat. "I've cured him of that."

"Really? Did you chop off half his head? Might do him some good."

"I thought you said he's helped you."

Brakisten sighed. "He did. He does. He's just a bit overeager." He knuckled his forehead. "In the end, I think Mother was happier having him as a son than me."

"Mother never would've stopped caring for you."

"Funny. I would've once thought the same of my sister."

Akina bit back harsh words. This was her brother's pain talking, not his true feelings. "What happened, Brakisten?"

"It's always easier to fall than climb, Kina." Silence draped over them until he hacked and spat to one side. "Sorry to be such a disappointment, but I haven't exactly been living every day on the off-chance you might pop up to judge my performance."

"I'm not judging. I'm trying to understand—"

He waved her off. "You really shouldn't have bothered coming home. No home to come home to, actually. Just a dead mother and a mad brother."

She flinched. "About this madness. Why are you talking about the duergar god at all? What's Droskar got to do with anything?"

His lips pinched shut and a challenge firmed his gaze.

She held out her hands. "Brakisten, talk to me. I'm home. I'm here. Can't we at least try and start patching a few cracks? Can't you tell me anything?"

He smiled sadly. "Nothing you'd really listen to."

They matched stares, hers dumbfounded, his bleary. Then he snapped the moment in two by stepping past and heading for the door.

She whirled. "Where do you think you're going?"

"Not really your business," he said over his shoulder, "but it involves balancing this nightmare with a few dreams."

She reached out to drag him back, but Ondorum raised a hand, cautioning her to wait. She trembled in place.

"I'm your elder sister," she shouted.

His weary laugh slapped her. "Not in any way that matters."

"Dammit, Brakisten, if you go anywhere near another—"

The door slammed shut in her face. She seethed a moment before stomping into the back room and punching the wall. Then she snagged the washbasin and broke it in half. When none of that helped, she grabbed up her helmet and strapped it on. She growled as she hefted her maulaxe.

"Right. While he's off to a lose a fight with a wine barrel, I'm off to win a few and get back some coin."

Ondorum rose and blocked the exit with his body.

Akina rolled her eyes. "I can control it. I just need more practice. You're always telling me perfection comes with repetition."

His skeptical look deepened.

"Ondorum, get out of my way before I—"

She tried to push past, but he grabbed and lifted her. As she kicked at his stomach and chest, he pinned her to the wall.

The door opened and Gromir poked his head in. "Brakisten, are you about?"

Chapter Six
Misunderstandings

Gromir shouted and leapt into the room. A small throwing axe appeared in one of his hands while he raised the other with curled fingers. The space between fingertips and palm flared with a knot of flame, which he aimed at the monk. A layer of frost crackled over the axe blade.

"Gromir, don't!" Akina cried.

Ondorum lurched sideways, dragging her along as Gromir attacked. The monk's robe flapped in the sudden movement, and a bolt of flame seared through the wool and charred the wall. Gromir flung the frosted axe. Ondorum ducked into the back room, carrying Akina with him. The axe ricocheted off the wall and floor, forming patches of ice.

Akina thrust away from Ondorum and caught her balance when she hit the floor. Gromir charged into the room, another rimed axe readied. She threw herself between the two men, arms wide.

"Stop!"

...e axe clacked against her breastplate and dropped to the floor. All three held still as a web of frost formed over her armor. The chill radiated across her breasts and stomach, but didn't penetrate further. She rapped at the affected metal and winced at the *ting*. She glared up at Gromir.

"If this is permanent, you're paying for a replacement."

Gromir had one hand halfway inside his robe, his bandolier of throwing axes now minus two. He withdrew the hand, while his other relaxed from whatever arcane symbol he'd been forming. His confused look swung from her to Ondorum and back.

"I thought he was attacking you."

Technically, he had been, but Akina decided not to press the point.

"Gromir, this is Ondorum. He's a monk I met while traveling. We've been together for a while, but I didn't have the chance to introduce you yet." She nodded to the monk. "Ondorum, this is Gromir. I told you about him, remember?" Only just recently, but she hoped Gromir assumed otherwise. "He and I trained together before the war. We were close."

"Close?" Gromir grunted the word. "That's really all you're going to say? After the time we spent together?"

She faced him. "I made my stance clear."

Ondorum pressed palms together and bowed.

Gromir stiffened. "He's an oread."

"Glad to see your eyes work."

"Why isn't he saying anything?"

"He's taken a vow of silence. It's a holy thing." Akina shook her head at Ondorum. "I'm going to find a giant slab of bronze, carve *I don't talk because I'm a halfwit, please spare a copper* on it, and chain it around your neck."

Gromir placed a hand on her arm. "Can I speak to you? In private?"

She shrugged him off, but nodded Ondorum toward the door. "Mind?"

Ondorum bowed again and exited, though without a calming touch or any of the small signs of affection she'd grown used to.

As soon as the door closed, Gromir gripped her shoulders. "What is he to you?"

She brushed his hands away and stepped out of reach. "Someone who understands personal space."

"I'm serious, Akina."

"So am I. What's it matter to you?"

"Everything."

"We've very different definitions of everything."

"Whatever you may think of me—" He chuckled darkly. "Or not think, for that matter, I can't believe you'd associate yourself with one of them. There's not a single oread in the world that's worth your time and attention."

She glowered. "Brakisten told me about your problem with them. Should I mention one of Torag's own clerics was happy to see Ondorum? Said it was a blessing to have him in the temple."

Gromir threw his hands up. "Yes, fine. They share some affinity with us. They fit in, but they're not our equals in any way. Human blood with diluted essence of the earth? It's like one person constructing a citadel of true stone while another builds one of hardened mud and tries to claim they hold the same value."

She opened and closed her mouth, trying to find the right words.

"I know it's not a popular perspective," he said, "but oreads have no real fire in their bellies like we do. They're weak clay, and we need to stop pretending otherwise."

She stabbed a finger at him. "It's sad to see all your studying's wasted. Ondorum's one of the strongest people I know. He's fought harder, worked harder, and done more to help others than anyone I've crossed paths with."

"Please. He may have fooled you, but it's obvious he's a brute, and his silly vow of silence is just a way to give himself an air of wounded virtue. He may have some strength, but so do ogres, and you don't see them contributing anything lasting to culture or civilization."

"He's saved my life more times than I can count."

"I've fought to save your family's name! In the end, your and your kin's place in the histories is what matters to future generations. They'll look to us, their ancestors, for inspiration. Can't you see that?"

"I've seen enough."

He glowered. "Yes, and then destroyed what you saw."

Akina shut her eyes briefly, trying to scatter the embers flaring within her. Violence couldn't solve everything, and rattling Gromir's skull wouldn't set his thoughts straight.

"You don't have any right to talk about Ondorum like this. You don't know him."

"Nor do I wish to, especially after seeing what knowing him has done to you."

The embers flared. She opened her eyes, hoping the heat shone through.

He reached for her again, but then hesitated and dropped his hand. "A lot has hit you at once. Coming home to find this," he glanced around the room, "discovering the things you hoped for having gone missing. Such shock can shake even the stoutest mind and heart."

"You saying I'm not in my right mind?"

"I'm saying you're sun-blind. That you've exchanged gold for pyrite. The surface world offered a lie you've bought into fully, and that galls me." Akina wanted to slap off his pained look, but he continued. "Your potential is wasted out in those lands. And on people like *him*."

"Keep talking like this and it'll be your *face* I pound to scrap next."

"See? Even your wit has been reduced to nothing but promises of violence."

"You once liked when I threatened you."

He bowed his head. "So I did. I often recall our sparring, learning the ways of war together, and our many meals in the training quarters. Then there was the time we spent stationed together out near Davarn. Those were the brightest points in my life."

The brightest times in his life occurred over a decade before, and revolved around her? She would've thought that one of the most tragic things she'd ever heard if it didn't cast a strange shadow through her. For her, the most glorious times were connected to losing herself in battle and the unexpected joy of surviving a brutal encounter.

"Why'd you even come here? What'd you want with Brakisten?" Akina squinted at him. "Or maybe you were looking for me, hm?"

He fiddled with the bandolier strapped to his chest. "I did come for Brakisten, to see how he was handling your return and offer him some food."

"Oh, he's so pleased to see me, he's out to raise a toast."

Gromir sighed. "I've tried to convince many tavern owners and merchants to deny him business. Only the greediest have refused, but no one will let him open a tab at least, so it's become harder to supply himself."

"How noble of you."

"As I've said, I care for your kin almost as much as I do for you. I just wish you'd see that."

"Want to show me you really care?"

When he nodded fervently, she pointed to the door. "Get to know Ondorum. Open your mind a little and admit you might be wrong about him."

His face crumpled. "Even if I were willing, how am I to do that when he's not speaking?"

Akina scrubbed a hand across her forehead. Didn't Ondorum realize how difficult he made this? "Point taken. But there's more ways to get to know someone than talking."

"None that I'd abide with one of his kind." He held out his hands in a begging posture. "What else can I do? Tell me. Anything. How can I prove that you belong here and that I'm worthy of your devotion?"

She knocked his hands aside and backed him up against a wall. She pressed a fist to his sternum so he might feel its weight combine with her words. "Bring my mother back and save Brakisten's lost soul." She pushed away. "Simple as that."

Gromir stood as if stunned. She waited for him to slink out so she could rejoin Ondorum and figure out their next steps. Instead, the tiniest smile twitched Gromir's beard. He bowed.

"As you command, m'lady."

Odd smile still fixed, he strode from the room and gathered the two thrown axes. On his way out the door, he almost knocked into Ondorum. He paused long enough to give the monk a venomous look, then continued on his way. Ondorum peered inside, curious. Akina exhaled. Then she shivered. The ice melting off her breastplate had sent a frigid rivulet tracking down her stomach and thigh.

Cursing, she searched for a rag to wipe off the remaining condensation before her underclothes got soaked. Maybe her armor could weep for Gromir, but she never would.

Chapter Seven
Fallen Faithful

The next day, Akina and Ondorum visited the ancestral vaults and met with a priest of Magrim, the dwarven god of the afterlife and restorer of souls. The priest expressed his sorrow and retrieved Jannasten's death etching. Brakisten's scrawl marked the thin bronze sheet, certifying their mother's demise. *Presumed death*, Akina kept reminding herself. Technically, Jannasten had just headed off and never come home. Much like her daughter—and everyone had started figuring Akina for dead, hadn't they?

Still, after staring at the certificate for several minutes, Akina asked for a guide into the catacombs. A steward led them to one of the ravines cutting through the city level. He lowered them by cage and winch to the entrance of a burial labyrinth built into the side of the trench.

He lit the winding tunnels with a lantern until, at last, they came to an arch marked by the Fairingot sigil: an engraved bar with an eye set in the middle, surrounded by rays of light. While they didn't have Jannasten's body, an empty stone coffin had still been interred in the generational vaults. Akina knelt and laid her maulaxe before this and tried to think of a fitting prayer. Yet she could only think, *Sorry. I'm so sorry.* She repeated this until her mind went numb and the words lost any meaning. Her hands shook as she retrieved her weapon and strapped it onto her back.

After leaving the catacombs and dismissing their guide, she wandered the city streets, Ondorum in tow. They wound up sitting on a low mushroom-garden wall overlooking the graveyard ravine. She leaned against him, taking comfort in his unwavering presence.

At last, she roused. "Coming back was a huge mistake; I shouldn't have dragged you into it." When he faced her, green eyes bright, she lifted a hand. "Let me finish, hm? I'm not giving up all hope. I just don't think I'll find it here like I figured."

She gazed across the city. "There's no place here for me. No purpose. Maybe that's what I really hoped to find. Place and purpose. When I fight, that savage joy fills me, but there's no sense behind it. Nothing besides ending one life and keeping mine. That can't be right. That can't be all there is to it. I want to find more, just not here. And staying would only make it worse for me and everyone else."

She stood, smiling wearily. "We'll leave. Maybe take Brakisten with us." She chuckled. "That'd be a good start, right? Some fresh air could clear his head. Then we find some work, bash some heads in, and only worry about whether our clients pay or not. Back to better times, hm?"

She hopped down from the wall with a clatter. He followed. It took them the better part of the day to track down the latest tavern Brakisten frequented. When Akina peeked inside and spotted her brother slumped in a corner, she sighed.

"Would you wait outside?" she asked Ondorum. "I'll try to talk sense into him."

He stepped aside and urged her on with an encouraging smile. Inside, Akina skirted tables and other drunks until she reached Brakisten. She sat beside her brother and eased the tankard out of his loose grip. A swig of the contents left her grimacing. Foul stuff. Hardly fit to call ale.

He stared at her with glazed eyes. "What're you doing here?" His focus drifted to the mug. "Hey, that's mine."

Deciding it was the lesser of two evils, she drained the swill in two gulps and wiped her mouth clean. She handed the mug back so he could pout into its depths. "Where'd you get the coin? Figured you for broke these days."

He hunched further. "There's always folks who'll take pity on those living lower than dirt."

"Begging, Brakisten? Really?"

"Like it's any worse than what I've already suffered."

"Tell me about that. Help me understand."

"Buy me another drink?"

"No." She forced a calm breath through her teeth. "Just talk to me. Please."

He dragged fingers through his knotted beard. "It's difficult to serve two gods at once. I gave over to worshiping the wrong one."

"No. I won't accept my brother betrayed everything he believed in to start worshiping the Dark Smith. You'd start following Zon-Kuthon the torture god before that."

He eyed her sidelong. "Not talking about Droskar. Talking Torag and . . ." He lifted the empty mug.

"Then why go around telling people Droskar's coming for their souls?"

He reached up and rapped his skull. "Ever feel like your head's so stuffed full of wrongness you've got to let it out or you'll crack and fall apart? That's what it was like for me. I started seeing things. Fire. Smoke. Hearing horrible screams, like the tortured dead calling for me. Chains rattling. Buildings and people would turn to ash and bone and rusting metal all around me for days at a time."

She laid a hand on his shoulder. "You worked in Torag's temple. Didn't other clerics get visions?"

He shoved her hand off. "Nothing like this! These're unholy visions, full of death and despair straight from the Abyss. Just like the stories we're told of Droskar's realm. I thought I'd go insane if it didn't stop. I told others, as much as it shamed me. Had them look for curses or any sort of wicked influence. Nothing. Some said it was all in my head, manifestations of doubt or some other blather."

"When did this start?"

"A couple years before Mother disappeared." His voice turned weepy. "I tried to hold it back. Tried to drink the nightmares away. Worked for a while, but then it just made it worse. I don't even remember half of what I did or said back then."

"You still get these visions?"

"They come and go. The less I remember, the better. Figure if I'm too drunk to walk or talk straight, I can't cause more trouble."

"Hell, Brakisten." She propped her chin on her clasped hands. "I know exactly how you feel."

His brow furrowed. "You do?"

A grimace. "During the war, I learned about Gorum. Saw him, actually."

Brakisten's eyes focused on her, the clearest his vision had been since their reunion. "You're joking. You saw a god."

"Didn't realize it at first. It was during one of the last, bloodiest battles with the goblin tribes in our area. I got separated from my squad and found myself surrounded by dozens of goblins and a few hobgoblins. I thought I was about to die. But as they closed in, a figure appeared by me. A giant man all dressed in dark iron armor, with eyes blazing like bloody fire. He touched my shoulder, vanished, and this pure, driving rage consumed me. I lost at least an hour in my mind and woke up to find myself painted in goblin remains with more than fifty of them dead around me."

Her brother paled. "Hell, Akina."

"It was incredible . . . at first. I gave over to it every chance I got. Learned more about the Lord in Iron and found my real calling for battle. That's what kept me from coming back right away. Out there," she waved vaguely, "offered me more chances to explore and fight as much as I wanted. I fell in with a band of mercenaries and made a good living."

"By killing whoever they paid you to kill."

"Wasn't mindless slaughter. We only took contracts on those who had good reason to die."

"Sure." Brakisten licked his lips and tilted his head as if seeing her from a new perspective. From the worried gleam in his eyes, whatever he saw frightened him. "What about now? Still a Gorumite?"

"No. But I still have some troubles."

"Such as?"

She reached back to feel the reassuring weight of her maulaxe. "Figure these days, it's less like giving myself over to the battlefury and more like it comes and goes as it wants; when it leaves, it takes a bit more of me each time."

He sniffed. "So you didn't come back for me or Mother or Gromir. You came back for you. Because you thought we'd be here to save you from yourself."

"No. I came home hoping to avoid fighting for a while. Besides, I brought home more than just myself, hm?"

He laughed raggedly. "Not sure Mother would've expected an oread lover as a homecoming gift."

She grinned despite herself. "Maybe not, but he's the best thing I've got. And I don't want to ruin that by wallowing here too long. I'm leaving soon."

"Leaving? You just got back."

"And see how well it's gone? I don't really belong here anymore."

His face crinkled. "Neither do I, if I'm honest."

"Which is why I want you to come with me."

Surprise flickered across his face. "With you?"

"You're my brother after all. We could wander the roads. See a few cities. Have a few adventures."

"Kill a few people."

She tried for a gentle smile, not wanting to scare him off. "Got to get paid somehow, but I'm not forcing you into that business. I just figure it'd be helpful to start climbing again—this time with folks there to catch you if you fall."

He pulled on a black curl so hard she feared he might tear it from his scalp. "Let me think about it, okay?" He rose on wobbly legs.

She snagged a corner of his robe. "Where are you going?"

"To think. And take a piss. I'll be back in just a few seconds, I promise."

He staggered off and out a side door, which clapped shut behind him.

Akina frowned after, instinct clamoring that he meant to ditch her and crawl into another drinking hole. She waited a few moments, then gave in and stood. Time to force the matter for his own good. He'd thank her later.

She slipped out the same side door into another short alley. Three dwarven figures gathered around Brakisten, who wavered in their midst. Two figures held his arms on either side, but her brother didn't appear to be resisting in the slightest. Akina groaned, anticipating more ruffians.

Then she recognized Gromir's golden hair and blue robe. These set him apart from the other two, who had matching bald heads, draping silver beards, and ashen skin. Nondescript gray leather outfits clad their stout bodies, and they gazed at her with obsidian eyes.

Duergar? Loose in Taggoret? It couldn't be. Dwarves were ever on the alert for infiltration by their treacherous kin. She'd only seen a handful of the abhorrent outcasts before going off to war, mostly as prisoners from failed assaults on dwarven territory. The wicked race had remained quiet in the past century, content to toil down in the Darklands in mindless devotion to Droskar.

Gromir whirled and goggled at her. "You shouldn't be here!"

Akina poised her maulaxe, blade edge out. "Get away from my brother."

Gromir glanced at the duergar. "Go. I'll meet you at the appointed place." He touched Brakisten's shoulder and her brother disappeared. The duergar appeared to continue holding unseen limbs. Before Akina took another step, the pair vanished as well.

"No!" Akina charged for where they'd stood. Some stories said duergar had an innate ability to turn invisible. If they'd done so rather than spirited themselves away with a spell, she could stop them before they got too far.

Gromir thrust a hand out, and a black glob flew from his fingertips; it splattered on the earth between Akina and her destination, coating the area with glistening film. Her feet went out from under her and she collapsed in a clatter. She scrabbled for purchase and lurched up to stare at him.

"Why are you doing this?"

He cringed, but then gathered himself. "You asked me to. It's for Brakisten's own good and yours. Farewell, Akina. My assistant will have a message for you explaining this."

One hand twisted into an arcane gesture, and he too vanished. Ondorum rounded the corner moments later. Grease streaking her armor, Akina regained her balance and bulled past the monk, looking every which way.

"Gromir . . . my brother . . . duergar took . . ." She caught her breath. "The shop. Need to get to my mother's shop."

They warned the first guard patrol they encountered. While not supported by any direct evidence, their claim of duergar within the city slapped alarm across the soldiers' faces. One jogged off to alert the nearest commander while the others spread out to search the area.

Akina raced on, Ondorum in her wake. She charged into the shop as Selvia emerged from the back rooms. Akina's bellow made the younger dwarf look like she wanted to cower behind the counter.

"Gromir! Where is he?"

Selvia wrung her hands, ruddy hair flopping back and forth. "N-not here, mistress. I haven't seen him since yesterday."

Ondorum placed a gentle hand on the girl's shoulder while Akina hunched to meet her eyes.

"If you're hiding him or doing anything to protect him, know he was just spotted with a couple of duergar. And they took my brother. So think carefully about what you say next."

Selvia's eyes widened in horror. "Duergar? Here? With him?"

"He said you'd have a message for me."

Selvia extended a quaking hand, making the parchment she held flutter like a bird's wing. "I found this in the room you destr—that he showed you the other day."

Akina snatched the paper away and unfolded it.

Beloved Akina,

I am fulfilling my promise to you and doing all that's left in my power to salvage the damage I've done to your family. And the only place I know to do so is within Nar-Voth. If all goes well, I should return within a matter of weeks with your mother restored and your brother redeemed. If not, then you can at least be at peace knowing you'll never have to deal with me again. Don't be frightened for my fate or for Brakisten's. He will serve a greater purpose alongside me, and I will care for him as I can along the way.

My only request is that you wait in Taggoret for two months. Seems a short time compared to ten years, does it not? If I've not returned by then, you can assume I've failed and live free from any burden you felt I imposed on you.

Yours,
Gromir Hokkelunst

Akina's roar made the other dwarf stagger. Selvia gripped Ondorum's bracing arm to hold herself upright. The monk took the letter and read it while Akina stamped about.

The growl in her throat resolved into words. "Unbelievable. Unbelievable! Into Nar-Voth? Taking my brother? Working with duergar?" She spun and shook a fist at Selvia. "You! Where's the nearest courier office? We need messages to every tunnel gate as fast as possible. They need to be on full alert so Gromir can't slip past any of the defenses."

Selvia made a shaky curtsy. "There's one just a few streets over, miss. But . . . um . . ." She chewed her lower lip.

"Spew it or stow it."

"I don't think Master Gromir's going down any of Taggoret's tunnels, miss."

"How would you know? And don't call him master anymore."

Selvia ducked her head. "Um . . . I . . . well, it's because of his stories and maps, miss."

"Stories? Maps? He's been down there before?"

"Yes, miss. Several times, I think. When business was slow and he was between carvings, he liked to talk about exploring Nar-Voth, and some of the creatures and sights he encountered there." She offered up shaking hands. "I don't know why he went down. He never said, but sometimes I'd see him working on strange bits of stone or studying old-looking carvings he must've brought back from there."

Ondorum rattled the parchment and Akina nodded.

"You mentioned maps," she said. "Of the Darklands?"

Selvia flushed. "I enjoy working at the shop, but I'm actually training to be a cartographer. I like to redraw maps I've seen of lands I've never visited. While cleaning the shop about a year ago, I discovered a bunch of maps Master—er, Gromir had stashed in one of the desks. From time to time, after he's gone home, I've pulled them out and practiced." She stared at her feet. "When I came in and found that note addressed to you waiting, I had an odd feeling. So I checked to ensure all our records were in order. Everything's in place except the maps. They're gone, but I still have the copies I made. I think they're pretty accurate."

"And you figure they show where he's going?"

The shop assistant perked up. "One of them notes a route to a surface gate northwest of here, not far from Davarn. There's another subterranean route linking from there to a series of unlabeled tunnels. It has various landmarks noted along the way."

"I know that gate. Gromir and I were stationed there together for a couple years. Before the war." Akina frowned. "Why would they go all the way there?"

"Maybe because he *was* stationed there, miss." Selvia flushed deeper at their attention. "I . . . I haven't even ever gone to Taggoret's lower gates, so I don't really know anything, but I just thought . . ."

Akina scratched her chin. "That's a good point, actually. Taggoret's undergates are extremely fortified. The surface gate near Davarn is secured, yes, but just against potential threats from below, not to protect a whole city. And Gromir knows the gate defenses. He might have an idea of how to get his duergar friends through without raising an alarm." She scowled at a wall. "Besides, a trip overland is actually the safer option."

"Safer?" Selvia's forehead scrunched.

"Compared to the tunnels, the surface is a wasteland. Plenty of unguarded territory. Lots of room to run and hide. In the tunnels, you can get cornered quick unless you're able to walk through solid stone." Akina clenched and unclenched her fists. "If they're heading to Davarn, we could catch up before they go under. But we've got to go immediately."

Ondorum grimaced in agreement.

"Miss?" Selvia raised a finger.

Akina huffed. "More?"

"Just one thing. Could I go with you?"

Akina and Ondorum shook their heads in unison.

"No. Absolutely not. You're staying here, and that's final."

Chapter Eight
Sundered Earth

Akina sighed and looked back at Selvia, who waved from atop her mule as the trio plodded along the mountain trail. The assistant acted as if this had become some grand adventure, while Akina hoped the furthest it'd take them would be Davarn. At worst, they'd catch up with Gromir and Brakisten in the shallow tunnels beyond the surface gate and drag them home.

Of course, this assumed their quarry had taken the path the maps indicated, and that Gromir's duergar friends didn't have a quicker route plotted.

She'd already spoken to the guards and patrols from the fortress at the bottom of Kingtower Pass, but they'd proven no help. If Gromir traveled with at least two duergar, they'd not likely be stopping in any dwarven settlements along the way, so she didn't bother side-tracking to question every post.

She glanced back at Selvia again. The other dwarf remained wide-eyed at all the natural wonder surrounding them. Probably hadn't left Taggoret her whole life. The shopkeeper cared for Gromir, that was obvious. She'd refused to give up the copied maps until Akina relented to her request to join them. That and the offer of using the workshop's coin cache to pay for journey supplies swayed the decision, though Ondorum still frowned whenever he looked Selvia's way.

Akina gazed ahead, remembering her first times beyond Taggoret's caverns, astounded by the sense of an endless sky speared by dozens of mountain peaks. The cliffs, gorges, and canyons made the region look like it had been carved by the hammers and chisels of the gods. Tundra fought for space against boulder fields, and they passed over numerous rivers swollen with snowmelt that poured down into natural and dwarf-made reservoirs in the upper valleys. The bleat of goats rolled off the cliffs from time to time. Even with all the passionate labor the dwarves had given to their mountains across the centuries, it remained a raw, untamed land. She loved it for that.

As had her mother. She easily pictured Jannasten traveling through this area, pack on her back, expression bright as she soaked in the same wild beauty.

As with any wilderness, it held its dangers. The main roads and passes tended to be safer, as patrols swept them at regular intervals. The city garrisons took regional defense seriously, considering it provided merchants and traders more peace of mind when bringing commerce to the area. But one couldn't keep an eye on every hillside or fill every vale with armed dwarves. Nor were bandits forever deterred by soldiers once the weather grew colder and their bellies emptier.

Roving beasts, trolls, giants, and ogres who also called the kingdom home all added potential complications.

As the shadows slipped toward evening, Akina scanned their surroundings for any sign of an ambush or tracks of any deadly beasts. So far, she'd spotted only a few wolf prints in the dried mud and a discarded set of antlers in a patch of brambles.

The sun dipped behind the nearest peak as they crested a ridge. The road continued through a narrow plain divided by a winding river and covered in swaths of wildflowers. Two days out of Taggoret. One more to Davarn. Their mules rode steady enough, laden with provisions, but they'd pushed the pace most of the day. It wouldn't do to have one or more pack animals get exhausted and leave them traveling all the slower.

When the others reached her, Akina pointed to a flat patch just above a river bend. A few scrub trees and bushes clustered there, offering minimal cover from the night winds that had howled over them the past couple stops. "Figure we'll camp there and be off at sunrise."

Ondorum headed down, but Selvia held back. Akina looked at her in question.

"Is it wise to camp out in the open like this?" Selvia had switched from her shop-keeping silks to a more sensible set of traveling clothes, with a leather vest that accentuated a trimmer figure than Akina would've guessed.

Akina nudged her mule forward, prompting Selvia to follow. "I prefer campsites in the open, most times. More freedom to move in a fight and lets me see my enemy coming. That, and it gives them a few extra moments to reconsider closing the gap."

"But if you can see them, can't they see you first? And couldn't they hit you with arrows or spells from afar?"

Akina shrugged. "Sure, but if something's out hunting you, it'll come whether you think you're safe or not. Hiding's for the weak."

Selvia shivered in the mild breeze. "It's hard to imagine constantly being exposed, though. Up here, it's like the gods are always staring down at you."

"Those are just stars. You get used to things on the surface. Or you don't, and it kills you sooner or later."

"Good thing we'll be back below soon." Selvia glanced around as if double-checking the wildflowers for hidden threats. "You must've learned a lot of things like that while traveling. How to face all sorts of unknowns and strange people and creatures. You really fought with mercenaries?"

"Gromir told you that, hm?"

"More complained about it, really. Said those sort of lowlifes weren't worthy of your presence."

"Sounds like him." She studied Selvia from under the rim of her helm. "Not my business, so tell me to stow it if you want. Were you and Gromir ever . . ."

Selvia started in her saddle. "Me and him? Oh, no. I'm just his assistant."

"And yet here you are, leaving home for the first time, braving camping in the open under the gods' own eyes, possibly heading down into the Darklands after him."

"What's down there?" Selvia asked. "How deep have you gone? Orv?"

Akina snorted. "You kidding? I've heard of folks going that deep and surviving, but I figure anyone who boasts about it is either a liar or madman." She mimed different layers with her hands. "You've got Nar-Voth, which is what most people mean when talking about the Darklands. I did a few training patrols there back when. Then there's Sekamina, which they say is over-run by dark elves. Orv is under all that, leagues deep, and I can't even begin to tell you what might be down there."

Selvia cocked her head. "What were your patrols like?"

Akina started to answer, then chuckled. She guided her mule off the road toward where Ondorum was already clearing space for a fire. "You almost did a damn good job of distracting me. I *was* talking about why you wanted to come along so much. I doubt it's for my brother."

The younger dwarf flushed. "Gromir's only ever had a mind for you."

"No straight answer is answer enough."

Selvia lowered her eyes.

Akina considered her as they rode on. If another woman ever appeared who had a history with Ondorum and turned his eyes away, Akina figured she might get a bit . . . snippy. Yet this youngling kept herself amicable, if occasionally flustered. Was she intimidated? Felt she wasn't good enough for Gromir?

They trotted up to where Ondorum had tied his mule to one of the scrub trees. Selvia hopped down from her mount and took Akina's reins.

"Um . . . is there anything I can help with for camp?"

Akina swung off her saddle. "Same as last night. See to the animals and then start gathering what dry wood you can find."

Akina joined Ondorum in putting up their small tents and hauling in rocks from an old slide nearby to use as a fire ring. Not much more entrenchment needed for one night; certainly nothing like sticking in one forest-bound clearing for months like they had with their former band. Things could get quite cozy at times, even when everyone lived out of tents and ate from the same pot and spit.

As Selvia fed the mules and watered them at the river, Akina pondered the many unknowns piling up. It'd been years since she felt at such an utter loss. Oddly, one of her mother's old exhortations rose to mind, urging her to turn to Torag for guidance. He'd led the dwarves up to the surface and guided them to strength and glory. Couldn't he still offer her direction and wisdom?

She thrust that thought aside. She hadn't prayed to Torag in years, and wasn't about to start now. Besides, it wasn't like he'd answer.

She hunkered down to stew in silence. By the time Selvia stumbled back into camp with an armload of dead scrub and twigs, darkness had truly fallen. Everything had gone shades of gray and muted whites to Akina's eyes, letting her clearly note the valley's layout even though the moon had just peeked over a low saddle. She rose to give the youngling a hand.

Ondorum lunged at Selvia from his crouch. The dwarf's eyes rounded and the wood dropped from her grasp right before the oread drove her to the ground. Akina stood dumbstruck for an instant before the earth burst open, showering dirt and rocks everywhere. A silvery form bigger than a horse shot through the air right where Selvia had been standing.

Akina drew her maulaxe, but the beast burrowed back down into the ground, disappearing in an instant despite its massive size. She glimpsed a spurred fin on its back and a ridged tail before it vanished into the hole dug by its claws. She spun, searching for any sign of where it might emerge. The beast's coming and going had shredded their tents to little more than scraps of leather and rope.

Ondorum rolled off Selvia, who lay gasping. She pushed up on an elbow, blood trickling from a scratch on her cheek.

"What was—? Was that—?"

"Landshark," Akina breathed in awe. She turned a circle, still seeking the beast.

The earth bulged a few paces over. She threw herself that way right as the landshark's head broke the surface. Encased in carapace that gleamed under the rising moon, it opened a maw filled with slavering fangs large enough to shred her in a single bite. Her blow whipped across its lower jaw, making its bite snap aside. It thrashed, and its skull slammed into her, sending her tumbling.

It clambered the rest of the way out of the earth. She rolled to her feet and braced herself. The creature raked the ground, parting it like water. Its eyes gleamed and its hiss threw ropy spittle at her. She circled to put its back to the others.

The beast charged, snapping wildly. She lashed her weapon back and forth to ward off the attacks, trying to stay just out of range. She struck a claw away with the hammer and then spun to slam the axe edge between its eyes.

The beast whirled with blinding speed, and its tail slapped her into the air. She somehow kept her grip on the maulaxe as she hit the ground. She spat blood and grinned as embers burst into flame within her.

The creature now raced toward Ondorum, who wielded a summoned iron quarterstaff. The staff blurred in his hands and lashed out to strike his foe multiple times in a moment, though it seemed to have little effect besides blunting the creature's bites. He took simple steps to evade its furious charges from all sides, almost as if taunting the creature. Of Selvia, there was no sign.

Akina used her maulaxe to push herself up. No hesitation this time. No worries about who to hit or not. She had a clear target, an open field, and all the strength she could muster to pound it back into the dirt it'd come from.

Akina howled death and thunder and closed the gap in two bounds, ramming her shoulder and helmet into the beast's scaly side. Then she staggered back, stunned, while it remained unmoved, focused on the monk. Claws lashed out and one clipped his shoulder. He whirled, planting the staff to keep from sprawling flat, but was exposed as the beast raised a claw.

Akina charged in, slamming the maulaxe up under its shoulder with all her might. The landshark roared as the hit flung it off its feet, skidding it across the grass. She followed and dealt hammer blows to its exposed underbelly.

The beast writhed to its feet, forcing her to leap back as it faced her. The spiked fin on its spine quivered and lifted, as if excited by the fight. Screeching, it lunged for Ondorum, who'd recovered and tried to come in from the side.

He ducked to let the beast leap over him, turning aside a tail lash with his staff. The landshark bulled ahead and dove into the ground. Akina charged for the hole in the earth, determined to crawl in after and slaughter the beast in its own tunnel.

Ondorum's staff blocked her way. She tried to bull past, but he just stood there, focused over her shoulder. Her gaze followed his.

The landshark reappeared over by where they'd tethered the animals. Two of the three mules were torn to shreds in instants, the beast gulping down chunks of muscle, organ, and bone. The last mule broke free of its tether and raced across the plain for freedom.

The landshark swallowed a last mouthful and then tunneled its way underground once more. It astounded Akina that something so huge could slip through the earth so easily.

Then she realized she should do less gaping and standing still. She jumped back right as the landshark speared up into the air where she'd just been standing. The ground trembled beneath its landing.

Akina dove aside as the maw snapped for her. She dug a heel in to reverse direction and threw herself up so the next bite stuck its head directly beneath her. A kick to the top of its skull sent her soaring above its back. She landed on its flexed haunches, bringing the full force of the maulaxe down to flatten the fin. The beast lurched at the last second, skewing her aim. Rather than striking the fin, the hammer pounded into a surprisingly soft patch of flesh behind it.

The creature's screech filled the night as it collapsed. Akina tumbled off its back and turned to see the creature thrashing, its back not quite aligning as it tried to regain purchase and dig to safety.

As it tried to roll upright, Ondorum darted in and rammed his staff into the exposed flesh behind the fin. The staff plunged deep, and the landshark's squirming flung chunks of dirt everywhere.

She sprinted up and landed a shuddering blow on the side of its face, cracking an eye socket. It raised a claw, but she knocked it away and rammed the axe edge at the same wounded eye. She hacked at the spot, ignoring it trying to scrabble at her. At last, its skull burst open, spewing black-and-red ichor across the ravaged earth. It gave a fading hiss and a final few twitches.

Chest heaving, Akina spun and looked for something else to slay. Ondorum stood a short distance away, looking wary as well, but of her, not more monsters.

She bared teeth and growled. "Don't worry. Know who you are."

At this admission and the lack of any other target, the inner flames flickered and died. Akina's bones cooled, and the weight of her armor and weapon doubled. She planted the maulaxe head to steady herself.

Then she realized she'd lost track of their companion. "Selvia?" Akina's tongue felt like a chunk of lead. "Shattered stone, she must've run."

"No, I'm h-here."

Selvia's head poked up from a large bush, twigs sticking to her hair and clothes. While Ondorum went over to help untangle her, Akina dropped to the ground and laid her maulaxe across her knees. The youngling stared over at the enormous corpse, now a jagged mound in the moonlight.

"What just happened?" she asked. "What was that?"

Akina worked on stilling her trembling muscles. "We call them landsharks. Figure them for beasts created by some fool of a wizard long ago. Who knows why." She unbuckled her helm and set it beside her. She swiped back her sweat-drenched hair and let the breeze soothe the blaze of her skin.

"Why'd it attack us?"

"Hungry. Angry. Bored. Take your pick. Dead now, at least." A hoarse laugh escaped her as she eyed the remains of the mules. "Even exchange, maybe. We lived, but it likely killed what chance we had of catching Gromir before Davarn."

With their tents ruined, they repositioned by one of the thicker trees, each with their back to it so they could rest while keeping an eye in every direction. Ondorum indicated he'd take the whole night's watch, but Akina laughed that off, saying she just needed a few hours to feel right and ready again. Selvia surprised her by offering to take a couple hours herself, claiming to be too shook up by the fight to sleep much anyways.

Once they settled in, Akina leaned her head back against the trunk and stared at the stars. The clear sky shone so polished and bright she figured it should've reflected a bit of the ruin and bloodshed down on the ground to be fair. As drowsiness crept in, her mind slipped back to her brief conversation with Selvia, and she wondered whether any of the stars might actually be the eyes of gods watching in silent judgment. Plenty to judge on her account.

One thought did niggle at her. Despite their savagery, landsharks were considered by some dwarves to be Torag's envoys. Elect of their kind were occasionally dispatched to send a message or work his will in the world. One in particular, an uplifted beast named Stoneriver, was said to swim in channels of magma the same way its lesser cousins did earth and stone.

If she were a more pious dwarf, she might take this as a sign. An indication of Torag's disapproval or a warning. But she figured that'd be overthinking the whole event.

She turned her head enough to see Ondorum sitting watch. At night, his form looked even more statuesque.

Whatever they had shared in battle, bed, and beyond, one of the biggest things she loved was how he never judged her. He'd disapproved of her methods at times, yes, but had never spoken out against her as a person. To him, the enlightened monk-god Irori was the ultimate judge, and people were only responsible for their own performance in life.

So did her methods matter so much as the results? Did it matter whether she fought under the blessing of Torag or Gorum or any others of the vast pantheon?

No answers came in the wind that sliced across the plain. She let the gust temporarily sweep away all worries and doubts as it filled her ears and mind with imagined cries of a horde about to charge into war.

To those pleasant thoughts, she at last fell into weary sleep.

Chapter Nine
Gladdringgar

Ondorum wished they had more time to experience the land, though he knew it to be a selfish desire. Even before meeting Akina, he found himself most at peace in the wilderness, or at least in places where people blended their structures with the earth, such as his old monastery.

As they often did, the thoughts of the monastery shot bolts of grief and regret through him. He briefly shut his eyes against memories of orc war cries, the sight of so many of his fellow monks fallen to their blades. He'd spent years attempting to purge the befuddled guilt the atrocity had left him with . . . and then the village incident had brought it all sweeping back to the fore.

At last, the memories receded, leaving him a measure of calm. Yet he knew they remained, waiting to pounce sooner or later. Would he never atone for either failure?

Since the loss of their mounts, they'd managed a steady pace on foot. Selvia impressed him with her determination and fortitude, never asking for rest despite the rough terrain they maneuvered through. They reached the fort south of Davarn by the end of the day, purchased new mules and supplies, and forged on as dusk encroached.

Ondorum questioned the wisdom of riding through the night—even though both dwarves and oreads could see well enough in the darkness, the mules were another story. Akina pushed to make up the lost time, though, and established in no uncertain terms that she'd be riding on and the others could follow later if they wanted to take a little nap, or perhaps sample some of the local brew. They journeyed north under a cloudy night sky, pausing at sunrise to give their beasts a brief respite before heading onward.

When they came in sight of Davarn, it struck Ondorum as similar to Taggoret in the manner of its construction and style, though on a smaller scale and with fewer adornments. More towers sprouted from the outer walls, the ridge of which had been fashioned into unevenly spaced triangles, suggesting a miniature mountain range. Ondorum studied the city's arched gates, wondering what the lower levels might be like.

He and Selvia hung back as Akina veered off to speak with the guards. When she rejoined them, her expression remained dour, but fresh determination gleamed in her eyes.

"They came this way, all right," she said. "Two days ago, sounds like. Means they've been moving faster than I guessed. One of the guards remembers Brakisten's stink, and that he acted strange when they came and went, like he wasn't quite in his right mind." She looked north and curled her upper lip. "They say the way's open, but there've been reports of a few people missing after going under."

"Do they know why?" Selvia asked.

"Not a clue. Maybe we'll find out." Akina nodded them forward. "Half a day and we're there."

They rode on, Selvia lagging slightly behind as she studied the maps to refresh her memory before they went under. She caught up right before they reached the surface gate at last. They came up between rows of enormous dwarven statues, with every second statue facing the opposite way. The first pair stared out over the path Akina and the others had come along, axes poised. The next pair looked up to the gate fortress itself, hammers planted as they stood watch. This repeated five more times until they reached the first set of gates, manned by six living dwarves, all in well-worn plate armor. Chunky towers stood on either side with archers peering down at the newcomers.

After Akina explained the reason for their journey and intent to descend, they were admitted into the first court. Another set of six guards met them on the other side of the gate. They held the same positions as the outer group, but faced inward.

A gate captain met them there, concern crinkling his brow.

"You're saying this Gromir fellow's been working with duergar?" he asked Akina. "And he came through here?"

She grunted. "That's what we're thinking."

"Well, we've had a few folks and teams pass through lately. Mostly dwarves heading down to explore or hunt. A few surveyors hoping to get lucky. None triggered any wards. The tunnels connect to duergar territory down far enough, which is why we keep such a close eye on it, but it's been quiet from their end for years." He frowned. "At least, we've thought so."

"We heard some travelers had gone missing," Selvia said.

The captain looked her way. "We defend the way from any real threat to our lands. If goodly folks want to go down for a treasure hunt, that's their business. They know the danger. The risk is all theirs, and there's plenty more than duergar in the Darklands to cause trouble."

"We're going after them, whatever the risk," Akina said. "They've got my brother."

The captain nodded. "You catch them, you give that traitor a good, painful bleeding."

They passed through four successive gates, each guarded by soldiers on either side. Dwarven warriors tromped along the top of the walls, as many studying the interior yards as peering out to the land beyond. Ondorum eyed the runes along the walls, wondering which ones anchored the wards and how many wizards maintained them. If the duergar had indeed taken this route, they must have had powerful magic of their own.

The actual surface gates themselves stood over a hundred feet high, controlled by massive bars and gears. Ondorum waited for them to swing wide, but was surprised again when guards opened a far smaller gate, ten feet tall and cunningly fashioned into the base of the larger ones. When they rode through, the arched tunnel they entered couldn't have stood more than twenty feet high. Why, then, had the dwarves created the illusion of a far larger entryway that must've concealed nothing but solid stone? Overeagerness on the part of the crafters?

He looked back just as the gate shut behind them, blocking out the sun. The *thoom* of its closing reverberated along the tunnel, and they followed its echoes down to find a set of inner entry points. Iron walls blocked the path with a bronze gateway allowing travelers through. They passed through two other gates until they reached a final checkpoint. There, Akina had them dismount and hand off their mules to a private, who agreed to see them stabled in hopes of their return. They divided their fresh water and food between themselves and then approached the last thick gate. The sergeant who unlocked this strode out beside them, where four soldiers saluted her before turning back to their duty. On this side of the wall, metal pikes had been drilled into the tunnel base, forming a jagged barrier that would impale anything foolish enough to assault the gate head-on.

The sergeant waved them ahead. "On your own from here. We've got patrols that go out several times a week and a few advance posts, but don't expect them to be right by your side if you encounter trouble."

"We can handle ourselves," Akina said.

The dwarf knocked a fist against her breastplate. "Stone endures."

"Stone endures," Akina replied, though with less enthusiasm.

The tunnel remained wide enough for Ondorum to stride by Akina's side as they descended, Selvia bringing up the rear. Lamps burned in sconces for the initial stretch, and then spaced out at greater intervals until they came to a last pair, beyond which lay darkness.

Akina marched across this transition point without pause. Ondorum took a moment to stand and pray to Irori, asking for guidance through the hollows of the earth.

"Worried?"

Selvia's whisper broke him out of the prayer. He smiled down at her, shrugging. Shadows cast her finer features into a craggy mask, but he read the anticipation on her expression well enough.

"We're not even really in Nar-Voth yet, according to her." Selvia watched Akina's receding back. "I'm sure things will get a bit more interesting the deeper we go. I look forward to seeing a map come to life."

Akina's words bounced back to them. "More life down here than maps. Best we remember that, hm?"

They trekked down through a series of switchback tunnels, which grew smaller and less refined with each step. At last, they passed through a jagged slant and into a larger cave that couldn't have been fashioned by any hands, dwarven or otherwise. Limestone columns poured down on either side and stalagmites of varying sizes formed chaotic fencings.

Since the darkness reduced his vision to shades of black and white, Ondorum wished for a bit of torchlight to determine the natural coloration of this new world. It couldn't lack all hue. While Akina had a torch strapped to her pack, the head remained sealed in wax. It not only preserved the fuel for when they might truly need it, but also avoided drawing the attention of things that preferred the dark and might be drawn to unnatural light sources.

He picked out other details as they descended. Mushrooms and slab-like fungus sprouted from some walls, forming miniature forests. Magnificent stalactites and stalagmites filled many of the caves, forcing the travelers to crouch or clamber past. In one section, he detected a distant dripping, with long, empty spaces between each drop. This stuck with them for a while. Though he never determined the source or even the particular direction it came from, he found it a meditative noise and felt saddened when it faded.

Certain walls and tunnel thresholds had been marked with dwarven runes and other scratchings in the stone. When Ondorum tapped Akina's shoulder and then tapped one such series of runes, she smiled slightly.

"It's an old *gladdringgar*. A rite of passage for more traditional dwarves." She traced the runes. "You delve the tunnels alone and carve your name into the deepest places you're brave enough to go. Then, to be considered adults, your younglings can track down the older mark and add theirs beside it. This one's hardly as deep as some, but with this being such dangerous territory, it'd take a hardy soul to go this far by their lonesome." Her expression softened. "Looks like it was never tracked down."

He pointed at her, and then the runes.

"No. Figured I might, but never got around to it. Don't even know when the last Fairingot did one, so I wouldn't have the faintest idea where to start looking. This one says, *Krovum Reklemoss stood here. Remember him.*" She turned away. "Never heard of him."

As she shuffled on, Ondorum placed a palm over the runes. *I'll remember you, Krovum. You carved these runes straight, which means your hands didn't tremble in the act. Well done.*

He kept on the lookout for more and found a handful, some hammered deep, some barely visible behind the limestone flowing over the walls. He tapped Akina's shoulder to get the names of each spoken to him, but after the fourth, her glare put him off from asking again. Perhaps they served as reminders of her mother's death. He made a mental note to be more sensitive about such things. If he couldn't comfort her with words, at least he could let her handle the grief in her own time.

At times, it seemed they'd entered an underground desert. They came upon broader caverns that appeared featureless but for the pebbles their boots brushed away. Some tunnels wound like coiled rope, and others shot down steep slopes that forced them to sit and slide, using occasional handholds to keep from gaining too much speed. In these portions, where no wind blew and no noise came except for their breathing and footsteps, the world felt empty, and they passed through it like ghosts.

Noisy ghosts, Ondorum amended at one point, when Akina jumped off a short ledge and sent clanking echoes all about.

In one of these barren stretches they reached their first major split in the tunnel. The path opened into a rounded hollow, where the ceiling vanished overhead, forming a chute up into nothingness. Ondorum motioned for the others to wait while he edged to the entrance. When nothing dropped from the darkness above, he waved for the others to join him.

Before them, twin openings slanted off in opposing directions. Akina planted fists on her hips.

"Your turn, mapmaker."

Selvia drew out a map. Unrolling it, she murmured to herself as she traced various lines. After just a few moments, she rolled it back up and pointed to the right opening. "This way."

Akina's brow rose. "You sure? Spend whatever time you need. I don't want us backtracking."

Selvia marched past the other dwarf. "I'm sure. Let's go."

Akina frowned but followed. In short order, they encountered several more spots where the tunnels diverged in as many as six offshoots at once, with some pointing back up toward the surface. Whenever they reached a junction, Selvia checked her maps but never needed more than a few seconds to confirm the direction. The deeper they went, the more she displayed confidence, as if seeing the route approved by her maps gave her a validation she'd not experienced before. She even took the lead from time to time.

As Ondorum attuned to their environment, he started noticing other inhabitants, most of which scattered or tried to hide from their approach. Beetles and spiders skittered across the walls, while the rare flitting insect buzzed past his ear. In one of the larger caves, wings fluttered above, though he never spotted their owners. As they passed out of that cavern into a narrow tunnel, he glanced back to see a dark serpent slither over where they'd just walked. At least nine feet long, but as thin as his little finger, it flowed into a crack in the floor and vanished.

Being underground quickly stole his sense of time. Selvia had pointed out their route before they left, saying it might take a week to reach the bottom of the initial tunnel network. There, it connected to a section known only as the Long Walk, a supposed Darklander thoroughfare. Of course, they hoped to catch up with Gromir and Brakisten before then.

Ondorum pondered how he might track their progress so he could gauge if they approached more perilous territory. The number of breaths or steps he took? How many caves they passed through? None of these seemed proper substitutes for day and night.

Akina dropped back by his side. "I can hear your thoughts knocking against each other from five paces. Care to share?"

So caught up in contemplation was he that he actually opened his mouth to reply before pinching his lips shut. He shot her a fierce glare.

She grunted. "Almost got you. Pity."

She tromped off again, and he swallowed a sigh. Disappointment bloomed inside him—not at her for trying to catch him off-guard, but at himself for the instinctive desire to break his vow. It would've been enjoyable to share his thoughts with her, and he doubted his ability to mime the concepts that flowed through his mind right then. At times such as these, his vow made him feel very alone.

Akina stopped and studied a spot on one side of the tunnel. Ondorum peered over her shoulder. Dull streaks stained the wall along with clumps that looked like drying scraps of meat. A faint rotten stench rose from it.

"What is that?" Selvia asked. "Blood?"

Ondorum frowned. Not blood. Detritus from some manner of kill, with the corpse dragged off? He looked around for signs of a struggle or further gore trails.

Akina leaned in and sniffed. She chuffed, shaking her head. "Dwarf puke. Couple days old."

Selvia held a hand to her mouth. "Er . . . how do you know?"

"You really want that story?"

Ondorum caught Selvia's eye and shook his head, making her hastily raise hands in denial.

Akina kicked at the dried mess. "And what dwarf besides my brother would've come this way and treated it like a back alley behind a slophouse? Looks like you've got us on the right track."

Selvia pouted. "Of course I do. But you really think Gromir's been keeping him sick-drunk this whole way? He would've had to haul a wagonload of ale along."

"Doubt it," Akina said. "I don't know how he's got Brakisten toddling along. Some sort of drug or spell, with the occasional slug from a tankard? Maybe his duergar friends are dragging him by his beard. Whatever it is, the stress of traveling must've caught up with him here."

"Hopefully we'll be the next thing that catches up with him," Selvia said.

"True enough."

Another interminable stretch of walking ensued. At last, Akina looked around and rolled her shoulders, leather and iron armor creaking.

"Guess we're well past due for a break, hm?"

"How long have we been going?" Selvia asked.

Akina grimaced. "Couple of days, I reckon."

Ondorum looked at her dubiously. A wild guess, or was she tuned into patterns he couldn't detect? He wished he could ask.

As the dwarves bickered over who'd take first watch, he found a clear patch of ground. He didn't need sleep yet, but he could use the time to bring order to his jumbled thoughts and emotions. Each disjointed instinct or desire could be a cobblestone that paved his soul's path to perfection. He just had to find out where it fit.

Akina groaned as she settled in against the cave wall. Ondorum sat a few feet away, already in his usual meditative position. Part of her had unthinkingly looked forward to resting for a few hours and maybe having some soft conversation with him. Nothing serious, just meaningless chatter to pass the time and ease her mind. Of course, he looked to be as rock-stubborn with his vow as ever. And what would she talk about down here, hm? The weather? Still, he would've come up with something, and his refusal to lower his wall of silence made her feel more alone than she cared to admit.

She tugged the brim of her helm over her eyes. Silly to do in the pervasive darkness, maybe, but it was a trick she'd picked up on surface marches and hunts, and it usually helped her fall asleep. Old habits must've followed her down these long tunnels, for she soon dropped into uncomfortable dreams she never quite remembered.

What felt like minutes later, Akina snorted awake and reached for her maulaxe on instinct. Where? When? Oh. Right.

Ondorum sat in the same position, though from the slight tilt of his head, she could tell he'd fallen asleep while meditating. Probably something he'd be kicking himself for days about, knowing him. Fine. Let him stew in guilty silence. He could ask her for sympathy when he was good and ready.

Selvia remained seated on the flat-topped boulder she'd picked as a sentry spot, where she could rotate to check for threats from any direction. With her back to Akina, she watched a tunnel leading out of the cave.

Akina took her hand from the maulaxe and eased it into one of her belt pouches, withdrawing Gromir's note. The parchment crackled as she unfolded it. She scanned its words for the dozenth time, trying to make sense of them.

... fulfilling my promise ... the damage I've done ... your mother restored and your brother redeemed ... serve a greater purpose ...

She wanted to crumple the note and cast it aside in disgust. Yet she folded it up and tucked it away again in case she could decipher it later on. Sounded like the ramblings of a madman, sure enough, but it couldn't be mere madness driving Gromir. He'd always been a bit off-kilter, torn between his love for magic and his interest in the fighting arts. It'd been her devotion to battle that drew him to the sparring rings, while his arcane bent caught her intrigue in return.

Yet she could never fully appreciate his use of magic. Back then, it slowed him down when he tried casting a spell during combat. During her years abroad, she'd grown even warier of spellcasters, partly thanks to the mercenary band's sorcerer—a gnome named

Piquwit—who'd once set the whole camp ablaze with a miscast ball of flame. Plenty of the mercenaries had charms and trinkets to enhance their edge in combat or bolster their health. Some even had enchanted armor and weapons; but to her, it felt like they always failed their wielders at just the wrong moment, or were cursed, or couldn't stand up to a good axe blow.

Ondorum had once tried to explain how magic held a natural place in the world and shouldn't be feared. She'd scoffed, denying any fear, but she'd take dwarven armor and weapons over a spell any day. He then reminded her how she herself had boasted of the ancestral magics some dwarven smiths used to forge their equipment. She'd told him to shut it and stomped off to find someone to bleed.

Thinking of making people bleed brought her mind around to Gromir again. She supposed she ought to ask Ondorum to make sure she didn't kill the bastard outright once they found him. She wanted plenty of explanations, and pounding answers out of a corpse never worked too well. Akina dragged her thoughts away from pleasant images of vengeance and shackled them in the back of her mind, to be released at a better time.

Selvia hadn't budged. Craning her neck, Akina realized the youngling leaned up against the limestone column at her side, head resting on its rippled surface. Ah. Poor kid had fallen asleep on watch—must've been far more tired than she let on. Akina smiled to herself, thinking of all the times she'd fallen asleep on watch during her first few months away at war. One night, she'd jerked awake to see a goblin skulking toward her, rusted dagger in hand. She'd never so much as yawned on duty again.

She stood and popped the cricks out of her neck, sending a dozen little echoes scurrying into their holes. Then she plodded over to Selvia and gave her shoulder a gentle shake, trying not to startle her too much.

"Hey, how about you—"

Selvia moaned and slumped off the rock, flopping onto her back. It took a stretched moment for Akina's gaze to flick from the bloody gash across Selvia's temple to realize the other thing wrong with the scene. Selvia's features had changed. Oh, they remained in all the right places—her hair even looked the same. But her skin appeared smudged and darker than usual in spots. Bruising?

Akina bent over and wiped a thumb across the other woman's cheek. The normal skin tone smeared off, revealing an ashen pallor beneath.

A duergar.

Akina turned to alert Ondorum, only to see a pale, spindly figure flip down from the jagged ceiling of the cave. The size of a halfling, the creature had bulging white eyes, and held a bloodstained sickle in one four-fingered hand. Spiky white hair covered its skull, which bobbed on a skinny neck. The teeth in its maniacally grinning mouth appeared filed to points. What armor it wore was cobbled together from random leather scraps.

Akina's maulaxe lay out of reach, so she roared and charged, intending to squash the interloper to pulp. It giggled disturbingly as it pranced away from the attack.

Something whistled through the air and her feet tangled, sending her crashing to the ground.

Ondorum's eyes snapped open and he leapt to his feet. Even as he reached to help her up, two darts sprouted from his neck. He slapped them away, but his arm wavered, and he stumbled and slammed against a wall. Two feet landed on Akina's back, and a sharp edge pricked under her jaw. The cut burned. Poison? She rolled, and the feet jumped off. As she sat up, her vision blurred and swam. Her breathing slowed, lungs and heart feeling compressed by giant fists. She tried to stand, but collapsed, helmet scraping on gravel. Her position let her see Ondorum, who'd slid down to the floor. His eyes had gone dull, staring at nothing, and his mouth hung agape.

With each breath and heartbeat, the following one came harder. Slower. Until she felt the next must be her last. She tried to lock the air in her lungs. Tried to keep her pulse from drumming one last time.

Pale feet scampered before her. Bulbous eyes lowered into view.

She worked her lips to spit in the creature's face. The final exhalation escaped and her eyes flickered shut.

Chapter Ten
Den of Madness

Black turned to gray turned to white turned to blue in Ondorum's mind. Had the eyes of his soul opened? Did he see beyond the curtain of the physical world? He struggled to make sense of anything. Shapeless shadows became shuffling figures about him. Others? With him? Who did he share this enlightenment with? As he tried to make sense, all the elements shattered and reformed at random.

Hope turned to confusion turned to despair. Not enlightenment. Chaos.

A cry of pain threatened to escape from his throat, but an unknown part of himself locked it down. Focus became memory became awareness. He had . . . vowed. Silence. He mustn't break the vow, and for some reason it felt doubly important not to make any noise here and now.

Where was here? When was now? To know, he must observe. To observe, he must gain control of his faculties.

Foremost, he assembled the components of his body, ignoring all else except the sensation of their existence. Hands, feet, legs, arms, hips, abdomen, chest, neck, head. All in place. Then he envisioned the golden ball of ki at his core and let lines of light twine through him. They bound his awareness tighter to the present moment, to the immediate predicament.

Pain flared brighter as he came to fuller consciousness. Muscle and bone screaming. Cords of fire painted across his chest and back. A choking bond around his neck, and tighter ones around his waist, wrists, and ankles.

Imprisoned. Which meant capture. Which, at last, revived the startled memory of the cave. Surging awake to see Akina fallen before him and a pale monster on her back. Then a spike of fire in his neck before hideous weakness stole his ability to stand, to see, to think.

Drugged, then. And brought where? For what purpose?

When his eyelids first failed to move, he feared them sewn or pasted shut. Flickers of light inspired him to force one eye open a crack. A harsh blue gleam speared straight into his mind, making him tear up and squeeze the eye shut. When he peeked again, though, both eyes opened, and the light dimmed to bearable levels. Each slow breath raked pain along one side of his abdomen. At last, he managed to focus and make sense of what he saw.

He lay bound on a rock slab at the far end of a winding room, at least a hundred feet from end to end. The light emanated from a strange bluish-white mold covering the ceiling and walls of the chamber. The mold illuminated ten other slabs set at random spots across the floor, with their surfaces tilted at awkward angles. Ondorum's happened to be angled up and to the right, as if he'd been put on display. He remained secured in place by ropes, his body stripped bare.

Most other slabs had creatures strapped to them as well, many of which he couldn't identify and most of which appeared unconscious or dead. There lay a lizardlike creature, with a scaly snout and talons. It had been flayed, and knotted organs dangled from its belly. There, a person wrapped all in black rags lay bound facedown. A brightly glowing crystal hung inches from their back by a silver string. There lay a human male whose chest had been carved into, revealing swaths of muscle, bone, and guts; his exposed organs continued to pulse and convulse, while his head twitched from side to side.

And there Akina lay, stripped of her armor and bound upside down to a slab halfway across the room. Eyes shut, breathing labored, hair dangling—yet she lived.

Across from her, Selvia had also been bound to a slab, looking unharmed except for her skin having turned dark gray. Lighter lines tracked around her neck and ears, but she appeared to have been made to look like a duergar, except for the hair.

The last wisps of fog blew from Ondorum's mind. His ears unclogged, and he became aware of a chorus of moans, screams, burbles, hisses, and a persistent scraping. The stink of raw meat and sewage jammed up his nose, along with another smell he couldn't quite identify, but which made him think of ice mingled with blood. At the same time, he realized other beings moved freely about the chamber. Four of the creatures that had ambushed them in the cave darted here and there, clutching pieces of glinting metal and glass. The mold cast everything about them—from their frizzes of white hair to the leather and cloth scraps that barely covered their stick-thin forms—in a blue light.

One appeared to be ordering the other three around as it stood over a slab. This table held a gnome woman covered in bleeding incisions from the neck down. The head creature held up a finger, which had a metal shard connected to the tip. He jabbed this into the flesh above one hip and sliced a ragged line across to the other. The gnome shuddered and, seeing her open-yet-glazed eyes, Ondorum realized she must be partially aware of the torture.

Her mutilator stuck several fingers into the gash he'd made and peeled it wide. The gnome's scream cut into Ondorum's ears. He trembled, straining against his bonds. The leader peered into the wound and then chattered at the others, waving a four-fingered hand in an impatient gesture. One darted over to a wall and tore off a fistful of mold. The leader took this and packed it into the cut until the gnome's gut bulged. He stepped back and turned to the others, pointing his bloody fingers at the gnome as if showing off a prized possession.

The other three creatures danced about, clapping and chirping. Then one raced over, drew a dagger from its belt, and jammed it into one of the gnome's eyes. The gnome went limp. The leader shrieked and lunged at the one who had destroyed his work. The remaining two ran out of sight at the far end of the chamber, while the mutilator and his offender clashed. They fought with vicious speed, darting and weaving as they slashed and cut. The fight devolved into a tangle of limbs and attempts to bite one another's ears and noses off. At last, the leader got his arms around the other's neck and snapped it with a noise like cracking glass.

Flinging the dead one on the ground, the winner jumped on the loser's corpse and stabbed it over and over, shrieking laughter. While it celebrated its victory, Ondorum redoubled his efforts to break free. The cords were roughly braided rope that looped through holes chiseled in the stone slab, no doubt knotting underneath. Ondorum gritted his teeth and flexed his left arm, curling the hand in while bracing at the elbow. The rope didn't snap, but when he relaxed, he found it loosened just enough to slip his hand through. Keeping his eyes on the cavorting creature, he reached across to grab his other hand and used the extra leverage to loosen that bond as well. With both hands freed, he dug fingers under the cord around his throat and snapped it like straw.

The creature froze. Ondorum dropped his arms back to his sides and closed his eyes to slivers. The creature's head swiveled from side to side, and then it turned around to scan the other specimens. Its gaze swept past Ondorum, making a full circle until it fixed back on the dead gnome. With a little wail, the creature ran over and hugged the corpse, weeping and caressing it.

Horror and disgust roiled in Ondorum's stomach like maggots. He reached down and jammed his hands through the rope around his waist, turning his forearms so the crystalline ridges on the outside ripped through the cord. This released his weight fully onto the ropes across his ankles, tightening them even more. Bracing, he reached down and raked his forearm ridges across these, cutting them quick enough. He dropped to the floor, and caught himself on one hand and knee. His legs tingled with renewed blood flow.

Pushing the pain to one side, he forced himself upright just as the creature raised its head and looked his way. It shrieked and gibbered, baring sharp teeth. Ondorum ran at it, dodging slabs. The creature grabbed a vial from a nearby ledge and flung it. It smashed a few feet in front of Ondorum, and when he passed by it, the rising vapors dizzied him for a second. He shook off the effects and closed the distance as the creature picked up its fallen opponent's dagger and slashed at him.

Ondorum slapped the weapon from its hand and brought a knee up under the monster's chin hard enough to drive it two feet into the air. Before it fell, he snapped an elbow out into its skull, sending it crashing into the wall. It slumped, head caved in, white eyes filming over.

Ondorum steadied himself, still not fully recovered from whatever these creatures had used to drug him. The concoction must not have affected his oread nature as they expected, though, letting him awaken faster than anticipated. He breathed deep, and cold agony lanced through his side. Looking down revealed the source—several rows of crystals had been gouged from his ribs, leaving puckering wounds. He cast about for some sort of medicine or magical healing, but though vials of liquids and powders lay scattered on ledges around the chamber, he didn't trust any of them, given what he'd seen of these creatures' poisonous natures.

Two of the creatures—perhaps the same two that ran off earlier—bounded back into the chamber. They halted, taking in the freed prisoner. Ondorum grabbed the two monstrous corpses near him and threw them at the others. As they ducked, he snatched up an assortment of vials and whipped the glassy missiles across the room. The creatures cried out, dodging the splashes and sprays. One ran screaming from the chamber, while the other drew a tiny crossbow from its back and took aim. A second later, a vial shattered in its face, and it went down clawing as fumes rose from its oversized eyes.

Pressing a hand to his wounded side, Ondorum hurried back to Akina's slab. He found a scalpel and sliced her bonds, then caught her before she hit the floor headfirst. She groaned in his arms as he shook her. At last, her eyes fluttered open and her voice rose muzzy.

"What brew was that again?"

He helped her sit up. She blinked about until she locked onto the eviscerated lizard-thing on the slab across from her.

"That's not right." She staggered to her feet, shaking her head as she took in the chamber's horrors. "Where are we?"

Ondorum pointed at the dead creatures lying at the far end.

She pressed a palm to her forehead. "Right. The cave. Heard of these things before—weird little blue people who live in the deepest tunnels and kidnap surface-dwellers for bizarre experiments. Of course, the folk who claim to have been taken by them always seem to be addled or unhinged, so most reasonable people assume their stories are just ramblings. Crack and shatter, this must be some kind of warren." Her eyes widened as she spotted Selvia. "Not a dream either; she's a duergar."

He frowned over at their guide. Had illusion magic or some other form of disguise cloaked Selvia's true nature? Or was this some transformation caused by their captors? Did this mean she was linked to Gromir's plot, whatever it involved? How had the wards at the gate not detected her true nature?

Akina ran her hands over herself, realizing she'd been reduced to smallclothes. "My gear. Got to find it."

Funneling his focus into the scalpel he held, Ondorum aligned himself with its earthen composition. Responding to his touch, the metal flowed and stretched into a solid quarterstaff.

Akina looked under slabs and in piles of jumbled rubbish. He joined in the search, seeking to clothe himself, and checking if any victims could be saved. He found another dwarf who'd been shaved from head to toe, but otherwise appeared unharmed. Ondorum cut the dwarf free and propped him up, but he just sat there drooling. Moving on, Ondorum freed the mutilated human, who wept, saying he "wouldn't fall for their tricks again." Two more dwarven prisoners proved to be corpses.

While hopes of saving others dwindled, he found a wide strip of filthy gray cloth crumpled in a corner. Better than nothing. As he tied it around his waist, Akina whirled about, throwing up her hands. "Shattered stone, none of it's anywhere!"

"I . . . know . . . where kept . . . treasure."

They turned. The rustling voice spoke in broken Taldane, the common trade language of the Inner Sea, or at least its surface nations. It came from the humanoid covered in strips of black cloth, who had turned its head to them. Strips wrapped around its head and lower face, leaving two black eyes squinting in a crease of white flesh as the only visible features. It made a hacking noise and waggled fingers.

"Please . . . I help . . ."

Ondorum strode over and had it freed in moments. Instead of sliding off the slab, it rolled over and raised bare palms, white as bone, to grab the glowing crystal above it. Its eyes closed, and it shuddered.

"Yes . . ."

"Who are you?" Akina asked. "How can you help?"

The creature drew its hands away from the crystal, which had lost its light and now hung as a dull chunk. The creature stood then, maybe a foot taller than Ondorum, but skeletally thin, like a distorted shadow peeled off a wall. Its tightly wrapped clothing seemed to be made entirely of strips of fine black cloth. When it spoke, its voice had gained substance.

"Better." It tapped its chest. "Here is Izthuri, mother of caligni tribe." She pointed at them. "There is?"

"People who need their armor and weapons back so we can get out of here."

Ondorum bowed, and Izthuri inclined her head in return. "Yes. Escape." She went to one of the ledges filled with vials and plucked up a selection.

"What're you doing?" Akina crossed her arms. "Those aren't our things."

Izthuri raised a vial. "Poison. Acid. Explosives. Weapons, yes?"

"How do you know?"

"Some used on me. Some I used on others."

"Oh."

Izthuri turned and held out several for Akina, who took them tentatively. She offered one to Ondorum, who abstained, indicating his staff.

"Throw in faces. On skin." Izthuri raised a slender finger. "Do not swallow."

Akina eyed the vials with trepidation. "Hold up a moment." Setting the vials down, she stalked over to Selvia and backhanded the woman. "Wake up."

Selvia groaned and shook her head. Then she jerked awake. She noted their surroundings first and then her revealed nature. "Ah."

Akina glowered. "So this is your real face, hm?"

The duergar sneered. "Isn't it lovely? Didn't you enjoy helping a young dwarf get her first glimpse of such a big, scary world? Must've been nice to comfort someone in need. You've got true motherly instincts."

A second blow snapped the duergar's head to the side. Selvia licked blood from a split lip and chuckled. "Make me bite off my tongue and I won't be able to whisper naughty secrets in your ear."

"No whispers. You're going to scream them."

"Get me out of here first."

"Why should we?"

Selvia huffed. "Try to be intelligent for once. Leave me here and you don't get answers. Even if you go off, planning to return, I'll be dead before you make it back. Your choice, of course."

"As if I'd trust a duergar's answers."

"Pity. I'm after Gromir as much as you are. I know where he's going and could show you a few shortcuts." Selvia smiled again. "And that's all I'll say until we get out of here."

Snarling, Akina used a jagged chunk of crystal to cut the duergar's hands free and then re-bound the wrists behind her back. After freeing her the rest of the way, Akina tied a length of rough rope to the wrist cords and gave the free end to Ondorum. Duergar in tow, they headed for the chamber exit. Ondorum tried once more to get the drooling dwarf and weeping human to join them, without success. Akina peered around the corner and waved them on. Izthuri hunched along on silent feet, her head almost brushing the ceiling.

The same blue mold continued down this tunnel and every one that branched off it, lighting their path. Izthuri took several quick turns, and then paused at a junction. She sniffed the air.

"They come. Hasten."

"I'd listen to her," Selvia muttered.

Izthuri darted down the left tunnel and they hurried after. This led into a larger chamber where the ground rose in stacked limestone tiers, creating a rough cone in the center. The top tier contained a luminescent pool of what Ondorum guessed to be water, ten feet across. Mounds of the glowing mold surrounded it, making this room the brightest yet. Holes of varying sizes honeycombed the uneven walls, most too high to reach.

Izthuri snapped a hand at the holes. "I get. They come. We fight." She dashed to one of the lower holes and grabbed at the darkness inside. She came out holding a sack of bones, which she threw aside with a clatter. Using the hole as a foothold, she clambered up a few feet and reached inside another. She withdrew a rusty, child-sized breastplate and held it up.

"This armor?"

"You've got to be joking." Akina raised her voice. "Iron and leather armor with a maulaxe. Like a hammer and axe in one. My size. Not trashed."

"Iron. Leather. Hammer. Axe." Izthuri flung the breastplate to the ground, where it crumbled into scrap. "I find."

"We should already be gone," Selvia said, glancing around.

Akina glared her way. "You're not the guide anymore."

A rabble of high-pitched voices made them turn as a horde of the white-eyed creatures swarmed down the hall. Ondorum and Akina backed up, moving around to one side of the tiered mound to avoid being surrounded right away. A dozen of the beastly things poured into the chamber, spreading out as they brandished everything from spears to small crossbows to an odd weapon that looked like a metal hook on a club with a long rope attached to the other end. A few held large chunks of crystal that had been chiseled into fist-sized wedges.

The duergar sighed. "You really should've listened to me."

Ondorum stomped and pounded his staff to keep them back. Akina held the vials poised to throw. Selvia edged away, not quite at the limit of her bonds.

The creatures held back. Ondorum remained steady but Akina kept twitching beside him, anticipating an attack at any moment. At last she hollered, "Right! What're you bastards waiting for?"

"They wait for me."

The speaker strode from the tunnel with regal bearing. He looked much like all the other warren denizens, but with slicked-back hair and a more devious gleam to his bulbous eyes.

"Who're you?"

He flapped back his purple and green robes and swept into a deep bow, one foot pointed in front of him, an arm poised over his head like a court dancer. "I am Nullick. I lead this warren." He twirled a full circle and then waved up at the dark figure halfway up the wall. "Greetings, Izthuri. Finally woke up, did you?"

Izthuri hissed down at him, but didn't stop rummaging in the latest hole she'd reached.

Nullick performed a little tap-dance around until he faced the duergar. "And greetings, Selvia. Sorry to see it come to this."

Selvia's eyes flashed in fury. "We had an agreement. The commander will have your scalp."

Nullick continued to spin about as he spoke, and Ondorum wondered how he didn't dizzy himself. "Our arrangement with Commander Vaskegar does not extend to you personally, and we've already seen your authorized representatives through to safety. I'm fully in accord with our compact."

"Who's Vaskegar?" Akina asked. "What agreement?"

"A mutually beneficial arrangement," Nullick said, stopping mid-spin so he looked at a wall, his back to them. "We kept a few ways to the surface clearer than most, and also eliminated any evidence of duergar passage so long as they brought us the occasional specimen."

"You mold-sucking spore rat," Selvia said. "I'll turn your skull inside-out."

Nullick tsked. "Name-calling? Such a bore. You know what I do to boring things, yes?"

The duergar's eyes widened. "You wouldn't dare—"

Nullick twirled, arms above his head. Then he snapped one down and flung a hand her way. His fingers glittered as crystalline shards sprouted from them and spewed at the duergar. Selvia tried to dodge, but she was already at the end of her leading rope, which jerked her back into place. Ondorum dropped his end too late. The cone of shards struck across her upper body, the crystals knifing into her flesh. Two larger chunks embedded in her chest and forehead. Blood streaming from dozens of gashes, Selvia flopped to the ground.

Akina cried out and ran over to check the body. A glance determined Selvia wouldn't be explaining anything unless they found a way to summon her spirit.

She shouted at the warren leader, "Damn you to the Abyss! I needed her alive."

Nullick tucked hands into his sleeves and rocked from foot to foot. "Fortunately, you three remain of keen interest to me. Take Izthuri, for example. She's been with us for a while now, yet remains one of our more promising subjects. Do you know her people can subsist on forms of light? It's fascinating. A true challenge for my intellectual prowess."

"So many big words," Akina said through clenched teeth.

"I find another cure for boredom to be a contest of wills." He resumed prancing in place, making her think of a manic child. "Do you like games?"

"Let's say we do."

"Then we shall play one. My people are quite fond of finding ways to survive in all environments we encounter. So why don't we engage in a game of survival? If my people can kill you before your new friend up there finds your gear, I win. Vice versa, you win, and will be allowed to leave."

Ondorum scowled, knowing this mad creature only meant to extend their suffering and feed his cruelty.

"Izthuri," Akina called without taking her eyes off Nullick, "want to speed it up a bit?"

"Yes."

"Good." A cock of her head. "That means you're going to, right?"

"Yes."

Nullick hopped, clapping. "Oh, I do love to play." At last, he collected himself and smoothed his robes down. "There is one rule."

Ondorum tightened his grip on the staff as Akina asked, "Which is?"

"I get to cheat."

Nullick raised hands that blazed with purple auras.

Chapter Eleven
Unfair Advantage

C hoke on your magic!" Akina snapped a vial straight at Nullick. He vanished, and it passed through the space he'd just occupied, striking the creatures behind. The glass shattered and green gobs sprayed in all directions. Those struck screeched as their skin sizzled and melted.

. "Good start," Nullick said, voice emanating from several directions. "I appreciate your zest."

The rest of his minions attacked as one, waving their weapons wildly. Ondorum's staff hummed as he spun it, knocking aside an initial flurry of crossbow bolts. The closest creatures took staff strikes to the chest and face, sending them tumbling.

Akina landed the other two vials in groups of charging creatures, taking down two more with the foul discharges they created. She leaped aside as one of the crystal wedges shattered at her feet, but slivers struck her face, stinging fiercely. She came up to see a spear-wielder charging her, crystalline tip rising to aim for her chest.

Her bellow drowned out all other noises as she raced in. She jumped and stomped on the spear shaft, pinning it. She grabbed the wielder's throat and yanked it in for a headbutt. As the creature fell away, cross-eyed, she stepped off the spear and snatched it up.

Several bolts of bright purple energy slammed into her side. Akina gasped and staggered, planting one hand to keep from falling.

"I'm winning," Nullick cried. He cartwheeled into view from the other side of the tiered mound, waved, and vanished again.

She stood and rammed the spear halfway through a creature running up to hack at her. The body dangled as she swept the spear around, knocking aside two other attackers. With a keening whistle, one of the hooked clubs shot through the air, but the hook embedded in the dead creature instead of her. The rope on the other end snapped taut and yanked both body and spear away.

Akina rounded on the one who'd made the snatch-and-grab. As it tried to pry the hooked weapon out of its comrade's body, she sprinted over and threw herself into a full-body slam. It raised an arm in futile defense. A few seconds of pummeling left it gushing blood out of every facial orifice.

She crushed its ribs with one last pound. Jumping to her feet, she loosed another bellow, stoking the blaze in her blood and bones. Let it burn everything here to cinders and—

Nullick appeared before her, holding a miniature storm cloud in his hands. A lightning bolt crackled out and struck her in the gut.

The world flickered black and white. When the sickly blue glow faded back into being, Akina found herself sitting on the floor. Smoke rose from her middle. She tried to move, and every muscle cramped. She fought to remain upright as a creature crept toward her, sickle in one hand, shortspear in another.

Beyond them, Ondorum struck down the last cross-bow-wielder and plowed toward an attacker who kept snapping his hooked club out and back. A streak of blazing green struck the oread in the back, and he stumbled. Nullick's cackle filled the chamber. The hooked club caught the staff on the next throw and tore it from Ondorum's hands. He planted his feet as the creature before him whirled its weapon and sent it whistling out again. Raising a forearm, he caught the hook on it, grabbed the club portion, and yanked. The minion holding the rope forgot to let go and found itself soaring toward the oread's waiting fist.

Akina smiled even as she smelled the unappetizing stench of her own cooked flesh. Then the creature advancing on her blocked the monk's ongoing fight. She strained again to force her stubborn limbs into motion. Right as her would-be-killer stepped in for the strike, an object slammed into the top of its head, crushing half its face and driving it to the ground.

Akina's maulaxe clanged down beside her. A clatter of armor pieces fell after it, with her ram's helm as the last to land.

Izthuri's call rang out. "Found it."

Akina grabbed the maulaxe handle and pulled herself up. "Lady, whatever you are, I like your timing."

Ignoring the rest of the armor for the moment, she slapped the helm over her head and hefted the maulaxe in trembling arms. Screaming wordless defiance, she ran for the nearest of Nullick's warriors. One flung crystal wedges at her as it backed away. Two wedges shattered as she ran past, spraying her with slivers. The third clipped her arm and spun away. She threw her maulaxe ahead, and it struck one of the little monsters aside. As the crystal-flinger drew another shard, she drove it to the floor and clamped a hand on its wrist. It struggled with wiry strength, but she flexed its arm until it gasped and dropped the crystal. She grabbed the wedge and crunched it through the waiting neck.

Nullick laughed. "Such a good game. But you've only found one set of gear and I've summoned more to play on my side. Shall we try for a second round?"

Akina looked around. Those who'd come with Nullick lay dead or dying. Ondorum stood by the entrance, leaning on his staff. Izthuri clambered about, shoving arms into one hole or another. The warren leader remained invisible, no doubt with reinforcements coming as claimed.

Akina retrieved her maulaxe and poised it. "Ondorum, any ideas?"

Ondorum held still for a moment, scanning the ground until his eyes locked on a particular patch of mold. Akina eyed this and spotted what he'd noticed: a few footprints well away from any fighting, where no one had been standing. Just as she noticed this,

Ondorum sprinted at an empty patch of air near the top of the mound.

"What?" Nullick's voice wavered. "Get back!"

Ondorum lashed out with the staff, spinning and thrusting it this way and that. He appeared to hit nothing, but he kept advancing while Nullick's wails rose to shrieks.

"No fair! You're cheating!"

All at once, Ondorum gripped his staff lengthwise in both hands and flung it out in front of him. It bounced off an unseen object, followed by a cry of pain from Nullick. Ondorum dashed forward—not bothering to catch the rebounding staff—and grabbed at that space. His arms locked around an invisible figure.

"No!" Nullick appeared, fighting to break the monk's hold. He scrabbled and bit and kicked, all for naught. Ondorum kept jerking him this way and that, disrupting his spellcasting attempts.

Akina bounded up the tiers. She grabbed Nullick's hair and Ondorum let go as she tore the warren leader loose. Nullick tried to writhe free until she smacked his stomach with the maulaxe.

She dragged him toward the pool. "Like I said before . . ." She slammed him against the lip, sending ripples across the surface. "Choke on it."

She plunged Nullick into the water and held him under until he stopped thrashing.

Chapter Twelve
Death's Stench

Akina didn't relax until the last of the blue-glowing tunnels faded from sight, replaced by the raw stone of uninhabited Darklands. They'd bumped into just two creatures while escaping the warren. Izthuri had hissed something in another tongue-clicking, tooth-gnashing language, and the others had bolted. Akina and Ondorum followed her, as she indicated she knew a safe place to rest.

Back in the warren, Izthuri had scrounged up Ondorum's robe, boots, and stash of iron chips from another hole in Nullick's little treasure trove. Other random items got dumped from the holes, including a tattered traveling pack, more rusted armor and weapons, moldy scrolls, and a bundle of rags. Akina grabbed the bundle up and stuffed them inside her armor for later. Then she checked Selvia's body for the maps, but Nullick's creatures must've removed them when they captured the group.

Izthuri continued searching until, with a raspy cry of joy, she drew out a blade unlike Akina had ever seen. It looked forged out of a piece of night itself; not a glossy obsidian, but a congealed darkness that made it feel like the blade leeched the sight from her eyes whenever she glanced at it. When the caligni—as she called herself—held it, they seemed to become a single form. When she paused and pressed against a wall or into a tunnel niche, her figure uncannily blended with the environment until she moved again. An eerie effect, and Akina wondered how she'd ever been caught by Nullick in the first place.

They hiked for a few hours, taking what would've seemed like random turns except for Izthuri's lack of hesitation. Then they entered a stretch where the tunnel ceiling sloped upward until it disappeared, making it feel like they walked at the bottom of a deep trench. They hurried down this until Izthuri stopped and patted the wall.

"Here."

The caligni pointed out a set of near-invisible hand and footholds set into the rock, leading up. She went first, climbing like a spider until she vanished over a ledge that otherwise couldn't be seen from the tunnel floor. Akina followed, jamming fingers and toes into the holds until she reached the ledge as well. When she peered over it, she started and nearly dropped, as Izthuri had crouched down to put their faces just inches apart. After an awkward moment, Akina hauled herself up over the edge.

"Why're you looking at me like that?"

Izthuri drew another long sniff. "You smell like him."

Akina brushed by her to study the small hollow. It went back a few yards, offering just enough sitting space.

"Who?" she asked. "Ondorum?"

"One I hunt. One who threatens my tribe." Izthuri sat, arms and legs jutting at awkward angles, marking her look like a giant grasshopper. "He came down. Woke evil among us. I come up to end him."

Akina frowned, but any questions stalled as Ondorum vaulted over the ledge. They shuffled about, trying to find the most comfortable arrangement. It wound up being Ondorum at the back, pressed into the curve of the wall, with Akina to his left and Izthuri on his right. Once the noise of their movement died off and they steadied their breaths, deep silence flowed into the gap. Akina felt like she would hear things miles off if they so much as kicked a pebble. Must've been the point of this hollow—to give someone not only a place to hide, but also a vantage point for any oncoming threats.

She scooted closer to Ondorum. "Loosen your robe a bit, hm? You took some nasty hits back there."

He gestured for her to do the same, and she grudgingly complied. The tight quarters made it difficult to maneuver, but Akina managed to unbuckle her vambraces and leather pauldrons and set them aside without too much clatter. She rolled up her mail sleeves, refusing to wince as pain started to poke its head out, asking if it was safe to emerge. The worst came from the crystal wedge that had clipped her shoulder. A flap of skin hung below her shoulder, but it proved a wide, shallow cut, rather than anything threatening the arm as a whole. She drew out some of the rags she'd salvaged earlier and let Ondorum bind the cut.

For himself, Ondorum slipped the robe back over his shoulders and let it pool around his waist. He bowed flat over crossed legs, letting her inspect his back. A fist-sized circle of blistered skin sat where Nullick's spell hit him. Acid of a sort, she guessed. Good thing he had such a tough hide. If he'd been human, the spell might've eaten straight through him. The wound might scar, at worst. He didn't flinch as she probed the bubbling's waxy texture. When he sat up, she spotted several rows of gashes on one side of his ribs, where a portion of his crystalline growths had gone missing.

She reached for this, but he caught her hand. With his other, he made a circling motion over the wounds and then patted them gently.

"They'll grow back?" she asked. "You're sure?" He nodded, but she clenched fists. "Wish we'd stayed for another round." He gave her a chiding look, and she bared teeth. "What's wrong with a bit of blood for blood? Would've taken a hundred of them to make up for each piece they carved from you. And you saw what they did to all those others."

His face darkened and one of his hands curled into a fist as well. Akina gripped this in both of her hands, though she could only cover a few knuckles on either side.

"See? Not always wrong to give people what they deserve."

He closed his eyes and drained his breath in one long sigh. His fist uncurled and he reached for her hands, but she pulled away. Scowling, she plunked her cheek down on a fist—and then jerked back up as stinging pain ripped through her face.

At her startled grunt, Ondorum leaned over and inspected her skin. Izthuri peered closer too, and Akina tensed to keep from shoving them both back. Even Ondorum's gentle touches sent off pings of flame, and she realized what it came from.

"Those bastards threw some crystals at me that broke when they hit. Must be from that."

"Should come out," Izthuri said. "Bad crystal. Hurts inside."

Ondorum drew out one of his iron chips and concentrated until it grew into a pair of long tweezers. Akina sighed but propped forward on her knees to set her profile to him. She tried to avoid making eye contact with the caligni, but Izthuri stared back, black eyes unblinking. Akina's grunts punctuated the stillness as the oread pried larger pieces loose and picked around for the smaller fragments. Nearly twenty shards had embedded in her face and throat. Lucky none had pierced an eye or gone so deep as to require cutting to retrieve. By the time he finished, her face felt swollen ten times over, and each twitch of her cheek or lips sent a crackle of flame across her skin.

"Thanks," she muttered, trying not to rub at the area. "I had Selvia pack a few healing quaffs in with our supplies, but I guess Nullick stashed all that elsewhere."

The mention of Selvia dropped a whole bunch of new, sticky questions to splat on her mind, and she started wondering them out loud. What had been the duergar woman's purpose in Taggoret? Was she connected to the duergar who'd helped Gromir abduct Brakisten?

If so, why had Selvia lured the pair down into the Darklands after Gromir indicated Akina should wait for him? He must've known Selvia's real identity, but his knowing didn't explain any of his actions.

What could've driven him to align himself with the duergar in the first place? That was one of the most obscene things any dwarf could do. It practically made him a non-dwarf in their people's minds.

Akina's head whirled with all the unknowns. By the time she finished rambling off all the whys and how-abouts and maybes, Ondorum looked as befuddled as she felt.

"And then there's Gromir's note . . ." Akina dug at her belt and, to her relief, found the parchment still tucked into the pouch. She drew it and held it up to illustrate her point.

Like a bat snatching a bug from midair, Izthuri reached over and clipped the parchment away.

"Hey, give that—"

Ondorum raised a hand and held a finger to his lips. He pointed down over the edge. Guess it didn't make much of a hidey-hole if she announced their presence by shouting. Akina forced herself to whisper, though still harsh enough to echo.

"Give that back."

Izthuri rubbed the parchment over the cloth masking her lower face. She snuffled; then she made a lip-smacking noise. "This. This smells like him. Strong. His touch."

Akina looked at her askance. "You're hunting some-one who . . . smells . . . like the person who wrote that?"

"Not like. Is. Him."

"Can you describe him some other way besides smell?"

Izthuri sniffled. "Sight is lie. Smell is truth." She shrugged a shoulder, almost hitting the top of the hollow. "Dwarf. Carries tiny axes." She drew a line diagonally across her chest and then plucked at her chin. "Gold face fur."

"Beard," Akina corrected. "Dust and drudgery, that's Gromir! You're talking about Gromir. He ran the shop Selvia worked at. We were following him before we got ambushed."

Izthuri's eyes narrowed to dark slits. Her hand went to the hilt of her light-sucking blade.

"Hold on, hang on now . . ." Akina fumbled for her own weapon, but didn't think she had room to draw or wield.

Ondorum thrust both arms between them like bars; he stared at Izthuri, making it clear who he'd go after if anyone attempted violence.

Izthuri eased her hand back, but her eyes remained suspicious. "Why you here?"

"I'd ask the same," Akina said. "You seem pretty sneaky and you claim to have a tribe off somewhere. So why leave them and let yourself get caught by Nullick and his little crazies?"

Izthuri hissed. "No *let*. Mistake." She kept Akina pinned with her eyes.

Akina tried to stare the caligni down, but then scowled and relented. "Right. I'll go first."

She told Izthuri of her return home and the plight she found her family in, and how Gromir had insinuated himself into her family's business, thinking he could win her affections back. How she'd rebuffed him, and he'd disappeared with her brother alongside the duergar. Then she read the note aloud, though it made no more sense to her than it had before. Izthuri's threatening air faded, replaced by wary curiosity. When Akina finished, the caligni's hiss sounded more thoughtful.

"He go back down. To my home. You follow . . . for brother? Not evil?"

"You're saying Gromir is evil?" Akina shook her head. "Why are you hunting him?"

Izthuri waggled fingers as she spoke. "Long time past, my tribe hunted by buggane."

"Buggane?"

"Mole beasts. They slaughter any of us they catch. We run. We hide. They follow. They find. They kill. Then tribe finds old ruins. We enter. Buggane stay out. We not know why. We make new home. We live quiet and deep and dark and safe. Old tribe leaders dead. I care for all."

Her eyes flared. "Then ruins wake up. Become hungry. I go to make ruins sleep and see dwarf. Gromir. I hide. He run away. But come back later with duergar. I hide from duergar. Duergar stay. Gromir come and go. My tribe hide, but some found. Killed by duergar. Gromir bring duergar. Gromir kill my tribe, I must kill Gromir. He leave ruins last time. I follow to kill. He go to surface, beyond gate. I wait below for him to come down again. Listen and wait. Watch travelers from darkness. They go up. They go down. I wait. Learn their words and hear their secrets."

"That's how you can speak Taldane?" Akina asked.

Izthuri nodded and shut her eyes. "I watch for Gromir. Not for Nullick. He catch me. You say Gromir go back down while I in warren. My tribe in danger."

Akina gnawed a knuckle until it bled. "So Gromir found the ruins your people live in and brought a bunch of duergar there. He's been going back and forth, working with them on something?"

"Hungry evil."

"The buggane?"

"No it . . ." Izthuri went still for several long moments. Then she waggled fingers faster, perhaps indicating she either didn't know or didn't have the words to explain in the surface-dwellers' tongue.

"Right. We'll work on that." Akina bent her head and hit the heel of her palm on the side of her helm, trying to knock answers loose. All the unknowns just kept rattling around. "I can't figure it yet, but I'm not about to let Gromir give my brother over to duergar who've gotten their hands on any sort of hungry evil. Whatever it is." She raised her head. "Izthuri, can you get us down to those ruins, to your tribe, so we can take care of Gromir?"

"You help my tribe?" Izthuri lowered her head to meet Akina's gaze on the same level. "You stop hungry evil?"

"We're going to stop Gromir and get my brother back. If that means dealing with duergar and knocking a few monsters to pulp, we'll handle it."

Izthuri stared at her for another instant, and then rolled sideways off the ledge.

Choking down a surprised shout, Akina leaned over to see her scrambling down the wall, not even using the larger handholds. When she reached the bottom, she looked up, white face a strip in a blotch of darkness.

"Come. We go. I show."

Chapter Thirteen
Darkness and Light

Izthuri set a frenetic pace and hardly seemed to remember she needed to remain close enough for the other two to follow. She whipped down tunnels like a black breeze, vanishing ahead only to hiss back, urging them to hurry. A few times, they'd hear or see nothing of her for so long, Akina felt sure the caligni had abandoned them. Then Izthuri would pop back up by her side, making Akina's fingers twitch for her maulaxe.

Her own urgency built the deeper they went, the new revelations spurring her almost as much as her need to get Brakisten back. With each step, the many questions they'd pondered back in the wall hollow flared in her mind, adding more steam to a growing pressure that would only be properly vented when she wrapped hands around Gromir's throat and squeezed the truth out from between his purpling lips.

Even Ondorum seemed gripped by a fresh energy. His jaw had locked tight, and he'd shed some of his usual grace for extra haste. She could well guess why: Knowing that not only her brother stood threatened by Gromir's scheme, but also an entire tribe of innocents, he'd likely be seeing this as a way to redeem himself from past mistakes. Whether or not Izthuri's people counted as actual innocents was another question, but if taking care of them soothed his tortured soul, maybe it'd also loosen his tongue at last.

She missed his voice, she had to admit. It went beyond wanting the convenience of talking again. Where his voice soothed, his silence grated. Where it had offered new perspectives and options, the silence made her feel trapped. She supposed there was reason to admire his dedication, but she'd have preferred the commitment be external—and extended to her—rather than internal. What if he started talking again but someday made a vow that bound them apart in more permanent ways? She tried to cast off her doubts, but they flitted after her like insects, nipping at her thoughts.

After the initial rush dulled, Akina realized they'd need fresh supplies if they intended to keep up the pace. She asked Izthuri where they might dredge up any resources, and the caligni started pointing out various molds or mosses they could gnaw on and taking them by puddles or pools of still water they could slurp up without fear of poison or anything lurking in the depths. Hardly tasty fare—in fact, most of it left a tang of stale dung in Akina's mouth—but it kept their legs moving.

More than a few times during their travels, the pitch darkness was broken up by patches of luminescent mold, glowing patches of water, or radiant crystals that speckled the wall with red and green starfields. Every so often, Izthuri would pause at such a spot and carefully unwrap the cloth around her hands to bare her palms. She held these over the light source and closed her eyes as if basking in their emanations. Akina recalled what Nullick said about Izthuri's people feeding off light itself, and since she never saw the caligni consuming anything else, she figured it for one of the few truths the warren leader had discovered in his madness. When Izthuri removed her hands, the light would be dimmer or gone altogether, while she sprang forward with renewed vigor.

Once, as they passed into a low cavern where the walls slanted off into the distance on either side, Izthuri made them stop. She hushed Akina's questions and shook her head, pointing to one side of the cavern, beyond where even dwarven eyes could penetrate the gloom. Then, through a series of gestures and her own posture, she indicated they must walk without making any noise whatsoever. When Akina took a step that clinked her armor, Izthuri made her stop again. She kept critiquing Akina's steps until she could take one without anything but the softest creak of leather or jingle of mail. Izthuri's eyes still narrowed at this, but she let her progress.

In this manner, it took them hours to cross what might've taken half of one at a steady walk. By the time they reached the other side and ducked back into new tunnels, Akina nearly vibrated with the craving to move faster. Her legs cramped at the effort of such a slow pace, and when Izthuri waved them on faster, she almost sprinted in relief. Izthuri never explained the purpose behind the snail's crawl through the cavern, but she kept casting relieved looks behind them for a while longer.

At another spot, the tunnel ended in a sudden drop-off, with the path resuming a hundred yards across the gap. The sound of rushing water emanated from below. Izthuri prowled the edge up and back, hissing to herself.

"Not like before. Flood took stone."

They had to double back almost half a day before cutting through a series of low tunnels that both Ondorum and Izthuri stooped to navigate. At one point, Ondorum even had to slide through on his belly. Izthuri crawled ahead, elbows and knees bent at right angles while her body lay flat, making Akina again think of a giant, underground insect.

One cavern held enormous mushrooms that shed a yellow glow as they towered over the group. While the glow did nothing to match the warmth of dwarven lamps, it at least struck the eyes softer than the blue mold from that hideous warren. Izthuri guided them around the densest clusters of mushroom-trees, and picked her way along with care. Akina wondered at this until she studied the forest-like clusters and noted the thick webbing strung between the mushroom stalks, and the occasional shadow of a multi-limbed creature skittering through the fungus. After that, she too chose her steps more carefully, cautious not to tromp on anything looking too much like a strand.

During a straighter trek, Izthuri came up short and motioned for them to do the same. At her aggressive posture, Akina drew her maulaxe and peered ahead.

Fifty feet down the tunnel, a length of the floor moved. What Akina had taken for rippled stone was, in fact, an enormous centipede stretched across their path. The beast lay twenty feet long and as wide as Akina stood tall, body supported by dozens of spear-thin legs. A pair of tendrils quivered up from the segmented end closest to them. The head on the other end bore enormous pincers, and it used these to tear chunks of mold off the wall, stuffing the scrapings into its maw with a set of smaller claws.

The caligni waggled fingers and whispered, "Back." She waited until they retreated a few paces and added, "Stay." Then she whipped out her blade and sprinted ahead.

Ondorum and Akina exchanged surprised looks.

Akina called after, "Wait, we can—"

The centipede writhed and coiled around at the noise, bunched body filling the tunnel. It chittered as it advanced, pincers clicking. Akina growled back and raised her maulaxe to join Izthuri's charge.

Before she took a step, an impenetrable cloud of darkness dropped over the area just ahead of them, cloaking the tunnel, Izthuri, and the beast. Akina scowled at the unnatural blackness, loathe to step inside. What sort of magic was this?

The insect's chittering rose in pitch, accompanying Izthuri's hissing and the ringing of a blade against shell. A loud crunch echoed. The darkness dissipated, revealing Izthuri perched on the dead centipede's body, sword embedded in the center of its head.

Akina sheathed her maulaxe, grousing. "Couldn't save any for me?"

In a smaller cave, they came across a patch of multi-colored crystals, shining bright enough to cast speckles of light over the whole area. They thrust in finger-length bunches out of a mound of dark earth. As Izthuri went over to feed, Akina hung back, wary. She could swear some of the gems were flawless diamonds, emeralds, and rubies, but the formation was clearly unnatural. And why were they glowing? "Izthuri . . ."

But Izthuri was already extending her hands. In response, the mound trembled and rose. The caligni hissed and tumbled back, drawing her sword as the mound resolved into a roughly humanoid shape formed of packed earth and rocks. Its boulder head rested just below the eight-foot ceiling, and its stony arms drooped to the ground, while hundreds of crystals protruded from its stooped back.

As Izthuri raised her blade, Ondorum ran in between her and the creature, arms extended to ward her off. When she hesitated, he turned and offered open palms to the creature, which Akina realized must be an earth elemental. Two gleaming rubies poked out from the front of the head boulder. It bowed until those gemstone eyes bathed Ondorum's face in red light, and she wondered if it sensed the earthen elements in his blood.

Ondorum tilted his head, as if listening to a voice the other two couldn't hear. Then he knelt and bowed low, palms pressed to the stone. The earth elemental formed a giant hand that drizzled dirt and laid it on the back of the oread's bent neck. The two remained like that for a time. Izthuri skulked on the other side of the cave, miffed at not getting a meal, while Akina kept her hands away from her maulaxe, not wanting to threaten the elemental and make it decide to crush Ondorum flat.

Then the elemental raised its hand and collapsed into a pile of rubble, sending a cloud of dust through the cave. Akina sneezed. She waved the air clear to see Ondorum rise, cradling a massive diamond in his hands. He turned and offered this to Izthuri with one of the widest grins she'd ever seen on him. Izthuri scuttled over and, after a wary look, plucked the gemstone from him. She bowed until her nose almost hit the floor. Then she took her time sucking the glow from the diamond, before setting it back on the ground where the elemental had been. Akina itched to grab it, but figured this might ruin the mood, and could be a huge insult to both her companions and the creature that bestowed the gift. Wouldn't do to have a cranky elemental pounding after them because she got a little greedy.

They moved on, Ondorum beaming to himself, Akina trudging after. She struggled with a strange jealousy, wondering how a random elemental could commune deeper with him than she had in a long while. Even Izthuri had been in on the action. She tried to be happy for the oread, but kept questioning why he got to be blessed and given a chance to make friends and give gifts, while she got touched by a god who gave her the ability to send more souls to the Boneyard in the most savage manner possible.

While the tunnel they headed down shot along straight, Izthuri waved them into a side corridor, where she drew them down a ways and then motioned for a stop. She checked every nook and cranny, sniffing around limestone columns and peering up at the bare ceiling. At last, she returned to them and kept her voice even lower than normal.

"We here. Long Walk not far."

Akina made fists. "About time. But it's a Darklander path, hm? Any other way to get to these ruins?"

"Fastest way. But not safe." She turned to Ondorum. "You, no worry. Seen your kind before. Her . . ." Lines formed around her eyes in what Akina now equated to a frown. "Her they kill or slave."

Akina scowled. "That's not happening."

Izthuri waggled a few fingers and reached under her rags. She came out holding a handful of what looked like thick flower petals. Akina poked one, and then pulled back, disturbed by the petal's fleshy texture.

"I gather. I crush. I paint." Izthuri waved a petal over Akina's face, filling her nose with an aroma of rot. "You look duergar. You no be killed or slave."

Akina crinkled her nose at the thought of looking like one of that fallen race, but realized there was no way around it. Aside from the ill fit of Ondorum's robe, wearing it to hood her features would just draw more suspicion from other travelers and any duergar patrols which, Izthuri assured her, were common. With painted skin, and her armor covering most of the rest of her, she'd blend in well enough to avoid raising an alarm. Still, it reminded her uncomfortably of Selvia's own dwarven disguise. Akina reassured herself that her motives were just while Selvia had been all about sabotage and murder.

So she waited while Izthuri used a rock to pound the petals to paste, and then kept still, eyes shut, as the caligni dabbed the slick mess over her face and neck. Izthuri had her remove her helm and worked a handful of rock dust into the remaining paste. This she used to conceal Akina's hair with its platinum streak, stroking it over with a sheen of gray that dried within moments. When it was finished, Akina turned to Ondorum.

"Well?"

Ondorum considered Akina's transformation. The simple act of turning Akina's skin and hair a grayish-purple had altered her appearance significantly, though no paint could mask her aggressive stance or the ever-kindling blaze in her eyes. Strangely, the disguise made her appear more earthy in nature, more akin to the rocks themselves. Add a few bits of stone or crystal and it might even look like she possessed some oread blood. It had an undeniable . . . appeal. However, he hardly needed Irori's wisdom to know he should never say such a thing to her.

He frowned and nodded, for once actually thankful he could hide behind his vow of silence.

Akina replaced her helm and gestured at Izthuri. "Ready now?"

The women took the lead. This tunnel reconnected with the larger one they'd left earlier. It broadened further as they went, and the ceiling rose, while the turns started to become sharper angles rather than the random meanderings many previous routes held. As Ondorum ducked through one lower opening, he glanced behind and paused.

On one side, the curve of the rock had appeared as a normal tunnel. On this side, it had been carved into an arched threshold, with strange glyphs, jagged runes, and images of serpentine creatures.

Ondorum studied the stone and wondered what names or events had been engraved on it, and if anyone cared to remember them. Then, accepting his ignorance for the time being, he followed the others around a corner and got his first glimpse of the Long Walk.

Chapter Fourteen
The Long Walk

Ondorum didn't know what to expect of the Long Walk. A slightly larger tunnel, maybe, or a series of huge caverns connected by shorter tunnels, similar to the dwarven city districts?

Instead, they emerged from under another archway and went up a flight of steps onto a broad stone platform, the sides of which dropped away into nothingness. Ondorum raised his eyes, and wondered at the scale of the place.

It could only be called a tunnel if all other tunnels, and even the caverns they'd marched through on their way down, were renamed as mere cracks or chips in the earth. While the ceiling remained visible, it hung broader and higher than that of Taggoret and seemed ready to pour down on their heads, dripping with enormous stalactites. Ondorum detected motion among those tremendous teeth of stone, flocks and swarms of winged creatures that darted here and there, nesting in the heights.

He at last dragged his gaze back down to the wide bridge thrusting from the platform they stood on, where it joined a perpendicular road that swept away in either direction like a river of gray stone until it flowed out of sight. At random intervals, other bridges and platforms connected with it on either side, with much of the space between a sheer drop into unknown depths. The road stood wide enough for a hundred humans to stand shoulder-to-shoulder across it—but Ondorum knew few humans ever had beheld this, and only then as slaves, most likely.

"Is it all like this?" Akina asked.

Izthuri looked at the Long Walk as if she saw a common mountain meadow. "Some. Not all. Nothing is all." She strode across the bridge and waved for them to follow.

As they crossed, distant motion resolved down the tunnel stretching off to their left; a group of creatures headed toward them from that direction. Ondorum wondered if they should hide and let those who approached pass. Then he realized the oncoming band would likely have spotted them as well, and any attempts to duck out of sight would be more suspicious than marching forward as if they belonged.

Instead, they reached the path proper and headed in the same direction the creatures were already going. He adjusted his pace to be slightly behind Akina, hoping to divert whatever attention might be thrown her way as the others neared. Izthuri remained ahead of them, though her gait had changed. Rather than the skulking and dashing about of the tunnels, she now stood erect and strode in a flowing manner, long limbs shimmying back and forth like ropes.

Noises reached his ears as the others gained on them: that of slapping feet, rattling chains, and a constant undercurrent of whimpering and murmuring peppered with harsher voices and the occasional mewl of pain. At last, the trio paused to watch them pass.

The newcomers resolved into a line of ten creatures all shackled together by chains around their necks and wrists. At the front of the line, a pair of reptilian humanoids held chains that connected with all the rest, and used these to guide the line along. Far different than the little lizard Ondorum had seen in Nullick's lair, these two walked erect, tails swinging thick and lined with spines. Crests rose from their heads and snouts, patterned with stripes of softly glowing paints. They wore ragged leather wraps around their waists and went bare-chested, showing off thick scarring. Each held a hefty club, though their claws and talons looked like weapons enough.

Behind them came the line of what Ondorum took to be prisoners, though whether by law or by coin, he could only guess. Try as he might, though, he couldn't find a single physical similarity between any of them. Ranging in size from rodents on hind legs to a furry behemoth that lumbered along on three stumpy limbs, each captive displayed an odd conglomeration of features and deformities. One had chains clamped to four multi-jointed arms, while another had hands on both arms and legs. Tails, scales, fur, horns—even fins were present, sometimes all on the same creature.

This strange menagerie lumbered past without so much as glancing at the trio. In their shuffling, many of them hooted or snuffled, a mourning sound that raked at Ondorum's soul. Did any of these creatures deserve to be in chains? What crimes had they committed? Were they captives from battle, or did they go to be sold to the highest bidder? He bristled at the last consideration.

Akina must've sensed the course of his thoughts, for she edged closer and whispered. "Can't save everyone."

He scowled, but tried to temper his unthinking fervency. True, things might work differently down here, but some things were either right or wrong, no matter whether they occurred in the darkness or under the sun.

When Izthuri checked to see if anything was the matter, Akina shrugged off her concern. "Just wondering what these creatures are."

"We call them tattered ones." Izthuri pointed an elbow backward. "Those who lead is called xulgaths. Their masters follow."

At the end of the line, two figures rode along on a set of giant furred spiders. The arachnids stood as high as Ondorum himself, their eight legs bound by leather and metal straps leading up to the hands of the duergar on their backs. The pair of ashen-skinned dwarves slumped in their saddles. Both bald, with flowing silver beards, they glared over their prisoners, occasionally adjusting the axes strapped to their backs. When a prisoner stumbled or slowed, they shouted at it in a hacking, choking language. It made Ondorum think of dwarven speech, but only in the roughest sense.

Where dwarven words might be compared to the crack of stone against stone or the thrum of a furnace bellows, the duergar spoke like gravel being stirred or the squeal of rusted metal.

When the duergar spotted the other travelers, one veered off and planted his arachnid mount before them. He pointed at Akina and rattled off incomprehensible words.

Ondorum strode in front of her and waved the duergar on. The duergar raised bushy brows and barked further babble. Ondorum just shook his head. The duergar's hand went to his axe, and the oread tensed. Izthuri came up, speaking rapidly in the duergar language. The duergar squinted as Izthuri bowed. He asked a few more questions and then sat back in his saddle, hand leaving his axe. With another verbal barrage, he steered to rejoin the slave caravan.

Once they were far enough away, Akina spat on the ground. "What'd he say? What'd you tell him?"

Izthuri snuffled. "He asked who you were. Then asked how much to buy your oread. Then wanted to kill your oread. Thought slave tried to make him leave. I say you refuse to sell and your oread is . . . one who guards. Attack him, attack you. His choice."

"Bodyguard, you mean?" Subtle mirth entered Akina's voice. "My oread, hm?"

Ondorum looked back at her in time to catch a wink. He tried to smile, but the image of the tattered ones in chains filled his mind. He fell into a solemn mood as they traveled on.

One of his monastery instructors had once used the illustration of an onion in a meditation session. Both the mind and the world could be seen as onions. They appeared as one whole and complete thing on the outside, easy to hold and understand. However, peeling back the layers revealed the complexity. Nothing was ever as simple as it appeared, especially not the pursuit of truth and perfection.

When the wounded orc had shown up on the monastery doorstep, Ondorum had thought it a simple thing to show mercy and tend to the creature, despite the other monks' misgivings. He'd even thought the orc receptive to the teachings he shared during its convalescence. While disappointed that the orc left rather than join their order, he'd felt quiet satisfaction in giving another soul the chance to follow a better path.

And then the orc warband had arrived a month later, ready to pillage the treasures they believed the monastery held. Many monks had been slaughtered, the monastery half-destroyed. In the aftermath, once the monks had recovered enough, Ondorum bid his home farewell and set to wandering, seeking clarity for his clouded mind. How did acts of kindness beget evil? How could offering hope to one life end so many others?

In the years that followed, he'd met Akina and the mercenary band and found himself surprisingly refreshed. He reveled in the varied perspectives they offered, the new experiences. He found a measure of solace in his and Akina's deepening relationship. She held both simplicity and complexity within her—the struggle with her growing rage and yet her single-mindedness when striking down ill-doers to save many more lives. She always claimed she just did it for the gold, but he knew better and had tried to help her see the same.

And then there was their parting from the band . . . the journey to Taggoret . . . the village along the way . . . his ill-spoken words and their ruinous results . . .

"Awake up there?" Akina asked. "You've been sleep-walking all day. More company's coming."

Ondorum snapped back to present awareness. In such dangerous territory, how could he let himself be so distracted by personal musings? He took a cleansing breath, sweeping it all aside to be dealt with later.

Company? He looked around and saw the newcomers as a gray mass behind them, filling the Walk from side to side and quickly catching up. The group didn't look to have any regimental order to it, and he prayed this meant it wasn't a military force. As they closed in, it consolidated into a caravan. At least a hundred people and creatures shambled along, forced to a quicker pace by their masters or just an urgency to get their destination as quickly as possible. Speed made profit.

Akina called a quick, quiet conference, and Ondorum grimaced in agreement with her assessment. While the crowded conditions might make for slower going, it could also help them blend in. No one would pay particular attention to one more group among the rabble.

The first to reach them was a duergar astride a giant beetle, its blue-green carapace gleaming like water under a night sky. He called something their way, which Izthuri answered in turn. With a guttural laugh, he rode on, and soon the rest of the caravan descended upon them.

After their time in the isolated wilds of Nar-Voth, being in the presence of so many others made for a jarring transition. Not a jostling experience, but more of a temporary sensory overload as he took in all the new sights and smells, and the many, many new sounds. The crack of whips and babble of voices struck him first, with the groans and lowings of underground beasts trained for labor. The rattle of wheels and creak of axles. A whiff of rotten produce lingered, and he wondered what manner of vegetation they grew down there, and what fruit or vegetables grown far from fresh sunlight or water might taste like.

Grim-faced duergar hauled loads of weaponry and drove carts laden with tarp-wrapped goods. One cage-on-wheels rattled along, filled with three cadaverous creatures with skull-like faces and monstrous claws on both their hands and feet. They snarled at every-one they passed and stuck out prehensile tongues at least two feet long. Three armed duergar marched on the cage's heels and kept a wary eye on anyone who got too close. The occasional xulgath scampered by, some on two legs, some on four. Several elven figures moved with lithe steps through the bustle, their skin a dark purple and their hair hanging to their waists like white drapes. Another group of deformed tattered ones tracked by, unchained this time. While they exhibited the same random assembly of limbs and features, Ondorum felt certain they shared a kinship with the prisoners who'd gone on before them not long before. In fact, looking up ahead, he could see that exact slaver chain had slowed enough to be absorbed into the car-avan proper, keeping to the further edge of the mass.

Ondorum had traveled with a few surface caravans, but this one lacked the camaraderie of those. Conversations remain muted except for arguments that broke out when groups got too close, even with the crowded conditions. Everyone watched everyone else, as if suspecting all to be potential thieves. Weapons hung at almost every waist, or stood clutched in fists. While they might be used to protect the caravan against the dangers spawned from the tunnels they passed, Ondorum guessed they might as easily be turned on one another. The lack of wind or any sort of weather and the ghostly palette the darkness enforced made it feel like a march of the damned more than anything else.

He noticed four tall, slim figures, all wrapped in black cloth. When he pointed them out to Izthuri, though, she hissed, "Not my tribe."

The three of them clustered together, Ondorum and Izthuri taking a slight point to look like Akina's bodyguards and dissuade anyone's approach.

"Do not follow," Izthuri said, a moment before she stepped aside and disappeared in the dismal bustle.

Ondorum exchanged a worried look with Akina, but they plodded on. Their fears were allayed when Izthuri reappeared and resumed her stroll as if she'd never left.

"Duergar squads. Soldiers come behind. Soldiers come ahead. Stop everyone."

"Why?" asked Akina, voice low.

"Pay to use Long Walk. All pay many times before end. We pay here and at gate."

"Gate?"

"Duergar gate," said Izthuri. "Blocks Long Walk. Tunnel we need on other side."

"Well, hell. Got nothing to pay with. What about that sword of yours? Seems valuable. I can get you a new one when we—"

Izthuri whirled and had the black blade to Akina's throat before Ondorum realized she'd moved. All three froze. Izthuri's eyes had gone wild. Akina stared up at the caligni, caught in mid-step.

Ondorum reached out and laid an open hand on Izthuri's wrist. He pushed down, slowly, and she let him move the blade away. At last, the tension went out of her arm and she spun around again, striding ahead. Ondorum nudged Akina into motion while checking to make sure they hadn't been exposed. Some of the nearer merchants and travelers glanced their way, but without further disruption, their attention withdrew.

Izthuri slid the blade into the looped rag she used as a sheath. "My blade."

Akina rubbed at her throat. "Fair enough." She glanced behind. "So what if we don't pay?"

"Be made slave. Or killed."

"What if we hop into an offshoot tunnel and wait for them to go by?"

Izthuri waggled fingers. "No tunnels here."

She spoke true. As far down as Ondorum could see, the Long Walk walls now looked solid, with no bridges, platforms, or otherwise offering a way off the main path. The duergar must've planned their sweep for this stretch, knowing travelers couldn't escape inspection.

"Figure bashing someone over the head and snagging their coin isn't the brightest, hm?"

Ondorum blew a low breath, fearing that'd be her next suggestion and thankful she saw the many flaws in it. She must've heard, because she glared up at him.

"What? I don't solve everything with bashing." When he looked back blankly, she jutted her chin out. "Shut it."

Ondorum tapped both their shoulders and indicated they should follow. Then he quickened his stride and guided them around numerous wagons and past a small group of duergar muttering among themselves. When they broke past a line of tattered ones, closer to the front of the caravan, he gestured ahead. The two women gave him curious looks.

"You just want to walk faster?" Akina asked. "She said they're up ahead too."

Ondorum took the horns of her ram's helm and forced her to look at a specific group. A moment later, her stillness told him she got the point. When he released her, she fixed him with a wondering look.

"You're cracked in the head."

He gave her helmet a reprimanding tap, which she shook off.

"Right." Akina directed Izthuri's attention to the set of duergar slavers. "How much do you think you can haggle for my oread?"

Chapter Fifteen
In Chains

Akina hung back, doing her best to look sullen while Izthuri finished sealing the deal with the slavers. She berated herself for not nabbing the elemental's diamond back in the tunnels. Would've been better daring the elemental's wrath than seeing Ondorum standing there, stripped to his loincloth and head bowed like a whipped slave. The wounds on his back and ribs made it easier for Izthuri to spin a tale of a duergar mistress displeased with her property and deciding she'd rather have a bit of extra spending coin than such a troublesome lout.

The exchange happened quickly enough, and the duergar grinned wide as they shackled Ondorum to the end of the line. Akina cringed as they added an extra precaution—several barbed loops went around his neck and were connected to an intricate system of interlinked chains that they fitted to his bonds in various spots. Multiple padlocks clinched the whole array. If he struggled too much or tried to snap the chains, the barbs would tighten, choking, puncturing, and eventually killing. It seemed a bit much, but Akina guessed they'd had trouble with oread slaves before or other creatures with prodigious strength.

Izthuri headed back toward Akina, while the slavers got their line moving again. This being Ondorum's idea didn't make it any easier. The thought of him in chains wrenched in directions she couldn't describe. He already chained himself up enough on the inside. Akina marked the two slavers in her mind and started pondering ways to see them dead once the scheme ended.

Izthuri didn't look at all disturbed at having just sold off one of her companions. To maintain the illusion, she bowed to Akina like a servant having completed a task. They rejoined the caravan flow, keeping enough distance from others to talk in low voices.

"He call your oread fine specimen. Said pity lost gems. Would pay extra. I tell him mistress has nasty bite."

Akina sighed. "Is it enough?"

Izthuri opened the pouch and withdrew two square pieces of silver, which she secured under her clothes. Then she handed Akina the rest of the heavy pouch. "I pay for you. Am servant. Keep rest. Pay again later."

Akina sighed. "At the gate?"

"Yes. A span from here. No pay after. Free oread and take tunnel."

"Perfect." Akina started to scrub her forehead, but then stopped, thinking this might blotch the skin dye. They had their plan in place to cause a diversion and give Ondorum a chance to escape, but who knew what could go wrong between now and then? Plus, Izthuri insisted they move out of sight of the slavers, otherwise Ondorum's new owners might get suspicious. She almost prayed to Torag, to ask him to keep the monk safe, but figured Torag wouldn't be all that pleased with her right then. Nor would Irori listen to someone as jagged-edged as she.

Noticing Akina's morose mood, Izthuri promised she'd slip up ahead every so often to make sure they weren't beating the oread to death or anything. They wouldn't notice her peeking around because, "Never tell us apart. Rag folk all alike."

The duergar squads came and went swiftly. Mounted on spiders and beetles, the soldiers wore black armor inlaid with silver. They worked the caravan from both ahead and behind, slowing progress to a crawl while scratching off numbers on a sheet of metal as they tallied and took the toll. Some of them even rode along the wall of the Long Walk, ten or twenty feet above the road, watching to make sure no one evaded their levy. Izthuri passed over the demanded two silver. Once the two collecting squads met and conferred, they all skittered to the sides, spiders and beetles clinging to the walls. They shot up into the thicker darkness near the tunnel's ceiling and navigated in between the stalactites, back the way the caravan had come. No doubt to wait until the next band of merchants passed through so they could repeat the process.

Akina grumbled a few choice curses in their wake. She tried to tell herself each step forward was another step toward getting Ondorum back at her side, but that didn't make them any lighter. She and Izthuri fell into an uneasy silence as the journey wore on. Their path lay clear, even when the deep gaps in the sides filled in and side tunnels started to connect with the Long Walk once more. Izthuri fulfilled her promise by slipping off every few hours and returning with a simple nod to indicate everything went well up with the slavers.

Akina tried to embrace the silence. That was what Ondorum did, right? Maybe if she took a temporary vow of silence until they got him back, it'd feel more like he remained nearby in spirit.

For a while, she reviewed Gromir's note in her mind, since she had it memorized by then. Then she imagined herself using the note itself in all sorts of amusing ways, including crumpling it up and punching it into Gromir's smirking mouth, or burning it and jamming the hot ashes up his nose. That almost got a smile out of her.

Soon, though, she went from the note to thinking about Selvia and all their interactions on the path underground. What had been the duergar woman's scheme? What was her real relationship with Gromir, and how did he get tangled up with duergar in the first place? What damage had he done to Akina's family, beyond making them a laughingstock of Taggoret with his art of her around the city?

For so many years, the main issues Akina had to deal with included, "Who do I hit?", "How hard do I hit him?", and "How much do I get when I bring the head back?" War and mercenary work simplified things. Now she needed to erupt with convoluted questions. She wanted to run to everyone around and shake them, screaming, "Why? Tell me why, you son-of-an-orc, before I bite your face off!"

Akina moaned and hung her head. Dust and drudgery, she hated silence. Made one think too much. All those thoughts tumbling over and over with nowhere to go. How did Ondorum stand it?

Izthuri laid a hand on her shoulder.

"There. Gate."

Akina blinked up. How long had they been walking? The realization of time slipping by without her realizing was disconcerting, akin to when she woke up after an intense fight and wondered how many had died, why she still lived, and where one of her boots had gone.

Nodding thanks to Izthuri, she studied the structure ahead. Spanning the Long Walk, it looked like a mingling of natural walls and artificial construction, yet all craggy and solid. In addition to stretching from wall to wall, it also reached up to the ceiling of the tunnel itself, blocking the way.

Metal spikes jutted through certain spots in the stone, making it look like a giant had pounded nails through from the other side. A couple dozen dark windows had been carved into the main structure, and Akina imagined these concealed guards or archers, watching for any travelers or trouble. At varying heights, thicker portions of stone had been fashioned into protected walkways that blended back into the structure on either end.

Akina wondered at the building technique, since the steel and stone appeared interwoven. Had they erected the barrier in an empty section of the tunnel and then used earthen magics to draw the stones around it, concealing its foundations? Or had they carved out a natural barrier and infused it with the metal?

At the base of it all, four arches stood spaced out, offering what looked to be the only way through. These were currently blocked by a double barrier of black iron portcullises and gates. Random holes and side-tunnels still broke up the walls leading up to the structure, but Akina figured these didn't offer routes that circumvented the gateway itself. Or, if they did, it'd take the traveler days or weeks out of the way through untenable terrain, making it an unprofitable and dangerous option.

As they neared, she could see that each gate had a symbol carved into it: an arch with a burning flame in the middle—the sign of the duergar god, Droskar.

This made her pause a second, thinking of Brakisten and the visions that had plagued him. How would he react to being taken down into the realm of the duergar, betrayed by the very dwarf who'd stolen their mother's affections? Would he be riddled with terror, believing his dreams of death were coming true?

The caravan started to converge into various lines, with a few merchants hastening to be at the front. Ondorum's slavers cut toward the rightmost gate. Akina headed that way, but Izthuri redirected her left.

"That slave gate," she said. "Traveler gate here."

Akina ground her teeth, but allowed herself to be led over to where more lone caravan members clustered, as well as groups of people who lacked any sort of visible goods to sell. People shuffled and shoved as more of the caravan arrived and tried to press them forward. But the gates themselves had yet to budge to admit them, nor had any guards emerged to shout down instructions or warnings. Soon, various caravan members began hollering up at the openings in the wall, or pounding weapons until the area resounded with cries or demands to open the way.

Akina peered through a gap in the crowd, glad to see Ondorum's slave line remained on this side, stuck with the rest of them. The wait would've been more torturous if he'd already gone through, plus it'd force them to scramble to catch up and retrieve him. Izthuri had mentioned the tunnel they needed lay just on the other side of the gateway.

"Does it always take this long?" She leaned in so Izthuri could hear her over the rising disgruntled chorus. Were the duergar who manned the place all drunk or sleeping? Not like they had to rush to ensure nobody slipped past them. She supposed the caravan could be made to wait for days and still have no recourse but to grumble or turn around; that seemed unlikely, given the ruthless efficiency with which the recent squads had processed them.

Izthuri frowned with her forehead. "No." She wove her head from side to side, trying to get a better look. "It quiet."

Quiet? Akina scowled at the noisemakers around them. The caligni must have meant the wall itself, rather than the general atmosphere, for not a peep sounded in reply.

"Something's wrong," she whispered to herself.

A robed figure appeared at one of the entrances to the uppermost walkway. The duergar stepped into sight, easing one foot in front of the other. He didn't look down at those assembled, but stared straight ahead as he approached the edge. A few caravan leaders called to him, but the duergar ignored all these, walking until he struck the low lip at the edge.

Then he toppled over it, and all saw the blade stuck in his back as he fell.

It must've been a sign, for a shrieking din erupted around them. Two dozen gray-scaled, black-speckled xulgaths filled notches and holes in the wall, shaking clubs and spears. Many of them wore ill-fitting black armor, which Akina realized must have been scavenged from the duergar who once manned this gateway.

The clamor of their war cries tripled as a hundred more xulgaths poured out of the tunnel openings around them and back up the road. As one, the lizards converged on the trapped caravan.

Chapter Sixteen
Ambush

Ondorum waited along with the rest of the slaves, wondering what might have delayed their progress. The gate remained closed ahead, its gleaming flame-within-the-arch sigil making Ondorum's head ache and stomach twist if he looked at it too long. He kept his head down, but still watched everything around him as much as he could without inciting the slavers' lashes, which they dispensed with glee for the smallest infraction. The line of tattered ones shuffled in place ahead of him, and it wrenched him to see their broken forms mirroring their broken spirits.

He didn't pay much thought to the rising shouts around them, but wondered if there might be any way for him to free some, if not all, of the slaves when Akina and Izthuri came to help him escape on the other side. It'd have to be near a side tunnel, otherwise any escapees wouldn't stand much of a chance of getting very far on the Long Walk before being chased down.

As he pondered the possibilities, a horde of xulgaths sprang into sight, and the caravan exploded into chaos. The two xulgaths who'd already been traveling with the caravan suddenly turned to Ondorum's line of slaves and began cutting down the nearest prisoners with vicious rakes of their claws. One then bounded off into the crowd, tearing out throats with its fangs and eviscerating with its talons.

The chain line jerked every which way as slaves bellowed and screamed and fought to escape. Ondorum gritted his teeth as the chain between him and the next slave yanked, tightening his barbed collar. He followed to ease the pressure and got close enough to grip the other slave's humped shoulders. The tattered one twisted around as much as it could. It had a drooping face and blubbery lips, through which it bleated plaintively. Wide-set eyes the color of yolk blinked at him, and its nose looked more like a beak. Ondorum clapped it on the shoulders again, trying to reassure it and get it to stay put. The tattered one trembled in his hold but didn't try to bolt, and he took the opportunity to survey the scene.

Xulgaths tumbled out of the wall openings ahead and above them, using the jagged stones and metal spikes to leap down. Some even clambered about the stalactites far above, using their claws to cling to the stone as they leapt from column to column before reaching the wall and scrambling down. More raced out of the tunnels to their back and swept in toward the exposed caravan flanks.

The duergar slavers raced by Ondorum on their spider mounts, shouting to one another as they headed to the front of the line. They leapt to the ground beside the treacherous xulgath, which had been gnawing on a dead slave's arm. The xulgath whipped around and snarled at them. It lashed out, but quickly fell to the axes, limbs and head flying away. As its body twitched at their feet, the slavers looked up at the descending tide of xulgaths, with the nearest being a series of leaps away. Ondorum tensed. Would they stand and fight for their property?

One duergar pointed his axe at the slaves and the other nodded. They turned and began hacking down the captives. Ondorum opened his mouth in a silent shout of denial.

The slave in front of him panicked and thrashed anew. Before its struggles could tighten his bonds and slice his throat open, Ondorum threw the slave to the ground. He grabbed one of the large iron links in the chain connecting his bonds to the other slave's. The metal flowed under his touch and the chain snapped apart, leaving him freed from the line and holding an iron quarterstaff. The tattered one stared up at him in wonder, before being dragged a few feet by the rest of the slaves. The slaves didn't even defend themselves. Some tried to flee, but became tangled in their chains, while others cowered and died beneath the axes.

Xulgaths shrieked all around as Ondorum briefly tested his bonds. He couldn't snap his chains without possibly killing himself in the process, and he couldn't repeat the link-breaking so soon. The shackles restricted his arms, but still gave his legs enough room. He charged down the line, keeping his staff tucked in tight.

The duergar slavers paused in their slaughter long enough to see him coming. Their eyes widened in shock, but they raised their axes as he rushed in. Right as he did, two xulgaths leapt onto the duergar to his right and bore him to the ground. More reptilian warriors dropped from overhead, downing caravan members or landing to hiss and attack others. The ones from the tunnels must've struck behind in full, for the cavernous tunnel roared with screams, mad laughter, and clashes of arms.

The surviving slaver ignored the xulgaths, ashen face twisted in rage as he raised his axe to strike Ondorum.

Holding his upper arms close to his chest to avoid tangling his chains, Ondorum used the crook of his wrists and palms to lever the staff around, maneuvering it through the fiercest attacks he could manage.

One end whipped across the slaver's face, cracking bone. As the duergar stumbled back, Ondorum kicked the axe from his fist and snapped a foot into his chest. He whirled and brought the staff down on the slaver's bald head. The duergar dropped into a motionless heap.

Ondorum turned just as the two xulgaths finished with the other slaver. They rounded on him, slavering jaws dripping with blood and gore. One dug claws into the duergar's body and used it to launch itself at him. Ondorum caught the creature in the chest with a staff end and directed it over his head. It slammed to the ground, and the staff crushed its ribcage. Ondorum ducked without looking and the second xulgath soared over him. As he came up, so did the staff, connecting under the creature's lower jaw and snapping its head back with skull-crunching power.

Xulgaths continued to drop about like wicked rain. He slammed one out of midair, swept the legs from another. His bare feet brushed across the ground, drawing intricate, invisible designs as he spun and whirled, kicked and crouched, creating a circle of death around him. The ground responded to his touch, sending strength up his legs and into his core, which glowed like a ball of molten steel. Power surged through him, following lines of energy to radiate from his toes to his fingertips to the top of his head.

The xulgaths seemed to move about him in slow motion. One lunged for his face, while another lashed at his ribs. He grabbed the incoming maw and clamped it shut with one hand, inches from biting his ear off. He speared the staff out twice to strike the other xulgath's arms in precise hits, breaking them both. Then he ducked and smashed the first xulgath's head into the ground with an elbow strike.

Three came at him from all sides, wearing mismatched black iron armor and swinging blades and cudgels. The clangs of his staff turned into a nonstop drumming as he ricocheted strikes off helmets, swords, and breastplates. Stomps and kicks broke their exposed knees and feet. As one went down, he turned and flung his staff sideways into the helmeted head of a second. As the staff rebounded into the air, he dodged the swipe of the third and threw a flurry of short punches into its side. Holding a palm upward, he caught the falling staff and used it to pound the second one flat. When the third opened its mouth, trying to suck in the air he'd driven from its lungs, a staff end drove out through the back of its head.

He halted, lacking an immediate target, and swept his gaze across the battleground—for that was what the Long Walk had become. The caravan faced more than equal its number, by his estimate. A dozen xulgaths remained perched on the wall itself, flinging bone javelins, shooting crude bows and arrows, or whipping stones from slings into the fray.

The fight had compressed the caravan into a shrinking circle as outer defenders met the swarm of reptilian attackers. Even with many of the caravan members armed, the xulgaths attacked two or three to a victim, slashing out eyes, hamstringing from behind, or gutting from crotch to beard.

Twenty duergar had transformed since the start of the attack, doubling themselves and their equipment in size. They bellowed as the ground shuddered beneath them. This change must've enhanced their strength as well, for they swept aside xulgaths and stomped several flat at a time. Even as Ondorum watched, though, one of these fell to xulgaths who converged on him from every direction. As the duergar's eyes dulled, his form shrank back to normal, and he lay in a growing pool of black blood.

A handful of xulgaths stood out from the rest. They remained further back from the fight, closer to the tunnels where they'd emerged. These displayed an assortment of fetishes—strings of metal and bone—and had sharp bones thrust through their arms and bare chests. To Ondorum's eyes, the whorled designs painted on their long faces suggested more of an arcane purpose than decorative. Each held some sort of wand or staff, which they waved about or thumped on the earth in a jerking rhythm.

In time with these rituals, bolts of bruise-colored power lanced out from pointed claws, striking duergar and their minions. Those hit fell in sprays of blood, or stumbled and began retching. Other shamans waved their bones, and the targets of their magic stood stunned or turned their weapons on allies they'd fought beside just before. Wagons burst aflame, scattering cargo and riders alike.

Ondorum looked to the base of the wall. The gates. He had to find a way to open the gates, otherwise everyone would be slaughtered.

He gauged the height of the arch above the gates, built to allow the passage of creatures much taller than a duergar. As he did, he noticed an even more horrible sight. A pair of xulgath shamans raised bone staffs above their heads and cried out in the culmination of an unknown spell, and below their feet, the stone swirled and cracked, detaching from the rest of the wall. The shards of stone formed into two earth elementals with emeralds for eyes. They stood no bigger than the xulgaths themselves—certainly nothing compared to the elemental he'd communed with in the cave. Nevertheless, they proved effective enough. One began tearing rubble from the wall and flinging it into the masses below. The other dove into the rock, reappearing on the ground by bursting up among a group of fighters and spraying shards in all directions.

Ondorum marked the summoners' position. He would not stand to see the earth itself a slave to these foul creatures. At the same time, he knew he needed to get the gates—or at least one of them—open. Not only would it let the surviving slaves flee to freedom, but his companions could reach the tunnel they needed on the other side. He could try to reach Akina and Izthuri and escape back the way they'd come, but what purpose would that serve? If the xulgaths kept the gates closed, there might not be another way to reach their destination.

He eyed the metal spikes that lined the curve of the gate archway, down to the ground. Readying his staff, he sprinted for the lowest spike.

With a bone-trembling roar, Akina mashed the xulgath to the earth with her maulaxe. She dodged another strike and then hacked a scaly head in half with a single blow. Izthuri fought by her side, dancing through the xulgaths. Her unearthly blade slit throats, slashed off limbs, and sliced stomachs wide. Every so often, she conjured one of her shadow clouds over a swath of the battlefield and darted inside. When the cloud dispersed, several of the beasts lay dead, and she danced on.

Sweat already drenched Akina's face and poured down the inside of her armor. Claws raked across her chest, and one xulgath grabbed her helm from behind and tried to yank it off. She rammed an elbow into its stomach and turned to drive the axe wedge straight into its heart. Lowering her head, she dashed forward and took another xulgath in the gut with her ram's horns, smashing it up against the side of a wagon—just as the cart burst into purple flames.

Snarling, she reeled from the blaze. These brutes had casters? Guess it figured they'd need some of their kind with more brains than brawn to coordinate this ambush. She looked around for the magic-users. A few xulgaths danced in place on the sidelines, shaking bone totems and staffs as they called upon whatever power they served.

She charged for the nearest one, bulling or knocking aside any xulgath that got in her path. The shaman must've seen her coming, for it paused in its frenetic hopping and pointed a claw at her.

Akina threw herself behind a pile of bodies. The earth blew apart in a swirl of chaotic color where she'd just been. As rock pattered down around her, Akina wiped across her face to clear the sweat dripping into her eyes. Then she looked to the side and found a duergar merchant huddled beside her. He clutched a dagger and peered at any nearby threats. When he returned her gaze, his gray eyes narrowed, and then popped wide again. Akina frowned, but then looked at her glove, which was smeared with purple-gray dye.

The merchant stumbled to his feet, trying to position his blade, but she beat him to it, standing and swinging up and over to mash him back down. Something moved behind her, and she spun, but checked her swing to avoid hitting Izthuri. The caligni waggled fingers at her face. Akina shrugged. Nothing to be done at this point but hope the frenzy of battle kept folks from noticing a little longer.

"Get to Ondorum," she shouted, aiming for where they'd last seen the slavers.

With Izthuri bringing up the rear, Akina rammed xulgaths aside, trampled over more, and cut others down as they lunged for her with claws and fangs extended. Sensing a danger from above, she jumped to the right just as a xulgath fell from nowhere to dash itself to mush.

The ground to their left exploded, throwing her aside as earthen fragments pelted the area and people. An earth elemental, little bigger than herself, rose into sight, and green flames lit in its emerald eyes. When it began attacking nearby duergar, she realized it must've been summoned by the xulgaths. Tricky bastards. What else did they have planned?

Izthuri appeared before her and offered a hand. Akina surprised herself by accepting, and the caligni hauled her up with unexpected strength. They barreled on. Arrows with stone heads struck around them. Beside her, a duergar fell when a bone spear sprouted from his eye. A rock whizzed past her head, and then another clanged off her helm.

Yelling against the odds, the pair sped up until they struck a line of xulgaths. They burst through, sending the beasts scattering, to see the rightmost gate. The two duergar slavers lay dead while their line of tattered ones cowered by the gate. Some of them had been cut down, leaving half a dozen chained to their mutilated kin. Akina tracked to the end of the line and saw a broken chain. Ondorum must've sprung himself early when the fighting started. A glance around revealed a measure of his handiwork in the felled xulgaths littering the area. Figured.

Then where . . .

Instinct made her look up.

The monk leapt from a thrusting rock to a metal spike. Chains still dangled from his neck, wrists, and ankles, but he balanced briefly before using an iron staff to shove off and soar up another length of stone toward the lowest walkway. She called after him, but doubted even her roaring voice could reach him above the clamor. With another leap, he disappeared over the edge.

Growling, Akina turned to find something to kill. The xulgath sprinting her way looked obliging enough. After dispatching it, she saw how the caravan numbers had dwindled. The xulgaths ran amok through groups of defenders who'd lost their centralized defensive position. Despite their own numerous dead, the reptiles appeared to not lack reinforcements, nor did their own losses dishearten them any or lessen their bestial attacks. Their shamans continued to chant around the edges, striking down unsuspecting fighters from afar and breaking up the earth underneath. They also cast their unholy magic over their own kind, sealing otherwise mortal wounds, shielding xulgaths from attacks by the enlarged duergar, or bolstering them with surges of power that drove them into ever-rising frenzies.

A set of three duergar had gathered near the other side of the tunnel and stood back-to-back. They wore crimson robes trimmed with black and had hands raised in a mutual chant. Icy lances thrust up from the earth, spearing xulgaths on all sides. Holes opened in the earth and swallowed screaming reptiles. Xulgaths that got too close struck an invisible barrier and were flung away by a spray of lightning. It didn't look like the duergar had singled out the opposing casters yet, though, being too busy defending themselves.

Akina drew Izthuri's attention to the duergar casters. Though the words burned like acid on her tongue, she said, "Got to help them."

Izthuri waggled fingers at her face again, denoting her failing disguise. Scowling, Akina ran over to one of the duergar slaver corpses and swiped her hand through the blood running thick from the wound in his skull. She slathered this over her face, and then waved for Izthuri to follow.

Whatever Ondorum intended, he better see it done quick.

Chapter Seventeen
Desperate Means

Ondorum rolled as he struck the walkway, chains bruising him as they ground against the stone. He channeled the pain aside as he rose and oriented himself. Two xulgath archers spotted him and turned their bows. His staff struck aside one arrow and smacked the xulgath from its perch in the next instant. The second didn't have a chance to even nock the crooked arrow in its hand before it sailed after its companion. A xulgath warrior in duergar armor appeared on the ledge above and jumped down, axe poised. Ondorum raised his staff, catching the axe between shaft and blade. However, the edge still slammed into the crisscross of the chains on his arms, making the barbs squeeze around his throat. Thrusting the blade away dug the points in further, and trickles of blood flowed over his shoulders.

He sidestepped two more axe cuts before kicking past the xulgath's guard and sending the creature clattering off several spikes below, then ran across the ledge and through the doorway at one end. The tumult of battle dulled as he charged into the depths of the structure. Within the wall, steel paths and steps led in several directions. Xulgath shrieks echoed and talons scraped along metal as several of the creatures raced down the hall he'd just entered.

In the narrower confines, he couldn't maneuver the staff as freely. Instead, he used it as a spear, jabbing the xulgaths back and crushing them against the walls. He took every downward set of stairs, searching for any gate control mechanism. The wall structure broadened as he went lower, and side rooms revealed little more than guard bunks and storerooms. He found one room filled with duergar bodies, presumably those stationed there before the xulgaths overwhelmed them. Some of them had been stripped to smallclothes, while others had armor still buckled on. Moving on, he found an armory in disarray, racks and stacks overturned, weapons scattered all about. A large crate sat in one corner, its lid tossed aside to reveal stacks of gleaming tubes.

Though time was short, Ondorum ducked into the room and inspected the crate further. The tubes looked familiar. Each had a waxy length of cord running from one end, with several tubes knotted to form bundles. He picked one tube up and sniffed at it. The smoky smell drew a vivid recollection to the surface of his mind.

During his time at the monastery, certain holy days had been celebrated with nonmagical devices called fireworks, which created all manner of explosive color and noise. The monastery masters had been gifted with a large number of them during a visit by peers from

Tian Xia. Curious, he'd tried to watch as they arranged them to launch from the walls. The operators had shooed him away, but not before he noted the metal and parchment tubes with fuses much like these. He didn't think the duergar used them to celebrate holidays, especially in such a remote outpost, but perhaps they'd constructed similar devices and used them for mining, clearing tunnels, or as a form of weaponry.

Even so, he had no idea what to expect if he lit one. Leaving the armory, he descended a few more levels, running from end to end on each. A few more xulgaths opposed him as he went, but he struck them down with kicks and staff strikes.

Then he found a large chamber filled with a giant gear assembly, fed into by four enormous chains that shot out into channels carved in the walls. Smaller chains trailed down into the floor. These must lead to the gate mechanism, with controls in the chamber below. Heart flaring with hope, Ondorum found the next set of stairs and flew down them. The hall cut along to a chamber where a swirl of green-and-yellow lights flared within. As he approached this room, the elemental magic he'd invested in his staff ran out. It shrank back into a simple chain link, which he tucked into his loincloth for later.

The chamber looked like it had once been used as a meeting room, with several limestone tables and dozens of chairs set about. A door at the far end suggested the gate controls waited beyond.

The furnishings had been pushed to the sides, making room for the largest xulgath he'd seen yet. A good head taller than him, with broad shoulders and massive thighs, it wore a horned, painted skull on its head, and a brown cape draped over its hunched back. One gnarled claw held a spear topped with a fresh duergar head. The shaman's eyes glowed green with power as it stooped and drew glowing runes on the chamber floor. Three other xulgath shamans stood around it, channeling purple rays from their claws into a knot of energy twisting above the one in the center.

Ondorum could sense the sickening power being wielded from where he stood. Did this empower the rest of the shamans outside the wall? Was this a summoning ceremony of sorts, intended to bring a fiend to the battlefront? The purpose didn't matter. Only stopping them did.

He gripped the chain that ran between his wrists. Sprinting into the chamber, he caught the near xulgath across the throat, wrapped the chain around and yanked in opposite directions. A snap, and the beast went limp. The other two smaller ones screeched at him. The purple auras faded from their hands as they gesticulated wildly to cast new spells.

One conjured a brilliant crystal that hurt his eyes to look at. He tilted a shoulder to let the missile fly past, and it shattered behind him, unleashing a chaotic flash of color. His fist drove deep into the shaman's chest before it could cast again.

A shard of the same energy caught him in the side. The force flipped him around and slammed him into a wall. Sucking in a breath, he shoved up to kneeling—and then dropped flat as another spell flashed by.

Somersaulting backward, he came up onto his feet. He grabbed the arm of a nearby limestone chair, spun, and flung it at the smaller shaman. The creature's spell cut off as it ducked. However, the larger shaman smacked the chair down with the spear, scattering chunks and shards. Ondorum had followed the chair's flight and vaulted the spear. He scooped up a long shard and rammed it through the third shaman's neck. Its last spell died in a gurgle and spray of blood.

He turned as the large xulgath's spear jabbed at him. Random colors writhed over the weapon, and the stone furniture and floor cracked and crumbled wherever the tip struck. Ondorum eluded several attacks, looking for an opening. With a screech, the shaman lunged at him, spear lashing out while its free claw flared with purple light. The oread evaded the spear once more, but the claw pointed at him and a beam of energy lanced out, striking his gut.

Nausea swept through his being, stronger than he'd ever felt before. Ondorum stumbled and fought for balance. He wavered, the room swimming in his vision, his stomach clenching. The very fabric of his being seized up.

Hissing in laughter, the shaman thrust the spear at Ondorum's heart.

Akina tried to focus as the stench of duergar blood filled her nostrils. It made her want to howl and lose herself in the joy of dismemberment and scream along with the music of grinding bones and popping ligaments. The embers in her gut, having simmered for so long, yearned to burst into flame.

She astonished herself by holding it at bay, keeping her thoughts intact a little longer. She and Izthuri approached the duergar casters, hacking and slicing and hammering their way through the xulgaths who tried to down the wizards. A minute of breathless fighting later, and they'd cleared the area of any immediate threat, though plenty of xulgaths closed in. Akina turned to the casters, keeping her distance so she didn't end up shocking herself on whatever barrier they'd erected.

Twisting her face up and praying the blood hid her features well enough, she caught the casters' eyes. She pointed out the xulgath shamans, shook her maulaxe, and roared. While they initially looked confused at her wordless instruction, they held a hurried consultation. When icy missiles flew from their fingertips once more, they soared out and struck one of the shamans, spearing it with icicles. Akina yelled again in approval and then whirled to keep the xulgaths off the casters until they could even the odds. Izthuri popped in and out of the fight, striking down a reptile or two and then whirling away to blend into the shadows.

Akina cast an eye toward the wall and its gates, looking for some sign of Ondorum. She had to refocus to avoid letting a xulgath ram a bone knife into one of her eyes. The fury called to her in a hiss of steam, begging her to unleash it. To become wrath incarnate.

Akina's voice thundered, defying the xulgaths she struck down and the idea of surrendering to anyone, even herself.

Not yet. Not yet . . .

As the spear came at him, Ondorum breathed in. The motion of the spear slowed as he visualized the orb of golden power at his core swelling. Cords of energy reached out, knotting through his flesh, fighting to restore him. He envisioned that central orb as being cupped in his hands, its purifying power going where he wished it. He coursed it through himself, touching every last portion of his mind, body, and spirit. The energy couldn't abide the imperfections inflicted on him and filled them in, restoring his balance. At the apex of his indrawn breath, he stood whole once more, with even the minor wounds erased from his skin.

The golden orb faded, leaving a core of stone.

He breathed out.

The spear sped up. He side-stepped and it thrust past. The shaman stumbled, its head lowered, horned skull helmet coming within reach. Ondorum grabbed two of the larger horns and wrenched them down. The shaman staggered and tried to claw at him once more. His knee cracked up under its chin, and then his foot caught the creature's forearm and stomped it to the ground.

The shaman wailed at the snap of bone, and its spear rolled away. Ondorum dropped one knee and drove a punch into the xulgath's throat, which crackled under his knuckles. The shaman's tail flapped, slapping the ground as it died.

Ondorum stepped around the body and went to the door at the far end of the chamber, dragging his chains along. Shoving it wide, he discovered another room to match the one above. The four main chains fed down into here, and then went through a series of pulleys to large wheels that could be turned, allowing a single person to operate each gate.

Every wheel and gear and chain and pulley in the room had been smashed and broken. He raced from one to the next, trying to turn each wheel or work any lever. They squealed and ground, but whatever physical or magical force the xulgaths used to accomplish this had been thorough in ruining the mechanisms. He leaped up and grabbed at the chains dangling from the ceiling, but his weight couldn't compare to the gates on the other end.

He dropped to his knees, mind swirling. The distant screams of the dying tore through to him. He trembled. Even opening the gates only provided a slim hope of escape, but at least it would be true hope, rather than a fool's hope. True hope could ignite the strength of the smallest army in the face of the most desperate odds. A fool's hope would merely blow away in the wind, like ashes and smoke.

Ashes and smoke . . .

Ondorum's chains rattled as he raced out and back up the stairs.

Akina realized the caravan stood doomed. While the wizards struck down several enemy shamans, enough xulgaths remained to harry the caravan survivors from all sides. A last motley assortment of Darklanders had been corralled into a thinning line of resistance, backing toward the wall. A few oversized duergar still lumbered about, chopping down xulgaths like dead grass, but even they slowed.

Akina felt a last flash of regret as the old familiar fire crept into her bones. This was how it ended? Death while disguised as a duergar, fighting to defend duergar against a bunch of scale-tailed savages who wouldn't know a good brew if it knocked them upside the head in a mithral tankard?

A rock pinged off her helm, and she spun to see which xulgath had flung it, ready to fling her maulaxe up at it.

A figure appeared on one of the lower wall ledges, near a pair of xulgath shamans. Her breath caught as she recognized Ondorum, still with broken chains clasped to him. The xulgaths had no chance to see him coming before his kicks sent them tumbling. One was impaled on a lower spike, while the other fell out of sight further down.

The monk held two bundles, one under either arm. Steadying these, he leaped from the ledge and caught himself on a lower spike shaft, then hurled himself from this to another tiny ledge, nimble as a mountain goat. A final jump from atop a gate, and he dropped out of sight.

Akina whacked aside a xulgath to clear her way. She pushed past a pair of dark-skinned elves and several tattered ones, at last reaching the gate. There, Ondorum crouched by the portcullis. She yelled his name. He glanced up, and a relieved smile flickered across his lips before he looked back down.

That was all the greeting she got? "Shattered stone! I thought you were dead!"

Ondorum remained bent over his work. He'd shoved two bundles of several dozen silver tubes through the gaps in the portcullis so they jammed up against the gate itself. Cords stuck out the ends of every tube, and each cord trailed down to a single thicker line. One of these already had a flame burning at the tip. As she watched, Ondorum struck a piece of scrap metal off what looked like a large chain link. Sparks flew, and several landed on the . . . the fuse. That's what it was.

The fuse he'd just caught fizzed, and the flames ate up toward both bundles of tubes with alarming speed.

Akina gaped. She'd seen enough mine blockage clearances to know what these were.

"Oh, hell." She reeled back at the same time Ondorum stood and caught her arm, hauling her away with him. Turning to get her feet under her, she saw Izthuri emerging from the ongoing chaos, and shouted, "Run!"

To her credit, Izthuri didn't question or hesitate, but fell in step as they sprinted for the next gate up. The trio pressed themselves under the archway there, up against the steel grate. A band of xulgaths raced for them, eager for cornered prey.

And then the earth screamed in agony.

The explosion ripped through the field of death, flinging duergar and xulgath alike through the air. A fireball blasted like dragon's breath down the Long Walk, roasting any creatures in its path and plowing up waves of rock before it. The eruption painted the walls in hellish hues, sending giant bats fleeing from their roosts in the heights, yet catching their wings on fire so they fell tumbling to the ground. The wall trembled as if an army of giants slammed against it, and the stones cracked all around them.

A blast of wind slapped the world and sent it spinning, scattering boulders and plates of iron like grains of sand before a wave. It knocked the three down even in their sheltered position. A screech of tortured metal and stone clawed across Akina's ears, and then the whole world went silent, but for a ringing in her head.

She realized she was roaring against the raging destruction around her, but couldn't hear herself. Fires guttered somewhere in the distance, and all had become a chaotic mingle of flames and shadow and blood and ruined earth. A hand grabbed hers. Ondorum dragged her upright, and Izthuri beside her. Even he looked stunned, and he stumbled at his first steps. With shaking hands, Akina secured her maulaxe in its sheathe and then staggered behind him. Izthuri kept wobbling back and forth as if she might collapse at any moment. As they came into the clear, Akina tried to make sense of what she saw.

The whole middle of the wall had vanished, leaving a V-shaped gap that cut up from where the gate once stood to the cavernous ceiling far above. Great rents in the tunnel roof showed where the duergar outpost had been connected with reinforcing beams and drilled into the stone before being torn away.

Wreckage and bodies were strewn about on both sides of the gap. Some of the fallen moved slowly, recovering their wits. Most did not. Akina and her companions picked their way toward the opening, leaning on one another for support. Sounds faded back into existence—mostly moans and screams and the clatter of rubble. As they crossed over, Izthuri extended a whip-thin arm and pointed at a tunnel entrance off to the right, not fifty strides away. Her voice sounded even thinner than usual to Akina's battered ears.

"There. Is there."

Akina plodded forward, eager to be off and gone, but something made her look up.

"Ondorum." Her voice ground inside her own head. She tugged at his arm again. "Ondorum."

The others stopped to see what she stared at. Cracks shot through the tunnel ceiling, all along the newly opened path and back the way they'd come. Crooked rents speared out from where the explosions had shattered the stone, where the duergar wall had connected to the upper regions.

And the cracks widened with every second.

Akina shoved the other two into motion. "Go!"

They dashed ahead as fast as their shaken senses allowed. As they ran, she dared to look back—and up.

Countless stalactites trembled and plummeted with a spray of broken earth. Ahead and behind, dozens of other formations, from stumpy blocks to long, dagger-like growths, tore from the ceiling.

Five steps later, the ground bucked and tried to throw her off. She planted a hand to catch herself and pushed on, just as a falling stone hit ahead. Tall as a tower, it shattered against the road, dissolving into columns that toppled in all directions. She veered toward the tunnel, following Izthuri's lead. With each second, the earth shuddered as if it might tear apart beneath them. The air filled further with dust and flying debris.

One stalactite drove into the road behind her with such force that it sent Akina soaring past Izthuri. The caligni somehow maintained her balance and grabbed her up, setting her running again. Ondorum labored beside them, chains rattling, blood oozing from under his barbed collar.

Spears and swords of stone rained down around them, while blocks and boulders sailed about. Existence shook to its roots. Another twenty steps and the tunnel entrance offered itself like a portal into another world.

Akina glanced up and saw the most massive formation yet loosen from the ravaged ceiling and fall straight for where the tunnel stood. The others must've seen it too, for the group sped up as one, racing to outdo gravity. She kept her eyes locked on the entrance, legs churning, lungs heaving, eyes tearing from the grit whipping through the air.

Then a last, desperate plant of the feet and leap. Passing over the threshold while a giant's fist of stone descended on her head. Striking a floor of rough rock. Rolling and skidding on her armor. Someone landing beside her.

A final quake. A spew of rock. A slide of crumbling, cold earth that buried her, and Akina wondered if a mountain had just become her tomb.

Chapter Eighteen
Parted Paths

A distant voice called Ondorum's name. He shifted on the monastery slab, vainly seeking comfort in its unforgiving surface. Though raw earth and stone often soothed him with its touch, the monastery beds had been fashioned with uneven surfaces in order to purge sleepers of requiring earthly comforts in order to rest.

His name again. The masters must have sent an apprentice to rouse him, which meant he'd missed the first or second meditation bells, calling all to rise and assemble. They would no doubt task him with extra labor in the kitchens or clearing the exterior walls of creeping vines to preserve the sanctity of the foundation stones. He grimaced at this, though he knew it was his fault for not being attentive to the hour. His body already ached in every joint from yesterday's work and martial practice. When would his body finally be able to bear the loads they placed on it?

He kept his eyes closed as he started to sit up, trying to set his thoughts aright before viewing the day, otherwise the hours that followed might be distorted by his shameful, flawed thinking. As he moved, metal rattled, and cold links slithered over his bare skin. He paused.

Chains?

"Ondorum? Where are you?"

He opened his eyes to a narrow tunnel, which ended near where he lay in a pile of granite and limestone rubble. Thick chains draped him, while barbs pricked his neck. The events in the Long Walk and the deadly ambush at the duergar checkpoint crashed over his mind like a wave. When he surfaced from the memories, he scrambled to his feet. Had Akina just called to him, or did that too remain in the realm of dreams? He peered down the tunnel, searching for his companions. Had they gone on ahead, unaware he lay behind them?

Something thudded faintly against the nearby wall. A muffled voice rose.

"Shattered stones and bones. Don't tell me he's dead. I'd know if he was. Don't ask me how I'd know. Shut it."

A low hissing noise formed words Ondorum couldn't catch. Izthuri. Both alive, then. But where? He went to the wall and rapped on it once. Then twice. Then pounded three times with a fist. He listened.

Scrabbling, and then Akina's voice came a little louder. "Ondorum? That you?"

He knocked in reply.

"You can hear me?"

Knock.

"Must be a crack in the wall somewhere." More hammering from the other side. "Where's the blasted thing? I'll pry it open."

Ondorum placed his palm on the wall. While her blows were audible, the stone didn't so much as tremble on this side. Far too solid and thick. A miracle they even heard one another. Akina could go at it all day with her maulaxe and might crack a few inches. And from the sound of it, she might attempt it anyway. However, after a few minutes of her hammering, a clang sounded, and frustration turned her words raw.

"No use." A pause. "Is it really you?"

Knock.

"If so, how many hobgoblins did we slay when we first met at the temple?"

Ondorum didn't hesitate. Eight knocks.

"Thank Torag." Another stretch. "You all right?"

Knock.

A rattle and curse, as if she'd just punched the wall. "Say something, damn you."

Ondorum stared at the stone. His lungs clenched and his heart pulsed in an unseen grip. His throat tightened as all the words he'd held back tried to rush up it at once. His chains hung as heavy as his thoughts as he lowered his eyes. Which should he feel more ashamed for? Getting so close to breaking his vow, or leaving her feeling that much more abandoned on the other side? The dilemma jeered at him no matter how many cleansing breaths he took or mantras he tried to cycle through to quiet the riot in his mind and heart.

"Oh for . . . Even now, Ondorum?" Another pounding. "Even now?"

He laid his forehead and palms against the wall, trying to stop her blows by force of will. They continued nonetheless, a distant thunder, until they cut off suddenly. He imagined her ragged breathing and mouthed, *I'm sorry*. Edging close to breaking his vow, but since she couldn't actually see anything, it might as well have remained his thoughts alone. Let Irori judge his actions and intents later.

"What good has it done? What harm would a single word do?" A scuffle and her voice tilted away. "Shush me once more and I'll turn those rags red. I don't care what might be down here."

The quiet felt worse than the maddening cacophony of the recent battle. Ondorum took a shuddering breath, feeling his refusal to speak hurt her more than any wound she might've taken from the xulgaths. The silence no longer felt pure, and he had to fill it with something. But the only compromise he could conjure was a questioning knock to ensure she hadn't tromped off in fury.

"Still here, you fool. Guess you'll get as much silence as you want now." She grumbled incoherently. "Fine. Fine. We're wasting time arguing." More mumbles. "With the ceiling falling on our heads, Izthuri forgot to mention the tunnel split off at the entrance. Funny thing is, you're in the one we needed. She says this one will get us there too, but it might take a little longer. Figure the plan is to try to meet up at the ruins. She's got directions. Hang on."

After a minute, her voice resumed.

"So. Go down. No tunnels that go up. Helpful. Take all left turns until you reach . . . the waterfall? Yes, a waterfall. Follow the current downstream a ways, but don't actually get in the water. Don't drink from it, don't even dip a toe, she says. Plus, if you see any green-glowing crystals, don't figure them for emeralds or another elemental for you to cuddle. Something called blightburn. Actually, she says it's best just to stay far away from any spot with green glows. When the river pours into a bottomless abyss, then head along the rightmost tunnel and stick with it. Don't take any side branches. None. Eventually you'll come to a few magma flows that have natural bridges across them . . ."

The instructions went on a little more, and Akina repeated them twice over, even though he caught the major landmarks and directions the first time. He thought she might be repeating them more for her sake, as if the more times she defined the proper route, the higher the chance of him making it through. She wrapped up the final talk-through.

"Got it?"

Knock.

"See you there then? Promise?"

Knock.

"Wait, are you knocking yes or—never mind. I'm getting waggled at to hurry. I guess . . . guess we're off."

Ondorum strained to hear sounds of her departing, but if any footsteps echoed on her side, they didn't make it across. He reviewed the instructions once more, ensuring they'd been engrained in the bedrock of his mind. Just before he turned from the wall, a murmur slipped through, so low he almost didn't catch it.

"Ondorum? Just . . . don't die, hm? I don't figure I'd handle it well."

He waited, but nothing more. He tried to loosen the barbed collar, but pulling it in one direction only cinched it from the other. At last, he clasped his hands before him and strode down, chains jangling, into the darkness and whatever waited for him there.

Akina plowed forward so fast she kept getting ahead of Izthuri, and the caligni kept hissing at her to avoid making a wrong turn or to stop making so much noise. If Ondorum's path got him to the ruins before them, who knew what he'd face there? Best if she double-marched and increased the odds of arriving as soon after he did as possible.

In time, though, even her steps slowed and her flustered thoughts settled like dust in the aftermath of the gate explosion. Different ideas started plinking into place, adding to the rattle inside her skull. She let Izthuri take the lead and followed without thought. As the two of them plumbed the darkest dens of stone she'd ever known, so she wandered into darker caverns of thought and started poking around to see if anything stirred. While she bellyached at Ondorum's refusal to budge on his vow, to admit she meant more to him than some self-imposed pledge, a harsh voice whispered, *Maybe he doesn't really care.*

Maybe they didn't mean as much to each other as she'd thought. While they'd increasingly relied on each other over the years, perhaps it'd been a relationship of convenience instead of devotion. And if his self-flagellation over past mistakes proved more important than their relationship—if he spurned a possibly final plea to give her a single word in such dire circumstances—did he deserve to be such a priority in her life?

Izthuri paused at a fork and sniffed the air down either passage. She slipped into the right. At the next junction of three passages, she sniffed two and recoiled so hard from the third she nearly toppled. They went down the middle, which proved narrow enough that Akina had to take most of it sideways, scraping her nose and armor as she went.

She continued to mull as they pushed on. If she and Ondorum remained bound together, would it do either of them any good in the long run? Or would they just find themselves following increasingly divided paths? Yet if she bound herself back to her kin and the Five Kings Mountains, what could she offer them? Her people were known for building lasting marvels, bringing great beauty and function to the world. They revered their ancestors and stuck beside their kin. Her? She reduced life to rubble and danced in the ashes. She abandoned her family for her own bloodthirsty wanderings. Some dwarf, her.

Izthuri halted and spun a circle. Her hiss went on longer than usual.

"What's wrong?" Akina asked. Despite the leagues they'd gone without any other sign or disturbance, she didn't figure their luck would hold forever. They'd paused in an oval-shaped cave with two main offshoots, one of which had deep claw marks in the stone around it. She reached for her maulaxe handle, but Izthuri waved her hands down.

"Wrong way."

"Don't tell me that." Akina made fists.

The skin around Izthuri's eyes crinkled. "Long time since here. You think always same? Always easy?"

"You call what we've been trotting easy?"

"We not dead. It easy."

"Figures. Did it just get harder?"

"We being followed."

"By what? For how long?"

Izthuri sniffed. "We need fast. I make fast. Not see signs."

"Of?"

The caligni crouched in the middle of the cave, knees up past her head. "We in buggane territory."

"Buggane? Those . . . what . . . mole beasts that killed some of your tribe?" At Izthuri's nod, Akina snorted and shifted her armor so it sat on her shoulders better. "I can handle a few moles."

"Several buggane kill . . ." Izthuri stared at her fingers. "Quarter of tribe. Most fighters and leaders. Why we weak. Why we hide."

"Oh." Akina cleared her throat. "Which way gets us past them?"

Izthuri rose and headed for the non-clawed-up path. "Here. If lucky . . . it easy. If not . . ."

"We dead. Got it."

Ondorum passed through the tunnels using the directions Akina gave him, forming them into a mantra that looped through his mind, making a path for his feet. Always down and left. Down and left. He tested his chains as he went, looking for flaws he might exploit to remove them. The shackles themselves offered no such opportunity, and he tired of feeling sharp fingers stab his neck whenever he flexed and stretched his arms too much. Even when he could transform another link, it would take multiple attempts before he'd be entirely free.

He tried to channel the discomfort aside, but it became a fraying presence—chafing, stinging, rattling, grinding. Just enough to set him on edge and forbid him true meditation.

Rather than see the chains and their nettling as an enemy of enlightenment, he tried to use them as a reminder of his flawed physicality and accept them as a learning opportunity. A temporary lesson, he hoped, as he had no intention of bearing them any longer than necessary.

A dull roar in the distance intrigued him as he traversed a narrow channel. A tingling in his feet spoke to a deep thrumming ahead, but it seemed to emanate from a single grand source rather than any sort of underground crowd. He emerged into a cavern with no ceiling, where water gushed from a hidden source high above. The waterfall cascaded over a hundred feet into a dark pool that filled much of the right side of the cavern. Clouds of mist billowed up from this, and water trickled over the walls and slicked the stone underfoot. A main channel wound away down the slope, offering the next portion of his path.

Ondorum gazed at the falling waters for a while, aching to plunge into them, to bathe, to drink. Dust caked his throat, and he gulped deep breaths, thinking the droplets in the air might soothe him some. Yet the effort teased his tongue and only heightened his cravings. Still, he heeded Izthuri's warning and did not so much as approach the edge of the rippling current. He noted how no vegetation grew in the area, despite such an abundant water source.

With a mighty leap, he crossed the channel, coming down on the other side with a sway of the chains. He followed the current as directed, keeping an eye out for any crystals and glowing spots around him, green or otherwise. He thought he spotted an emerald flash of light once in the distance, but it faded as he approached and he didn't see it again. Did his eyes jest with him? Not a comforting thought, and he began picking out nearby details, fixing them in his mind, and then turning after he passed to make sure they remained as he noted. After a while, he felt assured he saw clearly and did not walk fooled by illusions, conjured by himself or others.

At last, he came to a wide ledge where the ground dropped away before him into a bottomless expanse. The current flowed straight over the edge, forming another waterfall that plunged to depths unknown. This must be the abyss Izthuri spoke of. Heading off to the right, he found the proper tunnel—he hoped—and aimed down it. Following the main tunnel proved trickier than it sounded, as it hosted constant offshoots, from the slightest fissures to openings nearly as wide as the one he'd first taken. Multiple times, he had to pause at a forking of several paths and determine which deviated the least.

After such a gambling choice, he entered one of the largest caverns he'd encountered since the waterfall. Calcified mounds looked like miniature cities and fortresses, and the walls bulged out at the sides, forming natural side-caves hemmed in by rows of stalactites and stalagmites, many of which stood taller and thicker than him. Ondorum hesitated. Izthuri hadn't mentioned any significant caves before reaching the magma flows. Had he taken a wrong path? Did he now wander lost without knowing it?

He cycled through breaths to ease the flutter of alarm in his chest. As he stilled himself, tremors rippled through the floor and up into his bones. Not the muted thunder of the water from before, but of a creature moving through the earth nearby. After another tremor shook the area, he corrected himself: a *vast* creature, one he doubted he wished to meet. Random chance that it disturbed this very cavern as he entered it, or had his presence drawn it somehow?

He headed for a side hollow, determined to not be standing in the open if the beast appeared. He chose the largest stalagmite, broad enough to hide behind, and eased up against it, bracing on its frigid, grainy surface so his chains wouldn't rattle and give him away.

The rumblings grew into shudderings that made him grit his teeth as the creature's growing presence made his very core quake. Then the upper portion of the ceiling on the far side blew open in a boom of displaced rock. He glimpsed a maw large enough to swallow a horse, filled with grinding rows of teeth that would spear through the thickest shield. No visible eyes; just a dark, violet carapace covering every possible inch of the creature. Its maw thrust down into the floor, and it passed through like a worm threading through dirt. Its churning teeth turned stone to powder as it plunged on without pause.

Segment after armored segment slid by until Ondorum lost count. At last, the body dwindled and tapered off. At the very tip of its massive length, it displayed a bony stinger the size of a sword, and then this too slid out of sight. The rumblings went on for a time yet, and only when the last vibration faded did he step out from behind the cover of the stalagmite. He stared in awe at the rubble-strewn tunnels left in the creature's wake, which had reshaped the cavern itself. He wished Akina had been there with him to witness it. Despite the beast's no doubt brutish nature, it had been a marvel to behold.

He took a few steps forward, and then paused, considering the need to walk with more care, lest his heavy movements draw the creature back.

A voice like the drizzling of sand broke the silence behind him.

"A magnificent spectacle, I must say."

Chains rattling, Ondorum whirled just as the stalagmite he'd hidden behind flexed and bent toward him. Six thick strips peeled away from the column and flared into wriggling life. Four lashed out for him. He tried to leap backward, but a tip snagged a trailing chain and yanked him back with enough force to send fresh blood streaming down his neck. The other strands curled around his waist, left arm, and right thigh. They clenched and twisted, and Ondorum gasped as strength seeped from him, making him tremble where he stood.

"There, now. That's better. I did worry you'd leave without saying a proper farewell."

A crack formed near the base of the stalagmite and widened into a circular maw, bristling with dagger-like fangs. Near the top, shards of stone parted, revealing an enormous eye, glowing red with a black slit down the middle. This fixed on Ondorum as the mouth shifted into a monstrous grin.

"Greetings, traveler. I do hope you've had a pleasant journey so far. Tell me, what tidings of the surface do you bring?"

Chapter Nineteen
Buggane

No noise alerted her, but Akina glanced back, certain something followed them. A buggane? Yet the way behind her was empty.

A bulky creature walked out of the stone wall on one side and lumbered straight across the tunnel into the other wall, where it vanished.

Akina blinked. Had she seen right?

She turned and tried to catch up with Izthuri. The caligni's wheezing filled the air as she set a near-sprinting pace, and Akina barely kept her fluttering black rags in sight.

"Shattered stones," she called. "Leave me behind and I can't help your tribe."

Izthuri slowed enough for Akina to match her, though she continued to burst forward at odd intervals, as if the dwarf were a weight she strove to break free from.

"Can . . ." Akina gulped a breath. "Can bugganes walk through walls?"

Izthuri's head whipped around, her eyes obsidian disks. In answer, she picked up speed, ducking under ragged shelves, sidling along tight channels, and dancing through fields of spiked earth. Akina puffed as she fought to keep up, glad that while some of the narrower tunnels tried to wedge her in, she didn't have to hunch or crawl as often as her companion. Her heavy boots let her crunch over the jagged terrain without pause.

Twice more, Akina checked behind to see a shadowed mass scurry from wall to wall. Big—at least twice her size—but moving fast. She'd hoped the spaces she managed to barely push through might stall it, but solid earth impeded it not at all, and it paced them with unerring steps. No point trying to be quiet.

"How far to the ruins?" she asked the next time Izthuri deigned to let her close the gap. They hurried down a wider tunnel that at least let them run alongside one another.

"Not close. Not far." Izthuri's voice had gone reedy with fear. "Two tunnels. One cave. Ruins after."

Then Izthuri stopped so suddenly Akina smacked into her back and almost toppled them both. As she recoiled, Izthuri turned, eyes wide, and swayed in place.

"I . . . I doom my tribe."

Akina held up hands, trying to placate her. "What're you talking about? Why'd you stop?"

Izthuri plucked at her rags, which Akina took to be a sign of distress. "Last bugganes kill many of tribe. I not lead then. I hide then. I lead now. They hide now.

And . . ." She stared back up the tunnel. "I show bugganes where tribe hide. I might kill all."

"At this point, I'm guessing we'll have to deal with it sooner or later." Akina pushed past and tried to tug her along. "If the ruins are a few tunnels away, I'd rather face it there. Otherwise I might not be able to do much besides gnaw at its kneecaps. If it has knees."

Izthuri trembled like a branch in a high wind. Akina dared to press the matter further, sensing she could topple one way or the other.

"Your tribe already has duergar invading their territory, hm? If we lead the buggane away and die at its hands in some random hole, you'll leave them leaderless. The duergar will find them and we won't be around to protect them. We've got to get there. And I don't know the way, so we can't split up." She clasped one of the other woman's hands between hers. "Izthuri, I swear on . . . on the soul of my mother, Jannasten Fairingot, I'll see your people safe."

This locked Izthuri's eyes on her own. Akina met the gaze of those bottomless pits. She didn't see emptiness there, but a frightened soul who just wanted to protect her people at all costs.

"You fight for us?"

"I will. My life for your tribe. Just get us there."

Izthuri's trembling stilled and she drew her hand away. Then she nodded and zipped past Akina. Before she took ten steps, though, the buggane shifted out of the wall in front of them. Its appearance left neither ripple nor crack in its wake. Izthuri's rattling hiss echoed about as she drew her blade.

When the caligni had suggested "mole beast," Akina had imagined an oversized version of the surface creature plowing along after them on four legs, body soft and face ready for smashing.

What reared before them looked like a cross between a dire boar and an ogre. It had mole-like features with tiny, filmed-over eyes that looked blind by Akina's guess, as well as a narrowed snout and elongated incisors, but the similarities ended there. Tusks jutted from its lower jaw and a spike thrust from its chin. Its sloped back looked like a slab of rock with horns all down its spine, shoulders, and arms. Walking on elephantine hind legs, it could've held a dwarf in each of its muscled forepaws, which ended in six-inch claws.

The buggane opened its tusked mouth and made a noise somewhere between a growl and a bleat. It raised its arms and raked at the tunnel ceiling, digging furrows and crumbling slabs of rock onto its own head. They shattered and bounced off without the beast seeming to notice.

Akina realized she'd drawn her maulaxe. Izthuri shrieked, and a cloud of darkness engulfed the tunnel. In the midst of it, Akina stumbled and almost dropped her weapon. For the first time since coming into the Darklands, she *couldn't see*. Whatever magic Izthuri conjured, it blotted out even her vision. She flailed with one arm, not wanting to swing the maulaxe for fear of hitting the caligni in the confusion.

"Izthuri, I can't see! I can't fight in your darkness!"

Izthuri's screams hit a higher pitch. There came a dull clanging, and her cries cut off with a crunch and slap.

The darkness dissipated, revealing the buggane hunched over a prone Izthuri. Rivulets of blood streamed out of the caligni's side, where the cloth had been torn wide to reveal mangled flesh and bone.

"Not yours!" Akina launched herself at the buggane's back.

It turned in time to catch the brunt of her swipe across the snout. It didn't so much as stagger, but gave a little squeal as it wiped a claw over its nose. Then it came on, feet pounding, claws raking for her face. Akina backpedaled, trying to hammer one of its arms aside to get a clearer shot, but it felt like chipping away at petrified tree stumps.

A claw whipped at her head. She jerked to the side, and it hooked the top edge of a pauldron and tore it away as easily as tearing wings off a fly. The blow spun her around. She threw herself forward, and felt the air stir as another swipe just missed taking off her helmet—if not her head.

She struck a wall and used the rebounding energy to launch herself back all the faster. The buggane dropped to its front claws, head down, tusks poised to gore. She snarled as she struck first on the broad plates of its forehead. Its head jerked aside, and it grunted as she rammed into its side. Horns and ridges ground against her breastplate. She cracked the hammer side of the maulaxe across it, searching for a weakness.

The beast reared back up, taking her with it.

Akina hollered as the sudden rise scraped her across the ceiling. She reached back and dug fingers into its snout, using it as leverage to keep hammering away while aloft. The beast lurched, and a claw grabbed one of her flailing feet. A second later, her maulaxe went clanging away as she flew down the tunnel. Her helmet struck first, sending a gong through her head. She tumbled ass over armor until she hit a wall.

The tunnel wavered back into view. Izthuri lay a few feet away like a discarded strip of black silk. The buggane stomped toward them, snout crinkling as it snuffled, trying to get a fix on their position.

Akina licked blood from her lips. She swallowed a few drops and they slid down to sizzle in her gullet, striking fire to the embers. Hot blood, hot bones, hot breath . . . all coursed through her as she rose to face the monster.

"Much . . . better . . ."

Her maulaxe lay behind the beast, but she didn't give it more than a glance before flexing her arms and bellowing a challenge. She charged the buggane. It thrust claws into the walls on either side of it, digging in to brace itself as it lowered its tusks again.

Akina rammed her helm's horns straight into its tender snout and heard a satisfying crack deeper inside. With gauntleted fists, she grabbed the tusks and yanked down with all her might. She braced a shoulder against one tusk and jammed a foot against another. Then she kicked and pushed as hard as she could.

With a squelch and a horrendous pop, one tusk ripped free from the buggane's jaw. It went spinning across the floor, trailing gore.

The buggane's squeal rose into a full-fledged roar. Akina dropped flat and scrambled through between its legs. It smashed claws from side to side, carving up the floor and walls in its furious pain. Akina leapt to her feet and sprinted to grab up her maulaxe. Flipping to the axe edge, she raced back at the buggane, steam boiling her from the inside out.

The buggane staggered around and raised both claws. She veered left at the last second and let them crack down beside her. Spinning, she brought the whirling axe edge down on the creature's exposed right foot.

Two stumpy toes flew away as the axe bit into the stone below. The buggane roared again, but its cry became a bleat of pain and fear as it stumbled away. Squealing, it started limping off. When she realized where it headed, she growled, a noise like gargling rocks.

"No!"

She pounded after it, but the buggane slipped into the earth a second before she reached the wall and struck solid stone. The shock dropped her back, stunned for a moment before she shook herself back into motion. She hammered at the wall as if she could break it down and open up whatever passage it had taken, shouting in denial all the while.

Then a thought splashed over her mind and temporarily cooled the flow of magma within her veins. The beast could walk through stone. While she stood there dumbly trying to follow it, what if it circled around to attack her from behind or finish off Izthuri?

She turned to see Izthuri still lying prone. Strapping her maulaxe back on, she ran to the caligni and checked her wounds. The gash in her side oozed blood, but the woman's chest still rose and fell, if shallowly. If she lay near death, her main chance of survival stood in getting her among her people and hoping they had some manner of healing.

Nothing for it, then. Akina stared down the tunnel and tried to remember what Izthuri said. Two tunnels more, a cave, then ruins. First, she went over and retrieved the buggane's tusk, which she shoved down through her belt like a sword. After doing the same for Izthuri's blade, she dragged the woman up and draped her over both shoulders. Izthuri's feet still dragged, and Akina had to be careful not to whack her head against a wall, but she started off.

Izthuri weighed more than Akina might've guessed, and Akina's legs grew cold and heavy as the embers cooled within her. Yet she forged on, finding where this tunnel ended, hitched to the left, and followed a narrowing route. Several times as she eased through this, having to drag Izthuri by her arms in spots, she heard grunting, and the distant shadows rippled.

The buggane followed, she didn't doubt. Her leaden steps, Izthuri's blood, the tusk at her waist . . . all clear signals. Lures.

Her body refused to increase its pace. Her bones had gone to ice, while the embers in her gut refused to flare, no matter how much she tried to stoke them. At last, muscles congealing into mud and blood slowing to a heavy drumming, she stumbled out of a small cave and realized she had nowhere left to go. She laid Izthuri on the ground, and the caligni's eyes blinked open. A confused hiss wavered up.

"Where?"

"We're here," Akina said, trying not to collapse.

She looked up in wonder at the wall she'd stopped before. It reached halfway to the ceiling, a good fifty feet overhead. Down to the right a ways, an archway looked like it had once held a broad gate, and beyond this, she glimpsed squat towers and humped buildings in various states of disarray. Many of them had carvings along their borders, with the hint here and there of once-colorful mosaics. To her wearied mind, those looked almost like dwarven runes . . .

She jerked her attention back to the space before her. Ten or so figures had appeared from nowhere, staring at her as she crouched over Izthuri. While each of them wore an assembly of dark cloth and rags, and their black eyes glared from under pale brows, they all stood at least a couple feet shorter than their leader. On the heels of that realization came their stench—an eye-watering reek that made her think of raw sewage. Further unlike Izthuri, their rags appeared filthy, matted and crusted with unknown fluids.

As one, they drew a variety of weapons, mostly daggers or short swords. Akina backed off from Izthuri, who looked to have fallen unconscious again. She drew Izthuri's blade and tossed it over by her with a clank; then she raised palms to the others.

"Wait, see, I'm here to help."

They skulked forward, a couple going to Izthuri while the rest parted to come at Akina from either side. Akina groaned as she reached for her maulaxe. Then a rumbling from behind had her whipping it out as she spun.

The buggane limped from the cave entrance, leaving a bloody footprint with each step while ichor dribbled down its ridged chin. It blustered and slapped claws together, blasting loose earth up into a miniature whirlwind.

"No." Akina stepped forward, scowling against the grit. On an inspiration, she held her maulaxe in one hand and drew the severed tusk with the other. The buggane flinched as she raised the tusk and shook it. "Mine." She lunged forward. "Mine!"

The buggane shook its jowls once more and gave a final chuff. Then it receded into the shadows.

Akina stood panting, unable to believe it had worked. A slight noise from behind reminded her she didn't stand alone. She planted the maulaxe head on the ground and kept herself upright by bracing on the shaft as she turned.

Izthuri had risen, while the others of her kind had drawn back. The caligni leader crept forward and knelt, laying her black blade at Akina's feet. She spread her arms wide, indicating the tribe and the ruins beyond.

"Yours."

Chapter Twenty
Silent Conversation

Ondorum flexed as much as he could against the corded tentacles locking him in place. Yet the energy drained from his body. How could this be?

The living stalagmite bent toward him further, revealing flexibility beyond anything formed of rock should possess. Its solitary red eye gleamed with what he took to be wicked delight. Its voice whispered around the cavern like a snake slithering through grass.

"Ever it is the way of you humanoids: always quick to rush in, rush out. Never any consideration for manners or for taking the time to truly learn about your environment. I wonder, if the great worm hadn't given you reason to wait, would we be having this delightful conversation right now?" A tentacle tightened around his thigh, and his foot skidded an inch closer. "Though, I must correct myself, as a conversation implies a two-way exchange of information. So far, this would be a monologue, to be precise. But perhaps we can make it so much more?"

The strand about his arm slithered along further until the tip tapped his sealed lips. It had a gritty quality, like a sausage skin packed with sand.

"Come now. Don't be shy." The tip teased further, parting his lips and scraping along his teeth. "And let's not be rude, either. After all, manners are what set the civilized creature apart from the beast. I don't believe you to be a beast, despite the chains you've been clad in."

The rock-creature shook him, making the chains rattle. Ondorum tried to pull back, but could barely keep himself standing. If the creature chose to draw him into its jagged maw, he'd be lost.

Instead, the creature turned, dragging him around to plant him in a corner. It blocked any easy way to reach the chamber beyond. To his surprise, the tentacles then retracted, leaving him free, if unsteady.

"Let's make a bargain, you and I. You remain here, perfectly still, without attempting to leave, and I'll not fully paralyze and eat you. Should you attempt escape, I'll dispense with sating my curiosity and simply sate my baser appetites."

Ondorum firmed himself up, meeting its gaze in silence.

Its eye twitched and rolled. "Oh, I see. You must be surprised that I know your language. And yes, I detect the distinct glint of comprehension in those spongy orbs you call eyes, so don't try to pretend you don't understand or cannot reply in kind." It made a rattling noise, which Ondorum took to be a sigh. "Ah, but I know many languages—perhaps even more used by the dead than the living. Sometimes I wonder why I bother, since all those words and intonations and hidden double and triple and quadruple meanings take up so much room in the mind. I can't seem to make myself discard them, though."

It began to rotate through a number of different languages, most of which Ondorum couldn't identify. Birdlike chirrups switched to a guttural gurgling followed by knocking words that sounded slightly dwarven. Then it flipped to a soft murmur that sounded like the gibberings of a madman, making Ondorum wince as the disturbing noises slithered into his ears. The tip of its rocklike form curled forward, and tiny hairs twitched atop it.

"Do you wonder how I've come to speak your tongue? Of course you do. There's a trick to it, to be sure. Can you keep a secret? I'm trusting you on this, realize." One of its other tentacles reached out to caress the wall. "The truth of the matter is that no sound ever fully dies. To certain ears, it may fade and seem to vanish entirely. But it merely enters another form of existence. Another form of energy. Even when it is absorbed by a surrounding substance such as stone or wood—" It twitched, and its eye shut. "Ohhhh . . . wood. Tell me. Do you have much . . . wood . . . where you come from?"

After trying to determine the harm in answering, Ondorum relented with a slight nod. The rock-beast shivered again, creating a tremor which rippled all the way down its strands. It made a slurping noise, like a dog lapping at its own drool.

"Wood. Such exotic texture. Such delicate flavors. Such juicy sap, the blood of trees running through my teeth. It can make one feel so alive. And sawdust, the reduction of trees as old as the world itself into fine particles which you could practically breathe in . . ."

It gazed over him, apparently lost in visions of forests and of feasting on lumber. Then it perked back up.

"My pardon. I became distracted. When life's pleasures so rarely come your way of their own volition, it behooves one to relish even the vicarious mention of them. I fear I shall be slavering for days. But where was I? Ah, yes . . . the nature of sound." Its teeth clicked together. "Suffice it to say, we can hear you, you know. When one makes the effort to remove one's self from the noise and clamor of other creatures and sit entombed in silence, one learns to pick up on those sounds that might have otherwise passed one by. You learn to hear the dead speak. You hear gods speak. Demons speak. You even hear the void speak. And, over time, you learn to talk back. All the languages of surface dwellers, or those in Nar-Voth, Sekamina, Orv . . . All sound makes its way down, eventually." The rock-beast settled back into a more rigid position. "Speaking of the world and its many divisions, which one do you hail from?"

Ondorum clenched his teeth. While he might have been torn as to whether he should give Akina a parting word or two of comfort, no part of him considered surrendering to this creature's insinuating requests. Any response remained locked in his chest, and he tried to smooth over his face so it couldn't read his expression

"Why do you not speak? Has someone torn out your tongue?" It bent closer, eye blazing, voice rising into a screech. "No? Shall I do it for you, then?"

Ondorum didn't avert his gaze from the fiery light it cast over him. No heat radiated from the eye, but the malevolent alien intelligence within struck him with force enough.

Slowly, its gaze dimmed and its voice returned to the previous mildness. "I do beg your forgiveness. Is it because of my inconsiderate treatment? After all, who would wish to speak when they have barbs containing their throat? Would you allow discourse if I removed this ghastly instrument? Here. Let me get those for you."

Three tentacles curled over and around Ondorum's chains at various points. He shut his eyes, preparing to be choked or have his throat lacerated—and opened them again in surprise as the rock-beast dismantled the bonds with unexpected finesse. Links dropped away without a single chain tugging on another. With a flick of a prehensile tip, the collar too broke wide and slid off his back. The shackles around his ankles and wrists thudded by his feet.

He took a shuddering breath, feeling an incredible lightness that threatened to make him giddy. Then, aware of the creature's continued scrutiny, he blanked his face again.

The creature's eye became a crimson slit. "No gratitude for your freedom? Truly? The relief is there, but one would expect a bit of thanks considering I doubt you could've accomplished such on your own."

Ondorum inclined his head and waved at the beast before him and then the chamber beyond.

"I see. You define freedom by varying degrees, and are not happy unless you have it in full, is that so?" The base of its stalagmite-like form moved, gliding noiselessly over the ground to one side, opening the way for him to pass. "More freedom." Ondorum stepped forward, but then staggered back as it shifted back in front of him. "Less freedom. Do you see what a silly notion that is? One could argue that I could take you to the nearest pit and toss you in. As you fell to your death, completely unrestrained by myself or even the earth itself, that would be the ultimate freedom, would it not? But I don't believe that's the sort of freedom you desire. You must also realize freedom is a construct of the mind, not the body."

Ondorum frowned despite himself, disturbed to hear meditative truths echoed by this being. The creature's grin looked like a rent in raw earth, the tissue within like packed mud, ringed by teeth.

"I see that concept got your interest. Which tells me it isn't entirely foreign to you, or you at least have a mind that's considered such an approach before." It leaned closer. "You present a marvelous puzzle."

To his consternation, the rock-beast slid closer. He tried to back up, but hit the stone wall behind him. He could only stare up as its red eye loomed like a hideous sun.

"Back to the matter of your refusal to speak. Does it have something to do with your breeding? Are all your people so reticent? For that matter, before we proceed, what manner of being are you? I must say, you're the first of your kind I can recall encountering in my realm. Oh, and when I say my realm, don't saddle me with the silly notion that I aspire to heights of royalty or rulership. Just as with freedom, those are petty ideas, invisible boundaries with which smaller minds surround themselves to construct illusions of order and safety."

A tentacle shot out, coiled around his ankle, and flung him over the creature's top. He crashed out into the chamber proper, stunned by both the jarring impact and another portion of strength sapped by that insidious touch. As he tried to recover, the creature glided over and circled him slowly.

"Let's see. Oddly, my first instinct is to name you a strange sort of dwarf. You have the smell of mountains and deep stone about you. But you can't be dwarf or duergar, unless their kind have changed mightily without my noticing . . . and I pride myself on observational thoroughness. Not elf of any sort, though there is an ageless quality to you. You look, in part, human, but their flesh is far softer and they tend to be weeping or soiling themselves by this point in our talks. Hm. A miniature giant? No, pardon my ridiculousness. It is unbecoming of me. Golem?"

It paused. "Is that it? Golem? Is that why you won't speak? Are you a construct in service to another, thus the chains? Seeking to escape, and so you've fled into the depths, striving for freedom, unable to control your own tongue without your master's leave, and now you wind up here. Oh, that would be a delicious tale to remember."

It thrust the tip of a strand into the crusted wounds where the warren creatures had removed the gems from his side. Ondorum squeezed his eyes shut against the pain, pounding fists against the ground as an alternate to vocalizing the discomfort.

"However, I believe golems aren't intended to feel such pain, and I can tell that, despite your tough skin, vital organs lie underneath. A waste of effort to incorporate for a master who would wish a more durable servant. You lack the tail and scales of lizardfolk, and you seem too sane to be fleshwarped."

As it inspected him, considering and discarding a dozen other species, Ondorum came to a shaky crouch. If its tentacles grasped him for any extended period, he didn't doubt he'd lose all ability to move. Already weakened as he was, he had to get out of range before the beast latched onto him again. He needed a distraction.

While pretending to listen to the rock-beast's discourse, he rose. He stamped his feet and rubbed his arms as if chilled and warming himself. He glanced about, seeking the best avenue of esc—

Pain cut hot through him, radiating out from his arm. He bit down on his tongue in time to arrest a shocked cry. The creature had taken up a sharp rock and slashed it across one shoulder, gouging out a chunk of flesh which it now delicately retrieved from the ground. Blood flowed down his arm as the rock-beast held up the chunk. As it observed its prize, Ondorum lifted his feet and tromped as if in anger.

"I beg your pardon for the drastic methods, but you seemed to be losing interest and I wished to speed up my inspection a tad."

It flicked the scrap into its mouth, and its rows of teeth ground the gristle to paste in an instant. The rock-beast closed its eye and hummed to itself in a tone of dark echoes. Moments later, a fine mist sprayed from its maw, spattering Ondorum's face. The oread realized he'd just had his own masticated flesh spit back upon him. He stomped in disgust.

"Intriguing mix of flavors. I shall savor it for centuries, to be sure. It does have a smack of human after all, but a gritty aftertaste. Half-breed of some sort, then. The mystery deepens, but I shall have the answer sooner or later, never you fear. Now, for another test . . ."

It whacked a tentacle across his shoulders. Ondorum let the blow slam him to the floor. Half a dozen times, whenever he stood, it smacked him back down. He tried to anticipate and go with the blows, hitting the ground as hard as he could without injuring himself.

At last, the creature relented. "Quite durable. I'm pleased. I would've hated to break you too quickly. Now then, as to your continued silence. One might be tempted to use the old notion of claiming the simplest answer to be the truest one, but I find that's often not the case, what with such a strange variety of life in this world. Even for simple actions, there seems a near-infinite variety of motives and reasonings behind it. If we went that route, I'd say you grew up in a lower caste where you learned poor manners and never discovered the wisdom of obeying your elders. But it has nothing to do with manners or social status, does it? This . . . this is a choice. A rebellion, perhaps. A promise? It could be a moral boundary, such as defiance. Do you believe silence makes you noble in the face of death?"

Ondorum stared it down and lifted his chin. The creature whirled in place, tendrils thrashing. They crashed through stalactites and stalagmites, smashing them to powder in a show of frenzied strength. Its voice shrilled through the cavern.

"There are those of my kind who would have already stripped the flesh from you for such impudence!"

Tentacles whipped in from all sides, each one holding large stone shards as if to impale him. Ondorum held his ground and the razor-edged pieces stopped inches from his flesh. Tentacles quivered and Ondorum truly believed the rock-beast was about to flay him alive. He breathed slowly, trying to find a final peace. Yet the one thing filling his mind in that moment was regret—at not having a last exchange of words with Akina, and at failing to fulfill his promise that he'd meet her on the other end.

The rock-beast relaxed and dropped the shards, which cracked against the floor all around him.

"Fortunately, I prefer to not only take knowledge, but also impart it upon others, whatever their fate after they leave my presence. Therefore, let me tell you what I know of silence so you may be wiser for it." It drew closer so he had nowhere to look but that lambent red eye. "Silence is a poison. Oh yes, a poison of the mind and soul. Even more pernicious than any venom or toxin you might ingest." It quivered in place. "Oh, I do love that word. Pernicious."

Ondorum tried to divide his attention between the creature's lecture and the golden ball pulsing in his center once more. Slowly, Ondorum expanded the ki, letting it seep through his being until it filled the whole of him with a subtle gilded glow.

"I have basked in silence for centuries," the creature said. "I have gifted others with eternal silence, even without their asking. Am I not the epitome of graciousness? Yet in the end, I have come to realize that silence is not the sum of existence. Some say we came from silence, from the void, and that we shall all return there someday. I, though, have seen further than this. The void is not a beginning or an end, but a pause between universes. An indrawn breath before the next words are spoken and the eternal moment once more teems with life."

Ondorum nodded as he fixed his ki flow in place. While it bolstered what strength remained and might give him the element of surprise, he didn't expect it would survive much further abuse. Now he needed the moment to employ it.

Irori, if you can see into our very minds and souls, surely you can see this deep into the world. You've gifted me with years of training and refinement, but skill is nothing without the strength to execute it. I stand surrounded by the earth that is my birthright. I claim it now and pray you honor my effort.

"Those who give over to silence in this existence, however, are surrendering to the void," the rock-beast said. "Unnecessarily so! They deprive themselves of far more glorious experiences, no matter what noble or shameful reason gave them reason to still their tongues in the first place. Yes, I accept that a certain amount of deprivation may be good to enhance sensations you later allow yourself, but too many wallow in their silence as if it's a holy thing."

Ondorum's cheek twitched, and the creature's raspy laugh sliced at his ears.

"So. Holiness is your pursuit, then. You think me blathering foolishness, and yet here I've discerned your ultimate goal. Do you see how silence avails you nothing? Do you understand how much I've learned from you despite your efforts to the contrary? That this might have been a much more enjoyable experience if you'd let me remove not only your outward chains, but also the ones that bind you from within?"

While the oread knew the rock-beast meant to mock him, its words struck deeper than it could've guessed. Silence could be holy. He knew this. He'd felt it in the presence of others who'd given over their entire lives to the practice. However, this didn't ensure his own vow had achieved the same ends. What if he'd given himself a fool's hope, thinking depriving himself of one area of expression would automatically raise his regard in others? Or perhaps it had, but only in stubbornness and pride, rather than true virtue.

The creature made another rattling sigh as it inspected him. "I do appreciate the puzzle you've presented. It is one I shall mull over for decades yet. However, we all must admit our failings in the end, and I am nearing the limits of my patience. Yet I do wish to know the truth of you. And the best way to solve a puzzle is to disassemble it and try to work it out in reverse. A clever solution, don't you think?"

Ondorum set his doubts aside for later scrutiny. This was neither the time nor place. He tried to keep his muscles relaxed, maintaining the illusion of remaining within the creature's control. He'd have a single chance at escape, and if he fouled it, he doubted it would give him time to make another effort.

A single tentacle reached for him. He jumped back, heels thumping the ground. The rock-beast rattled again.

"Oh, don't resist. That'll just make this worse. I can tell how much your body already betrays you." Its eye slit narrowed. "But what if your mind is not your own? What if this body I see here is naught but a shell for one of those skull-infesting vermin?" The eye shimmered. "That must be it. The brain-feeders. I despise your kind. Hedonistic parasites, the lot of you! I will carve you out of this form and ensure you never claim another host again."

More tentacles wove his way and Ondorum dropped into a crouch, palms pressed to the floor. In that moment, the whole chamber seemed to thrum in response. He didn't have time to tell if it was his imagination or not. A strand whipped around his arms, pinning them to his torso. As soon as it grasped him, his strength began to ebb again. The rock-beast yanked him into the air above its peaked form. Its mouth churned and its eye raged with boiling light.

Ondorum drew in a breath and visualized his ki contracting into a blazing knot for just an instant. Then he breathed out, unleashing it all as he punched both arms straight up. The strand slid up over his head and released him. He dropped heavily to his feet, shaking and near to collapse. Yet the firm rock held him up, and he drew from that strength, pushing his body beyond what it could accomplish on its own.

He vaulted backward, flipping over two tentacles that snatched at him.

"Impossible!"

He ducked and spun on one foot. A tentacle whipped overhead. He stamped the floor, sending himself into the air over three more and into a roll. Coming up next to a shattered limestone column, he grounded himself, scooped up the nearest block, and flung it at the rock-beast. The creature smashed the first out of the air, but he continued to grab and throw chunks, forcing it to knock them down. It grabbed one and flung it back, and Ondorum shifted aside, letting it soar by and crash against the wall.

When the beast got too close, he bounded away again, footsteps thumping as he climbed up one of the larger calcified formations. It came on and grabbed the base of the rock. Ondorum threw himself off and past the creature as, with a heave of its strands, it crumbled the base, bringing the rest of it down in a roar and clatter.

Ondorum struck the floor behind it and rolled up to his feet. He started to run, but then his left leg caught, and he dropped to hands and knees. One tentacle had latched onto his ankle briefly, and the foot went dead. He dug fingers into the stone, calling on it to anchor him. He lurched forward and the numb foot slipped free. The beast glided toward him, and he pounded fists as he crawled forward as well, trying to keep himself out of range. He managed to stay just ahead as it advanced, until he reached a rocky shelf.

He grabbed the ledge and hauled himself upright. Turning, he found the rock-beast right before him, tentacles poised to grasp.

It leered down. "A fascinating and impressive attempt, but pointless. I should make your death quick for giving me so much to ponder after you're gone, but I find agonized writhing adds so much juice to the marrow."

The ground rumbled, and the rock-beast's eye twitched from side to side. "What . . . ?"

The cavern shook, and the shattered rocks all around began to quiver and slide, while the few remaining columns trembled in place.

Its shrill cry rose. "What is this? What have you done?"

Ondorum tumbled aside as the gigantic worm burst through the floor ten paces away. This time, it didn't continue on. Twenty feet of its purple-shelled body twisted into the cavern, almost filling it from floor to ceiling.

The rock-beast's strands coiled back around its body, while its eye and mouth snapped shut, camouflaging it once more as a harmless, if jagged, stalagmite. Ondorum stood before it, balanced on his remaining good foot. The worm's head wove around, seeking the source of the disturbance that had called it back this way. He thumped his numb foot against the floor, and the worm fixed on him. Its mammoth mouth widened, and the sides of its lower jaw split open even further, revealing extra rows of fangs and quadrupling the area it could engulf.

It hurtled for him. Ondorum threw himself sideways as the worm descended. There came a last screech of denial, which cut off with a massive crunch. The cavern shook a final time and fell still.

Ondorum raised his head to see the worm locked against the floor, body undulating as it choked down a troublesome morsel. He rose and spotted the tunnel entrance he needed behind the worm's coiled bulk, accessible so long as he didn't bump into the thing. Ondorum limped through the debris, placing his

unfeeling foot so it didn't disturb so much as a pebble.
He wished the worm a pleasant meal.

Once beyond the cavern, he discarded stealth and
shuffled faster. Despite being battered and weary, he
couldn't help a broad smile.

Free at last to fulfill a promise.

Chapter Twenty-One
In the Ruins

The caligni gathered around as Akina and Izthuri made proper introductions, though it seemed Izthuri was the only one among them to speak any surface tongue. Their collections of black rags, cloaks, hoods, and robes concealed most of their bodies. Here, a pale nose poked out, there, white feet or hands emerged from the wrappings. Their eyes were uniformly black, surrounded by gray and white skin.

When Izthuri finished relating whatever tale she told them, they all bowed to Akina, a gesture the dwarf returned to much hissing whispers on their part. Izthuri gently took her arm as she straightened.

"You lead. Not bow."

Akina cleared her throat and spat dust to one side. "Fine by me."

Still clutching her wounded side, Izthuri guided them over to the wall, where a set of half-hidden greenstone stairs led down into the ruin subsurface. Akina took a last look around before heading down. Guess the tour would have to wait.

The stairs cut under the wall and then down a tunnel—not one of raw rock or earth as they'd been traveling through for days upon end, but a true-and-true tunnel lined with fashioned blocks and capstones, with proper arches and decorative engravings depicting . . . Akina couldn't actually figure out what the faded figures and lines were meant to show, but they felt familiar. The uncertainty itched along her scalp.

A few caligni ran ahead to alert the colony proper to their arrival. As they walked, Akina noted the caligni didn't talk much among themselves. Instead, they waggled and flicked fingers at one another, while their body language remained animated. She turned to Izthuri and held up a hand, wiggling fingers at random.

"This is how you all talk?"

Izthuri seized her hand and shoved it down. "You make very rude sign. Any see, they attack."

"Right."

A caligni dashed back to Izthuri and they exchanged a feisty finger-flicking discussion. When he—Akina guessed it to be a he—sprinted away, Izthuri's eyes grew grim.

"What is it?" Akina asked. "Did Ondorum . . ."

"No oread. I tell of him. My people look. Will not attack."

"Thank you." *Dammit, Ondorum, where are you? You were supposed to beat us here.* "What's got you so worried, then?"

Izthuri fingered the hilt of her blade. "Evil wakes. Hungers."

"Isn't that why we're here?"

"Yes. But before, it wake and sleep again. Now wakes and does not sleep."

They took several turns in the tunnel, which started to be lit by green globules stuck to the walls. When Akina edged away from these, Izthuri waved a hand near one to show its harmlessness.

"Not blightburn. Just lights. No fear."

Akina recovered her poise and they strode on. As they took another corner, fresher-looking—though still ancient—carvings struck her again as strangely familiar. "Izthuri, are these dwarven runes?"

The caligni nodded. "Yes. Think so."

"So that makes these dwarven ruins?"

Izthuri gave her an odd look. "You wait. I show."

They entered a large room where two dozen or so caligni sat about a central pit, holding their palms to the green flame burning there. Tunnels cut away from the other walls, some lit by the green globs, others dark. The caligni stared at Akina as she strode through, and she tried not to sneeze or snort as their stink wrapped arms around her head and squeezed tight. Fortunately, Izthuri didn't linger, but led her down another short hall and into a side room set with several chairs and side tables carved out of the same greenstone as the buildings and tunnels. Izthuri waved for Akina to take a seat, which she did with relief.

She didn't realize how many aches and cuts and bruises she'd compiled until she stopped moving. Then every one of them clamored for attention in unison. Given the tribe's collective odor, she didn't bother asking if the place had any baths; the thought, though, brought to mind Taggoret's cunning network of hot plumbing or a dip in a natural spring, either of which sounded beyond delicious. She settled for loosening a few armor straps.

"What now?"

Izthuri draped over her chair, arms and legs dangling across the armrests. Despite this sloughed position and her still-seeping wound, for the first time, Akina noted an almost regal air to her.

"We eat. We rest. You learn. Then we fight."

Akina pounded a fist into her palm. "Good plan."

They waited for a bit until a pair of caligni entered, bearing stone plates of what she hoped was food. The servers bowed as they placed plates on the low tables before them. Akina smacked her lips as she leaned forward, but then cringed. Wherever the gray and green-speckled meat had come from, it had a distinct odor of rot, and the shriveled mushrooms didn't look any more appetizing. Izthuri's plate also had a glowing purple gem placed on it. She devoured the food, saving the gem for last, like a treat. Akina wondered how it compared to the elemental diamond Ondorum had given her. The thought of the oread started getting her far too maudlin, and she was thankful when her rumbling belly forced her to focus back on her immediate needs.

She nibbled on a few of the mushrooms, telling herself cheese was a mold, after all. When she didn't puke it straight back up, die, or start having visions of rivers of gold and mithral flowing from her fingertips, she declined the meat and asked for more fungus instead. Izthuri passed her a wineskin which contained a particularly sour fermentation, but she had to stop herself from guzzling it and save some for her host. While Izthuri also drank, Akina picked at her teeth, thinking wine definitely shouldn't have chunks in it.

A stooped caligni came up and presented herself with splayed palms. Akina found she'd started to note the subtle differences between male and female. It had less to do with any body structure, and more with the smell. The females had a muskier stink to them, like they'd been rummaging through refuse piles composed primarily of fruits and vegetables turned to slime. The men smelled more of carrion, like a few of the ugly giant buzzards she'd had the pleasure of getting up close and personal with back on the surface.

Izthuri spoke with the other caligni for a moment. The newcomer had sagging, wrinkled skin visible around her eyes, and Akina took her for an elder of some sort.

"She asks permission to heal," Izthuri said at last.

Akina sat up, uncertain about having such strange magic worked on her. She threw aside any misgivings, though, and nodded. The caligni healer came forward and clasped clammy hands to Akina's cheeks. A purple aura flashed over the dwarf's eyes, and the world went blurry. When the spell struck, it took all her self-control to not shove the old healer away. It felt like frozen grubs wriggling across her entire body, crawling in through her pores and scouring every last crook and crevice as they gnawed away dead, diseased, or damaged flesh. The embers in her gut flared for a moment against the invasive energy, but she tamped them down and let it wash over her, hoping she hadn't make a huge mistake in allowing this. When the sensation faded, Akina took stock. Anything missing? Anything changed? Anything hurting worse than it had before?

She worked her neck and arms and marveled at the sudden absence of soreness, twitching pains, and the underlying ache that had become such a constant companion. She even figured if she checked the bandage on her arm from the crystal fragments, it'd be healed over. The healer cringed as if expecting a strike, but Akina smiled.

"Thank you." She started to bow, but caught herself and just repeated, "Thank you."

Izthuri finger-waggled what Akina hoped was a more eloquent expression of gratitude. The healer repeated the process with Izthuri, and Akina watched the flesh on the caligni's side knit over the bone and seal into a pasty swath of skin marbled by blue-green veins. It might've been a trick of the light, but Akina could've sworn fluorescent pulses flickered along those veins. The other caligni shuffled off, and Izthuri splayed a palm over her exposed side as if embarrassed. She slipped out of the room for a few minutes, leaving Akina to revel in her restored strength. She didn't even feel like sleeping.

When Izthuri returned, new strips of clean black rags covered her abdomen, and she walked with fresh purpose.

"Come. I show now. We quiet. We careful. Duergar."

"Right." Akina rose and followed Izthuri along another series of tunnels. While she understood the need to keep the element of surprise, her new rush of energy had her fingers tingling, ready to crack a few duergar skulls if the opportunity arose.

They emerged inside a bare building, all worked stone. It looked like it could've been a small abode, and Akina noted the proportions appeared dwarven enough. Izthuri had to bend almost double to duck through the thresholds, while Akina plodded on without issue. They came out onto the slight rise of an ancient pathway, where the occasional cobblestone poked through the earth. Akina studied the buildings, clusters of low-lying structures, most with rounded tops like turtle shells, with random towers standing like stubby fingers. Everything stood packed side-by-side, but it felt like a cozy closeness rather than being jammed together.

Their position gave her a decent view of the ruins beyond. Portions of the buildings blended off into the distant cavern walls themselves, hewn straight from the earth. Above them, openings and blocky outcrops hinted at upper levels worked into the ceiling, and she guessed there might be whole warrens delved around and below the central chamber as well. While the cavern was already impressive enough, the entirety of these ruins might be several times larger than the initial glimpse suggested.

Izthuri paused at every corner and intersection, checking all directions before scurrying on. Akina came right behind, trying to keep her armor from making too much noise. Many of the buildings had collapsed walls or roofs exposing interior chambers, but some stood intact—though she doubted their integrity. They passed through a small square and down a tight knot of back alleys, all through a deathly hush that clung to everything like a pall of forgotten memories.

Izthuri studied the shadows once more before slipping into one of the larger nearby buildings, a circular, two-story establishment ringed with glassless windows. When Akina entered, she froze in the doorway until Izthuri pulled her all the way inside. Akina spun a slow circle.

"What is this place?"

Izthuri leaned against the wall by the threshold, peering out to watch the area they'd just come through. "Ruins."

Akina was too taken in by the sights on the walls to reply to what sounded like a sarcastic answer. Ruins. Oh, stone endures, yes. Dwarven ruins. This building must've been a temple or meeting hall of some sort, she figured, as graven murals covered every inch of the wall, ranging from runes to images of dwarves at work and celebration. She even spotted an icon of Torag with his warhammer, Kaglemros. She wandered deeper into the building, unable to absorb the enormity of it all, but unable to look away.

"You see?" Izthuri came up beside Akina and waggled fingers at a particular section on the lower wall. "You read?"

"It's confusing," Akina said. "I can read some, but other sections don't make sense. The runes are all there, but they're different somehow." She pointed out one set. "The part I can figure out says: *Here we served. Here Torag taught us. Here we fought. Here we died. Here we were born. Here we made. Here we left when the signs showed the way. Remember us.*" Her hand trembled at that last bit. "It's a farewell. A form of gladdringgar, almost." She squinted at the preserved carvings. "I'm not a historian, but . . ." She noticed Izthuri's confusion at the word. "Not a scholar." Tapped her helm. "No big thinker."

Izthuri hissed, and Akina couldn't tell if she was being laughed at or not. She refocused on the ancient script.

"I figure this goes back to before the Quest for Sky. This must've been one of our ancestral settlements before we headed to the surface. Or maybe a stop along the way. Not a major city, but still ours. And it's just been sitting here."

She found herself blinking back tears to think she stood in one of the original homes of the dwarves themselves. It felt like a holy place, sacred and worthy of protecting. She knuckled her eyes clear, wondering at her strong response. She hadn't realized she felt so deeply about this sort of thing. Had the healing spell made her more raw around the edges? Or did her connection to her people carve deeper channels through her soul than she'd believed? To be here, where it all began . . .

Her mother should've had the chance to see this. Jannasten had deserved this sort of discovery, not her wayward daughter. But maybe Akina could find a way to honor her memory here.

She turned. "I need to see more."

Izthuri slunk over and studied the mural. She reached up to an icon near the top, out of Akina's reach, and tapped it with a long finger. "Evil."

Akina strained to make out the image. A stylized flame rested atop an anvil, with two dwarven forge-masters standing on either side, one raising a hammer, one raising tongs. She could just make out the hint of a face within the flame.

"You saying something moved in after my people left, or that my people left something evil here?" But if it had moved in after, how had it been incorporated in this mural?

"Always been," Izthuri hissed.

Akina scowled. "My people didn't create evil."

Izthuri shrugged.

"Take me there."

They passed back out into the ancient settlement, and Akina couldn't shake the feeling of walking among the ghosts of her most ancient ancestors. Would she have fit in with those who once lived here, able to stride among them without drawing odd glances? Did any spirits linger, watching her even now? Did they like what they saw? Did they even recognize her as one of their own descendants?

As they went, Akina realized the city had been built in concentric circles, each inner district ringed by a solid wall with offset gates leading out to the larger neighborhood surrounding it. A defensive construction? A way to force any invaders down specific streets while dwarven defenders picked them off from preplanned routes? With each ring-wall they passed through, the buildings grew more elaborate, the structures more decorative. Columns and archways grew more abundant, with faces and figures worked over most surfaces, much like in Taggoret. These here had been somewhat worn by time, but the lack of weather and general exposure had preserved much of the original artwork, if not the gilding.

When they passed through the fourth such ring-wall, a distant glow caught her eye. It flickered against the cavern ceiling far above, and she figured the source had to be another ring or two away. Near the center of the place. Before they went through the next gateway, Izthuri ducked into a nearby swath of shadow and waved for Akina to do the same.

A band of four duergar marched by. The increasing light illuminated their black chainmail, strapped over with violet vambraces, breastplates, and helms, each one carrying a silver-etched axe. The duergar scouted on without spotting the intruders, and Izthuri waited until they walked out of sight before emerging from the shadows. Akina itched to stalk after the duergar and lay them all low, but she had to see the place first. She had to know what they faced.

Rather than take her closer to the glow, Izthuri crept inside a tower base and took Akina up a spiraling flight of stairs to the top. They edged out onto a walled landing and peeked over the edge.

The next ring over proved to be a large central circle, with three inner rings forming a clover shape inside it. One inner ring held a three-story building, a proportionate duplicate of the mural-filled temple Izthuri had showed her. The second ring held a massive hole. Whatever once sat there must have caved in long ago, as a rough shaft dropped straight out of sight into the earth.

The third ring contained an enormous forge, which sat on a raised rectangular platform with steps on either end. Dozens of duergar milled about the platform, accompanied by an assembly of earth and fire elementals, all of which looked to be hard at work.

Large archways crowned both sets of steps, and each arch had been fashioned in the guise of a helmed dwarf's head, with the walkway leading through the mouth—wide open as if roaring a battle cry. The top of their helms extended back to meet and form a roof across the whole platform. Long openings along the side of the forge indicated where metal gates might have once been installed, providing numerous stations for smiths to work, and more gaps in the top suggested old vent systems or hoist openings. Several fire elementals worked within the forge itself, stoking a blaze ever-hotter, ever-brighter, forming the light she'd seen on their approach.

On the near end stood a giant anvil, far too big to be of practical use—large enough for a troll to lay down for a nap, in fact. Beside the anvil lay a broad hearth and fire pit, where coals could be dumped and ignited. The oven housing extending from this could've been used as an actual house.

Duergar and their elemental minions chiseled on certain surfaces, bolstering others, filling in gaps and replacing stones. Others appeared to be casters, running their hands along the forge stones or standing back with arms raised, mouths wide in unknown chants. The whole process filled the ring with a constant din, while the flames of the forge added a throaty crackle.

Akina watched all this, dumbfounded. Four gates allowed access to this walled ring, each gate guarded by huge pairs of dwarven statues holding various smithing instruments. Below the platform, a duergar encampment had been established. Soldiers patrolled around the ring on foot as well as on spider, beetle, and reptilian mounts. From this distance, the duergar looked like beetles themselves, clad in their gleaming armor of black and silver and red.

Among all the glinting armor and ashen skin, a couple of figures stood out. One duergar sat astride an enormous beetle with an obsidian shell and a multipronged horn thrusting from its head. Unlike the other duergar, this one wore spiked, white armor. Bone? A pair of hook axes were strapped to his back, the blades weirdly pink. He oversaw the labor with an air of authority visible even across the distance.

On the ground beside him stood a gray-robed duergar, the first Akina had seen who was both entirely bald and beardless. He or she held a solemn poise, arms crossed within sleeves. A priest of some sort?

Next to them stood Gromir. Even if his dusty blue robes hadn't given the dwarf away, his face gleamed golden when he lifted his head to gaze up at the fires of the active forge.

Akina exchanged a look with Izthuri, and they crept backward until once more inside the tower. Then they retraced their steps all the way back to the caligni colony. Instead of retreating to the side room, they joined the rest of the tribe in the main room, where they conferred over everything she'd seen.

Akina scrubbed at her forehead, trying to make sense of it all. "That forge. That's the evil? Or the duergar?"

Izthuri wriggled fingers. "Forge hungry."

Akina clamped teeth down, biting a retort in half. "Forges need fuel, sure, but you realize it's just equipment."

At Izthuri and the tribe's blank stares, she plunked a chin on a fist and tried to sort out her thoughts. What could the duergar want with the place? Ever since the dwarves had left the Darklands for the surface, the duergar had gone to great lengths to overrun many of their ancient homes, making them their own and rebutting later attempts to reclaim them. It made some sense, then, that they'd show interest in undiscovered ruins linking back to that time period. What about the forge, in particular, had caught their attention?

Well, she knew one person who'd have answers. And where Gromir was, Brakisten should be as well, though she hadn't noted her brother's presence earlier. They'd likely drugged or enspelled him and stashed him somewhere.

She clapped hands on her knees. The noise made many caligni shy away, but Izthuri at least appeared used to their noisy companion.

"Right. We need a few diversions."

Chapter Twenty-Two
Fiery Crossing

Ondorum stared down at the molten river in dismay. While the first two magma flows he'd encountered offered natural bridges, as Izthuri said, this one lacked such as far as he could see. The ravine the lava flowed through also proved the deepest and widest yet.

When he'd found the lava-scoured cavern, he'd rejoiced at first, knowing he remained on the right path. However, he'd already trekked up and down a goodly length of this flow and saw no way to cross. The delay back in the rock-beast's cavern, and now this obstruction, compounded his anxiousness upon weariness. Even when he took cleansing breaths and worked through a series of mantras, he realize his struggles with the rock-beast had drained him more than he realized. At least his numb foot had regained sensation so he didn't have to hobble any longer.

Unlike the duergar wall back in the Long Walk, he couldn't leap this gap. He entertained a brief, desperate thought of jumping and trying to grab onto outcroppings halfway down the other side of the ravine, then climbing back up from there, but the opposing wall looked melted smooth by the magma's passage, with nary a crack nor ledge to be seen. Whatever stone the flow cut through, it had a glassy sheen that suggested no purchase whatsoever.

He considered the metal link still held in his loincloth, but any construct made from it couldn't extend more than ten feet, and the crossing looked to be at least five times that, even at its narrowest point. He jogged up, against the direction of the lava flow. It had to have a source somewhere.

What felt like hours later, he finally found it. The channel broadened into a molten river that rose out of the ravine and funneled up into the gaping opening of a giant lava tube. The size of it reminded him of dwarven city gates. Ondorum suppressed a groan; this discovery offered no solution. The magma still spanned further than he dared try to jump, and no stone bridge allowed for crossing anywhere.

Or did it? In the fiendish light, he studied the cavern wall surrounding the lava tube opening. The bottom had piles of rubble, but above, it turned smooth enough to defy climbing, with nothing to grab onto or kick off of. He placed palms against the rock. Roughened surface, yes, but any attempts to clamber up more than a few feet made it crumble under his weight and slide him back down.

He returned to the edge of the magma river and stood, arms crossed, to meditate on the problem. He would not allow this to defeat him. Nature, even the subterranean sort, provided as many answers as it did obstacles. It did so without regard for mortal convenience, though, so one had to learn to see the dilemma from a different perspective.

He looked up into the lava tube itself. Slowly, he bent over to one side until he pressed a hand to the ground and stared at the tube upside-down.

A different perspective indeed.

Unlike the channel the lava currently oozed through, the tube sides and ceiling hung craggy and ridged, rife with areas to cling to. Ondorum straightened and regarded his hands. Did they shake? Did they tremble? Did the strength remain within him to attempt such a feat? He spent a little while longer studying the area, ensuring no other option presented itself. Returning to the tube, he assayed the best starting point.

Heat waves and caustic fumes washed over him as he neared, and the stones themselves steamed along the edges. The fumes bit into the back of his throat and threatened to send him hacking, and he prayed his elemental heritage protected him from the worst of the effects. After all, what was magma but earth mingled with fire? Surely his nature could withstand it to a degree. Was he not, in some distant way, kin to the liquid stone flowing before him?

From the tube's entrance, a thin shelf of rock edged out along the base of the inner wall for twenty feet or so before ending. He eased out onto this, making sure it didn't crumble beneath his weight and end the attempt before it began. The rock burned against his bare feet, but not quite hot enough to start sizzling. This portion of the wall formed into blocky, black rock, with ridges sharp enough to cut if he gripped them wrong. He saw how a certain pressure flaked the edges, while pushing another way ground the flakes to coat his fingers and palms, forming a grit that improved friction between his hands and the stone.

The heat wove around him as he took a breath to steady his mind. *Irori, if failure is ever to impede my progress, let it not be here or now. May my skill be flawless for your glory.* Before doubt could seep in and the acrid air start to overwhelm his lungs, he climbed.

The lower portion proved relatively easy, but he refused to let overconfidence turn his efforts sloppy. Heat radiated into his palms and the soles of his feet as he scaled the first fifty feet. By the time he reached the first section curving overhead, sweat dribbled down his face, back, and thighs, cutting channels of their own into the dust caking his body. With two more advances, he shifted out over the lava flow. Falling now gave him no chance of dropping back onto the shelf where he'd begun. As his perspective inverted, the pressure required to remain aloft doubled, then trebled. Ondorum kept his stomach pressed close to the stone, not letting any sag in his form add to the strain.

He breathed as shallowly as possible through a thin gap between his lips. Still, the fumes built inside him, shoving out the fresh air and replacing it with a burning tingle throughout his neck and chest. His eyes stung and watered, forcing him to pause between each movement to blink the tears away, clearing his vision so he could see his next handhold well enough. The heat ripples played with his sense of distance, and more than once, he reached out to grasp a ridge or press a palm against a surface to find it an inch or two further than he estimated.

His world turned upside down, and he tried to trick his mind into thinking he crawled through a bowl of roughened earth while the sky above burned with a sunset. His body became a composite of opposing pressures, each perfectly balanced to offset the other. It felt as if someone had tied a rope around his waist with a heavy rock at the other end, trying to force him to buckle and drag him back to earth. His joints clicked as he locked them into place. He would not bend. He would not break. He would be perfect in this moment. And then the next. And the next.

With his back to a river of the earth's very blood, each advance became a series of precise calculations as he gauged direction, weight, balance, force. Each successful reposition of a foot and hand became its own minute victory.

Halfway across the ceiling, he braced his left hand, secured both feet, and reached for a thorny, black ridge to press the right palm against. As he did, the corner he gripped with his left crumbled. He jammed the reaching hand against the ridge, and the rocky spikes bit deep into the meat of his palm. Blood squeezed out between his fingers and slicked his whole hand. Keeping his breaths under control, refusing to let the pain master him, he sought a replacement hold for his left. Found it. Jammed fingertips into a crevice and prayed it held.

He withdrew his right hand and studied the damage: two puncture wounds, like fang bites, bruising already evident. He wiped the blood off on a leg, but by the time he repositioned it, more already welled. Nothing to be done but strive onward.

Below him, the lava burbled and hissed. A cloud of steam rose, enveloping him in a white haze. His arms and legs trembled as he tried to peer through it, unable to determine where next to move. Staying still would be his doom, but a blind leap would be equally disastrous.

The steam burned his eyes, blurring his vision further. How had the next portion of the ceiling looked before he lost sight of it? Which way should he go?

The steam congealed into a flat, white expanse; the exhaustion faded from his body. Any sense of up or down, of heat or chill, fled him, and it seemed as if he stood in an endless land without form or features. This must be death, then. Without realizing, he must've lost his hold and fallen into the lava. Now he waited in one of the realms beyond, where his soul would be weighed and parceled by Pharasma.

A vision wove into being before him, curling up like steam, yet with shadow and substance to set it apart from the rest of the nothingness. As it shivered into motion, he both saw and lived it in the same moment . . .

Ondorum and Akina slogged out of the swamp, mud and insects clinging to them with boot- and blood-sucking tenacity. Akina paused to scrape muck from her soles, but Ondorum trod straight for the village across the field, jaw set in barely checked fury.

Akina called after. "Maybe we should hear them out. What if it's not what it seems?"

"She spoke the truth," Ondorum called back. "And we are committed to our course. But I would still hear a full admission."

She grumbled behind him. "Good thing we got paid half up front."

As he stomped toward the human village, a couple denizens spotted him and called to the others. By the time he tracked mud into the main square, several dozen villagers gathered around the well. The man who called himself their mayor pushed to the front, buttoning up his vest.

"It's done, then?" he asked. "Our village will be at peace?"

The mayor squawked as Ondorum wrapped a hand around his throat.

"Look me in the eye and Irori take you if you lie," he said. "Those spirits you set us after, the ones haunting you and bringing madness and nightmares into your midst—were they or were they not the spirits of your own children? Ones you cast into the swamp to die?"

The mayor squirmed, but he couldn't budge Ondorum's grip or stance. Finally, he ceased struggling and drooped. "They were."

Murmurs twisted through the crowd; from the subdued noise, though, it sounded like few, if any, were surprised at this revelation. Akina jogged up in time to catch the confession, and she scowled as she joined Ondorum.

"You murdering bastards." She spat at the man's feet.

The mayor fixed Ondorum with a manic look. "They were cursed. Deformed at birth. Not of pure blood. Had we let them live, they would've brought even greater doom on our heads."

Ondorum shoved him back in disgust. The mayor cast nervous looks to the stooped, mossy trees forming the swamp border. "They're all gone, then?"

"We eliminated them all," Ondorum said. "They only had voices to wail and weep; if we had encountered them alone, we might've never learned the truth. But the witch responsible for their manifestations revealed herself. A naga."

That brought gasps from the crowd.

"A naga!" The mayor wrung his hands. "She's the one behind all our terror?"

"Yes." Ondorum glowered at those gathered. "She told us the truth of the situation. How she sensed the torment of your dying children. How their desperation for someone to care for them drew her here. In her own way, she did."

The crowd stirred, many clutching themselves as if chilled to the core.

"What was the naga's fate?" whispered the mayor.

"She lives."

The man paled. "Y-you can't leave her out there. She'll be our ruin."

"She may, yes." Ondorum stepped back. "But that's no longer our concern after the bargain she struck with us."

"What manner of bargain?" someone called.

"Just as you cast aside your own offspring, so you deserve to be cast aside." Ondorum's heart clenched, struggling with the path he must walk. "The naga took your children and made them her own. Now that you hired us to destroy them—as we have—she has claimed you in their stead." He shared a look with Akina. "We agreed to no longer interfere in your dealings with her. In return, she has agreed to stop interfering with your dead."

"Even if such a vile beast can be trusted, that won't stop her from attacking us directly." The leader fell to his knees. "Please, have mercy. We can't face a creature like this. We'll pay double if you go back and destroy her for good."

Akina's eyes lit up at the promise of more coin, but Ondorum cut her off with a growl. "No. You do not deserve such a mercy. You've fed this creature all these years, nurturing her power by sacrificing your children to her, whether you knew it or not. Now reap what you've sown." He spun on his heel and strode off.

Akina caught up with him on the village border. "Can't count how many times Durgan tried to abandon clients and you convinced him to give them a second chance. You've even fought for folks when they didn't pay a dull copper."

Ondorum cast a glance back at the villagers. The people had started to disperse back to their huts, heads and shoulders bowed. "There are times I fear certain souls don't deserve a chance to redeem themselves." He sighed and stared at the road they walked. "I also fear I erred in giving the naga my word. I spoke rashly, letting anger guide me rather than seeking the straighter path. It infuriated me to discover what the villagers had done, and that they'd try to pay their way out of their sins. It doesn't work that way. It can't. It shouldn't."

"You being the angry one for once is a nice change. It's a good look on you."

He glared her way. "But if I had at least measured my speech, I might not have bound us to wholly stand aside. The mayor is right. They remain vulnerable. We could defend them. Yet Irori teaches us to hold our word as oath, otherwise everything we say is inherently flawed."

"Not the first time I've paid for your beliefs. Doubt it's the last." She scratched her chin. "What if you go on while I head back and—"

"I told the naga *we* would not interfere."

"You're letting poor promises and single words carry a lot of weight."

"Then perhaps it'd be better if I were to not speak at all!"

"I've thought the same a few times." At his glower, she nudged him with an elbow. "Ondorum, we finished the job we were hired for. Not our fault there was a bit more mud in the stew than we figured. What happens next isn't our business."

They fell into silence as they headed down the road. As evening dusted the world in gray, they found a sheltered grove where they made camp and then pleasure, as they'd gotten into the habit of doing whenever their campfires only cast two shadows. A far cry from the constant winks and crude jokes they'd endured in the band, so they made the most of the solitary times they had.

Then distant screams tore the night in half. They lurched up from their bedrolls, Akina going for her maulaxe. Ondorum stared at the sky, which filled with flickering blue and green lights. They didn't have to guess where the sounds or sights emanated from. Nor did they doubt that if they raced to stop the slaughter, they'd arrive far, far too late.

Akina came up beside him and laid a hand on his back. "It's not your fault."

Ondorum knew better. And he believed he knew how to fix this mistake. He grasped her hand and faced her.

"Akina, from this moment on, I vow . . ."

The vision faded back into the swirling mists, and Ondorum found himself alone within the white void once more. He doubted he'd received a vision from Irori himself; more likely a vivid memory brought on by exhaustion and the fumes. Whatever the source, he now knew . . . he *knew* . . .

It hadn't been the act of speaking itself that doomed the villagers. The words only represented the underlying lie he'd allowed to skew his path. In fact, both his words and his actions had been based on falsehoods: The belief that the villagers were irredeemable. That he had the right to pronounce judgment on them. That their lives were of less value than his oath.

Just as he'd allowed Akina to believe she mattered less to him than his vow.

It was a lie he could no longer live by, and a mistake he needed to live to amend.

The steam faded, and Ondorum's vision blinked clear. The lava tube wavered into being around him with all its heat and fumes and promise of death. But with renewed vigor, he fixed on the next hold well enough, and the one after that. Feeling ebbed from his hands and feet as he contorted them into place. His joints seized, refusing to bend when he needed, and he broke them into submission, refusing to be defied by his own body. Through it all, somehow, his body felt lighter than it had when he started.

He crossed to the far ceiling slope and began a series of hitching turns to orient himself sideways, then upright. As he crept down, the other side of the lava flow coming into view through the red haze, he edged back toward the mouth of the tube. That's when he realized a key feature was missing in his descent.

This side offered him no shelf to land on.

His muscles and bones quivered, but he didn't pause at this observation, knowing any hesitation would buckle and drop him to plop into the churning magma below. Already, he could count the seconds left to him, before his body simply stopped responding to his mind's commands. With rapidly fading strength, he worked as close to the tube opening as he could. Twenty feet to the ground, by his estimate, but he could wait no longer.

Hooking a hand around the corner of the tube mouth, he threw himself out, flipping around so his back struck the outer wall. He tried to brace, digging hands and feet into the crumbling cavern slope to slow his descent as much as he could. The ground rushed up at him, and he rammed into the floor a step away from where it dipped into the lava.

Ondorum wavered, knees threatening to collapse and send him tumbling into the flow. Then he whirled away and threw himself prone. Uneven stone scraped his chest and cheek, but he lay there, spent, lacking even the strength to shut his eyes.

He had come through the furnace and been found worthy. After a time, he pushed himself to his knees and almost whispered audible thanks for this new understanding. Yet a touch on the back of his mind made him hesitate. Not yet. Not until he could share the joy of this new perception. Revelations proved worthless when savored alone.

So he sealed his lips a little while longer and cast out silent thanks to Irori. He also prayed this proved the last major obstacle between him and the ruins. Rising from the edge, he staggered far enough away to leave the heat behind, and then dropped into repose once more, where he rested for an immeasurable time. When his body at last cooled and the trembling left his limbs, he gathered himself and found the proper tunnel on this side to resume his journey.

Not two turns later, a skittering noise made him pause. He briefly shut his eyes, trying to quell his exasperation at such terrible fortune. He'd not recovered enough yet to face any significant foe, and he held no quarrel with any creature here. Just a traveler, passing through.

He checked the various nearby pathways, trying to determine where the noise originated. Plenty of sizable tunnels filled this area, all leading in vaguely the same direction. Perhaps that's why Izthuri had planned to go this way. If multiple routes led to the same place, there was less chance of error or getting lost.

A humped shape scuttled into view along the tunnel on his right. As large as a wild boar, the creature had a carapace made up of spike-edged plates that narrowed down into a lashing tail. Long, feathery antennae extended from below its obsidian eyes, and both the eyes and the antennae seemed to lock on him as it sped along on four multi-jointed legs. It spread notched mandibles.

Ondorum grabbed the chain link out of his loin-cloth and stretched it into a staff, thinking the sudden appearance of a weapon might give the creature pause. Instead, the insect rushed in even faster, and the burst of speed threw off his timing. As he side-stepped, letting its bite lash past, his strike bounced off hard shell. A leg joint thrust into his chest, throwing him back. He slammed against the wall while his staff went clattering away.

Ondorum tried to recover, thinking the creature would be on him. But the insect had raced to his fallen staff instead. Its antennae brushed the length of the staff and, from one blink to the next, the metal reduced to a line of rust. Ondorum struggled to his feet as the creature began munching on the corroded remains.

An insect that feasted on metal? He kept an eye on it as he shuffled around to the tunnel he'd been heading for before the interruption. As he backed away, he thought it fortunate the rock-beast had removed the rest of his chains. Otherwise, he might've been trampled in the insect's attempts to devour them. At least he no longer had any metal on his person.

The insect gnawed up the last of the staff. Then its antennae waved, and it scurried to the spot where he'd fallen. A splotch of blood from his wounded hand stained the stone, and the insect brushed its antennae over this before scraping mandibles across the stone.

Metal and . . . blood? Or an element present in both?

When the rock resisted its attempts to get at the bloodstain, the insect whirled and stared down the tunnel straight at him.

Ondorum engaged a tactic he rarely employed, except in the most dire circumstances.

He turned and fled.

Chapter Twenty-Three
Vaskegar

Stepping into view behind the duergar patrol, Akina raised her maulaxe and called out, "My hammer's missing a nail. Seen it? About your height and shaped like a skull."

The three duergar spun, and their surprise turned to wicked glee when they saw a lone dwarf challenging them. They hollered what she figured were indecent things about her parentage as they raced her way, axes and daggers readied. One vanished in mid-stride, employing their kind's disappearing tactic.

As the two visible duergar sprinted at her, three caligni dropped from above and cut them down. A ghostly hand appeared in front of Akina, glowing blue as it flew through the air and struck an unseen form. An axe appeared, falling from an unseen grip, and a large puff of dust indicated an invisible body striking the ground. It didn't stir.

Akina grinned as the caligni caster stepped out of an alley, blue glow fading from his true hand. Izthuri finished off the duergar on her left with a slash across the throat, and then rose to waggle fingers Akina's way. She nodded back. Right. Last patrol down. Time to get into position. Izthuri directed four of the caligni to split off, and they vanished back into the shadows. Then she, Akina, the caligni caster, and another fighter wove their way toward the nearest gate into the forge ring.

It had taken Izthuri a bit to convince any of her people to fight. Akina had watched as the tribe leader hissed and flicked fingers at the others. Seemed like most of the caligni had become used to hiding and didn't see any need to tip the stew pot, so long as the duergar stayed away from the district the caligni had chosen as home. Izthuri had punctuated her speech with gestures using the buggane tusk as well as numerous elbow jabs Akina's way. The dwarf felt uneasy at being painted as a savior, but she held to her promise to protect them. It just wouldn't hurt to have a little help along the way. Six caligni had joined them in the end, most armed with daggers and short swords. Another hadn't held any weaponry, but proved his usefulness soon enough with a knack for deadly magic.

Izthuri had asked if she wanted to wait a little while and see if Ondorum showed up to add to their number. Akina declined, which drew an odd look from the caligni leader. But they didn't know how much time Brakisten might have left. Besides, she figured it for a simple enough plan: Have a few caligni cause a distraction on one side of the forge ring. Draw away enough of the duergar for her and the others to sneak in from the opposite side, grab Gromir and Brakisten, and scoot back out. Akina also counted on the duergar thinking themselves alone in the ruins, with any disturbances coming from wild beasts roaming the area versus a coordinated attack. Once they had the other dwarves, they'd head back along Ondorum's route, leaving caligni behind to escort him to her if they somehow missed each other.

Izthuri led them into a small building near a gate, where they could see the set of duergar guards over the edge of a crumbled side wall. The light from the forge behind them turned their shadows into black giants looming over the street beyond. From Akina's position, the wall cut off much of the noise, but she could still pick up on the clang of hammers, the whoosh of flames, and duergar voices barking commands.

She hunkered down to wait. It might take the caligni a bit to navigate the ruins without being seen.

Just as she thought that, an unearthly howl rose off in the distance. Akina jerked up and looked to Izthuri, who nodded. Her people.

More howls twined together in a chorus that made her neck hairs prickle. Then came a long gong, like a bell struck by a hammer, followed by bloodcurdling screams. Akina tensed at a boom and rolling clatter of rock. Had they just collapsed a building? How did four caligni create so much ruckus?

Izthuri leaned in and hissed. "They in temple in next ring. Stand in center. Hole in top sends noise across all ruins. Loud."

The duergar at the gate had turned around to peer in the direction of the noises, which now echoed over the empty city. Duergar shouted deeper in, and shadows flashed by as troops moved about. These two stayed, though their tense postures indicated they wished to join the effort to hunt down the source of the disruption.

Mad laughter tore into Akina's ears, followed by a hissing gurgle of indecipherable words.

Izthuri tittered. "They say very rude things of duergar."

That did the trick. The guards hefted their axes and lumbered off into the ring. After counting off a few seconds, Akina signaled her companions forward. They sidled up to the gate and she peered around it. The duergar camp had gone into action, with many of the soldiers tromping along. Then a duergar ran into the middle of the opposite gate. He held up the decapitated head of another soldier and babbled in the duergar language. That spurred most of the rest to head over. Even the commander had his beetle mount in motion, heading around so the forge didn't block his sight of the far gate. As he went, the commander shouted up to the duergar working the forge, and they bent back to whatever tasks they'd been assigned.

She scanned for Gromir. The camp didn't have anything in the way of tents, what with no need to protect themselves from weather. However, cots, crates, and paths marked off various areas, including a small mess, piles of stores, and a makeshift meeting spot with chairs and a folding table in the middle. The dwarf sat in the last of these, head in his hands as a pair of guards stood watch.

Akina's breath hitched as she spotted Brakisten lying on the ground beside Gromir. Her brother stretched out on a bedroll, shaggy head propped in the crook of an elbow, as if asleep. After fearing him dead for so long, it felt unreal to see him alive. Now she just had to drag him to safety and ensure he stayed that way.

The chaotic banging, howls, crashes, screams, and laughter continued while the mass of duergar headed in that direction. They didn't all funnel out of the gates, leaving the camp undefended, but most at least wanted to see what was going on. Akina figured her group didn't have a better chance than this.

Caligni at her side, she darted across the gateway and inside the ring. She tried to ignore how the forge reared over them, an ancient structure resurrected by earth and flame. The fires blazing within it tried to draw her eyes, and its massive construction begged her to stand there, wondering at its purpose.

Yet she focused on remaining as hunched as possible as they clung to the inner wall and curved around until they had moved behind the meeting pavilion. With a last check to make sure no one had noticed them and raised the alarm, they swept in. The caligni caster propelled a phantom hand out to stun one duergar, while Izthuri raced up behind the other and jammed her black blade up through the nape of his neck and into his brain. Then the first took a blade between the shoulders to finish him off.

Gromir stared as his guards dropped around him. He pushed up from his chair, reaching inside his robe, but froze when Akina stepped in front of him. They stared at one another, her trying to figure a fitting hello, him switching from disbelief to shock to fear.

"You . . . you . . ." He flailed and tried to push her away. "You can't be here! No!"

He froze as Izthuri's blade caught under his throat.

"Quiet," she said. "Yes?"

"Akina? Who—? What—?"

Akina grabbed his beard and growled. "We're leaving. So much as cough on the way out and I'll bleed you myself, hm?"

Once she was sure Izthuri had him in hand, she went to Brakisten and shook him. For a strained moment, she feared him a corpse after all. Then he spluttered and squinted up at her. He stunk worse than the caligni tribe, his hair and beard snarled, his cracked lips bleeding as they quivered.

"Kina?" He groaned and clutched his stomach. "Been having such a nightmare."

She laid a hand on his back. "It's going to be all right, Brak. Time to go home."

Shouts erupted close by. Akina snapped her head up to see Gromir flinging throwing axes at a retreating Izthuri, who shifted around the attacks. The other caligni dashed in from the side, sword poised; Gromir whipped a hand out at the fighter, who went down in a spray of icy shards. The caligni's body contracted, as if he breathed in—and then the rags exploded, sending a dazzling burst of light through the area.

Akina tried to shield her face with an arm, but hot needles pricked her eyes and bloomed into white-red circles that blotted out all else. When her vision cleared, Izthuri and the caligni caster had disappeared. Gromir appeared to be recovering from a similar daze as he turned circles, throwing axes poised.

Akina twitched as a gray-robed figure appeared beside her. For half a heartbeat, she imagined Ondorum had arrived. Then she recognized the bald and beardless duergar she'd seen from the tower. Up close, the duergar woman had lean features and silvery eyes. She bowed, fist pressing against fist.

Akina snarled and swung her maulaxe. The duergar wove aside and let the weapon blur past. Akina spun and cut at the woman's head, but the duergar ducked and then stepped in and struck Akina's chest with an open palm. Akina staggered back several feet, while the other woman remained poised. Contemplative, even.

Not Ondorum, but she moved and fought like him. What in the blazing Hell?

One second, the duergar stood a few steps away. The next, she closed the distance and slapped Akina across the face, like one would an insolent child. Akina barked and tried to headbutt her. The duergar raised a hand to catch the brunt of her helm, and then made a twisting motion, diverting Akina's momentum to spin her around like a toy. A fist rammed into Akina's side with unbelievable force, even through her armor.

The maulaxe flew from her hands as she dropped to her knees, dazed by that single blow. She tried to regain focus, coherent thought dancing just outside of reach. A part of her knew she was vulnerable, but couldn't gather the wits to do anything about it.

"Stop!" someone cried. "Don't kill her."

A shove, and Akina fell over backward. The cavern ceiling glowed above her, and she stared up with blank eyes, wondering what had just happened. Figures moved nearby. Rough hands dragged her back to her knees. She started to struggle, but a ringing slap on the back of the head scrambled thoughts of resistance again. Scowling duergar clustered around her.

A voice boomed. "Bring her."

As they lifted her to her feet, Akina's eyes fell on Gromir standing off to one side. The dwarf ducked his head but followed as the duergar marched her over to the base of one of the forge stairways. The caligni's noise had died off at some point, and the soldiers and guards filed back to their positions around camp. Many stared at her, expressions promising death. She returned the favor.

They thrust her before the horned beetle mount of the commanding duergar. Soldiers gathered, but their leader hollered in the duergar tongue and waved most of them away. This left a few guards at his back, the robe who'd downed her, and Gromir.

Akina called over to the other dwarf. "Would've brought a few kegs if I'd known you were holding a party. You've been rude, not introducing everyone."

This elicited a chuckle from the head duergar, who spoke in smooth Dwarven. "You may call me Commander Vaskegar." He gestured to the hairless, gray-clad woman. "You've met Ularna."

Ularna pressed fist to fist again, while Akina glowered. Vaskegar swept down off the beetle and handed its reins to an attendant. As he approached, she confirmed his armor *was* bone, linked and interlocking, possibly reinforced with bolts and plates on the inside. A bone circlet formed from what looked like ribs adorned his bald brow. A jawbone had been fixed atop this, rimmed with broad, flat-topped teeth.

"Nice crown," she said. "You king around these parts?"

He swept the piece off and held it up so the forge light turned it a ruddy orange. "Do you like it? I fashioned it from my father's remains after defeating him in armed combat."

"Bit different from how we honor our dead."

"True." He frowned. "You stick them pretty boxes and hide them away in worthless catacombs where they wither into dust."

"That's not—"

"And then you decorate your halls with their false faces and forever wonder if they approve of your every word and action for the rest of your haunted lives." He replaced the crown. "I know my father respected me in the end, finding I was the stronger of us. I know he died proud, and I honor him in return for the strength he bestowed on me."

He turned and sauntered away. His axe blades gleamed, seemingly formed from semi-translucent pink quartz, with deeper red veins working through them.

"Gromir."

At his name, the dwarf hopped over without delay. It sickened Akina to see him acting as a servant to this duergar. "Yes, Commander?"

Vaskegar turned his head enough to reveal the glint of one amused eye. "Is this her?"

"I, ah, that is to say . . ." Gromir deflated. "Yes, my lord."

"How did she get here?"

"I have absolutely no idea, my lord. I never would've conceived of this possibility."

"Your note was helpful," Akina said. "Selvia, too. Remember her? Pretty little thing, Gromir, especially with her throat slit."

Gromir paled, but Vaskegar's expression pinched. "Care to clarify?"

"She means Gollvara."

"Ah." That brought recognition to the duergar's eyes. "You killed her?"

"Nullick did, actually. After he told me your name." Akina shrugged. "Whatever deal you had with them, those lunatics got a little greedy."

Vaskegar scowled. "Seems I need to remind them of their place."

"I already did. You owe me one."

"Hm." The commander turned to Gromir. "Tell me again why Gollvara remained behind while you returned ahead of schedule? It seems your mishandling of our arrangement got her killed."

Gromir shuffled in place. "As I said before, my lord, expediency has ever been my merit. I didn't have time to arrange details on my end, so I left Gollvara with instructions to continue that farce of a business in my absence. I can't understand why she would've felt it necessary to do otherwise. Akina did not need to be here to facilitate this next stage."

Vaskegar's bone gauntlets ended in metal hooks on the knuckles, and he stroked these through his beard. "I suppose that will remain a mystery, won't it? Hers wasn't a deserving death, but few of us get any say on the when or where of our passing." He clasped hands before him and studied Akina. "Have you ever wished you could control your destiny?"

Akina snorted. "Oh. You're one of those."

"One of what?"

"The type who thinks they're destined for something. Figure you see yourself as a hero, chosen by Droskar to bring glory to the Darklands."

The commander's laugh rang out. "Of course, a dwarf would fix on the word *destiny*. It's such a grandiose and yet vague word. Promising you everything in glittering piles, while leaving plenty of room to collapse beneath the weight of your hubris. No, the word you should've focused on is *control*." His gauntlet creaked as he made a fist. "Absolute, undeniable control. Wouldn't that be a marvelous thing? It's a progression, you see." He scraped a knuckle-hook down the bridge of his nose. "We start believing glory is the ultimate goal, however we define that. Maybe through the people we rule or in the deeds we accomplish. Then we realize reaching glory requires power, in some form or another. It may come in strength of arms, in the sharpness of one's tongue, in the application of arcane knowledge—or a mixture of all these and more. So we all seek power, whether we admit it or not. Because why wouldn't we? Why shouldn't we?"

He unhooked one of the axes from his back and brought it around to test the edge with a thumb. "Most of us remain in this state our entire lives, trying to accrue power, losing it, regaining it, wielding it . . . And for a time, it might suffice, because we're only among others who crave and pursue the same thing. We're rather like blind mole rats, each trying to carve out the bigger, longer, broader tunnel through the filth."

"Want to hear what I did to a mole recently?" she asked.

He ignored her and continued on. Akina glanced around, seeing how the others took this. Gromir, in particular, looked fascinated, while Ularna held the same placidity as before. Did the woman ever blink?

"Here's what separates certain of us from the rest of the rabble." Vaskegar caught her chin in the top crook of an axe blade and lifted her eyes to his. "Control. When power is not controlled, it is wasted. Uncontrolled flames become a consuming fire. Uncontrolled waters become a drowning flood. Uncontrolled hammering on the anvil can shatter the piece."

She hacked and spat in his face. "Uncontrolled tongues become fleshy catapults. Am I learning yet?"

Vaskegar stilled as the wad of mucus tracked down one cheek. Then he eased the axe back into place in its straps. He wiped the spittle off his face with his thumb, and then popped the thumb into his mouth. Once he sucked it clean, he reached out and swiped his own saliva under both her eyes. She tried to pull away, but her captors held her firm.

"You struggle with control." He leaned in until his nose almost touched hers. "It rages just beneath your surface. A never-ending tempest threatening to shake you to pieces."

Akina scowled, disliking this stone-shattered bastard talking about her in such intimate terms. "Exactly how drunk is Gromir when he talks about me?"

Vaskegar's laugh boomed out again. "She has a fine spirit, Gromir. I commend you for desiring one who is obviously far beyond your grasp."

Gromir flinched. "Thank you, my lord?"

The commander studied Akina a little longer before pursing his lips. "You're a chaotic element here. Chaos can be entertaining, but it's also disruptive by nature. The sooner I remove you, the sooner progress can be restored."

As Vaskegar reached for his axes again, Gromir stuck himself in front of Akina and bowed.

"My lord, please reconsider. Akina isn't entirely without reason. Despite her brutish behavior, which I apologize for, she is canny and possesses strength we could use. Let me show her the grandeur of what will be accomplished here. She may be convinced to aid us."

Akina considered snapping a kick into Gromir's kidneys, but as his simpering stood between her and a beheading, she figured it wise to let him yammer on a bit.

"Oh?" Vaskegar raised shaggy eyebrows. "Despite your past efforts, you think you could influence her still?"

"At least let me try. I deser—" Gromir swallowed at the commander's warning look. "I respectfully request the chance, given my rather vital contributions to this effort."

"If you think you can contain her, it'd be my pleasure to see such a feat." Vaskegar shouted commands to his guards, who moved into position at the bottom of the nearest forge stairway. "Go on, then. Show her around. Explain."

Her captors shoved her forward after Gromir, who headed up the stairs. They stopped beneath the main arch which formed the stylized mouth of the dwarven face on this side. The forge blazed beyond, and for the first time, Akina got an idea of what Izthuri meant by the place being hungry. With the raging fires kept going by the elementals and casters, it felt like a living thing, seeking to consume anything thrown into its maw. At this angle, the giant anvil rose to Akina's chest, and looked more like a broad altar than any functional workstation. A row of lumpy objects lay on top, but Gromir stood between her and them.

At Gromir's indication, the guards released her and backed off a few paces. She noticed Ularna standing in the shadow of a column, but ignored her presence for the time. Instead, she jabbed a finger at the other dwarf.

"You've got ten breaths before they peel me off you."

He held hands up. "Akina, please, try to be reasonable. Are you so set on death that you'd force Vaskegar's hand before even trying to understand what's happening in this place?"

"What's to understand? You're working for the duergar and going to use my brother in some obscene ritual because this lord of yours has probably offered you all the power or wealth you want in exchange. Am I close? If so, let's skip to the part where I make you swallow your own teeth."

"There are two things you need to see before you make any rash decisions."

"Five breaths, Gromir."

He sighed. "Do you have any idea what this place is?"

"Dwarven ruins," she said. "I may not be a scrollsnake like you, but I can figure some things out on my own."

He pointed up. "But don't you see? Haven't you noticed? Yes, it's a fantastic set of ruins, worthy of a lifetime's study. But it isn't just any dwarven settlement. It's yours."

She squinted one eye. "Mine?"

He kept pointing, and she followed his gesture. Then she spotted it. There, just visible on the sloping brow of the dwarf's stone face, sat the Fairingot sigil, a rectangle with a blazing eye in the center. He singled out a few other carvings on the walls ringing them, carved into the stones forming the forge foundation.

"This is your family's original home," he said. "Your ancestry traces itself all the way back here. And your ancestors didn't just found this settlement; they ruled it. Your family comes from a noble bloodline!"

In spite of everything, the words sent a thrill through Akina. Yet she refused to be distracted. She crossed her arms and glared. "So?"

He looked taken aback. "What do you mean?"

"So what, Gromir? You think this changes anything? Maybe my family did come from here, but what's that matter now? Right *now*, you're betraying our people. Right *now*, I'm being threatened by this duergar you serve. Right *now*, my brother lies over there looking half dead. So what are you going to do *right now* to fix all this?"

He wrung his hands. "That's the second thing I need to show you." He stepped aside and beckoned her toward the anvil, but raised a finger as she got close. "Whatever you do, don't touch the altar. Truly, don't. It will kill you instantly."

She stepped forward and craned her neck as he waved to the items arranged on the anvil. She finally

could make out a skeleton, laid out from toe knuckles
to skull. A dwarven skeleton.

Words choked out of Gromir.

"This is . . . these are your mother's bones."

Chapter Twenty-Four
The Forge

Akina trembled in place and couldn't stop her fingers curling into fists. "If you ever wanted a quick death at my hands, Gromir, you've found the perfect words."

"Can you stop with the pointless threats for once and just listen?"

She moved closer, but he blocked the way. "Don't! I swear, you'll die the instant you touch the altar."

She started to grab for him, to throw him aside. Out of the corner of one eye, she saw Ularna's gray form slide into view. Her expression remained calm as she stared over at Akina, but it had an expectant edge, as if intrigued by what would happen if the dwarf made contact with the metal surface. That, more than Gromir's pleadings, held her back.

Stepping away, she eyed what Gromir claimed to be her mother's remains.

"Altar?" She thrust a shaking finger at the bones. "Why do you say that's my mother?"

Gromir straightened his robes and then spread his arms to indicate the whole of the ruins. "During your absence from Taggoret, while I worked under Jannasten, it remained my hope you'd return one day and that we'd pick up where we left off. To that end, I wanted to offer you a gift on your homecoming, something grand." He paced before the altar. "During my studies of arcane lore, I also dabbled in various historical archives and genealogies. In these, I found references to the Fairingots and traced them back as far as I could, cross-referencing them with other accounts of our people's earliest days. I compared these records to as many maps as I could access, double-checking depths, tunnel markings, and ancient settlement references. It took several years, but I at last believed I'd pinpointed one of the first, if not the very first, Fairingot settlement. I'd hoped to make the journey down here with you, but . . . well . . ."

He sighed. "When another year passed, I instead showed my research to Jannasten." A smile flicked across his face. "She was overjoyed, to say the least. A possible direct connection to her ancestors? Evidence that she descended from nobility? It was a more marvelous discovery than she'd ever dreamed. She wanted to see this place as soon as possible. At the same time, she wanted it kept secret until we confirmed its existence. I left the city on a supposed errand to visit clients in Highhelm, while she set up rumors about another of her lone surveying trips and followed a little later. We met at the gates beyond Davarn and came below together. The journey wasn't without peril, but suffice it to say we reached this place and found far more than we'd conceived waiting for us. I'd thought perhaps a few crumbling buildings or monuments might be left. To find an entire city relatively intact, and with the Fairingot sigil emblazoned about for anyone to see . . ."

He closed his eyes, as if reliving those first moments of discovery. Despite herself, Akina got caught up in the telling, imagining her mother stepping into this cavern and being the first Fairingot to gaze upon their ancestral home in untold centuries. She imagined Jannasten striding through the long-dead streets, seeing the empty homes, the temple murals, the circling walls.

"You explored the city," she said, "and then found this forge."

Gromir's eyes opened, and it shocked her to see tears glistening in them. "Yes. Of course, the size of it confounded us." He flourished at the monstrous forge. "What might the ancient Fairingots have crafted here? Or was it a center of worship for Torag? As we pondered all these possibilities, Janna laid a hand on this anvil." He cringed. "And the forge tore her soul straight from her body."

Akina stepped back, a sour taste rising to her tongue. "How's that possible?

He wiped a hand over his face. "I didn't know at first. I only knew she lay dead and I lacked the power to bring her back. Then the forge awoke. Eldritch fires burned within it, and I heard the clamor of workers all around, saw fell spirits speaking in strange languages. A rift opened over the hearth and within it . . ." The knob of his throat bobbed. "Darkness. Then the spell ended and I fled. In fear. In shame. In despair, believing I'd caused her death in bringing her here.

I fled, yes, half-blind with grief, and tried to make it back to the surface. On the way, though, Vaskegar found me." He looked over to where the duergar commander stood alternating between speaking with his soldiers and watching the pair from afar. "He's a deposed lord, you know. Once wielded great influence throughout Hagegraf." He shook his head. "Can you imagine rising to that level of power? Being one of the most important figures in the duergar capital itself? He commanded the fate of thousands."

Akina aimed a flat look his way.

Gromir coughed. "Anyway, eventually some political manipulations and unfortunate military losses toppled him from favor. He was relegated to leading a number of patrols throughout the wilds—a shameful role for one so mighty. But he found me. His warriors captured me, and I thought myself a dead dwarf."

"You told him about this place," Akina guessed. "You bartered for your life."

"I told him everything. What more did I have to lose? He brought me back here and proved more intellectually aggressive than I would've guessed. He had several mages under his dwindled command and they discerned more about the nature and purpose of the forge. It's nothing short of an arcane device that transforms a soul into raw energy, using it to open a channel to other realms and make the power there accessible for—well, any number of ends depending on the operator's intent. We think it originally connected to Torag's realm, but became disconnected from that specific location in the time it's lain here in disuse." He waved a fist. "We couldn't get it to work, though. Nothing we tried summoned the energies or portal I'd seen. He even sacrificed one of his own soldiers on the altar—for that's what it is—but the forge remained dark."

Akina glanced at the anvil. "Then why'd you say it'd kill me to touch it?"

"We believe your mother's contact with the altar imprinted an echo of her soul within the construction. An alignment of Fairingot blood with the dormant energies of this place. As such, we believe it now requires another Fairingot to operate."

"Brakisten." She looked to her brother's rumpled form over by the pavilion. "You brought Brakisten as a sacrifice to get this thing working for Vaskegar?"

Gromir tugged the tip of his nose. "I didn't intend to get it working. I came to destroy it."

Akina frowned. "What?"

"When our initial efforts proved fruitless, Vaskegar realized we lacked too much insight into how the forge had originally been built and operated. There should've been a sort of arcane key, a way to unlock the forge without exposing the wielder to its deadly energies, but we couldn't figure out what it was. When he learned about Brakisten, he wanted me to bring him down here right away, to see if his soul could awaken it again."

Akina jerked his way. "You sold out my brother?"

Gromir waved off the idea. "I kept Brakisten alive this long by arguing such an attempt would be a waste. If we couldn't figure out the process within the span of his death, then we would've lost the only opportunity to harness the forge's power. I suggested the answers might lie in various dwarven archives, and that I could seek these out if only they would let me live and bestow on me a portion of the forge's power should he harness it. After some debate, he agreed, swore me to Droskar's service, and then let me return to the surface."

"You swore to Droskar's service!"

"In name only! To give myself enough time to figure out how to repair this disaster. Vaskegar plans to use the power of the forge to overrun Taggoret. Then he'd establish a power base for himself there and keep expanding, fueling his army with whatever weapons the forge can provide. Do you think I'd let that happen, knowing what he intended?"

"So he just let you go?"

"Of course not. Selvia—Gollvara, that is—and a couple others came along, disguised to keep an eye on me and ensure I held up my side of the bargain."

"The ones who helped you snatch Brakisten?"

Gromir nodded. "They also acted as the occasional go-betweens, watching the shop or escorting me back down here to confer with Vaskegar directly. Fortunately, that was rarely required. But if, at any point, I deviated from my efforts on Vaskegar's behalf, Gollvara was poised to kill me. I still wanted to understand Jannasten's death, so I played along, searching and studying and . . ."

His shoulders slumped. "I found it. A spellkey that would allow us to operate the forge under controlled conditions. I kept my discovery hidden from Gollvara for several months, feeding tales of delays and dead-ends, but I could tell she grew suspicious. It'd only be a matter of time before she tortured the information out of me and Vaskegar had all he needed to master the construction." He met her eyes for the first time since he'd begun his explanation. "And then you came home.

Gollvara argued that, with two Fairingots now available, Brakisten no longer needed to be spared. She pushed me to deliver him here so Vaskegar could further his experiments, not knowing I possessed the spellkey. Nor did I expect her to lure you here afterward."

"And you did bring him."

"I did, but only after I realized I could use him to end this. I only gave Vaskegar part of the spellkey and convinced him I was necessary for the rest, claiming at least one true dwarven operator was required. I planned to use Brakisten's soul to activate the forge, but divert the power and use it to resurrect Jannasten. Then I would release the energies, let it tumble into chaos, and wreck the forge for good, escaping with her in the wake of its destruction to return to you, triumphant." He sighed. "A foolhardy and desperate plan, I know, but it's all I had."

Akina struggled to absorb his tale, searching for further deception or hidden truths. Could Gromir really just be a victim of his own horrible mistakes and circumstances, or had he played a more vile part in her mother's death and now tried to conceal his hunger for the forge's power? Could he really destroy it? Did it absolutely require a soul sacrificed to its flames?

As she thought through it all, Ularna once more glided into view, seeming to study the forge while drifting in and out of earshot.

"What's her role?" Akina asked, gesturing.

Gromir plucked yellow hairs from his beard. "She's just one of Vaskegar's lieutenants, far as I can tell. Doesn't talk much, and I've not been too keen on the few conversations we've had."

She fell silent again, gaze drifting from the forge to her mother's bones to the duergar and elementals all around them. Gromir shuffled in place.

"Akina? Say something. Please."

She glared at him. "I can't forgive you for this."

He exhaled. "I don't suppose I expected you to, really, if you ever found out. Though I'd hoped to avoid telling you."

"And make yourself out as the hero, hm? Never mind that your 'rescue' involved sacrificing my brother!"

He looked away. "You can't make me feel more anguish than I've already suffered."

She popped her neck to one side. "Oh, I doubt that."

He held out his hands, pleading. "If you work with me, we can still get out of this. I'll tell Vaskegar you've agreed to help, and he'll let you live long enough for us to use Brakisten as I planned. Then we can escape together in the aftermath."

Akina stared at Jannasten's bones for another minute. Then she roused herself. "I'll help. But I won't let you sacrifice Brakisten."

"What do you mean?"

"You'll use me instead."

His eyes widened. "No! Absolutely not."

"It's either that, or I tell Vaskegar how you're planning to betray him, and we all die."

"But Brakisten is—"

"If you say anything that includes the words *worthless*, *hopeless*, or *doomed*, I'll bite your tongue out. I won't let my brother die for you or me."

Gromir's lips worked as he tried to summon further arguments; then he threw up his hands. "Very well. If that's what you wish, the least I can do is respect it. But won't you reconsider? I did all this to try and give you a better life, and now you're just throwing it away?"

"I'm not throwing anything away. I'll die with a purpose—keeping the duergar from stealing this power." She jutted a chin down at Vaskegar. "Go kiss his ass a bit more and convince him to kill me."

Chapter Twenty-Five
Perspective

Y ou realize she's obviously attempting a ploy of some
sort," Vaskegar said.

Bound again and under guard across the ring from
Brakisten, Akina listened to the argument. Gromir and
Vaskegar stood well within earshot, an indication the
commander didn't care whether she overheard.

"My lord," said Gromir, "Akina has always been the
most earnest person I've ever known." He glanced her
way. "Perhaps she errs in that somewhat, but whenever
she truly believes something, she charges ahead and
sees it through. Guile is not in her nature."

"It's been ten years since you saw her last," said
Vaskegar. "Even after she returned, you had barely any
time together before you came scrambling back here.
How much do you really know who she is now, Gromir?
How much did you really know her before she left?"

Gromir shifted in place. "We all change sooner or
later, my lord. Even you changed when you became an
outcast from Hagegraf."

Vaskegar cocked his head, and Akina half-expected him to attack Gromir then and there. Yet the commander shrugged as if it didn't matter. Of course—control. It wouldn't do to overreact to a tiny insult.

"And yes, I admit, there are aspects of her that have shifted. But not this." Gromir leaned in slightly. "She loves her brother. She's already lost her mother, and she'd rather die than see the rest of her family sacrificed before her eyes. If I could, I'd place myself in her stead, but only a Fairingot can—"

"Yes, yes." Vaskegar inspected his gauntlet hooks. "However, I cannot allow her to potentially disrupt our progress at such a delicate moment."

Gromir squared his slim shoulders. "Then I cannot allow you to complete the ceremony."

The commander stilled, eyes glinting in the forge light. "You dare?"

The dwarf half-smiled, as if even he disbelieved his audacity. "Without me, my lord, the forge will remain dormant. All your work will be for nothing."

Vaskegar turned to look off into the distance and held silent for several minutes. Akina barely caught his mutter when it came. "I will consider it. Now go before I kill you where you stand."

Gromir bowed and walked off, robes kicking up dust. Akina watched him go, wondering at the strength of his feelings for her still—putting his own life on the line to fight for her final request.

Once he'd gone, Vaskegar strode over to Akina. He folded arms across his broad chest.

"You want to take your brother's place. Why?"

Akina squared up with him. "Love for kin and kind. You wouldn't—"

"Wouldn't understand?" Vaskegar's laugh ruffled his beard. "You think duergar don't grasp the concept of love? You think our hearts are nothing but ash?" He caressed one of his crown's tooth-tines. "Oh, love is well known to us. It's one of many emotions we've conquered."

"Conquered?"

He thumped a fist against his breastplate. "All emotions must be tamed like wild beasts, lest they devour you. Love, fear, fury . . . these are powerful, but their power can be used against you. Better to leash them and use them to your own ends."

"Am I supposed to be learning again?"

He chuckled. "Can you prove me wrong? Trying to bluster past another's insights often means they see deeper than you wish to admit. What good has your flailing rage achieved? What good does aimless love accomplish? You have to anchor yourself to a greater purpose."

She tilted her head Brakisten's way. "I want to spare my brother's life. That's enough purpose for me."

"Even if I believe that, you think he'll thank you for it? He's obviously unworthy of the effort; you blind yourself to his many flaws, thinking a sacrifice will somehow fix yours." Vaskegar shifted one of the axes on his back. "Well, I can admire your devotion, at least. It's what defines us as duergar."

"I'm nothing like you."

"You like to think we're so different because our loyalties lie with different realms. Yet at our cores, we're more similar than you'll ever admit. If anything separates us, it's that we duergar are honest enough to accept reality. Droskar demands all from us, and we give it to him willingly. We accept that life is toil from beginning to end, unlike you and other surface races who try to distract themselves with shiny trinkets and useless accolades."

"Endless toil, hm? Sounds pretty pointless."

"Nothing is pointless. It may simply take certain things longer to come to fruition, or for you to realize what the point is in the first place. For the duergar, the only worthwhile results are those borne of our cease-less efforts."

She humphed. "Sounds like obsession, not devotion."

"What distinction is there in the end?" He waved to Brakisten. "Go. Talk to your brother. See if it makes any difference."

Vaskegar muttered to her guards in the duergar tongue, and they held back a few paces as she trudged over to Brakisten. He looked up as she plopped down beside him.

"My head hurts."

"Not surprising," she said. "Gromir says he got you down here with a string of persuasive charms. Once you got here, the duergar decided clubbing you uncon-scious would be just as effective. And more fun."

Brakisten winced as he studied the blazing forge. "At first, I thought I was having another nightmare vision. I wish I'd been right."

With her arms bound behind her, she could only bump a shoulder the forge's way. "Think this is what you were seeing all these years?"

"I'd bet a round on it."

"But how?"

Brakisten frowned. "Gromir talked to me a bit on the way down. I don't recall much, but I do remember him wondering the same thing. My dreams started right around when he began searching for this place. He thinks these ruins—this forge—*wanted* to be found. And once someone started paying attention to its existence, it reached out in return. He called it a . . . a resonance in me, seeing as we've got old blood here." He shivered. "Said I should've told him the details of what I was experiencing sooner, how he might've been able to help me make sense of it."

She scowled. "He's just trying to place his own guilt on you."

Brakisten looked crestfallen. "Maybe. But I sure as spit could've done better by myself and our family. I could've chosen different, but I didn't." He raised his gaze to hers and snuffled. "Forgive me, Kina?"

"Only if you do the same for me."

"Bad time to hold a grudge. You're my elder sister after all."

"In any way that matters?"

He coughed a laugh. "In every way that matters."

They fell silent for a minute until Brakisten roused again.

"Listen. I've heard them talking. Mostly their dark chatter, but I've caught a few things here and there. I know once they use this forge for whatever they think it does, they're aiming for Taggoret."

She frowned in thought. "Gromir mentioned Taggoret, too. Bet they're planning to come up the tunnels under the city."

"If you get the chance, you've got to get free and warn them. Don't worry about me. I'll just slow you down."

"I'm not leaving." She hastily added, "Not without you." A technically true statement.

He blinked, first in confusion and then suspicion. "What aren't you telling me?"

She was saved from answering by Gromir's approach, accompanied by Ularna. The dwarf bobbed his head to each of them and swallowed hard.

"It's time. We're ready."

Chapter Twenty-Six
Sacrifice

Ondorum stumbled on an unseen rock and caught himself against a wall. Only after he'd gathered his breath did he realize the formation was made of worked stone rather than raw earth. He leaned back to see the wall had fallen in on itself to his left, with mounded buildings and squat towers visible beyond.

Had he arrived? It seemed so, but he found himself at a loss as to where to go next. Izthuri hadn't noted any specific landmark he should aim for once he made it.

Chittering echoed behind him, followed by the scrape of chitinous legs on rock. He cast a look back, frowning. He thought he'd outdistanced the insect enough to dissuade further pursuit. Did the creature track him by scent? Or could it sense the vibrations of his steps, even as he tried to lighten his tread? Either way, it appeared hunger drove the beast to chase after whatever delights his blood contained, even across such a distance.

Clambering over the tumbled wall, he hurried along the road beyond, uncertain where to go within the ruins. He tried to track his turns, but his ignorance of the area's layout as well as his haste in fleeing his hunter served to quickly confuse him. Which direction did he face? Had he already gone down this side street? The empty buildings, made from uniform stone, all looked too similar, and he couldn't gain enough higher ground to get a better perspective.

A hiss caught his ear. At first, he shifted aside and crouched against a wall, fearing the insect had caught up with him. But when a black-clad figure shifted into sight instead, he relaxed, if slightly. The person's rags and glimpses of bone-white skin marked him or her as one of Izthuri's people; but he'd long ago learned that just because two people belonged to the same species didn't mean they could be depended on to extend the same civilities.

The caligni crept closer, and the hiss resolved into, "Un-dum?" The caligni showed empty hands—a sign of peace, the monk hoped.

Ondorum moved from his shelter and bowed, palms pressed together. The caligni mirrored the motion and then wriggled fingers at him and hissed more words he couldn't understand. When he tried to mime his confusion, the caligni put a hand flat about four feet in the air, scowled, and then pretended to swing a heavy object.

Akina. Ondorum nodded and pointed all about with a questioning look. The caligni waved for him to follow. They passed through several sets of walls and down a long, curving road until Ondorum was ushered inside a random building. Izthuri sat inside with a handful of other caligni. She leaped up at Ondorum's arrival and raised her black blade in salute. He looked around for Akina, then frowned at her absence.

Izthuri must've recognized his consternation, for she hissed, "Duergar take her. At forge."

Forge? He spread his hands. *Where?*

She looked over at the others. "My tribe fight. My tribe die. I show, but they not join."

Ondorum nodded. Of course, if one purpose of coming here was to keep her tribe safe, why should she expose them to combat?

Izthuri guided him back out into the city and deeper into its network of blocky constructions and ringed walls. A glow sat near what he gauged to be the center of the ruins, bright enough to cast the cavern roof into shadowy contrast and bring out some of the settlement's natural colorations. Green stone and black cobbles formed much of the structural foundations, though he imagined it had boasted far more decorative embellishments during its heyday.

As they approached, the glow flickered and then flared, ten times brighter than before. White and blue rays shot through every chink and gap of stone around them, turning the gloom into a false day. Izthuri cried out and flung herself into a nearby corner, shielding her eyes from the glare. Ondorum broke into a run, fearing he'd come too late.

Akina stood before the anvil as Vaskegar and Gromir finalized arrangements around the forge. She stared at her mother's bones as if their arrangement might hold a hidden message. Gromir had said that by the time Vaskegar had marched him back here, just a day or two after Jannasten's death, her body had decomposed entirely, slumped against the anvil. They'd tried using her remains as a focus for activating the forge, but without any soul left attached, it didn't make any difference.

Was this her fate, then? Not to be buried in her family's catacombs, but left as a heap for vermin to nibble on? She looked over to where Brakisten sat propped up against a stone column. While Vaskegar had accepted the exchange of intended sacrifices, he'd also ordered her brother kept nearby as a contingency.

Gromir assured her he had an escape route already planned for when he triggered the forge's destructions. And he whispered a promise on his own ancestors that he'd see Brakisten returned to Taggoret, and would nurse him back to health whether he wanted it or not.

She refocused on the altar. A single touch. After so many battlefields and narrow escapes, that's all it took to end her. Just one touch of an immobile object to rip her soul from her flesh and send her into the afterlife. It seemed . . . a relief. Vaskegar had mocked her with his talk of power and control and destiny, but she now took such control into her hands, accepting her death in this place, this moment.

She would do it as thanks to Torag for guiding her this far, even when she'd been too blind to see it. She would do it as thanks to her mother for inspiring her to seek out more in life, even if she'd done so without realizing they'd never see each other again. She would do it in thanks to Ondorum, who'd treated her with far more care and compassion than she ever deserved. And she would do it just to know her life ended with meaning, rather than as a random, senseless death.

"Are we ready?" Vaskegar asked.

Gromir inspected their preparations. He'd told the duergar he could keep the forge from killing Akina all at once, draining just enough of her soul to power it while keeping her alive to use multiple times . . . or at least give them the chance to see the forge in operation and divine how to operate it independent of the Fairingots.

The three of them stood in front of the anvil, with Ularna off beside Brakisten. Vaskegar's sorcerers stood ready according to whatever instructions Gromir had given them. The earth and fire elementals had been withdrawn, leaving the forge empty and dark. The rest of the duergar gathered below, except for a handful of guards who remained at their posts, alert for any caligni interruptions.

The forge ring gained an expectant air as the assembly prepared to see the culmination of their months' worth of effort. Her touch, her death, would start it all.

Gromir nodded. "We are, my lord. All glory to the Ashen Forge."

Vaskegar grunted and swept an arm out to Akina. "My lady? If you'd be so kind . . ."

Akina breathed deep and marched past without even a snide look his way. He didn't deserve the effort. Soon enough, his precious forge would be just another ruin among the rest. She kept her gaze fixed on the Fairingot sigil at the altar's base. In this moment, she should be fully focused on her family. Yet as she stretched out her hand, she found her final thoughts turning to

Ondorum. She was glad he wasn't here to see her go in such an ignoble fashion. Still, she wished she might've at least died by his side.

She pressed a palm against the anvil.

The metal lay cold beneath her touch. She flinched, not knowing what to expect. Burning hooks to latch onto her soul and drag it into the construction? Blinding pain to overwhelm all her senses? A glow for her to soar toward, leaving her body behind?

Nothing. The anvil remained dead, while not so much as a spark flickered within the forge itself. Akina pressed harder, as if she could force the spell to activate. Had Gromir done something wrong? Did he miscalculate how long it took for the magic to kick in?

"Excellent," Vaskegar said. "Thank you for your help."

Akina spun around. Gromir wore a confounded look, but the duergar commander looked more smug than ever.

"I don't understand," Gromir said.

Vaskegar sneered. "Like you, my mages pride themselves on their skill and intelligence. Unlike you, they are entirely loyal to me. While you dithered about with that spellkey nonsense, they studied the runes on the forge and determined which ones linked specific bloodlines to its operations. Since then, we've been laboriously eliminating those runes by any means possible."

"You could have brought the whole cavern down on your heads!" Gromir cried.

Vaskegar shrugged. "An acceptable risk. Not long before you came down, their divinations suggested the forge had finally been cleansed of the Fairingot taint and could be blocked from future imprintings. However, we couldn't be entirely sure, and what good is a weapon that could be snatched away with a touch and turned against you?" He bowed to Akina. "You've provided the final test. The forge is no longer anchored to your bloodline, and is now mine and mine alone. Completely under control. Now the real work can begin."

"No!" Akina said. "This is my home. I won't let you!"

She threw herself at him, ready to gouge his eyes out and rip his head off. Ularna intercepted her, gray robes making her look like a stone pillar suddenly placed between them. Akina battered at her, but the duergar knocked the blows aside and shot palm-heel strikes up her chest. Each hit staggered her back until a final strike snapped into her forehead. Her sense of balance swirled and her legs no longer held her weight.

Even as she fell, Gromir plucked throwing axes from his bandolier and made to fling them. Faster than Akina could've believed, Vaskegar whipped one of his own axes from his back and slashed across Gromir's chest. The dwarf collapsed, trying to hold in the blood and guts spilling from the gash. A disbelieving moan escaped him.

Vaskegar strode up to the altar and caressed it as one might a prize hound. With one arm, he swept Jannasten's bones away, sending them clattering all about. He gestured to the guards by Brakisten. They hauled the dwarf to his feet and dragged him over. Brakisten whimpered and jerked, struggling weakly.

"I just want to go home. Akina? I can't . . . please, I just want to go home. I'm so sorry."

She tried to reach for him. Ularna stepped on her ankle, grinding it against the stones, and Akina's leg went numb.

"Wait," Akina gasped. "You don't need him anymore."

"Not entirely true," said Vaskegar. "While any soul will now do, a soul is still necessary to begin the process. Why would I sacrifice my own followers while I have two perfectly viable options? And while I could certainly still use you, your brother is hardly lucid enough to grasp the significance of this moment. I want you to watch and despair for your people."

He grabbed Brakisten's tunic and threw him on top of the altar. Brakisten screamed as the gauntlet knuckle-hooks dug into his collarbone. He twisted his head to the side and his terror-filled eyes met Akina's. He flopped an arm over, trying to reach.

Akina stretched a hand out, but her legs still refused to obey her. "Brak! No, please, stop!" She braced to drag herself over, but Ularna grabbed her elbow and twisted. Agony popped through her bones and locked her in place.

Vaskegar drew an axe and poised it over her brother's neck. "Droskar, accept this offering and use it to further your glory."

He brought the axe down. Brakisten's head rolled off the anvil while his body twitched on top. Akina's scream drowned out all other noise, until a greater roar blasted it aside.

The forge woke.

The whole platform shuddered, and with a sweep of wind, the hearth burst into fiery life. The flames burned white and blue and black as they roiled within the forge housing. Twisting columns of flame erupted from the top while liquid fire splashed out from the gaps in the sides, forcing duergar to rush back to avoid being engulfed in the inferno. The roar and crackle deafened for a moment before subsiding, and the forge raged like a barely contained beast. A hungry one.

The anvil glowed white-hot under Brakisten, and she sensed his soul being pumped down into it, used as fuel for the forge. Vaskegar didn't seem affected by the molten glare. He raised his hands in exultation as a wave of heat blasted out, drying Akina's eyes and cracking her lips while basting her in sweat.

Above the enormous hearth, the air rent and widened into an obsidian portal limned with tongues of red flame. Another searing wind blew through the area, stinking of sulfur and char, with a saltier fetor suggestive of unwashed bodies. Anguished screams rang through her mind, accompanied by a horrendous, unceasing pounding, the clashing of metal on metal.

From her perspective on the ground, the portal ringed Vaskegar's head, crowning him in horrid glory. He turned and pointed to where Gromir lay dying, and his voice rumbled across the ringing walls. "You swore yourself to Droskar. Whether you ever meant to fulfill your oath, he still heard your words as a binding compact. The Dark Smith measures the works of all those who toil in his name, and metes out punishment to those who fail to live up to his standards." He snapped a hand back at the portal. "Now let your soul be weighed and found wanting by the fires of the Ashen Forge itself."

Blood smeared the stones as Gromir started to crawl away, as if to dump himself over the near edge and escape Vaskegar's wrath.

Motion within the portal caught Akina's eye. At first, she thought it some form of snake slithering forth, but then she realized it was a chain. With a life of its own, a many-barbed chain of black iron with a large hook on the end wove through the air. It wavered for a moment before homing in on Gromir. The dwarf screamed as the chain launched at him, dragging feet upon feet of its length after. The hook sank into his chest and yanked him into the air. It spun him about, the chain whipping and wrapping over him until the end whisked from the portal, trailing another hook. By the time Gromir dropped back to the ground in a heap, the chain had completely obscured his body.

The air quavered with a bestial growl. The chain clanked, sagging heavy from Gromir's limbs as he stamped and shoved to his feet. The metal coils fell away from his head, revealing a hairless lump of scab and charred flesh.

Akina cried out in horror. "Gromir!"

Gromir's eyes flared open, and Akina recoiled to see them gone as flat and gray as ash. He opened his mouth and black smoke billowed from his throat and nostrils, while the skin crackled and glowed orange, as if he burned from within. His roar sent ash billowing into the air, and the trailing ends of the hooked chain writhed back over his head, still possessed of a foul animation.

Vaskegar turned to his men and gestured to the transformed dwarf. "Behold the Forge Spurned! The fate of all those who fail Droskar in this life and the next. Behold the power with which Droskar gifts us, that we may march upon the mightiest city and bring death to any who defy us."

The duergar replied with a rousing chorus. Their shouts of worship continued as the portal disgorged another chained, smoking form. A second Forge Spurned stepped onto the hearth, and then down to join Gromir, who stood by the commander. More of the creatures strode from the rift in the forge, until a dozen packed the platform. As each spawn of the Ashen Forge joined their ranks, the duergar raised their voices higher.

A last Forge Spurned emerged, and a brief lull intervened. Akina held her breath with the duergar, waiting to see what horror might appear next.

Then the portal began to grow . . .

Ondorum watched the events at the forge in dismay, feeling helpless and insignificant in the face of their foes. The guards at the gate had turned their backs to him to watch the spectacle. They cheered with the rest as hideous creatures of chain and smoke issued forth from the gateway the duergar commander had summoned. Akina sprawled before the anvil altar, a spot of shadow within the forge's unending blaze.

Even if he rushed in now, in these moments of distraction as the duergar reveled in their ceremony, what could he accomplish? Likely, they'd both be cut down and the forge would churn out more living weapons for the duergar to employ without opposition.

Suddenly, the portal swelled to at least twenty feet in diameter. A giant metal foot thrust through, striking the platform with quaking force, followed by a boiler-shaped body as round as it was tall. An amalgamation of piping, bellows, and plates staggered into the space between the hearth and anvil, its stunted arms ending in levered spikes. The pig-like head on top held orange-glowing eyes and nostrils. When it opened its mouth, the flames boiling in the back of its throat cast rows of razor teeth into contrast.

A similar construct followed, and the earth trembled beneath their plodding steps as they lumbered to either side of the forge, then leaped to crash to the ground. The impact dropped dozens of duergar to their hands and knees, and forced Ondorum to cling to the threshold he peered through while ancient stone crumbled around him.

The duergar commander strode to the edge of the forge platform. He waved at the constructs, and as one they turned to face the duergar assembly. The soldiers shouted anew, and the commander's cry reached even Ondorum's ears.

"This is absolute control! This is just the first harvest of the fruit of our labors. With the blessing of the Dark Smith, we will drive the dwarves from their dens and claim our rightful place in their stead. This is the strength with which we will rule uncontested!"

Ondorum groaned. He at last recognized the crumpled form on the blazing anvil as Akina's brother. Too late to save one life, but if he waited much longer, they could sacrifice her as well. He had to try and get Akina away, even if it meant both their deaths. He slipped out from hiding, preparing to rush and disable the guards while the rest of the duergar remained distracted.

That's when the rust-devouring insect raced past him, chittering reaching a keening pitch as it dashed for the forge.

Chapter Twenty-Seven
Worthy Opponents

Hope had died, and Akina waited to follow in its wake. Ularna had left her lying before the altar as she followed her master to stand before the duergar troops, reveling in their god's affirmation. Akina didn't count as even the slightest threat to their plans. Nothing she did would ever matter. If anything, she'd be slaughtered like her brother, turned into raw fuel for the forge.

Numb, she stared up at the horrors Brakisten's death had conjured. She recognized the constructs now under Vaskegar's control. Scanderigs. She'd often been told of them as a child, when her mother would tease her with spook tales meant to frighten younglings into behaving. Never had she dreamed of actually seeing these forgefiends brought to repulsive life.

The scanderigs faced the forge, eyes and mouths blazing. Then their vast bellies split across the middle, revealing a second maw of spiked teeth, within which blazed an independent forge fire. Embers and ash spewed forth as the forgefiends bellowed at the portal from which they'd come.

Then screams echoed around the forge ring, breaking through her despair and inspiring her to sit up enough to see the cause. A bronze-shelled insect the size of a large wolf skittered toward one of the scanderigs. A number of the duergar turned to the disturbance, weapons readied, but then jumped back, faces twisted in horror as they let the beast scuttle straight past.

Vaskegar's dark face purpled near to black as he screamed, "Destroy it, you fools!"

Duergar converged on the insect, but it had already reached the scanderig and brushed feathery antennae across its lower bulk. Rust raced up the forgefiend's body, consuming one of its stumpy legs and the gnashing maw in its huge belly. A vast pile of glowing coals scattered across the ground, burying the insect as well as the duergar who'd tried to cut it down. The scanderig wavered on a single remaining leg—and then toppled to smash into the side of the forge housing. The roof and wall cracked and crumpled inward beneath the construct's weight. The portal to the Ashen Forge flickered, then died, though the anvil continued to glow and the purple-blue flames of the forge itself flared brighter, as if straining to be released.

The ruined scanderig thrashed about, casting rock and flames and slag metal across the camp. Chaos broke through the duergar ranks. Soldiers scattered as Vaskegar shouted to try and restore order. He leaped to the ground and strode through them, grabbing fleeing soldiers and striking them down, crying for them to regain their senses. All the while, his sorcerers wove gleaming shields of magic about the damaged forge, trying to contain its fluctuating energies. Gouts of flame struck the barriers they summoned, burning them away almost as fast as they could be conjured. Akina remained where she sat, mind detached from her body as she waited for the forge fires to break free and consume them all.

A figure landed on the platform beside her, and she found herself staring up at Ondorum.

"You can't be here," she said. "I must already be dead."

Despite the tension lining his angled features, he smiled and offered a hand. Then he spoke in a gravelly voice she hadn't heard in far too long.

"Not yet."

She gawped as she let him drag her upright. His touch loosened the knots and twists Ularna had inflicted on her muscles, and strength flushed through her. "Right. Not dead. I'm dreaming, because you just spoke."

"Ever observant, Akina." He pulled her toward a set of stairs. "Also observe that we should be going."

She spotted Vaskegar still bellowing for order and snatched her arm away. "No. We finish this here."

"Wait—"

Hurrying to the bottom of the stairs, she grabbed up a fallen axe and sought the duergar commander. Before she could take a step his way, Ularna interposed herself.

Akina raised her weapon. "Fine, I'll start with you."

The duergar looked bored, as if Akina wasn't worth the effort. Akina lashed out, but the other woman evaded as she had before. After another frustrated hack, Akina knew she'd already left herself exposed.

Yet as the duergar woman poised to strike her down again, Ondorum bulled between them and parried the hits, turning punches and palms aside like one might swat flies away. He lashed out with a kick and Ularna slipped back, letting his foot whiff past inches from her face.

He took up a defensive stance, fists cocked at the wrists. Ularna studied him for a moment. Fascination burned in her eyes, the first real emotion Akina had seen from the woman. She would've preferred the previous disinterest.

Ularna pulled back and bowed, fist to fist. To Akina's amazement, Ondorum returned the gesture, though with open palms.

"Go," he told Akina. "Do what you must."

Ondorum and Ularna launched at each other, becoming a gray blur of fists and feet. Akina was tempted to watch the fight, but realized they had limited time before the duergar recovered and concentrated on containing their captives. She spotted Vaskegar and furious heat flooded her, soothing aches and quickening muscles. He hadn't seemed to notice her yet, and she headed for him. But another figure landed in the way. The noise of clashing chains jarred Akina's skull as Gromir stood before her. The mutilated dwarf moaned as he pounded toward her, hooks swerving around his head.

Akina backed up, belly chilling at the sight. "Gromir, it's me."

The smoke surging from his mouth and nostrils thickened and darkened. He came on, chained limbs thrashing. She struck a fist with the axe, and the weapon whined as the chain deflected the edge. She tried to tell herself the dwarf had been taken beyond salvation, that she fought Gromir's shell, controlled by Droskar or a foul spirit from the Ashen Forge. She reared for a blow to his exposed head, but one of the hooks lashed out and knocked the axe down so it ricocheted off a shoulder. The two hooks then joined the fight, snapping out at her, clanging off her helm and breastplate as they sought to dig into her flesh. One snagged on a sleeve and jerked her about. Another narrowly missed stabbing her through the eye and caught under the rim of her helmet instead. The leather strap under her chin snapped, and her ram's helm tumbled away.

A hook snaked around her foot and yanked her down. Gromir's ashen eyes turned to burning coals as he dragged her closer, and his chain-wrapped fists rose to pummel her into the ground.

As they traded blows and blocks, Ondorum marveled at the duergar he faced, and realized she must've trained in a similar manner to him, learning to use the body itself as a unified weapon. He'd never realized duergar followed monastic paths, but how else to explain their rivaled styles as they flowed back and forth, dodging one another's kicks, letting bone-cracking punches shoot past each other's heads as they spun and stepped and whirled around one another.

For her part, the duergar looked intrigued. She tested his defenses with an avalanche of blows from all sides, then grounded herself and let him attack, fending off one strike after another with subtle movements. Neither of them gained nor gave ground.

Then, from one step to the next, she vanished. Ondorum's blow snapped through empty space. An unseen fist cracked against his wounded shoulder. He stumbled, but recovered the instant after. The duergar monk reappeared, now with the tiniest smile shading her otherwise calm expression.

A worthy opponent indeed. In any other time or place, even with one of her kind, he would've preferred to delay the confrontation, to confer with her, learn what her masters taught and how she perceived the world, and compare thoughts on the methods of ki channeling. Only then would they meet for a mortal exchange, having imparted one another's lessons and insights to ensure that at least the knowledge survived with the victor to be passed on to new students.

But this day afforded no such luxury, and Ondorum struggled to discern the most expedient way to disengage and rejoin Akina. The duergar held the advantage of being well-rested and unwounded, while he drew straight from his ki and the dregs of his physical strength to keep going. If the fight went too long, her endurance alone would overcome him. By the confident look in her eyes, she recognized this as well, and intended to extend the bout as long as necessary.

He rooted himself and let her next punch past his guard. The force rippled across his chest, but he absorbed the worst of it and grabbed her wrist, twisting to break. She flipped fully to follow the tension, slipping from his grasp as she did, but his kick connected with her hip right as she landed. She skidded backward a few feet. As she recovered, she noted the dusty footprint on her robe, almost blending perfectly. Another smile, another bow, and she strode in to resume the duel.

They'd turned so her back was to the forge, and she didn't see the flames boiling higher from the damaged mechanism. The largest surge of fire yet billowed from the forge and struck a shimmering barrier several duergar sorcerers fought to maintain. They collapsed, and the shield they'd woven vanished.

Ondorum threw himself backward into a braced crouch, arm raised to shield himself. The other monk paused, puzzled at the odd maneuver, until the suddenly uncontained flames tore through the ring like an explosion. The blast knocked her aside and shook the whole area, throwing the world into black-and-white relief.

An explosion staggered Gromir and spun him around. A lengthy piece of shrapnel embedded in his stomach, and the chain around Akina's ankle went limp. She waited for him to fall, but he just stared at the metal bar protruding from his gut. He gripped it in both hands and began hauling it out of his crackling flesh. Glowing embers drizzled from the wound, the edges charring and sealing over even as she watched.

Akina scrambled to her feet and lurched away before he recovered. Ondorum appeared at her side once more, shouting for them to go. She spared precious seconds to spot and scoop up her helm, slamming it over her head as they sprinted through the disoriented duergar. They passed within a few paces of Vaskegar, who wove in place, a hand pressed to his head. His eyes and nostrils flared as he spotted them, and he pointed all nearby duergar their way, yelling. Soldiers roused and charged after the fleeing pair.

The two sped through the gate and down the road, where a familiar figure in black rags waved for them to hurry, then whirled and sprinted ahead.

Akina dared to glance back. The other scanderig and all the Forge Spurned remained intact and ready to unleash destruction at Vaskegar's command. She returned her focus forward and bent her head to the race for survival, just as the final glow from the forge extinguished.

Chapter Twenty-Eight
Upward

The ruins dropped back into shades of black, white, and gray. The cries of the pursuing duergar remained far too close for comfort as Akina slogged on, neck and neck with Ondorum. Izthuri took them through several twists and turns, but the shouts never fully died off. She didn't lead them back to the caligni hideout, which Akina understood. If the duergar got a whiff of the tribe's location, they'd be hunted down and exterminated. Instead, Izthuri guided them to a series of fallen towers near the edge of the ruins.

They drew to a halt, two panting, one wheezing. Izthuri eyed the way they'd come. While calls echoed back and forth a few streets over, none had yet fixed on their location.

"What now?" Ondorum asked. "Hide and hope they pass us by?"

Akina shook her head. "Taggoret. Both Gromir and Brakisten . . ." She stumbled over her dead brother's name, but shoved the grief aside for the moment. "They said Vaskegar plans to attack Taggoret first."

"Could he take it with the forces he's summoned?" Ondorum asked.

Akina blinked, still not used to him voicing thoughts. "Maybe. If the city's caught off-guard. And if they fix the forge up, they might be able to call up even more."

"Then we must ensure the city is warned."

They held each other's gaze for a moment. She noted the chunk taken out of a shoulder, the still-oozing wounds over his ribs, and newer injuries. One hand sported several puncture wounds, while smaller cuts and burns coated his skin. Others might not have seen it, as he kept his frame strong, but his eyes hinted at utter exhaustion.

"You up for it?"

He rolled his shoulders back. "Only one way to know."

She grinned. "Right." She turned to Izthuri. "Do you know a path that will get us up to Taggoret before the duergar?"

Izthuri's eyes scrunched. "Where Taggoret?"

Keeping one ear to the noises of the encroaching duergar, Akina knelt and drew a crude map in the dirt. She noted Taggoret, Davarn, and the gate they came down. She tried to estimate where Nullick's warren had been in relation to the Long Walk, and where they stood now. Then she drew triangles to indicate the main peaks surrounding Taggoret itself. She tapped these. "Mount Langley, Mount Carissa, Mount Onik, and Mount Soryu. Have you been up this way at all?"

Izthuri muttered to herself as she studied the sketch. At last, her head bobbed. "Think so. Not in long while. A way is there. I think. But you said you protect my tribe."

Akina planted fists on hips. "I am, by leading the duergar away from here. I figure they'll stay and try to repair the forge some, see if they can bring in more for their army. But if they know we're off to raise a warning, they'll hurry to attack the city before we can be too prepared. Most of them will leave and you can pick off the rest here easy enough."

The caligni looked doubtful, but nodded again. "The way is there. Goes up fast. But way is watched. Dangerous."

"More buggane?" Akina asked.

Izthuri wriggled fingers. "Not know. See some duergar go up. Not come back."

Ondorum frowned, but Akina leaned out to check that the area remained clear. "If it gets us there in time to raise a defense, we'll take any risk."

Izthuri reached into her rags and pulled out a pair of tiny glass vials. The liquid within slid about like gobs of oil and glimmered with luminescent blue-and-green motes suspended within the otherwise clear fluid. Oddly, it reminded Akina of the glimpse she'd gotten of Izthuri's freshly healed skin. Izthuri cupped these in her hands and offered them in the same way Ondorum had once presented her with the elemental's diamond.

"You gift life from stone. I gift life from light. Drink. Run. Live."

They took the vials, scraped thumbnails across the wax-sealed openings, and quaffed the contents. Expecting a repeat of the earlier healing spell, Akin braced to gag but found herself pleasantly surprised when the liquid dropped down her throat like a glob of warm honey. It struck her stomach and heat lit her up from the inside-out—not the marrow-burning deluge she'd felt too often of late, but an energizing burst that flushed her cheeks and renewed the vigor in her limbs. She huffed and shook her head as her scalp tingled.

"That's got a kick."

Ondorum flexed his arms and bounced on his toes, showing he felt the same effects. The wounds on his shoulder and arms faded to slate scars on his gray skin, while the many minor cuts and burns vanished. He briskly rubbed his palms together in a manner so unlike his normal composure that Akina almost laughed. "Quite agreeable."

Izthuri waggled fingers. "Follow."

She took them to an outer wall on the opposite side of the city from where she and Akina had entered. There, a set of tunnels led away from the cavern.

"Take only up. Steeper, better. Faster. Remember, is watched now. Dangerous. Don't know what. But dwarf roads above."

As they studied the entrance to the route, a clatter rose two blocks down. Ularna ran into view, leading a squad of duergar. She pointed out their targets and the group picked up speed.

"Shattered stones and bones, how'd they find us?"

Izthuri held a pale palm toward them, both a farewell and an urging on. "Fight well. Live."

Akina mirrored the gesture. "Stone endures."

The caligni melded back into shadow. The pair spun and fled up the tunnels.

Akina quickly discovered the main and crucial difference between entering Nar-Voth and leaving it as expediently as possible. On the way into the Darklands, most of the tunnels had sloped down, with only the occasional rise before falling once more. It lent a subtle ease to the journey, despite the obstacles they'd encountered along the way. Now every footfall became a bit more strained. Every leg muscle worked under just a bit more of a burden. Akina almost started to appreciate not having had the chance to retrieve her maulaxe, but the thought of facing enemies without it rid her of that line of thinking quick enough.

The rousing effects of the potion had faded long ago, leaving them to forge on under their own endurance and willpower. After the first half day, by her estimate, their initial pace slowed and they alternated a steady run with a rapid stride on the steeper portions. When they took a brief rest, she squatted to catch her breath.

"We lose them?" she asked.

Ondorum shut his eyes and stood perfectly still. He frowned after a little bit. "I may hear distant echoes, but am unsure. Either way, it would be wise to assume the duergar still follow, and that they will protect their secrets at all cost."

"How in Hell could they be tracking us?"

"One of their number must have some skill in the matter. I saw their monk, but don't know the abilities of those with her."

"That trull's name is Ularna."

"Is it?" He gave a half bow. "Thank you. It would be a discourtesy to leave such a worthy opponent nameless."

Akina scowled. "Right. Duergar behind, unknown nasties ahead. And me without any weapon. Don't figure you've got one of your metal nubs still, hm? Summon me a hammer?"

He spread his hands. "Alas. But perhaps we'll be able to move ahead without being molested. So long as we don't encounter any majestic worms."

"Majestic whats?"

He started up again. "Another tale, another time. If they follow, we should hasten."

Any attempts at conversation died off as they labored on. The only good aspect of the race came from Izthuri's instructions, which eliminated any confusion about the route. Up went up. At one point, Akina imagined these tunnels were some of the original paths from the Quest for Sky, when her ancestors strode ever-higher, seeking the surface. Visualizing their spirits marching along beside her imbued Akina with a sense of retracing their steps, reliving history as it happened. She imagined their hopeful conversations as they explored and progressed, wondering what they might discover when they reached the end of their journey. She became lost in this uplifting vision for a time, letting it ease her weariness and keep her feet steady.

Then her brother's face rose in her mind, joining those of the envisioned dead. Her stride flagged. *Brakisten. Shattered stones, you deserved better.* Fists curled at her side, and she ground her teeth in silent prayer. *Torag, sorry it's been so long since I gave you your due. But if you help us reach Taggoret in time, I'll slaughter Brak's killers and make sure they never hurt anyone again.*

Ondorum looked at her in question, but she waved him on. There'd be time to mourn later. For now, surviving this mad dash to the city mattered most.

They reached a rare level stretch and rested a moment, leaning against the walls, sweat dripping off noses and chins. Once her breath returned, Akina huffed.

"On we go."

As she charged ahead, her footsteps gained an odd echo. Something in the back of her brain recognized it, and she did her best to reverse direction. "Oh sh—"

Rock crumbled beneath her, sending her plummeting. She crashed and rolled, clutching her helm to keep it from flying off. Good fortune for her as, on a final tumble, her head struck a hard outcropping that rattled all sense loose. When her wits returned, Ondorum crouched over her, flinty features cracked with concern.

She grumbled as she sat up. "Fine. I'm fine."

She studied the lower tunnel she'd fallen into. The texture and composition of the tunnels had changed repeatedly as they raced upward, switching between veined rock to chunky slabs to slick limestone. The path she'd just fallen from had held rows of tiny stalagmites that crunched underfoot, but this new section looked more granular than anything they'd seen so far. Packed gravel lined the curving walls here, spotted with larger rocks that looked ready to tumble out at a touch. From what she could tell, the area had been dug out to form a thin sheet of stone between it and the tunnel above. Some sort of burrowing creature? Buggane after all?

Stretches of the walls, floor, and ceiling looked daubed over with thick streaks and clumps of an unknown substance. Not mud, but not natural stone, either. Akina ran a hand over one such spot and found it held firm, with the looser rock around it embedded in the daubing.

"At least it still goes up," she said, looking to the tunnels winding off from this one.

As they continued, she spotted a handful of shell pieces strewn about, from chitinous plates as large as her head to a club-like length of what might've been an oversized antenna or leg. She paused to pick up the latter, thinking she might use it as a weapon, but it crumbled in her grip.

They entered an area where several tunnels converged. The walls of these had been worn away, creating passages that wove back and forth between them until the whole place looked like one big maze. Larger columns of the muck-daubing looked to be all that supported the ceiling in some spots.

In the middle of one wide stretch, Ondorum halted their run.

Akina stumbled to followed suit and stared back at him. "Why'd you stop?"

"Movement ahead."

With a click of claws, three giant insects strove into sight. Twice as large as the strange rust-eating creature that had invaded the duergar camp, they spread out as they came on, mandibles flaring. Six barbed, hook-clawed legs propelled each one forward. Broad chitinous heads sloped down into segmented bodies, every inch covered with the same brown shell she'd seen discarded before—though she doubted theirs would crumble at a touch. Their mandibles were shaped like axe blades with curving spikes at the tips, and beady eyes fixed on the intruders. Mucus oozed from their wriggling mouths, dripping to sizzle on the rock.

Considering a tactical retreat, Akina looked behind to see Ularna and four duergar soldiers run up the way they'd just come, blocking off any escape. She put her back to Ondorum's and waited to see which set of foes reached them first.

Chapter Twenty-Nine
Tunnel Pests

Ondorum rooted himself as their enemies closed the distance. Beside him, Akina tore her helm off and clutched the ruined straps in one fist. She bared teeth at both oncoming parties and loosed a rock-quaking shout.

The duergar would reach them a few strides ahead of the insects. Ondorum shifted his balance, ready to face Ularna and resume their previous battle.

To his surprise, the duergar monk darted toward Akina while the four soldiers raced at him. They hacked axes and thrust daggers as he spun away from the rush of attacks. He used his palms to push and slap their blades aside. Nearby, Akina used her helm as a make-shift flail to ward off Ularna. The monk shifted from side to side, looking for an opening.

Ondorum snapped a kick into one duergar's chin, thrusting him back. An axe swished past his nose, and he took an armored elbow to the side while shifting past an attempt to cleave his guts. He stopped a descending blow by ducking under the duergar's arm. Spinning in place, he grabbed the wrist and shot up, wrenching the arm down across one shoulder. The duergar bawled as his elbow crunched and he went flipping over Ondorum's shoulder.

Then Ondorum found himself face-to-face with one of the charging insects. He flung himself to the side, wheeling over a planted arm. The insect barreled through the space he'd just occupied and into the duergar who'd come up to stab him from behind.

He righted as a second insect rushed at him. Planting his feet, he reached up and grabbed the two main mandibles gnashing for his face. The insect surged forward, skidding him back on the looser rock. It bucked and jerked to try and dislodge his grip. As it reared, he yanked on the mandibles and used the leverage to launch himself over its head. He landed on its ridged back, near the narrowed segment where its front half connected with the rear.

The insect scrabbled forward, legs pumping as it tried to dislodge the unwanted rider. Ondorum balanced and then leaped off to plow both feet into the back of a duergar bearing twin battleaxes. The soldier collapsed in a rattle of mail and hardened leather, one axe spinning away. Unaware it had already lost its victim, the insect spun and slammed its back end into one of the daubing columns. The column cracked, and the whole area shook, scree drizzling from the ceiling.

After running over to grab the fallen axe, Ondorum took in the situation with a glance. Two duergar hacked at one of the insects, harrying it from either side as they tried to lop off its legs. The other two duergar soldiers—including the one he'd just downed—had vanished.

Near the far side of the open area, Akina fought desperately to meet Ularna's attack. She tried to grab the duergar monk's flapping sleeve to keep her from constantly pulling out of range of the helmet horns. But the monk chopped a hand into the dwarf's wrist, knocking it away. Akina barked and jerked back, shaking her hand as if it'd gone numb.

One of the insects rushed the two women and slashed at them with jagged mandibles, but it seemed confused as to which one it wanted to kill most, and its divided attacks reduced their effectiveness. This distraction also kept the monk from getting the advantage over Akina, as Ularna kept having to dodge claw swipes as well as the helm that whipped at her head from all angles.

Fury flared in Akina's eyes, and Ondorum sensed her getting close to when she would fling the helmet aside and launch herself at either opponent to try and break them with her own body. It might work against ordinary adversaries, but the monk would turn such a reckless attack to her advantage.

He sprinted over, axe poised. Ularna sensed his approach at the last second and tumbled away, leaving him to lash out at the insect as it turned on him. His blow took off one of its antennae, and the creature's shrill, rattling cry jammed rusting nails into his ears. Gurgling noises came from deeper within its carapace, and its mandibles flared.

Ondorum threw himself at Akina, knocking her aside as the insect sprayed a stream of steaming liquid across the area. Some splashed over an unseen figure, revealing portions of a face and torso. The duergar reappeared as he screamed and lashed out blindly with his remaining battleaxe, then dropped the weapon to claw at the acidic spray eating into his skin.

Froth flecked Akina's lips and she shoved Ondorum off her. She heaved to her feet, only pausing to snatch the axe away from him and slap her helm on. Gripping the weapon in both hands, she loosed another shout and charged the two duergar already occupied with an insect. The soldiers had managed to carve off one multijointed limb while suffering only a few cuts in return. The nearer one turned just as Akina bulled into him, using the axe as a battering ram. He went flying backward, and the wounded insect whirled to bear down on the remaining soldier, while a second insect skittered in to try and overwhelm him. That duergar swelled in size, almost doubling in height and girth as he tried to bludgeon both creatures into submission.

To one side, Akina went to work on the fallen duergar, chopping away as if he were a log for the fire.

The fourth, the one whose arm Ondorum had damaged earlier, remained hidden. But Ondorum had no time to search as Ularna hastened his way. They didn't bother with bows this time. Their meeting had occurred already, and each clash now only continued the encounter, forming an unbroken vein of ore to be mined and added to either's wealth of skill and knowledge.

"Ondorum," he said as they traded initial blows. "You are Ularna."

He blocked a battering flurry of kicks at his shins and thighs. She swiped an ankle, trying to trip, but he planted his feet and her strike bounced away.

"Why protect the dwarf?" Her hushed voice barely reached him over the clamor of the ongoing fight, each word smooth and polished, like pebbles from a riverbed.

"Why serve such a bloodthirsty master?" Ondorum let a punch pass his side and tried to trap her arm. Instead of pulling away, she lunged forward, driving a shoulder into his chest. He spun with the hit, letting her drive by. She recovered and they circled for a few moments.

"The stones led me to him. Said I would learn much beside him. To learn is to live, true?"

"True, but what good is it to only learn of death and destruction?"

Her gaze flicked to Akina and back. "Have you learned otherwise from such a flawed stone?"

"She is not stone, but living flesh," he said. "As we all are. She grows. I grow. She learns. I learn. We live."

"Flesh is weak." She illustrated her point by turning her attacks into all hard angles, using elbow and knee strikes to push him back.

Ondorum made himself a wall and rebuffed further hits. "Flesh can be strengthened."

He tried to repay by jabbing into a pressure point to lock her arm. Her skin hardened under the attack, however, and she smirked as a vicious punch struck his inner thigh. Ondorum used the offered momentum to spin and launch a kick at her head. As she ducked, he redirected the kick in midair and brought it down toward the top of her skull. She tried to pull back, but his heel snapped down her face and chest.

She stumbled. Recovering her balance, she wiped a sleeve across the blood trickling from her nose and eyed the stain it left. A strange look passed over her face.

"The stones are already pure," she said. "Pure in form. Pure in strength. Pure in silence."

"Silence is a poison," he replied. "Emptiness that leeches substance from the mind and body and soul."

Her expression turned pitying. "Then you haven't listened to it long enough."

Before they could continue either their physical or verbal debate, one of the insects slammed into the earth between them. The enlarged duergar stomped after and embedded his axe in the creature's head. Ichor spewed from the wound, and the insect's screeches died away as it curled in on itself. The duergar yanked his blade free and turned to face Ondorum, axe dripping with gore. Behind him, a second insect had engaged Ularna, who landed punches and kicks with shell-cracking force.

Akina had grabbed her duergar up by his beard and mashed his head repeatedly against a daubing column. More pebbles and larger rocks clattered from the ceiling with each hit, until the column and the duergar's head cracked at the same time. She flung him away and searched for a new victim, eyes glazed with fury. The insect missing one antennae obliged by scuttling her way, mandibles clacking.

Ondorum spun aside as the overgrown duergar charged. The duergar tromped past and rammed into a thin wall of stone and daubing. This shattered beneath the hit, and the ceiling sagged. When the duergar turned and raised his axe, it struck the roof and broke through. Rock and dirt cascaded over his head. As the duergar tried to stumble clear of the miniature avalanche, Ondorum ran in and drove palm-heel strikes into his exposed side. Ribs cracked beneath the duergar's mail tunic, but he kept on swinging. Ondorum retreated before the savage blows. Half whiffed through air, while the others chopped into more daubed columns.

Another section of the roof caved in, billowing dust everywhere. Ondorum's opponent bellowed as he tried to close the distance. Ondorum led him in a wide sweep, circling toward Akina. As he maneuvered, Ondorum spotted a set of footsteps appearing in the fresh debris. The tracks aimed for Akina's back as she battled her giant insect, but didn't coincide with any visible form. Ondorum waited until the person took one more step, and then exclaimed, "Akina! Behind! Head level!"

She whirled without question, axe lashing out. Blood sprayed and a cry sounded. She followed through, spinning aside as the insect lunged into the gap, antennae quivering. It landed on an invisible form, trampling it. Acidic spray coated the duergar a moment later, sending more screams across the chamber.

Akina joined him in facing the giant duergar. She hacked at his legs from behind while Ondorum kept his attention, dodging blows that would cut him in half if one landed. At last, when she planted an axe edge into his lower back, the soldier stumbled and went down. A kick crushed his throat, and his form shrank back to normal size in death.

An enormous crack resounded. Ondorum looked up to see Ularna wrench her insect's upper half away from its lower. The upper body continued to writhe and gnash as vital fluids drained, staining the ground about it. The oread met Ularna's eyes as she straightened from the kill. Akina spotted the other woman at the same time and barked her name. The duergar's lips twisted in a half-smile, half-grimace, and she vanished.

Akina charged where she'd stood, swinging wildly. Ondorum held a defensive form, but was at a loss when no more attacks came. He wondered at the monk's retreat, not thinking her one for cowardice.

Then the whole area shuddered under another small cave-in.

He timed Akina's cuts and caught the axe haft on a backswing, forcing her stop. "We must go. Unless you wish to be buried."

She tried to pull away, but he held firm. A few moments later, her eyes cleared somewhat and she rumbled. "Almost had her."

"Next time, no doubt."

He urged her to ignore the final insect, which continued to savage the fallen duergar's body. As they hurried by, heading for the upward slopes, a mound of rock collapsed and buried the creature. As they dodged further falls, rushing for the other end of the tunnels, it reminded Ondorum of the battle in the Long Walk, and the subsequent sprint for survival before the plummeting stalactites crushed them. A couple sheets of stone cracked against Akina's helm, but she didn't falter. He kept a forearm raised over his head to deflect the worst of it. Rock thundered down as the whole area collapsed on their heels. Dust blasted past them, shoving them forward and into a firmer set of tunnels.

They stopped on the edge of the destruction, looking back at the area sealed off by rubble. To have been caught in there would've meant a slow crushing death or agonized suffocation for either of them. Knowing this, they advanced, aiming to get clear of the area in case other sections proved unstable. The insect-daubed tunnels ended after a little while longer, and they began cutting through more level tunnels, to their relief.

From then on, they barely paused for rest; when they did, it was mostly to gather edible fungus or slake their parched throats from small pools of water. During one such short break, Akina worked knots out of her neck and groaned.

"How much further, you figure?"

Ondorum gazed up the tunnel. "Perhaps two or three more days? My sense of time underground remains unreliable."

She sighed. "You're supposed to tell me we're almost there."

He shot a sharp look her way. "I'm not comfortable with stating such a falsehood."

"We'll work on that. Comforting lies can be a big help."

They resumed the seemingly endless trek upward. Ondorum kept a wary eye on every large stalagmite they passed, but none so much as winked a red eye his way. Another stretch of tunnels looked honeycombed with side passages, but whatever creature formed them didn't make an appearance as they skulked through the area.

At last, after several long marches punctuated by short periods of sleep, Akina pointed out chisel marks along the sides of a tunnel—dwarven-worked. Soon after, runes spotted various thresholds, and she used these to guide them along until they came out into a broader tunnel with a smooth floor and arched ceiling. Their pace quickened in anticipation as they worked up through a series of right-angled, narrow halls meant to file possible invaders into more easily defended routes. This let out into another wide path. Up ahead, a gate blocked the way, lit by torches and guarded by four dwarves in plate armor. They must've heard echoes of the pair's approach, for they had weapons unsheathed. Akina waved her axe and hollered hoarsely.

"Hail, Taggoret!"

A crossbow quarrel pinged off the nearby wall, and a dwarven voice barked.

"Don't be moving!"

Akina lowered her axe and cupped a hand to shout. "Stone endures! We're friends."

"Step into the torchlight. Slow and steady now. We've already got blades at your back."

Ondorum glanced behind and noted several armed, grim-faced dwarves blocking the last turn they'd taken. There must've been hidden posts on the way in, and they'd been too exhausted to notice.

They eased ahead, letting the guards inspect them. Even when the dwarves waved them closer, they continued to eye Akina and Ondorum with suspicion, especially the weapon Akina carried.

"Where are you coming from?" asked one.

Akina thrust her chin out. "Deeper than you'd guess. If you want to keep Taggoret from being overrun, you'll tell the king a duergar army is on its way."

Chapter Thirty
Taggoret

A kina paced in the chambers they'd been given, muttering to herself. The axe had been taken from her on admittance to Taggoret, with a promise to return it if the king and his advisors decided she was to be trusted. Most of these worthies gathered in a council room, where she and Ondorum had related all they could of their experience in Nar-Voth. They'd warned of Vaskegar's small yet powerful army and his intent to march on the area. She'd recounted the forces he had available—at least a couple hundred duergar if he didn't gather more along the way, plus his gifted scanderigs and Forge Spurned. Not to mention the casters in his service.

The leaders had then presented Akina and Ondorum with maps and asked them to detail their journey, looking for flaws in their story or other reasons to doubt an immediate threat. As she tracked from Taggoret, down to the Long Walk, and back up to the main tunnels, their questioning grew into concern. The gate they'd come to wasn't a major entrance to the city. The largest tunnel offered itself to the south, and she guessed this would be where Vaskegar made his primary advance, considering he'd want to bring his hulking constructs to bear. When the councilors began pointing out different defenses to activate and pulling up lists of reserve troops, Akina felt the slightest relief, knowing she'd been believed. The council thanked them for bringing the warning at such a high risk to themselves and assured they'd be involved once preparations were fully underway. Then they were dismissed as the dwarves set about the task of protecting their city.

They'd been attended to by a cleric who gave them Torag's blessings in healing, restoring their spirits and strength. After a gloriously hot bath, Ondorum received a robe which fit him surprisingly well, while she begrudgingly handed over her armor in exchange for a simple cloth tunic and pants. The attendant who took her gear to be repaired swore he'd have it back before any conflict broke out. He suggested they rest while the council conferred. However, once deposited in a room, Akina found herself more restless than ever.

Her thoughts filled with her lost mother and brother, everything she might've done better or different to save them, and the army marching on the city. Could this whole series of events have been averted if she'd returned home right after the war ended? What would her life be like if she'd never joined the mercenaries, never met Ondorum, simply reintegrated herself into Taggoret to form the next link in her family line? Would Brakisten have fallen into drunkenness and out of the faith? Would Gromir have turned her into an object to be coveted from afar? Would he have ever discovered the ruins and led Jannasten down there to an unwitting doom?

Or, if she'd never returned at all, would Gromir have found the courage to defy the duergar and reveal the spy in their midst? Without her interference, would he have found a way to break the forge and keep Vaskegar from employing it? Whatever path her mind took, it always seemed to end in disaster, always her fault.

"You can't blame yourself," Ondorum said.

She started and looked over to where he lounged on a cushioned stone bench, watching her pace.

"What's that?"

"You can't blame yourself for others' decisions," he said, sitting up. "You can only be responsible for the choices you make here and now."

She snorted. "Look who's talking. Why do you think I'm blaming myself for anything?"

He nodded at her hands. "The way your fists curl while you're thinking, like you need to strike your own thoughts down."

She forced her fingers to relax. "Isn't that what you do? Find what you don't like about yourself and destroy it? Break away the flaws until they're all gone?"

"Not quite. Think of it like a stonemason. If one took a block of stone—even a heavily flawed one—and simply attacked it with hammer and chisel, chunking away portions without considering what elements deserved to remain, eventually you'd be left with nothing but rubble. You must work slow and steady, refining rather than shattering. Even if you find a portion to be removed, you take time to find materials to replace it, otherwise you threaten the durability of the entire piece." He held up a flat palm, as if supporting an invisible object. "In the same way, we must work in increments, lest our whole selves crumble beneath the pressure."

She rubbed the back of her neck. "Makes sense, I guess. Never heard you explain it like that before, though. This have anything to do with why you started talking again?"

He brushed a hand over his side. After the healing, the barest tips of purple crystals had poked up through his skin. "Somewhat. I realized my error in following the path of silence. I removed too much of myself without anything to replace it. I left myself incomplete, no longer able to express myself in essential ways." His gaze dropped, as if ashamed. "Nor could I fully share myself with those I truly care for."

The silence swelled until it started to choke her. She cleared her throat. "So it's all back to normal? You drop the vow and we move on?"

"Almost." His eyes met hers again, earnest and steady. "The time spent silent wasn't entirely in vain. Something's different."

"How so?"

"I'm not quite sure, yet. I feel the change, but haven't determined how best to manifest it." He peered at her. "In the meantime, it's more than just guilt bothering you, isn't it?"

Akina turned and scowled at the wall. "I guess I'm just wondering more and more . . ." She puffed a sigh. "What's the point of all this, Ondorum?"

"Quite the encompassing question. The point of what, specifically?"

She flung a hand out, indicating everything they'd passed through recently. "The fighting. The deaths. The struggle. Is there a point? Is there anything beyond just knowing you're still going and your enemy isn't? Why do *you* fight?" She raised a hand. "Wait, don't tell me. It all has to do with perfection, hm?"

"That's part of it," he said slowly. "But I've come to realize the singular pursuit of perfection in myself is a lesser goal. It's only when I apply what I learn to other lives that it matters. If I withdraw myself and achieve perfection in isolation, never interacting with the world, what value would it have?"

"But don't you figure it'd be easier to reach your goal alone? Isn't it difficult to find perfection when everything around you is so broken?"

"Yes, it's a struggle. A constant battle between the ideal and the real." He formed a circle with his hands. "Just as life and death are forever entwined. Without one, the other would be meaningless. Our lives give substance to our deaths, and death makes life worth delighting in while we're blessed to possess it."

"But when my life is all about bringing death to others," she said, "doesn't that defeat the purpose?"

"Death and destruction may seem futile to some, but they make room for new life and growth to occur in their wake. You fixate on the lives you've taken, rather than the ones you've saved or helped flourish."

"Who have I saved, Ondorum? I don't know their names. I don't know their faces."

"There are many I could name from our time with Durgan's band and beyond. Whole towns, even a few cities whose paths could've led to the grave had you not interfered. Think also of Izthuri and her tribe. Might they not now have a better chance of survival? And what of Taggoret itself? We fought to reach this city in time. If we'd simply accepted our deaths down below, then your people would've been caught unawares and likely slaughtered. They now have a chance to live."

She grunted and went over to sit by him. Leaning against his solid build, she tried to relax. The strain in her mind eased as they sat there, taking comfort in just being alive and together in the moment.

"You really think my death will have meaning?" she whispered. "That I'll have made a difference?"

"Whenever it comes—may it be many years from now—I've no doubt of it."

She yawned, welcoming a sleepy fog that stole over her. Before she surrendered to it, she used his shoulders to pull herself up and him down into a long, full kiss. When they broke away, his malachite-tinged eyes had brightened, and her drowsiness pulled back for a moment.

"I know you just started again, but can we stop talking for a little while?"

He chuckled. "They say action holds more substance than words."

"Right."

Afterward, she slept—for how long, she didn't know. When she woke, he rumbled on the cushions beside her, lost in an unknown dream. She sat up, wondering what had roused her. Then another knock sounded on the chamber door. She nudged Ondorum awake with an elbow and retrieved her clothes while he donned his robe. The attendant from before waited outside.

He returned her armor—dents hammered out of the breastplate, leather oiled, straps repaired, helm buffed to a gleam—and stated that a local armorer would be delivering a maulaxe soon, as she'd noted losing hers during the Darklands trek. As she strapped her equipment on, he conveyed a brief message from the royal council.

"They've requested your presence at the main undergates to take part in the defense. They understand if you wish to abstain, considering the sacrifices you've already made, but believe your knowledge of the invaders will be invaluable to the effort."

"We'll be there," she said. "What time is it? How long has it been?"

"It's been a day and a half since your arrival, and is now ten strokes into the evening. Advance scouts have returned and report the duergar force should strike the city by morning."

Chapter Thirty-One
Forge Spurned

Akina studied the city defenses, looking for any gap, any hole Vaskegar could exploit. Fortunately, after centuries of underground warfare, dwarves had gained more than a keen understanding of how to protect their stonebound dwellings.

The main tunnel leading down into the depths had three successive gates leading up to the city proper. They'd been spaced a couple hundred yards from each other to form potential killing grounds in between. The walls and yards were guarded by five hundred dwarven defenders, their armor polished and weapons sharpened. Two hundred had been stationed at the deepest gate, with the other three split between the reserve gates. While the tunnel beyond stood nowhere near as high or broad as the Long Walk, it provided enough room that the Darklands caravan Akina and Ondorum once hid within could've passed through with ease. Any obstacles had long been cleared away, creating a straight shot down the main approach, and this had been littered with deathtraps.

The ground leading up to the first gate had been dug out in spots and covered in metal grates, which were now concealed by false patches of earth or illusion. The space below these had been filled with oil or simmering embers. According to the council's plans, piping fed into the base of the ember pits, and was connected to enormous bellows further up, which, when pumped, would spew fire over any attackers. Spellcasters would set the oil pits alight at the right moment to catch duergar within the flames.

Metal and stone barricades had been erected, forming a maze for the attackers to wind through, directing them across the trapped portions and giving the dwarven archers time to pick off the first waves. Spiked pits were rigged to drop open, sections of the ceiling poised to fall, and other nasty tricks readied to kill as many duergar as possible before they even reached the gates.

If worst came to it and the attackers somehow broke through the first two gates, the tunnel ceiling just beyond the third had been cored through in spots and rigged with mining explosives. These could be discharged to collapse the tunnel, sending countless tons of rock thundering down. It would bury any defenders left fighting outside the gate, but at least the city itself would be spared—for a time.

Akina and Ondorum joined the warriors at the first gate lookout stations, determined to halt the attack there. Through an observation slot, they watched the tunnel stretch away. Torches and enchanted lights blazed all along it, while sorcerers and wizards worked constant dispellings to ensure no duergar tried to sneak up under invisibility or any sort of camouflage.

The gate itself blocked the whole tunnel, wall to wall, floor to ceiling. Central double-doors provided the only external access, and this had been bolted shut, barred, and sealed further with chains secured by a complex network of gears. Aside from slit windows for archers, the only other openings were larger hatches that allowed heavy ballistae to fire if the attackers got close enough—though these were currently latched shut and appeared seamless from the outside.

After getting a sense of the defenses, Akina scrutinized the defenders themselves. To the last dwarf, they wore the same foreboding expression, and the few who moved about, checking last-minute preparations, did so with dour determination. This was their home, and no duergar would take it from them while they lived. She didn't doubt their courage and strength, but wondered how well it would hold when faced with Vaskegar's unholy forces. She fought down a faint echo of horror within herself as she thought of Gromir's fate, and the twisted, chained forms of the Forge Spurned.

If they didn't stop Vaskegar here, he'd have the opportunity to consolidate even greater power, and his victories would draw more duergar to him, eventually rivaling the lords of Hagegraf itself. The whole of the Five Kings Mountains would be shaken as city after city fell to his replenishing army, fueled by the forge.

She drew her new maulaxe and studied the head for the dozenth time. One of the councilors must've recognized the Fairingot name, for the maulaxe had been emblazoned on one side with her family's sigil, while they'd engraved the peaks and crown emblem of the Five Kings Mountains on the other. The end of the haft had also been capped with a spiked iron ball. She carried the weapon proudly, honored at such an unexpected gift. Planting its head on the ground, she bowed her own.

Since we're talking again, Torag, I figure I should try it once more before I might be able to do it in person. If . . . if I die here, know that it's for my people. For the lives they've got beyond these gates. If I'm lost in battle, let it at least matter. Help me give them a chance at a happy future, even if I don't get to see it.

She lifted her head as the ground trembled underfoot. She glanced at Ondorum, who held an iron staff engraved with dwarven runes and the Five Kings Mountains sigil, also gifted by the city weaponsmiths. His nod confirmed her feeling. Most of the other dwarves didn't so much as shuffle in their positions.

She looked out at the tunnel again as the first duergar ranks marched into view. Rows upon rows of black-and-red armored duergar tromped along, eyes like grave dust. A handful of large fire and earth elementals came alongside them, and Vaskegar led them all on his horned beetle, bone armor gleaming in the conjured lights.

Behind them came duergar artillery riding giant beetles and spiders, weapons strapped to their saddles while they hefted crossbows. Further ranks appeared behind them, and a roil of black smoke appeared as Forge Spurned mingled with the soldiers. Dwarven oaths rose from other watchers as the Forge Spurned lumbered closer. Their hooked chains writhed across their misshapen bodies while endless smoke belched from their open mouths. The fumes rose and coated the roof with soot, forming a low-hanging cloud of darkness that matched their advance. All of the Forge Spurned had been armed, most with hammers, but others with axes and blades.

Akina searched for Gromir among them, but couldn't distinguish him from the rest. She prayed his soul had been cast out of the tortured wreck of a body during the transformation, and that he didn't suffer inside, watching as his old self was forced to serve Droskar.

Two scanderigs brought up the rear, lighting up the far end of the tunnel with the fiendish glows visible through their eyes, nostrils, and mouths. Several other strange-looking constructs lumbered beside them. As round as the scanderigs but lacking the forgefiends' inner fire, these newcomers had sculpted heads dominated by enormous, gaping maws, creating the disturbing impression of screaming duergar. Apparently Vaskegar had gotten the forge working again after all, at least for a bit.

The trembling in the ground became a pounding, reverberating up through Akina's legs and forming a penetrating pressure at the back of her skull, as if someone pounded a thick nail in there. She squinted, trying to see through the growing cloud of ash. Something more was going on toward the back of the army.

The scanderigs had turned to the tunnel walls and began using their metal claws to gouge huge chunks of stone, which they then carried along as if bearing gifts.

Akina frowned. The constructs were deadly enough on their own. Why would they . . .

The answer rolled into view behind the constructs themselves. A trio of massive metal trebuchets set on spiked metal wheels ground forward, moved and manned by teams of duergar. The main throwing arms of the devices were inscribed with hot-white glowing runes that hurt Akina's eyes.

Akina gaped in horror, realizing the terrible error the defenders had made. "Oh, gods."

Ondorum looked at her in question, but she whirled and shouted down to the gate guards.

"Open the gate," she cried. "Get troops out in front! Ready an assault!"

The gate captain, a white-haired dwarf with a face full of scars, raced over. "What're you about?"

She dragged him to an arrowslit and pointed out. "See those constructs with the rocks? I'm thinking they can fling those a long way. And those trebuchets behind them? I'll bet my armor they're magical ones straight from Droskar's realm, more powerful than any we're used to. The duergar aren't going to just smash themselves face-first into the gates. They're going to batter it down from a distance and then march right on in."

Scars twisted as he peered out at the duergar. "How can you be sure?"

"Vaskegar's smart," she said, hating as she admitted it. "He's not going to waste his forces attacking these gates. Instead, he's going to throw rocks harder and farther than we can, until we either go out and meet him or this whole place comes down on our heads."

The gate captain straightened and glared around at the rest of the defenders watching them. "That'd mean compromising our whole defense plan."

"Sticking to that plan means sitting here and getting buried alive. Our best chance is a preemptive strike."

He yanked at his beard. "I don't know. I need to confer with—"

"There's no time." She froze for a moment. "But I'll give you some."

She ran past the gate captain before he could argue further. Spotting a ballista hatch, she smashed it open with the maulaxe and leaped out. Dwarves raised a cry as she dropped into the trapped field, planting her maulaxe and going to one knee to catch herself. Before she even rose, a second thud told her Ondorum had landed at her side. She hid a grin. He hadn't hesitated a second in following. Gods, she was going to make his bones quake after this was all over.

Bellows went up from behind the wall. Lever and gears clanked and chains rattled, indicating the gates were being unlocked from within. Akina silently urged the defenders to hurry.

Beside her, Ondorum studied the enemy. He gave her a calm look, nodded in encouragement, and then lifted his gaze again to Vaskegar, who'd halted with the first duergar line just beyond where the killing field began.

The duergar commander studied the two standing between him and the gate. His voice rang out.

"Come to surrender?"

Akina stepped forward and called back. "Come to shatter your bones and use them for kindling!"

He adjusted his jawbone crown. "A touching sentiment, but you're hardly equal to the task. Your ancestors proved their unworthiness, their inability to control their own destinies by fleeing the depths when the first tremors shook the world." His smirk was visible across the distance. "And you, dustling, surrendered any inheritance to this power when you fled weeping before me down below."

"You're a coward and a thief, Vaskegar," she cried. "You've invaded our ancient homes. You've murdered our kin. And now you're here with stolen weapons to take what belongs to us. The stones here are ours. Come any closer and you'll bleed out on them."

"The stones?" He waved back at the earth elementals with his ranks. "I happen to command them myself."

"You don't command your own bowels!" Akina shook her maulaxe.

At last, the great gates swung wide, admitting a rush of dwarves. Their pounding steps echoed as they spread across the field, taking up positions behind barricades, forming ranks of squads and preparing to charge. Once the fore positions had emptied, the gates swung shut again. Horns sounded, hopefully signals for the rear guard to move up as reinforcements.

Vaskegar waited until all had quieted again. Then his harsh laughter broke the stillness.

"I see a cluster of rats before me, with twitching beards instead of twitching tails. You squat in shallow dens, too afraid to commit yourselves to one world or another. Fear and uncertainty rule you."

He drew one axe and held it high. To Akina's eyes, it held a deeper crimson hue than before, as if it had soaked up someone's blood.

Maybe Brakisten's.

"I am here to free you," Vaskegar cried, "either by dominance or death. Your choice is clear. Have spirit enough to make one. But know that every choice has its consequences. See now the price of defiance."

One of the Forge Spurned staggered up through the lines until it reached Vaskegar's side. Smoke chugged from its mouth and nostrils, obscuring much of its features, but Akina thought she could just make out a thinner face and anguished eyes she might've once known.

"This dwarf was once such as yourselves," Vaskegar shouted. "Do you see? All who defy me will suffer the same fate. You will rise to serve Droskar, whether you wish it or not, and so serve me in his stead, wrapped in unbreakable chains and given over to an eternity of torment, burned from within by the shame of your miserable failure."

Dwarven defenders shifted and mutters rose, but Akina shouted over them.

"Liar! You're showing off nothing but a traitor. Those here are true dwarves, and any who fall today will be welcomed into Torag's realm."

"So you condemn them to death," Vaskegar said. "Very well." He yanked his second axe over his head and stabbed both forth. "For the glory of the Dark Smith!"

At the same time, Akina whirled her maulaxe overhead. "Stone endures!"

Grasping the weapon shaft in both hands, she screamed in defiance and charged.

Dwarves and duergar sent up a mighty roar as they surged toward each other. From the back of Vaskegar's troops, the scanderig flung a first salvo of boulders, and one of the devilish trebuchets rocked as it its arm whirled.

Boulders landed among the dwarves, smashing squads and sending stone shrapnel in every direction.

Powdered rock plumed, momentarily blocking sight of the duergar.

As the smoke thinned, duergar, elementals, and Forge Spurned plowed across the field. Once enough duergar were in range, a distant horn rang out and traps engaged. Duergar screamed as waves of fire and molten metal poured out across the stones. Spouts of flame engulfed soldiers, while others fell into pits that opened beneath them without warning. Massive blocks dropped from the ceiling, crushing multiple enemies at a time.

Dozens continued to rush in. Another horn blast, and crossbow quarrels flew over the advancing dwarves' heads to rain down on the attackers. Bolts bounced off duergar breastplates or struck stone. Others embedded in eyes, in throats, in chinks of armor, sending duergar toppling or forcing them to stagger on as blood streamed down their bodies. Quarrels striking the elementals proved ineffective, while those embedded in Forge Spurned flesh were ignored or yanked out and cast aside without slowing their steps.

The surviving first wave of duergar clashed with the main line of dwarven warriors. Axe met axe met shield met sword and a riotous cry filled the air. At the same time, lances and bolts of frost, fire, lightning, and acid landed in the fray from the duergar side as Vaskegar's casters unleashed their spells. Many of these were dispelled by Taggoret's arcane ranks, or struck and dissipated across invisible barriers. Many more tore into the dwarven ranks. Then the dwarven casters unleashed their own attacks, firing swerving missiles of pure energy, grabbing duergar with disembodied fists, and hitting the encroaching elementals with curses meant to banish them from the physical realm.

Akina claimed her first duergar with a sprint and smash of her horned helm straight into his chest. Two more quickly fell to strokes of her maulaxe. Ondorum fought by her side, casting down duergar with sweeping kicks and devastating staff strikes.

They created a circle where duergar entered but didn't leave alive. All around them, dwarf and duergar fought and died. Earth and fire elementals bore down through them, smashing aside shields, stomping bones, and roasting dwarves where they stood.

Ondorum pointed at one of the nearby earth elementals, which had backed a handful of dwarves against a barricade. Akina nodded, struck down a final duergar, and joined the oread in the assault. Her strike cracked one of the elemental's stony legs, and it swung around to face her. Ondorum hit it from the other side, staggering it. It slammed an arm down, trying to crush the monk, but he tumbled aside. Akina struck its other arm at the shoulder. Countless cracks formed over the joint, which instantly started to reform—until Ondorum's staff thrust popped the limb off entirely. The elemental bent over, off-balance. She slammed it full in the face, shattering the gems forming its eyes. With that, the rest of its body shuddered and began to disintegrate.

As the elemental crumbled beneath them, Akina spared a look to determine the attack's effectiveness so far. Forge Spurned stood like smoking pillars, lashing everywhere with their hammers and chains. Those dwarves who got too close soon found their legs or arms tangled in the black links, dragged in until the Forge

Spurned bashed them down with unrelenting fury. On the other side of the tunnel, a band of six defenders ganged up on a single Forge Spurned. Several fought its living chains while the others charged in and hacked at its chain-armored body. The Forge Spurned crushed one dwarf's head with a fist, tore the throat out of another with a chain hook.

Then an axe blow split the chain loops down the Forge Spurned's back. It staggered, and cinders flew from the wound. The remaining attackers fell upon it in a frenzy, chopping and hammering the gap in its link armor, widening the opening until the Forge Spurned fell apart in a chaos of lashing chains and bursts of flame. In the wake of its death, a blast of foul smoke obscured the air.

So they could be destroyed. Right.

Two more trebuchets fired. One stone struck the gate itself. The barrier shook, but held. The other obliterated an iron barricade and scattered the dwarves behind it.

Ondorum directed her attention to another earth elemental, which had stomped through the front lines to pound boulder-sized fists on the gate itself. Spells and crossbow bolts bounced off it, while a squad tried to cut it down from below. At the same time, the scander-igs launched more rock slabs, which exploded against the gate walls. Beneath these hits, a few cracks formed in the barrier.

Akina followed Ondorum, intending to help down the next elemental, but then a chain whistled through the air in front of her. A hook snagged a dwarf and hauled him off screaming. She diverted that way, letting Ondorum assist the dwarves already attacking the elemental. By the time she reached the Forge Spurned, the dwarf it caught lay crushed to pulp at its feet. The creature roared at her, fresh smoke issuing from its mouth.

She bellowed back. All she had to do was envision the dead dwarf before her as Brakisten, and the rage came to her as easy as breathing.

The realization thundered through her mind: *It* had come to *her*. Rather than succumbing to the tempest of her fury, she wielded it like another weapon. She held it within her instead of being choked in its grasp.

The air turned as thick and hot as magma. Her bones turned molten and her armor and maulaxe melded with her until she couldn't tell where she ended and her gear began.

Barbed chains lashed out at her, but she forced past them as she plowed into the creature. The Forge Spurned stumbled back. It raised its hammer. She struck it aside. Her axe edge hacked at its exposed head, cleaving the skull. Hooks tried to tear into her armor. She grabbed one hook in an armored fist and used it to haul the Forge Spurned closer, then bludgeoned it with hammer blow after hammer blow. Heavy fists beat against her, but she shrugged them off. Another hit; one of its legs buckled.

She dragged the chain she held down, then stomped on it. It writhed underfoot like a metal serpent. She batted away the other hook and caught the Forge Spurned across the face with the axe side. It moaned like a dumb beast and lunged, arms spread in an attempt to smash her flat. She hopped away, letting it reel by, and then lashed into its exposed back with all her might.

The chain coils burst apart, revealing charred flesh beneath. The creature dropped, and Akina hacked away until flesh and bone and chain all broke beneath her. Ash and fire plumed from the corpse, and she lurched away, eyes squeezed shut against the blast. As the smoke and her vision cleared, a handful of defenders around her gawked at the sight—a lone dwarf taking down a Forge Spurned. They roused with cheers and launched themselves into the battle with renewed vigor.

Akina coughed, trying to clear her lungs. The battle fury dwindled to flickering embers, yet didn't recede completely. Her strength wavered, but she forced herself to stand firm; rest could come after victory had been assured.

Duergar and dwarves raged across the tunnel, but it seemed they had held the attackers off the first gate so far. Ondorum stood amidst the rubble of the elemental he'd help take down. He raised his staff to signal her. Akina headed his way.

A slab of rock exploded against the wall above him, and he went down in a spray of shrapnel. Her cry of denial was lost under further deafening crashes and booms. The gate buckled under a direct trebuchet strike, then shattered from a second hit.

Hundreds more duergar and another dozen Forge Spurned charged through the dust and ash. Behind them, the scanderigs and other constructs thumped into sight, joining the battle in earnest.

Chapter Thirty-Two
Old Friends

Rubble fell from Ondorum's back as he shoved out of the pile of ruined wall. Spitting dust, he dragged his staff from the heap and assayed the situation. The defenders edged back toward the second gate, their numbers cut at least in half from the opening engagement. Akina left a dead Forge Spurned in her wake as she hammered and chopped her way through duergar toward him.

Recovering his balance, Ondorum threw himself back into the fight, angling his attacks to meet her halfway. Boulder crashes continued to deafen him as the duergar army heaved forward. The foregate had been reduced to scrap, and now the constructs turned their attention to the defenders.

The forgefiends entered the fray, enormous bellies splitting wide into razor-edged maws, spewing sparks from the furnace glow in their depths. Any dwarves caught in those hellish teeth were gnashed to shreds in moments. The scanderigs also used their massive claws, shooting them out to spear defenders straight through their armor. As each dwarf died, the glow of the scanderigs' eyes and nostrils flared all the brighter.

The other constructs trod about, mostly trying to trample anyone in their way. One, though, snagged a defender in an iron fist and tossed the soldier into its huge mouth. The mouth clamped shut a moment later, sealing the unfortunate dwarf inside as the construct fought on. Other dwarves rushed to attack the construct, hammering and bashing to try and free their compatriot, but their attacks glanced off without effect.

More traps had been set along this stretch, but until most of the dwarves cleared the area, they couldn't be triggered without causing friendly casualties.

The full duergar ranks looked committed to the fight. The mounted artillery brought up the rear while teams edged the trebuchets closer to prepare an assault on the second gate. The trebuchets paused to fire as they came, flinging welded clusters of smaller shot that broke apart and scattered, ravaging the withdrawing ranks.

Ondorum slapped a crossbow bolt aside as it soared at him. He dashed Akina's way, pausing to help a pair of dwarven soldiers lay three duergar low in a brutal exchange. When the last dropped, Akina stood before him, chest heaving, teeth bared. Her own collection of corpses lay at her feet, several duergar with heads and chests smashed in. Putting his lips close to her ear, he shouted over the bedlam.

"Constructs first? Siege machines? Leader?"

She set her jaw and they surveyed their options. Vaskegar had dismounted and added his fury to the fight, with Ularna nearby. The pair struck down any dwarves who dared stand in their way. Blood spattered Vaskegar's bone armor, making him look like a monster stripped of skin and muscle. Ularna engaged every foe with deadly grace, turning aside the most vicious blows while returning strikes that seemed to ignore even the thickest plate armor.

A forgefiend plodded across the battlefield just behind them. Dwarven defenders had erected several ballista in front of the second gate and winched steel bolts into place. They launched one at the scanderig, and it struck dead-center in its open belly. The blow barely made it pause, and the chomping teeth scrapped the bolt within seconds.

Akina used her maulaxe to indicate the other scanderig coming up the left side. The dwarven line hadn't quite collapsed there, with a thinner band of duergar warriors between them and the construct. She and the oread stormed across the battlefield, cutting down duergar as they went until they reached the front line.

"The construct," she shouted to the other dwarves. "Make it fall!"

She rammed a duergar aside, and they began slashing a path straight to the forgefiend. Dwarves bellowed battle cries as they fought along with them. The construct stamped to a halt as they neared, and the flames of its face gained a violet hue.

Sensing that change signaled an imminent threat, Ondorum roared, "Scatter!"

The dwarves lunged in all directions just as a wall of purple fire flashed into existence in their midst. Only one warrior got caught in the blaze, but her horrendous screams battered their ears. The heat of the wall slapped Ondorum as the defenders reconverged from various sides. The construct stood still a moment, as if studying an anthill it wanted to smash. Then it began stomping all about, trying to pulp its attackers or catch them in its fiery maw. Several dwarves were crushed beneath its bulk before they could back off.

Duergar came to defend their construct, and the outer ring of dwarves spun to hold them off. The rest hammered at its legs and feet, trying to bring it down. Akina joined in, screaming as she rained blows on the Abyss-forged metal. The construct continued spearing dwarves with its claws, tossing their corpses into its furnace-like belly.

Ondorum took up a position behind the construct, spinning his staff into a blur to shield the dwarves, deflecting incoming crossbow volleys from the rear artillery.

He glanced back as Akina lunged by him. With a furious howl, she leapt onto the scanderig's back. She held on with one hand and wielded the maulaxe with the other, whacking away at the many pipes and pistons across its form. Steam erupted and metal squealed as she wrecked the construct's upper framework. The forgefiend stamped in a circle, claws straining to pluck her off. She clambered higher and struck blow after blow atop its head. At last, a hit dented its brow and closed one of its eyes.

As she distracted it, the dwarves pressed their attack, jamming their blades and weapon shafts into its joints and pipeworks. The construct stabbed a hand into the ground, piercing a dwarf in half. However, its claws jammed in the earth as it tried to pull back out. Soldiers raced to that side and bashed it until, with a shriek of tortured metal, the arm snapped off wholly.

The construct reared, fought for balance, and lost. With an earth-quaking crash, it struck the tunnel floor and rolled onto its back. It wobbled like an overturned beetle as the dwarves swarmed over it and beat it into a motionless heap.

Akina staggered out from the chaos, looking both crazed and dazed at the same time. She licked her lips, and Ondorum had no trouble reading what she mouthed.

Again.

They looked across the battlefield. Several Forge Spurned lay pinned by ballista bolts, but others engaged the dwarves at the second gate. The siege engines had begun firing anew, battering the second gate as well with each awful shot. Already the walls had started to sunder; several major dents formed a gap down the middle of the double-doors. Reaching the trebuchets required fighting through the larger mass of duergar.

The defenders on the far side were busy trying to repeat the construct takedown with the second scanderig. The forgefiend picked off dwarves by the handful, adding to the forge fire raging within it. As each dwarf fell into its belly, the maw spewed hot ash and embers over the dwarves attacking it up close. This blinded them long enough for the forgefiend to scoop up another screaming victim.

Ondorum pointed his staff at the trebuchets. They needed to give the dwarves some manner of reprieve if they were to rally. He headed that way, Akina on his heels.

Then she cried out, "Wait!"

Akina stared at a particular Forge Spurned thumping across the field. Unlike the rest, it didn't attack anyone as it came. Its dark eyes fixed on her and no other. It held a pair of small axes as it lumbered closer, smoke churning from its gaping mouth.

"Gromir," she whispered.

As if in answer, the Forge Spurned spread its arms and wailed, ash forming a fresh cloud about its tortured form.

Ondorum moved to intercede, but she waved him away. "No! Mine!"

He jerked a nod and turned to engage anyone in range.

Akina gripped her maulaxe with renewed strength and set her feet to charge. Images of Jannasten and Brakisten seared her thoughts. Molten ore pumped through her veins as she dashed toward the creature.

Living chains writhed toward her. She slashed one aside. The other coiled around her wrist and yanked, trying to throw her off-balance. Instead of fighting the pull, she let it jerk her closer to the Forge Spurned. She whipped the handle of her maulaxe up and thrust the spiked ball at the end into the creature's throat.

A spike slipped through the choking chains and rammed deep into the flesh beneath. Smoke poured from the wound as she tried to throw the creature to the ground. It stumbled back and the chain around her wrist loosened. At the same time, the other slithered along the ground for her ankle.

She slammed the maulaxe hammer down onto the latter, sundering the links and sending the hook spinning away. As she straightened, an axe flashed toward her face. At the last second, the hit turned so the Forge Spurned's chain-wrapped fist struck instead. The blow knocked her sideways.

Working her jaw, she planted a foot and lunged back at the creature, chopping as she neared. Its jerky motions held her at bay for just a moment, before she discarded any pretense of defense and barreled straight in. An axe struck her right arm, and the blade bit through leather and mail, hit bone. She howled as the hot pain stoked her fury even higher. When she wrenched away, the axe remained stuck in her arm, but she barely noticed.

She spun full around and brought the maulaxe sweeping across, axe edge first. It sliced through the chains across the Forge Spurned's chest and drove deep. The Forge Spurned rocked back and she threw herself forward, slamming the creature to the ground. She jammed a knee into its side to pin it.

It looked up at her and stretched out a hand. The constant moan from its gaping mouth resolved into a brief screech.

"... *keeennnaaaa* ...."

Akina stared down into its dead eyes. The maulaxe trembled in her grip, the weapon still embedded in the creature's chest.

"Damn you, Gromir! I still can't forgive you." She felt unexpected tears well up. "But I can free you."

Letting go of her weapon, she mashed fists into its skull until bone crunched and shattered. As the Forge

Spurned went limp, a last ashen gust erupted from its ruined head, making her eyes sting.

She heaved to her feet and tore the axe from her arm, throwing it aside. Then she wrenched the maulaxe free. Ondorum remained poised nearby, dead duergar sprawled all about him. They shared a nod and then turned to assault the trebuchets once more.

As they did, two figures emerged from the smoking fray, striking down defenders until no more stood between them, Akina, and Ondorum. Vaskegar stood covered in gore, while Ularna's robes merely looked a little dustier than normal.

The duergar commander clashed his axes and launched himself at Akina. Face serene, Ularna moved between Ondorum and the other combatants and beckoned him forward.

Chapter Thirty-Three
Control

The crystal blades of Vaskegar's twin axes pulsed with a crimson light. Combined with the ichor-smeared mess of his armor, it made him a hideous sight, straight from Hell itself. He spun at Akina, blades chopping at her face and neck. She parried, only to have him swing both axes around in unison, looping them up and under her guard. She reeled back. An edge clanged off the front of her helm.

And just like that, she was on the defensive, knocking aside cuts with the maulaxe head and trying to ram the spiked ball on the other end into his face. A manic grin fixed on his face as he smashed these attempts away. Another blow slammed into her head. He thrust an axe straight out, catching her in the chest.

She rallied and tried to drive him back with frenzied strikes, but he proved too strong. He used one axe like a shield, absorbing the blows until he dashed past her guard and rammed his lowered head into hers. The toothed tines of his jawbone crown drove up under her helm and into her forehead with dizzying force. She stumbled. An axe blade slashed into her leg and sliced straight through her armor. An unnatural chill lanced through her thigh, tendrils of ice driving further in. The crimson glow of the axe deepened, congealing as it sucked away her very blood.

She staggered and barely dodged a hack at her neck. Her wounded leg threatened to collapse under her as she backed away. Vaskegar laughed and slipped taunts in between his teeth-jarring attacks.

"I've ended countless lives. What does one more matter?"

"Shut it!"

He turned one axe and used the flat of it to drive her to the side. His other axe came in opposite. She screamed as its edge caught the wound Gromir had inflicted. It drank from her arm and the strength in that limb flew away like ash on the wind. She struggled to keep from dropping her maulaxe. Ondorum? Where was Ondorum? She needed him . . .

"Droskar is here with me. Where is your pathetic god?"

"Burn in the Abyss!"

She dropped low and cut at his knees, but he swept both axes down, deflecting the attack. His boot caught her in the face, and she lurched back, spitting blood.

"When I break the last gate, I will slaughter the children first."

"Die, you bastard!"

If anything, his attacks increased in pace and power, making him a whirlwind of destruction. As she retreated, she caught sight of Ondorum a short distance away, trading blows with the other monk. She wanted to call out to him, to find a way to reach him, yet she had no breath with which to do so.

Vaskegar forced her back past the ruined scanderig, toward the tunnel wall. She knew that once he trapped her there, it'd only be a matter of time before his axes drank her blood to the last drop.

The duergar monk came in with such speed and ferocity, Ondorum wondered if she'd held back during their previous bouts. Staff whirling, he averted blows that had shattered the shells of giant insects and dwarven armor alike. Kicks whipped at his head, stomach, and knees so fast that instinct alone kept him alive, despite his extra reach.

In the briefest moment, he glimpsed Akina off to the side, battling Vaskegar. Ondorum could tell she struggled to overcome the commander. He ached to fight by her side, yet Ularna gave him no opportunity to disengage. Her face held no expression, as if she wore a mask of painted stone. No words, this time.

Yet no silence, either. Their strikes connected with smacks of flesh and snaps of their robes. Loose rock sprayed as they swept feet. Armor jangled as they vaulted fallen bodies. Metal and stone ground together as they leapt onto and over ruined barricades. She carried no weapon, but didn't seem to need one, even as he battered her with half a dozen blows in mere seconds. The hits rebounded as if he struck stone.

As they dueled, the pandemonium of the battlefield seemed to withdraw from his senses. They fought in a gray haze, surrounded by shades of war. Two mountains in motion, each trying to chip the other down into oblivion.

The staff caught her over the head; she dropped to all fours. An instant later, though, she lunged up, open palms leading. He snapped the staff out horizontal, but she latched onto it. Her feet came up and planted on his chest. A mule couldn't have kicked harder, and the staff tore from his grasp as she launched away. When she landed, she cast the staff aside and sped in again.

Fist to fist, foot to foot, they circled and planted, ducked and sprang. Her bare toes grazed his cheek. His palm struck robe, but nothing beneath. Her elbow cracked a shin raised to block a kick. He somersaulted backward, rose and lashed kicks up her body—low, middle, high. Then he switched legs and made the same strikes in reverse. She deflected all but the second kick into her side, but just grimaced against the impact.

Her ki rapped against his, energy alike yet unalike, sending miniature shockwaves through him whenever they connected. Their stomps and poundings vibrated the earth around them, reflecting and building until they seemed to fight in the epicenter of an earthquake.

Then a greater impact shook the area. The unexpected tremor threw off both their balances for a breath.

One of the ponderous, gape-mouthed constructs loomed over Ondorum. It had staggered up behind him, unnoticed as he focused on Ularna. It grabbed for him. He pivoted to avoid being snagged, but lost the poise necessary to avoid Ularna's follow-up attack.

Her kick caught him full in the chest and sent him soaring straight into the construct's maw.

Vaskegar raised his axes to drive Akina into the tunnel wall. Over his shoulder, Akina saw Ondorum vanish into the construct's belly. The maw clanged shut.

No.

No!

The rage swelled beyond all bounds, transforming her into living flame. Sight became etched in shades of black, every motion causing gray lines to waver around forms and figures. Sound dropped away except a single distant drumbeat. The lines of icy cold skewering her body evaporated and steam seemed to pour off her skin and from every ragged tear in her flesh.

The duergar commander moved achingly slowly; his axes drifted toward her head. She watched them come, baking in the heat of her own fury. Once more, it threatened to devour all sense of self and place, all ability to discern between friend and foe, all intent except for mindless butchery.

In that moment, she saw past Vaskegar to the construct that had taken Ondorum. To the monk who'd doomed him. To the duergar and dwarves fighting beyond. To the trebuchets taking aim at the remains of the second gate. To the Forge Spurned tearing the defenders apart with barbed chains and filling the tunnel with ungodly smoke.

She could let the rage take her. Let it devour her completely, surrendering all cares and worries and weariness until she burnt out from the inside. Yet if she did, it meant not only abandoning herself but also abandoning Ondorum to whatever fate awaited him inside the construct. Abandoning her people to the invaders. Abandoning the promises and prayers she'd made.

Or she could choose control. At least, just enough to make a difference.

Her hands tightened on the maulaxe shaft. That distant drumbeat sounded again, louder—though now it sounded more like a hammer pounding an anvil.

She dodged.

The axes flashed past. Vaskegar looked stunned at having missed.

Akina heard an elongated scream, growing louder until it tore from her throat.

A glancing hit off Vaskegar's shoulder cracked the bone pauldron. He brought his axes together to deflect, but she kicked and clobbered through the flimsy defense. He tried to cut in from the side. She caught the hooked axe on her hilt and swung around, dragging him along until his back faced the wall instead.

He cut his axes in from both sides. She jumped, let them intersect beneath her, and then brought her maulaxe down on the center of the axe blades.

They shattered beneath the blow, chunks of blood-soaked crystal exploding outward. Vaskegar reared up and lashed out empty-handed. The hooked knuckles of one gauntlet tore into Akina's cheek. She batted his hands aside and thrust the maulaxe head into his neck. He choked and brought his hands up to grip his crushed trachea. His eyes went wide with disbelief as she swung across.

At the last second, she spun the shaft so the axe edge sliced in. She sheared through in a single, clean cut. His severed head went flying, jawbone crown soaring ahead of it. His body slumped to the earth.

She wanted to leap onto his corpse, howling and shrieking. She trembled, wanting to pound the bones he wore into so much dust, then start on the ones inside his body.

Instead, she turned and spotted the construct that'd taken Ondorum. It waddled across the field, aiming toward one of the pits of flaming oil.

Calling on the fury to quicken her steps, Akina raced to rescue the one she loved.

Inside the construct, Ondorum tried to regain clarity. The construct's gut appeared to be an empty round chamber, just tall enough for him to stand. A line above indicated where its mouth had clamped shut, but so far no effort could pry it open.

A handful of other lines formed a square shape across the construct's belly. A tiny hole was set above this, like where a key might fit. A hatch? Ondorum pressed a palm to this, trying to determine if it offered a flaw he could exploit.

The chamber shifted, making him brace against the curved surface. The construct was moving. Back into battle? He thought of Akina. Without him opposing Ularna, the duergar monk could join Vaskegar and easily overwhelm her.

With a centering breath, he fell into a grounded stance and pummeled iron. His fists hammered the construct's stomach a dozen times over, to no avail. He launched fierce kicks, only to send himself bouncing off the back of the chamber.

He redoubled the attack until his fists spattered blood across the metal. He pulled back, wincing as the pain shooting up one arm informed him of several broken knuckles.

Ondorum shut his eyes, trying to focus as the construct continued trudging along. There was always a way. He simply might not be strong enough nor skilled enough to find it.

The construct rang and vibrated as something hit it from the outside. Akina's voice came through, hoarse yet recognizable.

"Ondorum!"

Akina struck the construct's body time and again. Every blow bounced or glanced off, yet she refused to stop. She raced around it, raining strikes from all sides, seeking a weak spot. The construct didn't so much as pause.

As she fought, some deep instinct told Akina that letting the molten fury drive her for much longer would kill her, forcing her body beyond any ability to recover. She accepted it. Embraced it, letting it fill every dark crevice of herself with liquid stone burning as bright as the sun. She only needed to hang on a little longer. To help Ondorum. To give him even the slightest chance.

She hesitated as several Forge Spurned lumbered in. They clustered around her, blocking further attacks on the construct. Akina whirled her maulaxe and charged. She couldn't afford to be distracted. Not now.

Akina struck the nearest monster with such force that she split the chain loops around its neck with the first blow. It reached for her, but she knocked the hammer from its grip and ran in under its waving hooks. She drove it to the ground, then spun and slammed the hammer side down on its head. Smoke gushed from its broken form as the other two closed in.

She darted in at the closest, dodging from side to side as hooks snapped out at her, one after the other. Grabbing a fistful of the Forge Spurned's chains, she hoicked the creature over her head with one arm and sent it soaring toward a group of dwarven defenders. Something popped in her shoulder, but the pain blended into the tempestuous riot already within her. The dwarves set into the Forge Spurned, hacking it to bits, while she dove at the third.

Spinning her maulaxe around, she rammed the spiked ball into its gaping mouth, piercing its skull. When she tore the weapon loose, the monster shuddered and dropped to its knees. A hammer blow laid it flat.

Her path clear, and she sprinted to catch up with the construct. She reached it and raised her maulaxe to renew her assault.

As she did, one of the construct's iron fists lashed out and caught her full on. She flew through the air several yards, maulaxe tumbling from her grip. She hit. Rolled until she crashed against a pile of bodies.

Akina forced herself up, but her right arm collapsed, dropping her again. Her body shook uncontrollably. She gritted her teeth and rose, one agonized lurch at a time. Her vision spun, and she staggered for balance. Turning circles, she tried to clear her sight and orient herself.

She regained her senses in time to see the construct standing above a flaming oil pit, body glowing red-hot.

Ondorum breathed in the stench of his baking flesh. The chamber burned around him, heated by some external source.

Even as he realized his fate, the metal turned searing beneath his feet. Jumping about would only waste energy, and he now needed every last bit he could summon. All his punches and kicks had barely dented the metal. He didn't have any more time to waste.

He pressed palms together, shut his eyes, and drew in a cleansing breath. It rushed into his lungs, both cool and steaming at the same time. He locked the air in. The golden ball of ki at his core flared as he retracted cords of energy from throughout his body, twining them into a singular focus.

The heat rose about him. His feet and legs blistered. His hair shriveled and fell away. The crystals across his body cracked and shattered, one by one. He felt and accepted it all. Every last painful sensation escalating, accelerating toward the point where his entire body would melt or combust. He waited until the last spark of gleaming power consolidated in his center.

He opened his eyes and studied the expanse of black iron before him. The curve of it, the way the hatch aligned with the rest of the surface, leaving no gap for escape. The heat became part of him, its energy adding to his even as it consumed him.

Now.

His soles tore away as he stepped forward. He drew arms back tight to his waist, even as the skin stretched and split. Hands bent at the wrists, fingertips charred black. Eyes fixed on his target, too dry and tight to blink. All angles proper. All power directed in unison, in synch with everything around him.

He aimed at the center of construct's belly. Breathed out. And struck a single, perfect blow.

Every last glimmer of ki rushed out through his palms and into the metal form. The wave of force rippled outward. The construct shuddered. The hatch groaned as it fell open, admitting a blast of chilled air.

Ondorum tumbled out. He somehow landed on his hands and knees and crawled a few feet further, smoke rising from his scorched palms.

The construct lurched off from where it had stood above a flaming pit. It staggered away, crushing several duergar as it went.

Ondorum tried to stop his shaking. Tried to slow his gasping. His head lolled, and he fought to control his tormented body before it gave out on him completely.

But he had nothing left to fight with. The ground rose to him.

A pair of hands caught under his arms.

Akina grabbed Ondorum and kept him up long enough to sit herself. Once positioned, she tugged him closer so his head rested in her lap.

She spat out a tooth knocked loose sometime in the battle. Grit and flakes of dried blood fell from her eyes as she blinked about. Hundreds of dwarves and duergar lay dead. The first and second gates had been obliterated, but the third remained. Both scanderigs lay in heaps, their forge fires burnt out.

Looking the other direction showed one of the trebuchets listing to the side, its rigging smashed. Another stood devoid of any duergar team. The third remained active, but the operators were busy fending off a squad of dwarves who'd reached their position. Many duergar fled down the tunnel, while defenders rallied to rout the rest.

Akina's soft chuckle scoured her throat. They'd live. They'd be safe. They'd rebuild and move on.

The embers within her guttered and died. Her bones became rods of ice, the chill seeping through to clutch at her heart, which beat slower with every breath. Only a handful left, she guessed.

She caressed Ondorum's face with a trembling hand. His eyes opened, meeting hers. His burnt and bleeding lips twitched.

A shadow fell over them. Akina raised her head.

Ularna stood there. Her stolid expression had broken into shock, and she stared down as if not understanding what she saw.

Akina raised shaking fists. Ondorum shivered in her lap, also gazing up at the duergar monk. They waited for the final blows.

Ularna blinked, once, slowly. Then she bowed, fist pressed to fist. She turned and strode away, passing by all ongoing fights without regard until she walked straight into the stone wall of the tunnel and disappeared.

Akina looked back at Ondorum, and they shared the slightest of disbelieving smiles.

With another shudder, his eyelids fluttered closed.

She bent to kiss his brow, but the motion tipped her over into an endless fall.

Epilogue
Vows

Akina opened her eyes to find herself in a simple bed, woolen blanket drawn to her chin. A fire blazed in a nearby hearth. She lay in a room of rough-hewn walls, undecorated, with a clay jug, cup, and washbasin set on a low table. Off in the distance, a soothing din of dwarven voices chanted in rhythm with bellows and hammers.

Recalling her last moments, Akina quirked a smile. This must be the afterlife. Plain comforts welcomed her to a new realm, where she'd join in endless revelry and craftsmanship under Torag's provenance, alongside all those who'd gone before her. Would she see her mother and brother? Would her father be in attendance, ready to embrace her after so long apart?

She took a quaking breath, longing for her departed family and eternal rest.

But . . . would Ondorum be here as well? Or had his soul taken a different path? What if they'd parted forever?

Tears sprang to her eyes at the thought of spending eternity without seeing him again. To her surprise, the tears stung before tracking down her cheek. Quite an irritating sensation for a spirit such as herself. She reached up to brush the tears away.

At the movement, a figure leaned into view near the head of her bed. A hand settled on her shoulder.

She stared at the hand for the longest time. Whole and strong, the gray skin unmarred. A healthy ridge of amethyst crystals tracked up the forearm. She reached over and ran a fingertip along these. Ondorum's face bent into view, half-shaded by the firelight. His burnt-away hair had been replaced by dark gray stubble.

"I told you they'd grow back," he said.

She swallowed past the rock in the back of her throat. "Where . . . How . . ."

"We're in a convalescence chamber in Taggoret's temple to Torag. The cleric has been by several times. Despite the healing, he . . ." Ondorum glanced aside. "He was not sure if you'd wake." A corner of his mouth tugged up. "I'm glad you chose to do so."

He stood and poured water from the jug into the cup. When he tried to lift it to her lips, she struggled upright and took the cup for herself. Taking a few sips gave her a chance to analyze her own body. She expected a few twinges here and there, a few deeper aches, but . . . nothing. No tearing or splitting or spilling her guts into her lap, or other more worrisome symptoms. She could've dreamt the whole battle.

She slugged back the rest of the water and held the cup out for more. "What happened after?"

He explained as he refilled. "It's been four days since the battle ended."

"Four days!"

"The duergar fled and the city stood." He bowed his head. "Still, we lost . . . many. Their names are now being inscribed in the tunnel walls as repairs are made. Clerics tended to those they could save and, fortunately, found us before we faded too far."

Clasping hands behind his back made the front of his robe part, revealing his muscled chest. Akina eyed it hungrily, remembering what she'd promised herself right before the battle began.

"Scouting parties are working through the lower tunnels to root out any lingering duergar. Envoys have been sent to all major cities and fortresses near any surface gates, putting them on alert for possible increased Darklands activities." He met her gaze at last. "And in the wake of it all, I realized what my silence helped me discover."

She peered up at him. "Oh?"

"Truth." He held a hand up, palm outward. "From this moment forward, in your presence and beneath the eyes of Irori, I swear a vow of truth. No matter the circumstances, no falsehood shall pass between my lips. No deceit will lurk within my heart, and I will strive to strike down lies wherever they exist."

Akina scrubbed her forehead and sighed. "Can't figure if this is better or worse than your first vow."

He locked eyes with her. "For as long as you'll have me, Akina Fairingot, I promise to be by your side, to fight for you, to learn to love what you love, to inspire dread in your enemies and be your shield in battle. These words and all the actions they may prompt are true."

She stared, the speechless one for once. Then a grin crept up her cheeks, along with a deep flush she hoped the firelight hid. When her tongue started working again, her voice had gone husky.

"Ondorum, that sounded an awful lot like a betrothal oath."

He blinked. "Did it? I'm not familiar with dwarven customs."

She shook her head and swung her feet out from under the blanket. The plain shift she wore should've left her chilled, but the blaze drove all drafts from the room. "We'll figure it out as we go, hm?"

He hastened to her side. "What're you doing?"

She pushed him back, determined not to be treated like a youngling just learning to walk. The first few steps went wobbly, but her muscles and bones soon got reacquainted and she stood firm. "I'd like to see the city we helped save."

"The cleric said you should continue resting when you woke. Injuries can be more than physical."

"I'll rest when I'm dead." She caught his look and returned it with a grin. "Which I don't plan to be for quite a while. If there's work to be done, I'm taking part."

He chuckled. "I told them you'd say as much. They didn't believe me."

"Good thing you know me so well. Otherwise you'd already have to go back on being truth-sworn. Now, where's my armor?"

Before he could answer, there came a rap on the door, and a middle-aged dwarf bustled in. He wore silver robes and had gold rings threaded through his oiled, black beard. He hesitated, seeing her standing in the plain garment, but she crossed her arms and raised an eyebrow.

"Well?"

He swept a bow. "Stone endures, m'lady. It's a relief to see you up and about. My name is Ruckle, and I represent several of the more vested parties who are indebted to the great service you and your companion performed on our behalf."

"Didn't do it to put anyone in my debt," she said. "If anything, I had to work a few off myself."

"As you say." His teeth gleamed. "But if there's anything we can do to repay you for such noble deeds, you have but to ask."

"Right. I'd like to volunteer." Ondorum shifted beside her, and she corrected herself. "*We'd* like to volunteer."

Ruckle's brow drew down, puzzled. "For what, may I ask?"

"To join one of the patrols hunting the duergar."

Puzzlement turned to concern. "The cleric says you're barely recovered. Are you sure you're fit for that sort of duty?"

"Fitter than anyone you've already got out there." She thumbed at her companion. "Just ask him."

Ondorum grimaced. "If she says she's ready, there's little point in arguing."

"Figure that for the truth."

Ruckle combed his beard, studying them as if assuring himself they didn't jest at his expense. "Actually, I had come to make another request that might still satisfy yours."

"Hm?"

"Ondorum has spoken with us more about the ruins you found, and the details he remembers are quite striking. Especially this forge the duergar sought to corrupt to their own ends. An expedition is being discussed, with the intent of visiting the site and surveying it for our official records." He held out an upturned hand. "My patrons were of the hope that you'd consider joining the effort, perhaps provide some guidance along the routes you know and offer a measure of protection. You'd be quite well compensated, of course."

Akina and Ondorum exchanged a look, and she figured the gleam in his eyes matched her own. She thought of Izthuri and the caligni tribe and wondered how they'd fared. What dangers still threatened the ancient settlement, and what more might they discover within its walls and beneath its foundations? What might she learn about her ancestors and her place among them? Her mother's bones and brother's body waited to be properly honored and buried, and she now knew where to carve a gladdringgar of her own.

Clapping Ruckle on the shoulder, she guided him out the door. "Tell your masters we'll give it some serious thought, so long as the pay's as grand as I'm thinking."

He murmured thanks and headed off to deliver the message. She remained at the doorway, looking down the hall to where flames and shadows rose from a set of forges. The temple thrummed with song and the tumult of dwarves turning raw ore and alloys into pieces worth admiring for generations to come.

"What do you see?" Ondorum asked.

"Choices," she said. "Opportunities. More than I ever imagined having." She turned and flashed a grin. "What say we make something of them, hm?"

About the Author

Josh Vogt is an author and full-time freelance writer whose work has been published in dozens of genre markets, with stories covering fantasy, science fiction, horror, humor, pulp, and any combination of the above. This is his debut novel.

Akina and Ondorum also appear in "The Price Paid," a prequel web fiction story available for free on **paizo. com**. Additional Pathfinder Tales shorts available on the website include "The Weeping Blade" and "Hunter's Folly." For other novels, look to his forthcoming urban fantasy series, *The Cleaners*, which commences with *Enter the Janitor* (2015) and *The Maids of Wrath* (2016).

As a copywriter, Josh works with a roster of international clients, crafting advertising and sales copy, content marketing campaigns, and more. He also writes for a wide variety of RPG developers and publishers such as Modiphius, Privateer Press, Gun Metal Games, and Raging Swan Press, producing game manuals, sourcebooks, campaigns, adventure modules, worldbuilding materials, and tie-in fiction.

He's a member of SFWA as well as the International Association of Media Tie-In Writers. You can find him at **JRVogt.com** or on Twitter **@JRVogt**. He lives in Denver, Colorado.

Acknowledgements

Let me begin with enormous gratitude for my editor, James Sutter, who gave me the chance to journey into Golarion and add to the endless adventures there. His keen insight concerning the plot and characters, plus his constant willingness to hammer out the raw details, helped make this book what it is. It's been a great joy to work with him.

I'm incredibly grateful to Jenelle Tosaya, who cheered me on throughout the whole process of sitting down and actually writing this story, despite the crazy and exhausting hours involved. And to my loving family, who shared in the excitement as I experienced having a novel published for the very first time

Further thanks to Dave Gross, for his invaluable feedback during the novel's early development and drafting. To the many other Pathfinder Tales authors I've met along the way, thank you as well for your encouragement!

Of course, every novel needs plenty of tough love to whip it into shape. I'm appreciative of my Denver critique group, which kept me in the loop even when I could only attend via Skype. Finally, I'm indebted to the beta readers who took the time to cast their eyes across these pages: James Sams, Travis Heermann, Holly Roberds, Michael Stewart, Mike Kalar, Michael Pack, Rob Haines, Tony Peak, Dr. Jennifer Kincheloe, and Melisa Ford (apologies if I missed anyone!).

Thank you, one and all.

Glossary

All Pathfinder Tales novels are set in the rich and vibrant world of the Pathfinder campaign setting. Below are explanations of several key terms used in this book. For more information on the world of Golarion and the strange monsters, people, and deities that make it their home, see *The Inner Sea World Guide*, or dive into the game and begin playing your own adventures with the *Pathfinder Roleplaying Game Core Rulebook* or the *Pathfinder Roleplaying Game Beginner Box*, all available at **paizo.com**.

Abyss: Plane of evil and chaos ruled by demons, where many evil souls go after they die.

Arcane: Magic that comes from mystical sources rather than the direct intervention of a god; secular magic.

Ashen Forge: The realm of the afterlife ruled by Droskar. Located in the Abyss.

Avistan: The northern continent of the Inner Sea region, on which the Five Kings Mountains are located.

Blightburn: Dangerous radioactive crystals found in the Darklands.

Boneyard: Pharasma's realm, where all souls go to be judged after death.

Bugganes: Race of monstrous mole-like beasts that live deep underground.

Caligni: Race of reclusive humanoids who live in tribes deep underground and swaddle themselves in strips of cloth.

Cleric: A religious spellcaster whose magical powers are granted by his or her god.

Construct: Mechanical creature given life through magical means.

Dark Elves: Race of elves who left the surface long ago and turned to the worship of demons.

Dark Smith: Droskar.

Darklander: Resident of the Darklands.

Darklands: Extensive series of subterranean caverns crisscrossing much of the Inner Sea region, known to be inhabited by monsters. Generally divided into three sections: Nar-Voth, Sekamina, and Orv.

Davarn: Small city in the Five Kings Mountains.

Droskar: Evil dwarven deity dedicated to toil, slavery, and cheating. Patron god of the duergar.

Duergar: Race of gray-skinned dwarves that remained in the Darklands instead of ascending to the surface during the Quest for Sky, and who turned to the evil god Droskar for protection.

Dwarves: Short, stocky humanoids who excel at physical labor, mining, and craftsmanship. Originally from the Darklands, the dwarves ascended to the surface millennia ago during the Quest for Sky.

Elemental: Being of pure elemental energy, such as air, earth, fire, or water.

Elves: Long-lived, beautiful humanoids who abandoned Golarion millennia ago and have only recently returned. Identifiable by their pointed ears, lithe bodies, and pupils so large their eyes appear to be one color.

Father of Creation: Torag.

Five Kings Mountains: A large and ancient mountain range in southeastern Avistan. Primarily inhabited by the dwarven nation of the same name.

Fleshwarp: Creatures that were once normal humanoids but have been magically twisted into horrifying shapes by dark elf magic.

Forge Spurned: Damned souls sworn to Droskar and turned into powerful chain-wrapped monstrosities in order to do the god's bidding.

Forgefiends: Scanderigs.

Giants: Race of brawny humanoids many times larger than humans.

Gladdringgar: Dwarven symbols carved in hard-to-reach subterranean places as a rite of passage.

Gnomes: Small humanoids with strange mindsets, big eyes, and often wildly colored hair.

Goblins: Race of small and maniacal humanoids who live to burn, pillage, and sift through the refuse of more civilized races.

Goblinblood Wars: Series of wars that only recently ended, in which goblinoids rampaged through southern Avistan, forcing many different humanoid nations and organizations to band together in order to finally defeat them.

Golem: Type of magical construct, usually humanoid in shape, built to mindlessly serve a master.

Gorum: God of battle, strength, and weapons. Also known as Our Lord In Iron.

Gorumite: Someone who worships Gorum.

Hagegraf: Subterranean capital city of the duergar.

Hell: Plane of evil and tyrannical order ruled by devils, where many evil souls go after they die.

Hobgoblin: Larger, more intelligent kin of regular goblins. Highly organized and militant.

Inner Sea: The vast inland sea whose northern continent, Avistan, and southern continent, Garund, as well as the seas and nearby lands, are the primary focus of the Pathfinder campaign setting.

Irori: God of history, knowledge, self-perfection, and enlightenment. Popular with monks.

Ki: Mystical force or life essence which warrior monks often learn to master, allowing them to perform exceptional feats of strength and agility.

King Taggrick: Founder and first ruler of Taggoret.

Kingtower Pass: Famous mountain pass in the Five Kings Mountains, home to a massive memorial for King Taggrick.

Landshark: Ferocious monster that burrows through solid earth and eats almost anything.

Lizardfolk: Race of reptilian humanoids; often viewed as backward by more "civilized" races.

Long Walk: Massive tunnel thoroughfare through parts of the Darklands, crucial to trade between local subterranean races.

Lord in Iron: Gorum.

Magrim: Lesser-known dwarven deity.

Monk: Someone who devotes himself or herself to enlightenment and self-perfection, often through mastery of the physical body and its use as a weapon.

Naga: Race of intelligent, magical creatures with the heads of humans and bodies of snakes.

Nar-Voth: Level of the Darklands closest to the surface.

Ogres: Hulking, half-witted humanoid monsters with violent tendencies and repulsive lusts.

Orc: Race of green- or gray-skinned humanoids with protruding tusks and warlike tendencies. Generally seen as savage and dangerous by other races.

Oread: Humans whose ancestry includes elemental earth magic, resulting in stony or crystalline skin.

Orv: Deepest level of the Darklands, characterized by enormous caverns called Vaults.

Pharasma: The goddess of birth, death, and prophecy, who judges mortal souls after their deaths and sends them on to the appropriate afterlife; also known as the Lady of Graves.

Quest for Sky: Centuries-long journey in which the dwarven race, following a prophecy from Torag, journeyed upward from the depths of the Darklands to settle on the surface.

Scanderigs: Metal giants from another plane of existence that exist only to feed ore into their forge-like bellies. Sometimes used as servants by Droskar.

Sekamina: Middle level of the Darklands, characterized by seemingly unending caverns and tunnels that can span continents.

Sky Citadels: Ten great fortress cities built when the dwarves first emerged onto the surface following their origins in the Darklands.

Sorcerer: Someone who casts spells through natural ability rather than faith or study.

Taggoret: Dwarven city in the Five Kings Mountains.

Tattered Ones: Race of subterranean creatures that can breed with any humanoids, resulting in a bizarre spread of genetic traits even between siblings.

Tian Xia: Continent on the opposite side of the world from the Inner Sea region.

Torag: Stoic and serious dwarven god of the forge, protection, and strategy. Viewed by dwarves as the Father of Creation.

Trolls: Large, stooped humanoids with sharp claws and amazing regenerative powers that are overcome only by fire.

Warg: Larger, more intelligent versions of wolves. Usually evil.

Wizard: Someone who casts spells through careful study and rigorous scientific methods rather than faith or innate talent, recording the necessary incantations in a spellbook.

Xulgaths: Intelligent and evil reptilian humanoids that dwell in caves. One of the oldest intelligent races, long since outstripped by other humanoids, and now viewed as feral savages by most civilized races.

Zon-Kuthon: The twisted god of envy, pain, darkness, and loss. Was once a good god, along with his sister Shelyn, before unknown forces turned him to evil.

THE ADVENTURE JUST GOT BIGGER!

Paizo Inc. is teaming up with Tor Books to take the Pathfinder Tales novels farther than they've ever gone before! Beginning with Dave Gross's *Lord of Runes*, each new Pathfinder Tales novel will now be published in a bigger, bolder trade paperback format. What's more, Pathfinder Tales ebooks will also be available online in a wider variety of formats—including Kindle!

So keep your eyes peeled for the new Pathfinder Tales format—because when you're going up against giants and dragons...

BIGGER IS BETTER!

TOR paizo

Torius Vin is perfectly happy with his life as a pirate captain, sailing the Inner Sea with a bold crew of buccaneers and Celeste, his snake-bodied navigator and one true love. Yet all that changes when his sometime friend Vreva Jhafae—a high-powered courtesan and abolitionist spy in the slaver stronghold of Okeno—draws him into her shadowy network of secret agents. Caught between the slavers he hates and a navy that sees him as a criminal, can Torius continue to choose the path of piracy? Or will he sign on as a privateer, bringing freedom to others—at the price of his own?

From critically acclaimed author Chris A. Jackson comes a fantastical tale of love, espionage, and high-seas adventure, set in the award-winning world of the *Pathfinder Roleplaying Game*.

Pirate's Promise print edition: $9.99
ISBN: 978-1-60125-664-5

Pirate's Promise ebook edition:
ISBN: 978-1-60125-665-2

PATHFINDER TALES

Pirate's Promise

CHRIS A. JACKSON

PATHFINDER TALES

Raised as a wizard-priest in the church of the dark god Zon-Kuthon, Isiem escaped his sadistic masters and became a rebel, leaving behind everything he knew in order to follow his conscience. Now, his unique heritage makes him perfect for a dangerous mission into an ancient dungeon said to hold a magical weapon capable of slaying demons and devils by the thousands and freeing the world of their fiendish taint. Accompanied by companions ranging from a righteous paladin to mercantile mercenaries, Isiem will lead the expedition back into shadowed lands that are all too familiar. And what the adventurers find at the dungeon's heart will change them all forever.

From acclaimed author Liane Merciel comes a dark tale of survival, horror, and second chances set in the award-winning world of the Pathfinder Roleplaying Game.

Nightblade print edition: $9.99
ISBN: 978-1-60125-662-1

Nightblade ebook edition:
ISBN: 978-1-60125-663-8

PATHFINDER TALES

Nightblade

LIANE MERCIEL

W hen the leader of the ruthless Technic League calls in a favor, the mild-mannered alchemist Alaeron has no choice but to face a life he thought he'd left behind long ago. Accompanied by his only friend, a street-savvy thief named Skiver, Alaeron must head north into Numeria, a land where brilliant and evil arcanists rule over the local barbarian tribes with technology looted from a crashed spaceship. Can Alaeron and Skiver survive long enough to unlock the secrets of the stars? Or will the backstabbing scientists of the Technic League make Alaeron's curiosity his own undoing?

From Hugo Award winner Tim Pratt comes a fantastic adventure of technology and treachery, set against the backdrop of the Iron Gods Adventure Path in the award-winning world of the Pathfinder Roleplaying Game.

Reign of Stars print edition: $9.99
ISBN: 978-1-60125-660-7

Reign of Stars ebook edition:
ISBN: 978-1-60125-661-4

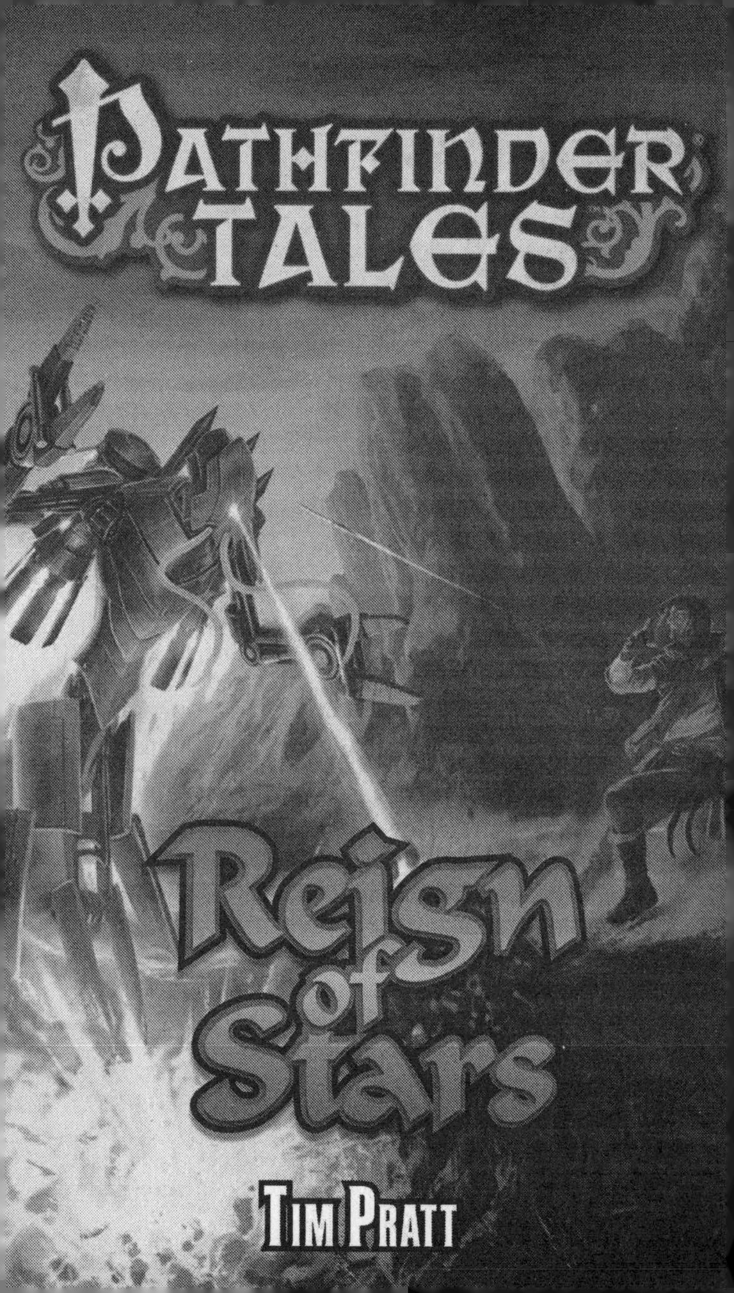

Pathfinder Tales
Reign of Stars
Tim Pratt

When the aristocratic Vishov family is banished from Ustalav due to underhanded politics, Lady Tyressa Vishov is faced with a choice: fade slowly into obscurity, or strike out for the nearby River Kingdoms and establish a new holding on the untamed frontier. Together with her children and loyal retainers, she'll forge a new life in the infamous Echo Wood, and neither bloodthirsty monsters nor local despots will stop her from reclaiming her family honor. Yet the shadow of Ustalavic politics is long, and even in a remote and lawless territory, there may be those determined to see the Vishov family fail . . .

From *New York Times* best-selling author Michael A. Stackpole comes a new novel of frontier adventure set in the world of the Pathfinder Roleplaying Game and the new *Pathfinder Online* massively multiplayer online roleplaying game.

The Crusader Road print edition: $9.99
ISBN: 978-1-60125-657-7

The Crusader Road ebook edition:
ISBN: 978-1-60125-658-4

PATHFINDER TALES

THE CRUSADER ROAD

MICHAEL A. STACKPOLE

When murdered sinners fail to show up in Hell, it's up to Salim Ghadafar, an atheist soldier conscripted by the goddess of death, to track down the missing souls. In order to do so, Salim will need to descend into the anarchic city of Kaer Maga, following a trail that ranges from Hell's iron cities to the gleaming gates of Heaven itself. Along the way, he'll be aided by a menagerie of otherworldly creatures, a streetwise teenager, and two warriors of the mysterious Iridian Fold. But when the missing souls are the scum of the earth, and the victims devils themselves, can anyone really be trusted?

From James L. Sutter, author of the critically acclaimed novel *Death's Heretic*, comes a new adventure of magic, monsters, and morality, set in the award-winning world of the Pathfinder Roleplaying Game.

***The Redemption Engine* print edition: $9.99**
ISBN: 978-1-60125-618-8

***The Redemption Engine* ebook edition:**
ISBN: 978-1-60125-619-5